In eleven stories

that span Florida marshes, North Carolina mountains, and Southern metropolitan cities, *Make Your
Way Home* follows Black men and women who
grapple with the homes that have eluded them. A
preteen pregnant alongside her mother refuses to
let convention dictate who she names as the father
of her child. Centuries after slavery separated his
ancestors, a native Texan tries to win over the love
of his life despite the grip of a family curse. A young
deaconess who falls for a new church member wonders what it means when God stops speaking to her.
And at the very end of the South as we know it, two
sisters seek to escape North to freedom, to promises
of a more stable climate.

Artfully and precisely drawn, and steeped in
place and history as it explores themes of belonging,
inheritance, and deep intimacy, Carrie R. Moore's
debut collection announces an extraordinary new
talent in American fiction, inviting us all to examine how the past shapes our present—and how our
present choices will echo for years to come.

"Each story in Carrie R. Moore's *Make Your Way Home* is remarkable, gorgeously written, complicated, deep, continually surprising—and each a page turner, too, propulsive and heartbreaking in all directions. Her characters are so real you come to know them, body and soul. *Make Your Way Home* is a collection that is much more than the considerable sum of its beautiful parts. It is a book that has the force of life itself, all its hurts and love and betrayal, the little intimacies, terrible mistakes, reconciliations, moments of transcendence, the ways we can and cannot change. It is an astonishing debut."

—**ELIZABETH MCCRACKEN**,
author of *The Hero of This Book*

"Carrie R. Moore's arresting Southern stories pulse with the kind of intimacy, beauty, and intensity that the best art conjures. Her characters and their voices linger and arouse, long after their final moments on the page. *Make Your Way Home* is a deeply satisfying, glorious debut."

—**DEESHA PHILYAW**,
author of *The Secret Lives of Church Ladies*

"Carrie R. Moore's stories are gorgeous, resonant, and startling. It's rare for a new writer to have such profound emotional wisdom; in *Make Your Way Home,* a single small ripple in a character's interior life can build strength to become a huge wave that crashes over them. What a thrilling new talent, and what a beautiful collection of short stories."

—**LAUREN GROFF,**
author of *The Vaster Wilds*

"With pitch-perfect attention to place, belonging, and the reverberations of history through several generations of Black men, women, and families in the American South, *Make Your Way Home* is a collection that moved me to my core. Carrie R. Moore conjures the complicated longing for home and connection with nuance, compassion, and grace. In the story 'The Happy Land,' our protagonist maintains, 'It was nearly impossible to have everything you wanted in one place, at one time, prolonged.' This book is a fervent exploration of this impossibility, giving space to the desire for true belonging and abundance from which this search takes root. A powerful meditation on ancestral inheritance and contemporary love, *Make Your Way Home* is an extraordinary and luminous debut by a singular talent."

—**MEGAN KAMALEI KAKIMOTO,**
author of *Every Drop Is a Man's Nightmare*

MAKE
YOUR WAY
HOME

MAKE YOUR WAY HOME

STORIES

CARRIE R. MOORE

TIN HOUSE / PORTLAND, OREGON

Copyright © 2025 by Carrie R. Moore

First US Edition 2025
Printed in the United States of America

Epigraph © Jesmyn Ward, 2013, *Men We Reaped: A Memoir*, Bloomsbury Publishing Inc.

The stories in this collection appeared, in slightly different form, in the following publications: "When We Go, We Go Downstream" in *American Short Fiction*; "Cottonmouths" as "Vipers" in *The Normal School*; "All Skin Is Clothing" in EPOCH; "Surfacing" and "Till It and Keep It" in *The Sewanee Review*; "Morning by Morning" as "The Rest of the Morning" in *The Southern Review*; "Gather Here Again" in *Virginia Quarterly Review*; "In the Swirl" in *New England Review*; "Naturale" in *One Story*

Manufacturing by Kingery Printing Company
Interior design by Beth Steidle

Library of Congress Cataloging-in-Publication Data

Names: Moore, Carrie R, 1993– author
Title: Make your way home : stories / Carrie R. Moore.
Description: First US edition. | Portland, Oregon : Tin House, 2025.
Identifiers: LCCN 2025007759 | ISBN 9781963108286 paperback | ISBN 9781963108354 ebook
Subjects: LCGFT: Short stories
Classification: LCC PS3613.O554546 M35 | DDC 813/.6—dc23/eng/20250324
LC record available at https://lccn.loc.gov/2025007759

Tin House
2617 NW Thurman Street, Portland, OR 97210
www.tinhouse.com

DISTRIBUTED BY W. W. NORTON & COMPANY

1 2 3 4 5 6 7 8 9 0

For Jonathan, my home, anywhere.

*And for Hannah, who was there
from the very first story.*

How could I know then that this would be my life: yearning to leave the South and doing so again and again, but perpetually called back to home by a love so thick it choked me?

—**JESMYN WARD,**
Men We Reaped

TABLE OF CONTENTS

WHEN WE GO, WE GO DOWNSTREAM

I

IN THE RESTAURANT'S FADING LIGHT, he tells the story to his woman. Warily, the way his father told it to him:

There once lived a man named Elijah. A man who, among many other things—blacksmith, singer, lover of russet pears—had been born a slave. In those days, Texas had yet again changed its mind about what it was. It had belonged to Mexico, then became its own fearsome land, then joined Polk's America, then splintered off with the rest of the rebellious South. Texas dreamed of cotton and the hands to pick it. Elijah dreamed of Evaline, whom his master forbade him to call wife.

On that plantation by the Brazos River, they met by night, Elijah approaching the women's cabin and unfolding the back of his throat to announce his arrival. Evaline heard the low, guttural trill of a nightjar and came out to meet him. They must've talked in that starry darkness. Perhaps she confessed that on the nights he did not come, she heard hundreds of such birds in the woods and believed him everywhere at once. Perhaps he told her about the extra minutes he spent playing with the horses instead of forging their shoes. Small victories against the master who was also his father. The man owned him in neither manner.

Still, it was hard to give love in such a place. For twenty years, Elijah had seen his master-father keep his mother in a cabin apart from the other slaves, bringing her shawls in winter and apple dumplings in summer. Then, either tired of her or goaded by the plantation mistress, Master Roberts sold her to a trader heading to Arkansas. In watching her vanish against the horizon, Elijah learned how hard it was to keep anything in this life.

After, Evaline held him close, enveloping him against the trunk of a wax myrtle. In his mind, he held his mother's scent. She'd smelled of butter, which she'd used to keep her hands smooth.

One night, Elijah did not go to Evaline's cabin, instead seeking his freedom under a half-moon. He waded through the river's shallows, not only so the dogs couldn't track his scent but also to let the water shake loose what memories he had of his fine-boned father. Those lingering cabin visits. The whispers of making his slave-son a driver over the others. None of it had offered protection. Elijah had only the certainty of his feet taking him away, toward a self he could claim.

Evaline hadn't expected his leaving without her. He couldn't have been the first man she'd lost. But he was the first to leave by choice. His name rose again and again in the whispers of other slaves, a taunt.

So she visited a witch who lived in a grove of bald cypresses, making her way there on a night when no birds sang. She brought with her Elijah's shirt, cream colored and made of homespun linen, thick with his smell and therefore his memory. The witch tied three knots in it.

Now this would be true: Any lovers Elijah had would grow to despise him, would find in him faults that he did not possess. They would leave him, his name rotting in their mouths. And if he had sons and daughters, the same would be true for them.

Though, a witch was a witch and could give no gift without a blade. Because as Evaline made her way back to the cabin, she didn't yet know she carried Elijah's child. That babe was born the year before freedom, then grew older and sharecropped that same plantation—up until his wife accused him of hoarding what little they had, then left him for a farmer with his own land in West Texas.

And when that sharecropper's youngest son grew up and moved to Austin to work as a porter, his wife said she couldn't abide a man who lived in the bottom of a bottle—though he drank only on Friday nights, the law being what it was.

And neither that porter's sons nor daughters nor grandchildren could keep anyone around for long. Always, their lovers ran off with their paychecks or mailed divorce papers without warning or decided, out of nowhere, that dating a Roberts made them want to live somewhere more mountainous and cold.

Which was the end of the story, as far as it went, Ever Roberts III tells the woman sitting across from him on the restaurant patio. Except to say that Elijah was his third-great-grandfather, and it is still a story his family tells from time to time.

He has talked for longer than he'd have liked, but Amari, whom he'd like to call his woman, has asked him to share a family story, and he will do anything to keep her here. They're on the patio of a barbecue spot off Cesar Chavez, the restaurant packed on a Friday night. He can't stop trying to memorize her face. Her twists hang in a long ponytail, the strands fine and dark and numerous, like the night behind her is still dripping, not yet dried.

"Can't imagine my father telling me something like that," she says, tugging on her neckerchief. "Be too easy to believe it, as a child."

"I think he was scared somebody else would tell it if he didn't. He always wanted to frame things for my sister and me."

"But as a doctor, he should've known better. Kids and their impressionable minds."

"You could say that."

He doesn't mention that his father told the story the year of his divorce from their mother. His father had made tofu burgers, sat him and his twin, Leela, at the dining table in their old home off Chicon. The place felt too large in their mother's absence. They could sense her new duplex in Hyde Park, off in the distance. "I don't believe in it," their father had said, a strange smudge on his glasses, "but I wanted you to hear."

At the restaurant, the ceiling fans whir overhead. Amari swats a fly and says, "Well, I'm looking forward to meeting your old man. And everybody."

He mops sauce with his white bread. "You say that now."

"Seriously. The longer I stay, the less it feels like I've been talking to a ghost all this time."

He knows what she means. She's been in his city only an hour, coming to him in the bus station light before he drove them here. Yet the longer she talks and pulls the pickled onions from her brisket sandwich, the more he can match this person in front of him with the woman he's messaged online for three years. Back then, she'd posted in all caps on Reddit, PLS, DOES ANYONE DO EMERGENCY WEB DESIGN? and he'd responded, assembling her home page and listing her publications ahead of her job interview with a major DC newspaper. He'd gotten sucked into her writing, the windows of her life appearing on his screen some thirteen hundred miles away: Only child. Former Park View resident. Howard alum. Her city had grown less familiar to her, she wrote, but she loved it still, like a troubled cousin sure to get himself together someday.

Read your work, Ever had messaged her. *Place means something to you, huh?*

She'd responded: *Says the guy with his area code in his username.*

From there, from their shared profiles and eventual video chats, he'd learned that other things mattered to her too. Like volunteering with her sorors or buying her parents an elaborate cruise for their twenty-fifth anniversary or bussing everywhere instead of flying, so she could see where she was in the world. She went months thinking he was named after Medgar Evers, then realized Ever was his grandfather's name, his father's too. Sometimes, he thought they both found it easier to grow intimate with someone partially an illusion, a mirage conjured up by screen and code and careful curation. They'd held each other down through boyfriends who called her out of her name and girlfriends who asked him to pack his things. Through insurgents storming the Capitol twenty minutes from her apartment. Through his grandfather's move to the memory care facility. He'd turned twenty-nine, thirty, thirty-one. She remained always ahead of him, two years older. Most recently, he'd talked her through her layoff from that newspaper where she'd once been so eager to work.

This break is why she's here, his guest on this April weekend of his sister's wedding. They have three days to see who they are to each other at a breath's distance.

As they eat, he wants to ask: *So, am I what you thought?* Perhaps he is shorter than she wanted, too hairy in the face and arms. But he lets her chat about the wildflowers on the ride in. She isn't as smooth faced or curvy as she'd seemed online. The version of her in his mind becomes less imagined, more real. Forehead wrinkles. Smaller breasts. All this, he's discovering.

"What?" she asks. "You changing your mind about me?" Before he can answer, she goes, "No, wait. I'll change my mind about *you*, right?"

He doesn't laugh. Above them, the grackles keep squawking, those birds forever in thirst.

WHAT HE BELIEVES: Love swells like a thundercloud, makes a whole lot of troublesome noise up close. Part of him fears that this weekend has started a countdown toward their inevitable end.

Too soon, he's driving them into the Hill Country, Austin's city lights collecting into an orange lake in the dark basin of the rearview. He's been careful about this weekend, has even surrendered his suite so Amari can stay at the lodge hosting Leela's wedding, a fifteen-room property with a terrace overlooking gentle savanna and distant salt-pink granite. A small venue, in the end, with all the other rooms taken by travelers from out of town. After he drops Amari off, he'll have to make the hour and a half drive back down to his grandfather's old place in East Austin, where he's been living since his last girlfriend kicked him out of their apartment six months ago. "We just aren't sexually compatible," she'd said. "Who has time for twice a week?" Now the last thing he wants is for Amari to feel pressured by the idea of sharing a room. Though he's had fantasies of her gripping his fingers and pulling him through the suite door. *You're too patient,* she'd say. *I came all this way.*

In the passenger seat, she says, "You know, at dinner, I thought there'd be more people in bolos and cowboy boots."

"Keep waiting. Though I'm guessing you've seen too many movies."

"Not so many. It's just easy to get ideas about Texas. To be honest, I was hoping you'd have some rodeo-star relative up here. Or somebody willing to bring a broke girl to his ranch."

"Got a cousin in Houston with a horse. Best I can do."

"Disappointing."

"Now you know how I felt when you told me your sister didn't work for the president."

If the mention of "work" presses something sore in her, she doesn't betray it. Instead, she toys with her neckerchief, and he wonders if she's done this during their phone calls, in moments she hid her nerves. Once, she'd admitted to always wearing a scarf or bandanna because of the neck folds that had appeared in her thirties. Maybe it means something for her to tug at the fabric now, exposing some flaw bit by bit.

"I should be up-front with you," she says. "I got a job offer."

"Congrats. You finally tricked somebody else into hiring you."

"Funny. I'm saying the gig's for a local paper. Here in Austin, I mean."

He drags a thumb over the wheel and waits for his breath to catch up. Their three days together expand, a narrow hallway tunneling off his life. It's all too easy to imagine an exit on the other side. "Don't know if I should feel relieved," he manages. "Or like a bum for not offering to move to DC."

"Nothing's set in stone. We'll see how this visit goes." She fusses with the dial on the dash, and he adjusts the air for her, lowering the temperature in the car.

They sit within their first silence. Always, they've announced they were logging off or hanging up, though she seems calm in the quiet, one toe nudging her sandal's bed. The voices in his mind grow in volume like the pinpricks of stars through the windshield. All his former girlfriends' complaints: "You're a god-awful listener. . . . Why is your stuff everywhere, *all* the time? . . . Honestly, I can't pretend anymore that there's any attraction here." In his early twenties, one girlfriend accused him of being careless with his money, and another said that not buying gifts was a way of withholding affection. He'd kept trying to change, to be whatever they needed. Yet they always said he cared too much or too little about family, that he dressed too casually or else wasn't as cute as he thought he was—and therefore didn't need so long in the mornings to get himself together.

Even Leela, his younger sister by nine minutes, had recently cooled to him. Last December, when she announced her engagement to her girlfriend of two years, he'd joked, "So how much do you need?" She'd changed professions more often than anyone he knew: waitress, temp, elementary school teacher, nursing assistant, flight attendant, half-time student of veterinary medicine. He'd bailed her out of late credit card payments a handful of times.

"You don't get to speak to me like that," she'd said, pursing her lips like their mother. "We don't need your money. And you don't get to be smug because some of us take longer to figure things out."

Smug. Out of his own sister's mouth.

After another half hour, a crown of pink appears in the darkness, growing into a lodge with front-lit adobe walls, an entrance that curves outward. The gravel drive leads their car under a walkway connecting the lodge's two halves, then into a lot near an overhang with its invisible leap into night. He parks beside several trucks and sedans: his family members, already arrived, their presence felt in the lodge's windows, glowing yellow.

"Somebody's eager," Amari says, and he sees the stick-legged figure in a hoodie. His sister is coming out to meet them.

Beside the car, he watches them hug, these two women in his life. "If I were you," Leela says to Amari as she pulls back, "I wouldn't be able to stand another long ride for years."

A little sting, that his sister does not hug him too. Her crossed arms feel like an argument, as do the wreaths of verbena and bluebell on the lodge's bottom windows. A reminder that she's made her wedding happen without his help.

Yet—his sister's insistence on intimacy has long been her gift. She adjusts Amari's twists, calls her "sis," says they have a long weekend ahead of them, but she's hoping everybody will relax and enjoy being here. In the morning, there'll be a dip in a nearby swimming hole, then an afternoon of floral arranging for the tables, then the rehearsal dinner. But she'll make sure they find time to talk. Too bad her brother's secret girl isn't staying longer.

"Who's a secret?" Ever asks, and Amari says, "Good to know you feel that way."

Leela attempts a smile, which fails at the corners. She's done something to her face ahead of the wedding, her round cheeks oddly buffed. She's holding something in.

He cocks his head to one side, their old twin ritual: *You good?* But Leela only says, "Amari, want to see your room? I'll talk to my brother after."

A small hole forms in the air. "You're not staying?" Amari asks him.

"I've got to head back down."

Wrong answer, he realizes, as a quiet light retracts in her pupils. Suddenly, he can hear her saying, *I get the sense I'm investing more than you in all this.*

"Ever's doing me a few favors," Leela says, and maybe she is saving him. "And he's got to pick up Grandaddy ahead of the services. He's turning a hundred next month, and I've got a surprise for him."

"Surprises all around," Amari says.

When she hugs him goodbye, it's too quick. The shape of their bodies never sets in.

THE WAIT FOR LEELA'S RETURN is too long, something in him twisting like the fabric awning above. There's the constant work of being a good brother, a good son, a man no woman will call a "disappointment." He's tried to make up for his earlier teasing by dropping off Leela's wedding invitations and assembling her arch and offering to pick up Grandaddy. He even took her and Kiki to a celebratory dinner, where they went on about colors and seating charts in a restaurant that put four-petaled flowers on enchiladas.

Despite his joke about Leela's flightiness, he likes Kiki for her, likes his sister with an introvert who works too much. He and Leela met her for the first time in a bar off Rainey Street, Leela returning from the women's bathroom and leading a crying woman to their table. "You can let it out," Leela said, "but, deal is, I buy you a drink." Kiki sat, dressed in all white, wiping her face like a kitten pulled from a ravine. Leela bought her a rum and Coke, then signaled to him to *play it cool*. He was already doing his best to keep an even face, though it was hard with a woman crying in front of him. Kiki nursed her drinks with both hands, like she rarely drank, like the crowd of two-steppers was overwhelming.

"I messed up with a client," Kiki confessed. "So here's to proving the office right. All those times they looked at me and thought: *Diversity hire*."

"Don't even give that your energy," Leela said. "They love to tell themselves that."

In the red light, Kiki slowly nodded, deciding to agree.

She'd worn a rhinestone cowboy hat, Ever remembers. He should've told Amari.

By the time his sister returns, he's already crafted Amari an apology text: *Sorry if I misread. Didn't know how you felt about sharing rooms.* The dots on her side of the thread load: *So thoughtful . . . haha. Good night.*

"She's pretty." Leela folds her hands into her hoodie. "And clearly into you."

He waits to respond. Suddenly, after months of being cool toward him, his sister wants something. There's a tent of wariness they both stand under, each at opposite sides.

"You ever think about what Dad told us?" Leela says finally. "It's been on my mind with the wedding and everything."

"It's just some story."

"You've decided that for sure?"

A moth draws uneven circles over the string lights. Over the years, he and his sister have mentioned the story to each other a handful of times, mostly as a joke. Like after three of Leela's girlfriends claimed she was too much of a class clown. Or when a premed major in undergrad called her selfish for not choosing a career path that could benefit her whole family. In her twenties, Leela had met the first woman she'd ever been serious about, a bookseller who kayaked religiously along the Colorado on weekends. *You're just too young for me,* the woman had emailed. *You've got to get some experience under your belt.* After Leela had been silent for two days, he told her, "Everybody's got commitment issues, right?" and they shared a joint on her apartment balcony. Eventually, Leela asked, "You think you're madder at Elijah or Evaline?" Then laughed through the drift of smoke.

Tonight, Ever says, "It's just something our family likes to say now and again. It doesn't . . . operate on the level I like to operate on."

"Why? Lot of stories are at least half-true."

"What about Grandaddy? He was married forty-five years."

"Sure."

Neither of them says the rest. Their grandmother had died a year before they were born, in a car accident. She'd been in the middle of nowhere, on an interstate connector near Marfa, half a day's journey from home and from anybody she knew.

"I wanted to ask," his sister goes on, over the endless crickets, "if you ever found anything at Grandaddy's place."

"Other than a bunch of old furniture and boxes?"

"You know what I mean. If there's some . . . record of something. Why all this feels real or . . . how he got around it. I should've asked him when his mind was still good. I wish I'd asked him a lot of things, honestly."

"It's just family lore," he repeats. "We don't have to go down this road."

"It's my wedding." She pulls her hoodie around herself, the wind moving over the hills, over the invisible canyons in the distance and their own stubborn figures. "I'm asking for a gift."

II

HIS FAMILY HAS ALWAYS FOCUSED on the love lost, always told the moment of Elijah's departure and what followed. It would take over a decade for Ever to hear more. Winter. His twenty-second year filled with the warmth of having earned his degree and launched himself into a good tech job, managing the interface for a grocery delivery app. His father's siblings, Uncle Dell and Auntie Charlee, were living together in that house in Pflugerville, and he sat with them on the back porch, its screen turning the overhead bulb into a net of light against the floorboards. Uncle Dell's woman had recently left him, saying he'd been broke as long as she'd known him. Auntie Charlee had lost her fiancé at the mall, turning around to show him a cashmere sweater, only to find him gone and, later, his truck missing from the parking lot.

Relationships weren't everything, Ever thought as he drank his coffee. You didn't need them to be happy. For the past year, he'd been allowing himself only strangers and late nights. But he supposed you wanted the option of another person, to help bear everything else.

"I can see why she did it," Auntie Charlee said, stroking her mug's handle. "Evaline. I can see why it hurt so doggone much."

"Shoot." Uncle Dell crossed one ankle over his knee, which disturbed the drape of his corduroy jacket. "If she couldn't understand running, there was a lot she didn't get."

"Impossible choices."

But her voice trailed, and Ever sensed his father's siblings holding something back. He pressed them. They hesitated. He pressed again. "What?" Auntie Charlee said. "You don't know the rest of it?" Like he could know things he hadn't been told about, that weren't even written down.

Evaline, Auntie Charlee said, had more trouble to deal with after Elijah left. Old Master Roberts, more slave owner than wounded father, kept badgering her about where Elijah had gone. As if she must've helped him prepare. It was all she could do to sleep at night with the babe a turned-over stone within her. Yet Roberts was outside the cabin every evening when the field work was done, threatening to sell her farther South soon as the babe was born.

Then—sudden as a downpour wearing itself out, Roberts stopped coming. Instead, he sat on the front porch overlooking the fields, lazing in his own contentment. At first, the whispers in the quarters said it was because Texas had just won at Sabine Pass, which meant Roberts had wrapped yet another finger around his wealth.

But rumors came from a woman hired out to a nearby plantation. She'd seen Elijah there, she said, toiling away on the iron fences. For punishment, he was wearing the horns and had to mind their bells and rods knocking against the bars. At Primrose, the woman said. Not even a two hours' walk. Imagine being gone half a year and hardly any distance away.

That night, in the women's cabin, Evaline turned her face to the wall. She could see Elijah with that collar round his neck, the rods jutting out a cattail's length and making any sort of peace impossible. She felt cold from the inside out, sweltering from the outside in. Perhaps she had cursed the wrong person. But Elijah had been the only one she'd expected anything from.

"Of course, she'd see him again," Aunt Charlee went on. She looked out into the small backyard, where the mountain laurels made dull heaps against the wooden fence. "Freedom being so soon, less than a year out. And we know he was buried out there in '67. After yellow fever got him."

Ever had finished his coffee, his mind drained after thinking of many things at once. What must it have been like, when Elijah and Evaline first saw each other again? Perhaps too much would have happened in their absence from each other. Either his father hadn't known that part, or it hadn't been the story he wanted him and Leela to hear.

As he watched his aunt and uncle exchange heavy glances, he didn't ask if they believed in curses or witches. Or if they mulled over such family stories because they could draw a wobbly line from Elijah's misfortune to their own. But maybe it wasn't about them. Maybe you needed to hold close the truth of your ancestors' love, chosen despite their circumstances.

Instead, he leaned forward, elbows on his knees. Asked: "How'd you learn all that?"

"Our grandmother," Auntie Charlee said. She smiled, remembering. "Shame you never met her. Bet you've never even seen a picture."

"She was a blunt one," Uncle Dell said. "Always said Elijah didn't have any sense. She couldn't get over how, before he got caught, he ran south." Uncle Dell's breath made faint puffs in the air. He looked into the shape as if something would reveal itself.

"She always said: 'Why wouldn't you listen to the stars, telling you where to go?'"

GRANDADDY'S HOUSE HAS ALWAYS FELT like the last scrape of the past. In the indigo of early morning, Ever moves through its low rooms, searching for God knows what. It's like parts of Grandaddy's mind have been leaking out of the man for years, filling the small Victorian off Navasota. The main hallway forms one trail, its photographs evolving from sepia to color, ending in a picture of his grandparents cuddling outside a Billie Holiday performance at Victory Grill. There's the cherrywood chifforobe that holds the suits Grandaddy wore to the Baptist church each Sunday. And, finally, the loose pine floorboard in the kitchen, where Grandaddy used to hide the tallies from his decades of running numbers in the Negro District, before the Texas Lottery came along and killed his business.

There's no disappearing in old age, Ever thinks. You simply grow more diffuse.

What sort of record is Leela even looking for? Some photo album or diary? Some discarded family history report? He combs through boxes of clothes in the bedroom and VHS tapes in the TV stand, through old Bibles in their pile on the credenza desk and gold-rimmed glassware in the kitchen cabinets. With every meaningless object he puts down, a knot in his chest unwinds. A relief.

By midmorning, Amari has already texted, which he must've missed while digging through Grandaddy's things. *You coming?* she's sent. The attached photo shows him more of her body than he's ever seen. Before the foamy spill of a waterfall, she exists only from the waist up: Damp patches on her tangerine bikini. Twists pulled back. Her neck bare, the soft lines there like another nakedness, separate from the crevice between her breasts.

He texts: *On the way.*

She replies: *Hurry.*

And he wishes chivalry had never been invented.

He tries one more avenue, given that he has to make the call to Magnolia Terrace anyway, ahead of signing out Grandaddy for the wedding. As the phone rings, he toys with the latch on the sash windows until the nurse answers. Yes, she says, everything looks to be in order for tomorrow. Before he can even get out his question, she adds, "Your grandfather's having a good day. Maybe you'd like to speak to him?"

"Ever?" Grandaddy asks on the line. His baritone's both rough and velvety, like layers in bedrock. "They say you're coming to get me."

"They're telling the truth." He thinks of Grandaddy keeping him and Leela when their parents had to meet with the lawyers. All those hotcake dinners beside checker games. The way Grandaddy encouraged them to draw dollar bills on cardstock, which he called "the only time in their lives making money would be easy." But habit has taught Ever that Grandaddy doesn't remember this. To Grandaddy, it's Ever Roberts II on the line. Still, Ever says, "I'll be there tomorrow."

"Who's getting hitched?"

"Leela. Roberts."

"Let's hope the weather has mercy. Be some ceremony if the garbage starts smelling."

"No going to Wheatville tomorrow. I'll be driving you up to the Hill Country."

"Oh."

Grandaddy goes quiet, back in his boyhood on Austin's west side, back in the 1920s, when the city forced Black families to go without water and sanitation services until they moved to their allotted six square miles. "I know people don't learn about it, but that's what happened," his father has warned them all. "When Pops is back there, don't try to pull him out."

Ever murmurs, "You remember Maisie?"

His grandfather sucks his teeth. "Why wouldn't I remember my wife? Only flaw she had was her driving, how she always got distracted by whatever was on the radio. And don't let Billie be playing, neither, or she'd have to pull over. Made me feel better just to take her up the street to the grocery store."

"You were married a long time."

"Not long enough, if you ask me."

"What got you through?"

The silence returns, deeper. Over the line, Ever hears a strong wind.

"God," his grandfather answers. "I know that for a fact."

BECAUSE OF AN ACCIDENT on 290, it takes Ever two hours to return to the lodge, ridged as a shell emerging through the meadow's surface. The whole ride, he's been rehearsing one apology to his sister (*Listen, there was nothing, but that's not bad news.*) and another to Amari (*Wasn't standing you up. Got behind on some wedding business.*). But the guests are already returning from their swim, filing beneath the lodge's walkway. Pale sunscreen streaks dark shoulders. His mother, in her sarong and gold bracelets, waves tensely at his car, and his father stands a little ways from her in a striped polo, hands in his cargo pockets. There's something unreadable in his face, though perhaps it is only his usual discomfort with swimming holes, their unpredictable bacteria.

And at the edge of the windshield: Amari. He parks next to her and climbs out. Apart from the others, she ties a sheer cloth around her upper body, like she contains an inner breeze at odds with the afternoon glare.

"You missed a lot," she says. "Really, you couldn't have worse timing."

"The traffic getting up here was—"

"Nobody can get in touch with Kiki." She's staring, relaying the entire morning he's missed. "She was supposed to be here for the swim, and your sister's been calling her. And now everything's going straight to voicemail."

It's slow, the return to a moment he's experienced several times before. Like driving the same daily route and knowing the house on the corner is dilapidated, collapsing in on itself. You keep hoping somebody's fixed it.

"I'm sure," he says, "that she was caught in the same traffic I was."

"Don't think your sister sees it that way. It's been a morning you wouldn't believe." Amari looks over his shoulder, toward his waiting parents.

She's not thinking about any family story, he realizes. She's pissed he wasn't here. Spine tight and cold, he pictures her introducing herself to everyone: *I'm Amari? Ever invited me?*

Apparently, Leela has decided to skip lunch, is hiding in her room. He bides his time in going after her, wanting to soothe Amari, who hovers at his elbow as they make rounds in the circular courtyard. Sweat collars his neck. His sister and Kiki have planned a small wedding, fewer than thirty guests, mostly family and a handful of friends from Leela's various jobs and Kiki's firm. So there aren't many people to greet on the patio with its tables of bagged lunches, and therefore only so many times he can mutter compliments about the venue, the paintbrush and bluebonnets glimpsed on the drive in. The guests sneak glances toward the lodge, take their sandwiches toward the long farmhouse tables. Everyone waits for one of the brides to appear.

Then there's his father's side. Uncle Dell, who believes whole-heartedly in the curse, helps himself to more champagne, as if the only choice is to make the best of things. Auntie Charlee, who wants not to believe, takes a wooden bench by the lodge's entrance, to better greet Kiki when she arrives. His father mutters to his stepfather all the reasonable possibilities for Kiki's absence: the traffic, ordinary cold feet, something unexpected at work.

Only his mother smiles, muscling everyone into cheer and dragging up an extra chair to sit beside Amari. "I have to admire your home training," his mother says. Her coral sundress matches her blush. "Most girls wouldn't be so calm about not getting a proper introduction." Amari smiles, faintly. Turns the conversation to their rival sororities. Without him, they've crossed entire territories of conversation.

The afternoon moves on, indifferent to the growing confusion. As the sun pours out an endless bucket of heat, Amari turns to him and says, "Shouldn't you go check on your sister?"

Like he has to be told. Like he hasn't been trying all afternoon to weigh the things he can control against the things he can't.

AFTER SEVERAL KNOCKS, Leela lets him into her room, then slumps wordlessly back through the all-white suite, to the balcony overlooking the corner of the lodge. The grasses bow under the force of the wind, pointing toward the granite and sycamores beyond.

"I could hear y'all talking," Leela says, plopping into a cushioned chair. Her hair's still swim-knotted in its bun. All this time, she's been arranging her bridal bouquet on a low table, which he remembers her deciding to do herself in order to cut down on costs. Dried thistle, buttercups, lavender sprigs wrapped in brown crepe paper. "I'm guessing you don't have something to tell me."

"I spoke to Grandaddy." He takes his own seat. "Though he didn't give me much."

"Should've asked you to look sooner."

"C'mon now. Kiki wouldn't go out like this."

"You know what you haven't said? *Of course she's coming, Lee.* Or, *It's normal for people to act weird the day before the wedding.* Or, *She'll be here before the rehearsal.*" For the first time, her gaze meets his full on. A dead quality coats her mouth, her flat eyes. She hasn't put on her eyelashes. "You've been believing in this story longer than you'd care to admit to me."

"We're not kids anymore. Not a couple of eleven-year-olds needing to explain our parents."

Yet—there's a small box within him, its flaps opening into the air in his chest. Those hours he spent searching his grandfather's belongings. That . . . *relief* when he'd found nothing. He'd felt some small delight in not putting an end to talk of curses.

"You're going to be alright, Lee," he says.

And she's shaking her head, right as somebody whistles from below.

Over the balcony railing, their father stands beneath them. "Good news," he says, though there's a question in his voice. "Kiki's folks heard from her."

KIKI IS SAFE, their father tells them. Alive. Apparently wanting to finish a project for a client ahead of the honeymoon. This is what she has texted her parents.

In the bridal suite, Ever watches his sister's shoulder blades draw together, two doors closing. This time, when Leela dials, Kiki answers right away and mutters apologies: Of course she will be there tomorrow. She'd sent a message earlier, saying she wanted to use the time she has *today*, she will be *useless* after wearing herself out with guests. The message must not have gone through.

"Didn't go through?" Leela says after the call. "I ring her a million times, and she's saying a text didn't go through?"

"I know," he says. And his sister whips around and slams the bedroom door, and maybe it will make things worse, to question tomorrow. It'd be smart to be the first to leave, he thinks, watching his father head back to the courtyard. If you knew what was coming.

The tension hangs over the rehearsal in the dusk. The parents practice walking down the aisle, and, next to Leela, a shaken Amari fills in for Kiki, the officiant with a black bob curtly telling them where to stand. In the rows of Chiavari chairs, the guests chatter and play cards on the cushions, watching the rehearsal and pretending not to.

Ever stays in his seat, flinching inside every time his sister checks her phone. He knows the balance of her thoughts: Perhaps Kiki didn't want all the celebrations. Or really was working. Yet—she texted her parents first.

"I'm going up for the night," Leela tells him when the rehearsal's over. She steps out of reach of his touch. "Enjoy the food for me, okay?"

When darkness has settled in and everyone has eaten a solemn dinner, the guests file back to their rooms, and Ever helps the catering staff clean the remains of smoked chicken and potato salad. His mother catches his father by the elbow and mutters something to him beneath the carriage lights. His parents' polite distance. Their heads cocked together. It is like seeing them the way he did his eleventh year, when they'd argued in the kitchen. "Tell me, who signs up to be in a marriage by themselves?" his mother had whispered. "Who would take such a raw deal?" Which hadn't made sense to him then. Whenever he and Leela had wondered if their father would return from his hospital shift in time for dinner, his mother had said, "We have to call ourselves lucky that we have somebody capable of saving a life."

Eventually, even his parents decide there is nothing to do but turn in. His mother kisses his cheek. His father asks if he's still getting Grandaddy in the morning. *Perhaps,* his father's weary eyes say, *the best thing to do is to hope tomorrow keeps its promises.* When they leave, Amari lingers at the edge of the patio, toeing one of the loose rocks.

Before she can say anything, he goes, "Don't be mad, about this morning."

"*Mad*'s a big word," she says. "I can be annoyed that you missed all those hours. And . . . still question myself for feeling pawned off on your family. Though I felt guiltier as the day got worse."

She thumbs her wrists. With the night cooling, the faint hairs on her arm lift. He wonders if some part of her has linked the day's events to the story he told her. *Does any of this feel like evidence?* he wants to ask her. *Can somebody's life be the evidence?*

He says only, "Come back with me. Tonight."

Amari swallows, the shape a faint shudder within her throat.

AFTER A LONG DRIVE that passes in polite conversation, they are at his grandfather's. She slips out of her sandals at the threshold, and he can sense her taking in the place, measuring his life as he turns on the lights, which snap over the old furniture, the burgundy walls. What must it have been like, to be the first Roberts to believe in curses? It couldn't have been Elijah, a man who spent the darkest nights of his life in quarters with the endless reshuffling of family. Any belief would've come from his children or grandchildren, comparing notes. The regular troubles: The shorter life expectancy of a boyfriend with prostate cancer or a wife with a womb leaking after childbirth. The sudden absence of a spouse with heart disease. Then, all the love yanked away. Losses echoed across generations.

Some family member would've seen too many stories play out and put stock in the telling. Somebody would've fearfully touched a body in the dark, the way he touches Amari now, hand on the small of her back, seeking at least a moment.

"Turn the lights off," Amari commands, and he obeys.

He guides her through the cramped den and into the bedroom, until she's on the tan ottoman before the sash windows. The streetlights stripe her dark skin through the blinds.

"I didn't come here to sleep with you," Amari says. "I've just learned that talking in dim light makes people speak truthfully."

"Alright."

"I mean it. Half the time, I feel like I know everything about you, and the other half, I feel like I'm out here on my knees for some guy who's unserious."

"I am serious. Want me to get on my knees?"

"Don't be stupid. And don't even try to be cute." She strokes her duffel beside her. Scary, to ask her what more she's thinking, if she's already planning to turn down the job offer. "Is it normal for you to invite women places, and then skip out?"

"It wasn't skipping out."

"So you weren't . . . with somebody else?"

"I wouldn't do that. It was only a favor. For Leela."

"And when it comes to your sister, do you normally ignore her when she's upset?"

"Leela just . . . processes on her own. You've got to wait 'til she's ready."

"Hmmm. And if you'd gone with us this morning, to that swimming hole, would you have eased in? Or jumped?" She removes her neckerchief. Then removes the tie from her twists.

"I don't know," he says. "I would've had to be there."

She keeps asking questions as they brush their teeth, as she pulls her bonnet over her hair. By the time they lie beside each other in his grandfather's bed, she has asked him a million: If he hates weddings or if they make him swell with feeling. If he loves some relatives more than others. If he's happy seeing his mother remarried or if part of him wishes she'd stayed with his father.

He answers: He's never let himself think too hard about weddings. There's a sadness in Auntie Charlee he hates himself for fleeing. He wishes his father had something like his mother's contentment. The man never remarried, too skittish now that he knows the difficulty of untethering your life from someone else's.

Amari lies against him, chin tucked into his shoulder. She unburdens herself of the questions she's carried this far to meet him. He is learning her shape, its hard and soft places. Whenever she speaks, her back hums.

"You haven't asked me if I want you to take the job," he says, after midnight.

"'Cause that's for me to decide."

"Kinda feel like I get to say something, given how much I've been asked."

"I took the bus, spent all day keeping your family's spirits high. I'm owed." She shifts against him. "But let me try something. Let's see if I can guess what's on your mind."

He waits in the darkness, the shadows in his grandfather's place longer than the objects that cast them. His mind's on so much that she's likely to guess correctly. Part of him keeps waiting for his cell to chime, for Leela to text him that Kiki's made it to the lodge and really was finishing a project. Yet—what is this faint stirring in him? It will answer some question if Kiki doesn't show.

"You were thinking about that story you told me," Amari mumbles against his skin. "How that'd be . . . such a weird coincidence."

The understanding arrives as heavily as the weight of her head sinking against him in sleep. His earlier relief: If there is a curse on his family, even on the dust mote of his particular life, then he cannot be blamed, nobody's leaving can be his fault. How hard it is, to take full possession of yourself. And how impossible to anticipate the choices of somebody else.

Amari snores against him, another detail he hadn't known.

He lies awake, listening, trying to guess at the course of her dreams.

III

IF HIS RECOLLECTION IS TRUE, there was a period of his life when talk of curses unnerved him. In the year after their splitting, his parents seemed to be made of thinner material, formed of skin but no bone, at the whim of the wind. They moved so carefully in those days: hushed phone calls and heavy glances and prolonged weekend drop-offs. As if they didn't want him and Leela to feel the change all at once, they'd meet for breakfast at their usual place, dining as a family in a café with orange-tile floors and linoleum tables. The same routine, accompanied by a scheduled splitting.

One such morning, Leela and Dad had gone to the counter to place their order, leaving him and his mother at the table. His mother always looked like a different person on the Saturdays he was being returned to her. Fresh-faced, a grace to her fingers as she pulled napkins from the holder to make them place mats. She'd shaved her head, which called more attention to the elegance of her mouth, the calm there.

What did it feel like to be moved to leave somebody? Was it an itch in your hip's back corner? Or an idea that wouldn't let go until you'd obeyed?

"I'm going back with Dad," he said.

Her eyelids quivered, faintly lined and rimmed in black. Like a small wave turning over within her. "It's not his week. And he has to clear his schedule with the hospital."

"Well, I'm asking."

"You can't," she said. "And I'm sorry for making you feel this way."

In another stage of his life, such an attempt to wound her would wreck his idea of himself. But he was twelve. She'd left his father, and she deserved to know what it felt like.

"It wasn't a decision," his mother said, "that I made lightly, you know."

He shrugged. Wondered if his father had told her the story he'd told him and Leela. Or if his mother was loving the three of them through the fence of what she knew.

"I mean it," his mother went on. "Maybe . . . when I was in the thick of making up my mind, I could've chosen differently. Your father's the best for you, and, at the same time, not the best for me. As a husband. Which I tried to live with."

"Tried."

Some ten feet away, Leela cocked her hip to one side and pointed at a kolache in the display case. Their father tugged her back by her purple hood.

"Would it help if I explained?" his mother asked, and when he said nothing, she went, "It was like I kept hearing everything I wasn't getting. At the highest volume imaginable. The time we weren't spending. The same old apologies. How much help I needed. All that got so . . . loud. I could barely hear my own name over it. I just kept getting flattened beneath that feeling."

He ripped a corner of his napkin. So his mother had a feeling. Which was maybe something you could control and maybe something you couldn't.

His mother glanced left, where Dad and Leela were returning with paper bags.

"I felt things could be better for everybody," she said, her voice quiet. "And you should know, whatever I felt, it had nothing to do with you and your sister."

SOMEHOW, HE'S MANAGED TO SLEEP because when he wakes in his grandfather's bedroom, Amari is gone. He hadn't heard her rise. Hadn't heard her collect her duffel from the ottoman. Yet he senses her absence before his eyes adjust to the gray morning. He's almost expected it.

He rises and searches the house—smell of coffee, eggshells in the garbage disposal—though he doesn't relax until, through the den window, he sees her sitting on the front steps. She's in a concert tee and jean shorts, sipping from a mug next to his grandfather's yellow agaritas, her knees balancing her diary. He's forgotten that she told him she's an early riser, that she seeks at least an hour alone every morning, before her phone starts buzzing.

This thought in him, which he hates himself for having: How thoroughly she has her life together, even when in turmoil. There's a relentless pressure to earn his place.

Her ritual calls others to mind. Dad making vegan strawberry smoothies and Mom reading her horoscope at the counter and

Leela needing to set three alarms to be awake in time for school. On those nights Ever and Leela had stayed with him, Grandaddy's ritual had been reading his Bible.

"God," the man had said. "I know that for a fact."

The suspicion arrives slowly, taking its time to reach him through his worries about Amari, through his fears for Leela. His grandfather has owned many Bibles, though the one he read from each morning was a black tome with its spine warped and cracked as tree bark. It was so heavy it rarely got moved from its place beneath the others on the desk.

When Ever uncovers it, the Bible releases its dust into the air. Grandaddy's skin cells and who knows who else's. Carefully, Ever lays it on the kitchen table. The spine's so broken, the glue eroded, that the thing barely holds together.

There's nothing inside. Just the same details he's seen a million times before, the penciled underlines and marginalia Grandaddy's left behind. Almost all of it restates Scripture in his own words or contains lines from spirituals: *Don't you let nobody turn you aroun'*.

But when Ever traces the split spine, his thumb detects a sharp point. A tip. He opens the Bible to its last page and sees an envelope jutting through the binding, tucked in the back amid centuries of family names.

The envelope is full of time-faded documents. Which he's grateful for, so what he holds can make itself known to him slowly. Bills of sale. A crude sketch of plantation land, complete with a grand manor and smaller cabin squares. A sharecropping contract signed with an *X*. All preserved from sunlight, tucked within a volume older than Grandaddy's hundred years. And in the very back of the envelope, there's a paper with more writing on it than any other. A letter.

Something ancient reaches toward him, the paper fully unfurling like a long yellow finger. It reveals a delicate, fading cursive:

Dear Th. Roberts—

With any other gentleman, I'd hesitate to send this letter, yet for some twenty years, you and I have had a good deal of success balancing our friendship and finances. A number of factors can account for our mutual respect. Your understandings of how to manage the slaves, for one, which have been instrumental in helping me maintain order as we await news of our Confederate victory. Further, as you expressed during my visit last Christmas, you admire my willingness to be forthright, when it'd be easy to coat my tongue in pleasantries.

He sits down. What comes over him is the same feeling he often has in museums dedicated to painful histories, a feeling that the world has sucked him back in time through a straw, to remind him how small he once was. There isn't even glass to temper the sensation.

By now you'll have realized that these words accompany my man, William, and the blacksmith Elijah. It is with great discomfort that I am returning him to you and annulling our agreement. I will of course explain my reasoning, but I must say first that Elijah's punishment has done him good. He did unimpeachable work in restoring the fencing around the property, and though I have not let him travel to obtain more materials, I believe that such journeys would no longer be out of the question.

Nevertheless, he has caused trouble among my slaves. He spent some time with my Adell, and after some months, she escaped south, our men failing to capture her before she crossed the Mexico border. Then Jenny got it in her head to go after a negro long sold to my cousin in Louisiana, and when you consider our bringing Malinda back from loitering at the Haywood plantation last week, that means some idea has caught fire among my slaves—a fire perhaps less dangerous than revolt, but a fire nonetheless. I fear Elijah is upsetting the delicate balance I've established at Primrose Grove. A balance you have taught me to keep, especially during these tumultuous years for our Texas.

Normally, I would not put stock in superstition. I leave such talk to my kitchen wench, who has been recounting a story your Dido shared on her last visit to my cookhouse, a concerning tale involving witches and curses and other fancies negroes like to entertain. I know the God I serve. Yet even Pharaoh was not immune to plagues or storms that defied reason.

Make of this what you will. Elijah is returned to you, and I am convinced he will cause you far less trouble than he has caused me.

Your good friend and neighbor,
H. R. Glenn

Ever rereads the words, faded and searing. They've had to make room to enter him, as if through a slit now too wide to close. The curse. Not some yarn spun by his family, in need of a laugh during their troubles. Some haunting—and not freedom—had even returned Elijah to that same Roberts land he'd once fled. How on earth could Grandaddy have read this and come away with enough belief to sustain him for forty-five years?

The sliding door lets in a fresh gulp of air. From someplace beyond him, Amari says good morning, that she woke and wanted to get down her impressions of Texas, the morning in the city looked so different from the morning in the Hill Country, completely cleansed of stars. She almost wishes she could've experienced things the other way around.

"What?" she asks, when she sees his face. "Is it Leela?"

Which it is. And also, this woman standing before him with sleep in her eyes. It feels like a promise, now, how he will lose even more than what he has.

AMARI IS CHATTY AND OBLIVIOUS as they drive to Magnolia Terrace to pick up his grandfather. Three minutes down the streets that backdropped his blissfully ignorant childhood, where Black and Brown children rode their bikes up Comal, speeding past the church ladies telling them to watch out this Saturday morning, the funeral home was jumping and didn't need any more death today. Then another two minutes past the modern farmhouses and metal cottages that have replaced the craftsman bungalows, then down East Eleventh Street with its coffee shops and new boutiques in boxes of glass. "This doesn't look anything how it used to, huh?" Amari asks. He reaches for her fingers, feels her startle when he squeezes. It isn't right how some things get to be lost, and others don't.

After another half hour, they've reached the facility that looks like student housing, apartments with grid windows and wisteria and no balconies. The nurses have already brought out his grandfather. Despite the spring warmth, the old man has chosen his Sunday oil-black suit and shining wing tips. He looks dressed for a funeral. Part of Ever remembers that he was supposed to bring Grandaddy's lighter suit. But too many things have been going on.

Let's get out of here, Ever wants to tell Amari when they climb out to greet him. *Let's go back to the house, to DC, wherever. Let's have what we can, while we can.*

But Grandaddy is already saying, "Let me see here, now. Who is this lady?" and holding Amari by the wrist, inspecting her like fine cloth.

"A girl Ever wishes he had," she says.

He hears everything she's not saying, every term they have not used for each other. Perhaps he hasn't been clear enough about what he wants with her.

"Sounds about right," Grandaddy says, white brows knotting. "You're too pretty and clever to fall for his tricks."

On the freeway, Grandaddy stews in the back seat and Amari asks about the buildings in the distance, the endless construction and cranes. In her voice, Ever hears the disappointments of other women, which eventually, he knows now, will become her disappointments. That he either wants too much sex or never initiates. That he either never pays them any attention or else is too intense, his affection overwhelming. That he is either messy or anal about keeping a home clean. That he is simply not who he appeared to be.

"Why are you so quiet, all of a sudden?" Amari asks, taking a break. "Your gears are turning so hard over there, I'm half tempted to roll down this window."

"Leela's not answering my texts," he responds.

Amari touches his knee, a thread of concern.

"Ole pigtailed Leela Mae Roberts," Grandaddy says, and starts humming Sam Cooke's "Bring It on Home to Me," the B-side on a record of his that Leela often requested in her girlhood.

At least it is a good day for somebody.

The city melts around them, gnarled mesquites and bluestem meadows following them all the way to the lodge's exit, even when Grandaddy has stopped singing and fallen asleep, even when Amari begins to worry about the wrinkles in her silk dress. Ever has only allowed himself to look at her in glimpses, as if he can slowly siphon off their time together. How happy she looks in his car, with the morning entering her hair and revealing its currents of light brown. How stupid that, out of habit, she keeps hiding her neck with her palm, when there are so many other things to worry about.

Ten minutes out, he pulls onto the road's shoulder, along a patch of prickly pears. He kisses her right through the surprise of her mouth parting, right over Grandaddy's silent sleeping.

"Stay," he says. "Here."

"I hear you," she says. But she's only half laughing.

"I just need you to know where I stand."

"Thanks for telling me." For several seconds, she says nothing else. Her face contracts as the words sort themselves within her. It takes too long. Finally, she says. "I don't know, Ever."

He's still leaning close to her, his mouth warm. He knows something in his face changes because something in hers does too. The radiance she's had all morning retreats behind her even expression, part of herself tucked away someplace safe.

"It isn't you," she says, glancing toward the back seat. "What we have . . . feels different from anything I've ever had to understand."

"Uh-huh."

"I'm serious. It was just . . . what happened yesterday. Being alone up here with your family. I could see how everything could go wrong. I could come all the way out here, and we might not work, and there'd be nothing I could do about it. I can . . . only control myself. No matter the answers I try to get out of you."

Everything she's saying is rational, full of truths. And he hasn't convinced her otherwise.

"I'm sorry," she says. "The job once felt more right than it does now."

"It's alright." He pulls back. In the rearview, Grandaddy's thin eyelids twitch in sleep. Like moth wings. "We ought to go. Before we're late."

"I still want to be close the way we were."

"I mean, I don't think this weekend's let us off the hook for anything."

As he switches the car's gears, he senses her draw in a breath. Only when he's pulling away does she place her fingers over his on the wheel. She's sweating. She opens her mouth and closes it again.

"I can't believe how far this is," she says eventually. "You've made two trips up here now."

Three. But he doesn't correct her. It is all he can do to keep driving.

Bursts of activity await them at the lodge, which only makes him feel like everything through the windshield is happening far away, on a screen. Guests navigate the gravel in their heels, balancing wrapped gifts. Two caterers haul in a two-tiered lavender cake, and a photographer in a beige suit snaps away. As he parks and helps his grandfather out of the car, Ever keeps trying to focus on what's happening, as if he can make it stick. Amari steps out into the fresh air and sighs, too deep. His father rushes over, unblinking, a little sweaty in his suit and purple boutonniere.

"It's alright," his father says, reading his mind. He helps Grandaddy steady himself. "Everyone's here."

But Ever doesn't believe it, not even when all the guests have gathered in the courtyard, everybody but Grandaddy dressed in the white the brides have requested. He hardly believes when the music starts and everyone stands. There is no wedding party, no extra gowns or bouquets. From the front row, Amari tense on his left and Grandaddy relaxed on his right, he stares at the runner of dried blooms, leading from the lodge doors.

Kiki steps forward in her lilac gown, flanked by her parents on each side. She has chosen a lace veil, which flares in the wind like a bell. It hides her face, exaggerates her determined walk. *I'm here*, her steps say. *I did what I had to do, to be here.* A good thing, he reminds himself. At least his sister can have what she's planned, for now.

Then—the music changes. Leela has withheld many of the wedding details from him. But this is the moment she's been leading everyone toward: Piano and Billie Holiday. His grandfather's shoulders relaxing. "Softly" is the song, played at their grandparents' wedding. Billie sings that she understands who she is, that she can tell her lover how to be.

"Mmhmm, that's alright now," Grandaddy says. Once, then again.

Perhaps the old man can see them too, Leela's fearful steps below the purple tulle of her wide gown, her wedding colors darker than Kiki's. She shrinks between their parents, Mom beaming beneath her wide hat and Dad making sure to walk slowly, as if to deposit Leela gently into her chosen life.

The surrounding guests wipe their eyes, yesterday's events forgotten. For some. Uncle Dell and Auntie Charlee track Leela's steps. Their father hesitates, just for a moment, as they reach the end of the aisle.

"There she goes," Grandaddy says. "No easy journey, so you've got to do it on purpose."

Which sounds like the rambling of a man who doesn't remember how he achieved his happiness. But Grandaddy has spoken right as Leela reaches Kiki, right as the bride at the altar extends a hand to the one with gloved, trembling fingers.

And, in his grandfather's words, Ever hears another meaning. *On purpose.* Like Mexico, he remembers. Like heading south. Or—at least in that general direction, toward the mouth of the Brazos. Elijah had gone the same way others went. Not blindly, not without intention, the way his great-grandmother thought, but because free land was close enough to learn the way and come back.

There must be more to the story than what's been told, Ever thinks as Amari leans against him, clutching his sleeve. So many versions not passed down.

Say Elijah always planned on returning to his woman. That he would've traveled three times to get to the border, to retrieve his would-be wife, then take them both to freedom, had he not been captured.

Say that, if Evaline were clever and determined enough to seek out a witch, then she could've been clever enough to invent the story of said witch. Say she sent it by way of gossip, to spook a white man already war-skittish and fearful of slave rebellion. *Everyone will leave,* she'd said, by which she could've meant, *Return to me what's not yours.*

She and Elijah had met again on that terrible land. Before freedom, when owning themselves had to be done in secrets and cleverness. Before yellow fever had arrived. Before time could let them prove how things would turn out.

Tell the whole story like this: That, once, a man sang a birdsong to a woman, changing the sounds a human could make. He sang even when told to leave her alone, when life had other plans. That man's descendant would find another song for a woman who loved jazz, and perhaps that woman had not quit him. Perhaps she wanted to drive to Marfa merely to witness the ghost lights. Or to visit a place she'd never been.

Say what these people left in their wake: A line of men and women looking for ways to have more than what was allotted. So many truths have been withheld. So many have been warped into what's convenient for the teller.

Ever's breath fills him, thick. Like something within him has shaken off dust.

Beside him, Amari tightens her grip on his sleeve. He adjusts so her hand loops through his arm. The hills surge behind the violet brides, their altar, the force of their decision.

"What about a few more days?" he murmurs to Amari. "If you stay—just a little longer?"

She waits a moment. Then steps so close her heels scrape his shoes. "Yes," she says. "Now be good."

The music fades. When his sister scans the crowd and finds him, he nods. She catches it, the assurance he tries to give her from this distance. Her face—shining and done up and not completely her own—relaxes. One chair over, Grandaddy sighs and sits down.

As if following him, the rest of the guests sit too, the endless crackling of chairs, the weight held. The officiant taps the mic. Says she's never seen it before, a crowd so ready to bear witness.

COTTONMOUTHS

THE SUMMER MOMMA AND I SHARE PREGNANCIES, THE cottonmouths come crawling out of the marshes. It's a wonder to watch, the way those snakes float their own weight, curving over the brown water and nosing into the mud. They slip all the way through the sawgrass. Work themselves into lazy balls on our land. *I ain't going no place*, you imagine them saying, *now that I'm all comfortable here.* And you kind of get what they mean.

Sometimes, I watch them from the back porch, 'specially when it's too hot to move—much less go carrying a baby inside you, thrashing in your belly like it's trying to shrug off your body heat. Every spring and summer, we get them, same as the other folks in Collier County, though they like our house best because of the way water collects in a little dip not far from our porch. Not so much water that we get eaten alive by mosquitoes, but enough for a Florida cottonmouth to stay cool.

Two years ago, one of Daddy's friends was helping to clear them out and he got bit, right on the calf. I remember him sitting in Momma's kitchen, his boot sideways on the floor and dripping clumps of mud on the wood, his right hand clutching a glass of whiskey. Daddy had lanced the wound and wrapped it, the red blurring over the white. Momma couldn't take her eyes off that spot, kept murmuring, "Thank you, Mr. Dursey. Getting out there like that." And he grinned at her through slitted eyes, grateful. He didn't die, and the next time the men came back from laying the Tamiami Trail, that highway they worked before switching to railroads, he and my father were out there again, glancing toward the house to see if Momma was watching.

MOMMA DOESN'T REALLY LIKE when I sit out alone. "You got two people to think about now," she's said before, "and you can't go focusing on yourself."

She worries a lot, about cottonmouths and heat waves and sickness, about money and the work she's missing in the orchard, now that she's too big to pick grapefruits at Deep Lake. Sometimes, she pulls me off the porch to help her around the house. She presses lavender into the rag cloths we carry around, holding the rough fabric over our nostrils as we search the hen pen for eggs or shake sea grapes off the trees or manage the harvest in Daddy's absence—things I'm expected to do every day now. After we boat into town for tea from the supply store, she brews it with ginger on our potbellied stove, and we rest the cups on our thighs, pointing as we watch the cottonmouths carve symbols in the dirt with their bodies, which look like Miss Davis' cursive on the classroom chalkboard.

It doesn't help, really, all this holding up and mixing in. We're always sick somehow, whether we take lavender or not, trading off days when our feet ache or our breasts throb. I look at Momma high on the porch steps. She rests her hand on her balloon of a belly and watches the trees like Daddy's gonna come back any minute. Every now and then, she gets a little smile on her face, and I think of me tumbling around in her womb way back when, somersaulting at the idea of her. I pat my belly, praying for my own baby to flip around. Even with the nausea, we're at peace in such moments—until Momma thinks she sees something moving in the grass.

"Don't you go messing with those," she says, if we see a stripe draped over a log. "When your daddy's back, he'll take care of 'em."

She is always saying things like this. Never mind that Daddy can be gone for weeks at a time, or that her callused feet, now swollen past their usual size, could squash any cottonmouth if she weren't so afraid. Her body is as muscled as my father's. All that farming and grapefruit picking. Yet he has a way of making it soft. Soft enough for her to groan when he takes her feet into his hands and teases the soreness from them. "I'm glad it was you," she tells him, when she thinks I'm out of earshot. He kisses her belly.

Really, she only wants me to hear the important things:

"You might try putting your feet up to get that swelling down. Or squeezing a little grapefruit in your bathwater."

Or, "No, cross the stitches this way for a hat. So it stays on your baby's head as best it can."

Or even, when I stand behind her, braiding her thick, dark hair into twists as fat as the cottonmouths: "If it's a girl, you want to tease the scalp like this so the hair will grow."

"Wouldn't I do the same if it was a boy?"

She tilts her head back, her smooth skin darkened.

"I think," she says, "you've been spending too much time teasing boys as it is."

WHAT SHE DOESN'T EXPLAIN to me is where the babies will sleep. In July, when he slips away from the Atlantic Coast Line, my father returns and brings us back watermelons. He's quiet, watching me eat, his cheeks pitted and sun beaten. Then he gets the crib from the shed and wipes down the dust and owl droppings. He doesn't look at me when he sets it up in the bedroom, close to my parents' bed. A few years ago, I was small enough to sleep there too. Though now I've got my own bed in the front room.

"Such a cute little thing," I say, running my hands over the crib's wood. There's a mattress inside, a small pillow with some orange stitches. I picture both of our babies sleeping there, my sister and my daughter, tiny fists touching.

My mother sighs behind me. She's on the bed, her knees slightly parted. "Cute alright. Until it starts waking you up."

"Maybe they won't cry," I say, peering down into the crib, reaching in a hand like there is already something to soothe. "They'll look over at each other and just grin."

When I turn around, Daddy's in the doorway, studying Momma. He rubs the back of his neck and looks more tired than anything.

"Oh, Twyla," my mother says. "Both of them can't fit in that little thing."

WHEN DADDY LEAVES AGAIN, it's like he takes some of Momma up the road with him. Sometimes, I can feel her growing tired of me, like when she suddenly dumps the lemons on the table and storms out of the kitchen or when I see her squinting at me under the clothesline, whipping the sheets into neat squares before dropping them into the basket.

"Who is it, Twy?" she whispers with that look on her face, and my mouth goes kind of dry and I shrug and say, "Can I have some water?"

She brings it to me and sits me down and brushes her fingers over my hair. I ask her how things are changing, what things were like when this was Calusa territory, then Seminole, then eventually Lee County, then split off into Collier, and she lets me go.

One day in early August, when I'm on the back porch and trying to count how many cottonmouths there must be, figuring the ones Daddy's gotten rid of, she comes up behind me and mimics my posture on the railing. It can't be easy, with her belly hanging so low in her blue dress.

"Twy," she says, real slow. "Twy, did someone *make* you? Can't you tell me that much, baby?"

And when I look at her from this angle, at the skin lined under her eyes, it feels like I've got a wad of lovegrass wedged in my throat. My tongue prods the roof of my mouth, and I think about how wet boys' tongues are, wet and surprisingly warm, when you thought your own mouth was warm enough.

"Twy," she says again, her fingers on my wrist.

I shake my head. "No."

"No?" She brings her face closer to mine. "Then tell me who it was."

She is so close to me that our foreheads nearly touch, and I wonder if she can see all of it, these boys I can't really explain, except to say that maybe everything began that moment seven months ago when I came in for a glass of water and saw her with Daddy in the kitchen. He was sitting at our old table, trying to sew up some buttons on his dress shirt. She came up behind him and ran one finger down the line of his neck, and I saw the way he turned to her. "Look straight," she said, and he obeyed, the needle still in his hand. She slid her fingers over his hair, passing his shoulders, gliding along his back. Then she did it again, trailing her mouth after her touch. He groaned. I stared at the part in her scalp as she leaned over him. And then I crept back to my room, ignoring my thirst because I knew this was a part of her I wasn't supposed to see.

But when Momma's so close to me now, eyes questioning, it's hard to keep these sorts of things away from her. Part of me wants her to see. 'Specially since I can't fix my mouth to explain. The game that stopped being a game. That first Tuesday. One of the boys in Miss Davis' class, Perlie, the Thompsons' youngest, was walking home in front of me. I followed him for a while and watched his neck peeking out his collar, and I put my finger there. He kind of froze. Then looked back at me, and when he twitched his mouth, the little hairs there twitched too. I could tell the way he looked at me wasn't the way it had been with Momma and Daddy in the kitchen, but he still took my hand and walked me the rest of the way back to the house. That's how we were for a few weeks, the tip of my finger just above his collar and his hand grabbing it quick, until one day I put my lips on his neck too. He gasped a little and reached around for my waist. Then he walked us off the road and to the old Williams farm, and we went inside the barn—then things hurt, then stopped hurting, and, at the end, when his face tightened, things seemed like they hurt for him. "It's 'cause I helped you with your reading that time, isn't it?" he asked when he pulled back. Though I didn't know what he was talking about. When we did our reading together, it hadn't felt like either of us was helping the other. He must've seen that I didn't remember the way he did because then his face didn't show me anything at all. After that, on school days, he didn't walk slow enough for me to catch him.

So I tried putting my finger on Wesley's neck, and when his face, yellow and smooth all over, broke into laughter, he said, "I guess nobody's telling lies" and led me to the barn right away. After, he lay beside me for so long that I wondered if this was what Momma enjoyed, the feeling that she could lead a man to some smaller place within himself. Wesley was bonier than Perlie, his ribs small, thin claws around his quivering lungs. Though I'd later understand what Wesley had meant by people telling lies. Because, soon, all the girls kind of sniffed when I walked by. And some of the boys started saying they'd taken me to that barn, though most of them had not.

It makes the back of my knees ache to think Momma can see all this in me. My dress grows sticky and damp, clinging like willow. "I don't know," I say. "I don't know."

She looks at me real hard. "What do you mean you don't know?"

"I mean," I say, "I don't know which."

She watches me a minute. Then, she understands.

ONE NIGHT, MOMMA TAKES ME outside and we sit on the porch, the moonlight revealing the roof on the next farm. She's got a thing for Bessie Smith, who's wearing out our radio with the "Lost Your Head Blues."

Even in the half-light, it's easy to see how Momma and I have swelled up something fierce, our twin stomachs the way we most resemble each other now. I cross my legs and pick at the scars I got from playing tag last winter. My mother fusses with the navel that sticks up under her dress.

"I'm not one of your friends, Twyla," she tells me, though she says it like she really means she's my *best* friend. "And so I can tell you what nobody else wants to." She runs a hand over my belly. Inside me, the baby leaps to her touch, and at this, her hand slows. "You can be clever once the baby's born, once you see who it looks like. Better to wait until then, anyway, since people will be kinder to a girl with a newborn."

"What you mean 'be kinder'?" I ask, though there's already a heat on my face.

"I'm saying that you'll probably have a choice about who to come to. Main thing is, you don't want a boy with smooth hands and arms no bigger than twigs. You want someone willing to work hard and who'll do what he can to keep a roof over your heads. That's how you decide who to name."

"For what?"

She looks at me like I am one of the earthworms always inching around the porch railing, slow and ridiculous.

"Don't be stupid, Twyla," she says. "You've got to have more help than me."

My mouth has never been so dry. I imagine Perlie or Wesley dressed in my father's overalls, coming back to a house like Momma's. But that feels wrong. Because of course it won't be the same house. I'll have to stand alone at the sink or with some woman who won't touch me when she talks or let me braid her hair. I'll have to pull clothes off a laundry line absent of Momma's dresses. I'll have to take care of this baby on some porch far from where Momma rocks hers, and though they might still grow to be close, it will not be the same because she will have held one of them more than the other.

From the dirt road, laughter rises. I can see the boys coming back from fishing, swiping their poles at one another and lunging. They act so different when they're together. In the barn, you could tell what worried them. Both Perlie and Wesley had started talking about what their daddies would bring them when they came back—and if they'd grow up to build railroads too. Or if they could pick grapefruits or work at the cannery or wait for the next job. Everybody around here knows by now how railroads bite. A screw in the hand. A blast gone the wrong way. The poison of heatstroke or catching some sickness from draining swamp water.

"All that noise wears me out," Momma says, waving in the boys' direction, but before I can agree she says, "I guess you have to have it while you can. The fun, I'm saying."

She grips the armrests and pushes herself up. Though she's breathing heavy, I don't help her, don't even look in her direction, and she rocks herself forward and moves into the house.

I LET THE NIGHT GROW cool before I go back inside, but when I do I have to wonder why Momma's standing on the chair.

"*Twyla*," she whispers, harsh, and she's got her skirt gathered in her fists, raised above her knees. Her legs have hardly a scar.

Then I see her. The cottonmouth wide as my arm. She's coiled right by the edge of the table. Perfectly still. Her speckled body so long and fat that I know I can't wrap my hand around her. If she's the kind of snake to work her way around a neck, she'd have to loop several times. Something in my throat squeezes and I have to slow my breathing.

"Twyla," Momma whispers. "Twyla, go back outside and get some help. Get *somebody*."

I watch the cottonmouth. Keep even my lips still, in case it thinks I want to make trouble. Momma says my name louder, and is it the sound of her voice making my skin tighten? I shrink back from Momma, from the cottonmouth. Until I barely fit around my baby.

The cottonmouth stays still. But Momma is waving. "Twyla, listen to me," she says. She lets her skirt fall a little. Puts her hands on her knees and tries to steady her voice. "Go on outside and get one of them to do something about it."

I don't move. I try to picture myself going up to Perlie and Wesley and the other boys. They'll stop playfighting and look at my stomach. Then I'll have to ask for help, and I don't even know, really, if they would do it.

"I can get it," I say, though my voice shakes. "Just let me get it."

"Twyla. Listen to me. Get—"

"I am listening," I say. I'm looking at the cottonmouth, the black slits for eyes, the curve of her mouth. She lowers her head, and I think, Oh. She's tired. She's much more worn out than you'd guess at first glance. "I'm listening. I'm listening, and I'm talking too."

Momma talks over me as I go to the walls and pull down the quilts that have hung there long as I can remember. When I come back, the snake still waits and Momma whispers, "Oh Lord, oh Lord, oh Lord."

I roll each quilt into a rope and make two lines, two blue-and-red-and-purple rows stretching a path from the door to the kitchen table. I keep my eye on the cottonmouth and it's watching me, unblinking.

"Come on," I say, and Momma says, "What you talking to it for?"

The cottonmouth doesn't move at first, then unfurls a little.

"It's gon' bite you," Momma says. "It's gon' bite you and then where will you be?"

I see the broom in the corner, useless. Then I remember standing water, things being the right heat or too much. I crack the front door and light all the lamps and load all the wood we have into the potbellied stove, orange brightening inside. I shut every window.

It takes a while. Momma has to ease herself onto the kitchen table, down on all fours, and sweat collects on the back of my neck and in every fold of my body. We could pass out, inside this place. All this time feels like being halfway between safety and something I don't even want to think about. But the snake moves, hesitant at first, stretching out so the heat isn't bunched up around it. Then I crack the front door farther, and after a few minutes, it noses in that direction, tongue flickering. I see the inside of its mouth, the gummy white cave.

"Go on, now," I say, and it shudders along, its head out the door before the long line of its body, bobbing between the patched quilts.

I wait until it's disappeared completely, then a few more seconds. I stick my head out the door, and for once the world is cooler by comparison. There's nothing on the porch, nothing weaving down the stairs. The grasses above the marsh in the distance wave back and forth, whether from wind or from something farther away, I can't tell. I stand there a long time, feeling my skin relax, my dress dry with my sweat.

WHEN I GO BACK into the kitchen, Momma is easing herself off the chair, one leg down and then the other. She turns to me, her eyes scanning my ankles.

"Nothing bit me," I say. "But we're gonna have to wash this dress."

"Let me see you," Momma says, and I let her spin me around, our stomachs brushing when she stops. "You got lucky. You should've done as I asked."

"Momma, I'm not going anywhere," I say. "I'm not going to live with one of them."

She doesn't take her hands from my shoulders. She studies my face and her nostrils are flaring and I can see something pulsing in her neck.

"I'm not going," I say. "I'm just not."

She doesn't say anything. I move her to another chair, where she places her arms on the table, slow and unsure.

"You're upset," I say. "Don't go getting upset." I turn to the stove and dampen the fire. Then I put on some tea. I swipe ginger from the cupboard and press into it with a knife. The sharp, sweet smell burns my nose a little. "Alright, now," I say. "You sit there."

Through the back window, there's no light in the other houses, only the moon like someone's erased a hole into the sky. The tea steams up and the air in the kitchen is so unbearable that I blow out the lamps and open the windows again. It's just that I've made something happen in this place. Or that here is where kind things happen to me.

I turn back to my mother, placing the tea before her. She stares down into it. I drink mine, imagining us sitting at this table months from now, two bundles in our arms, talking over whatever we have boiled or brewed or made. We'll lay our babies down in two cribs side-by-side, wherever we've found room. I'll wrap my fingers around Momma's wrist. I'll say: *Here, now isn't this better?*

ALL SKIN IS CLOTHING

THE BULLET SHATTERED THE WINDOW. MOONLIGHT fell in shards as the air split cool above their beds. When he could look up, a tiny mouth gaped in the white paint above the headboard. A hole.

Had the bullet missed him? His sister? Through the window's emptiness, he saw headlights swerving into the Kentucky night. One set, then two. Yellow light so harsh it scraped the house across the street, its peeling charcoal paint.

Across the room, Cadence swooped out of her sheets, unharmed. A flash of dark limbs and a lone muscle of stomach. She pulled him against her, and he felt his six years crouching against her fifteen. Her shell-tipped braids covered his knees seconds before her arms belted him into her powder-sweat smell. Her whole body hummed his name—*Brayden*—even as his voice sunk deep into his chest.

The door banged open, and Momma screamed, clutching her gown's pink folds. He thought the bullet had passed into his parents' room, lodging in her shoulder. A tiny wound blooming against her gown's embroidered lace. Their shotgun house finally bowing to its namesake.

But Momma rushed toward him. Squeezed him so tight he knew the bullet hadn't touched her. Maybe she screamed because *he* was dead. Or dying. He couldn't find his voice. A pit had opened in his chest and swallowed him.

"He's fine, Momma, see?" Cadence said. "See?"

She held her hands up to the moonlight. They were clean of blood. Shaking a little.

He believed he was alive only because she did.

"Bray, baby?" Momma said. She pulled him into the doorway, squeezing his legs and stomach and arms. "Say something, *please*."

He couldn't. Below him, Cadence hunched round as a stone. When he blinked again, she was standing, a silhouette in pale light, bits of glass glittering in her tank. She'd thrown herself across the floor for him. His sister, impossibly unafraid.

"No one outside," his father said, coming up behind Momma. He carried a knife, its silver tip quivering, a rhythm that traveled up the sleeve of his T-shirt. "Walked around the whole house and there's not a soul."

"Everyone needs to calm down," Cadence said, pushing them out of the room. "Everyone needs to breathe before they give themselves a heart attack. Everyone needs to let me change."

They slept as a family after, their bedroom doors closed, sealing them in the hallway's tunnel. His father had called the police, but it was a busy night and no one was hurt and the bullet was probably a stray and so an officer would come by in the morning, best they could do. A comforter wrapped his father to his mother. Another cocooned Cadence against him. His sister's breathing nudged his ear, a wash of solid air.

He'd come so close to becoming the others. Boys who caught bullets in their spines. Who got jumped, their split ribs puncturing their lungs. Who went impossibly quiet after officers knelt on their necks. He searched for his own voice and found nothing.

"We're moving," Momma said in the darkness. "I don't care if your mother did raise you in this house."

His father leaned back against the wall. "You'd have to stop homeschooling. You really going to put them in public school? Go back to adjuncting?"

"What else am I supposed to do? Spend all my time trying to better my children, and they get shot at in our own house? What *is* that? I thought Bray—"

"I know," his father said.

"You didn't see Cadence holding him. He was so quiet I thought—"

"Don't."

Beside him, Cadence shifted. He curled into the shield of her.

"I'll sell the place," his father said. "It's okay. I can let it go."

Cadence breathed out as if she agreed. Or, as if what she heard took her breath away.

THEY MOVED WITHIN THREE MONTHS. The old house sold for less than it was worth. The new one bought at a premium, rooms petaling off its center. He circled through, watching his family. Momma and Cadence painting the kitchen butter yellow. Daddy cleaning the skylights in the master bedroom, dead leaves peeled from the glass. The three of them organizing the VHS collection, setting up the new computer in the den. No creaking floorboards here. No chipped doorframes, exposed wood peeking through. Yet— this house sat only fifteen minutes from their old one. What was so different, across a few painted lines and sidewalks, new zip codes?

His own room felt so far from his sister's on the opposite side of the house. They'd painted his walls a blue that sometimes went black as deep water, night lowering the entire room down, down, dark, before the sun pulled it to the surface again. Away from her, he didn't sleep much.

But there were no bullets here. Only his parents' worries rippling against him.

"He hasn't said anything in so long," Momma said over dinner. Spicy chili oozed over spaghetti noodles.

His father sipped his tea before he answered, his sweet breath blanketing the table. "Give the boy time. We just got settled."

Across the table, Cadence gave him a smile that said: *Your voice'll come back. Nothing hurt you, Bray.* They took turns holding him, passing him from lap to lap, though it was Cadence's he wanted.

His sister's voice remained bright, ever present. Talks of school in the fall. Peers she'd debate in classrooms. Girls to swap secrets with. And *please*, could she visit people in their own houses, for once? Go out past eight, even, since this neighborhood was safer?

Their father palmed his face, his beard buzzed low. "I don't want you to think of things like that. Our old neighborhood—the people were still people, wanting different things. You shouldn't—"

"Of course you can go out," their mother said, and their father fell silent. Brayden couldn't trace the line of his father's thoughts as the man stared out the window at the block of red-brick homes and empty driveways. Except—maybe his father was thinking that everyone seemed so separate from one another here, no grandparents and cousins filling rooms, no line of cars along the curb. Already, they'd seen their own relatives far less than they'd thought they would.

After his sister's questioning, their parents' wary nods, Cadence looked down at him. Grinned. Unlike Momma and Daddy, she didn't expect him to say anything.

In early June, he spoke to her first. The two of them stood in the sunroom, watching the creek that ran into the Ohio. Brown water lapped against the dip below the backyard fence, and he imagined it flowing over Louisville's spine, past this new house and the university and the automobile plant south of the city, where his father assembled cars.

"Drown," Brayden said, pointing.

Cadence squatted beside him, a sheen coating her brown skin. After showering in her new bathroom, she'd rubbed lotion into her face and neck, the skin sliding beneath her fingertips before bouncing back. Firm now, though what if she grew into his mother? His mother, who had screamed, the loose skin around her mouth echoing the shape, as if he could peel it back and she'd be only shrill sound and bone.

"You're not going to drown," his sister said. "The water's too low."

He wanted to tell her about other fears, nightmares where he played checkers with dead boys, their blood-stained sneakers nudging his under the table. Dreams where he watched Cadence play at a different board, where she didn't hear him calling: *Over here!*

But she picked him up and he didn't have to say anything. Humming, she carried him into the kitchen. Made him pancakes with honey, as many as he wanted, until his voice rose on their fluff.

"Are you gonna move your bed?" he asked when they'd finished eating and Cadence had started back toward her room.

"Move my bed?"

"From the window."

She paused, then turned around. Kissed his forehead, hopeful. "No, Bray," she said. "No one dies here."

SHE WAS RIGHT for about two weeks. He woke one morning to find Cadence and Momma watching the neighbors from the den, wrists floured as they sipped coffee. They'd made a mess of the kitchen: half lemons with tentacles of pulp and cracked eggs dripping yolk. Practice, he remembered, for his father's birthday cake. They'd baked him one every year since he'd turned forty, older than his own father had been when he passed. A different flavor each time, as many trial runs as necessary to make it perfect. His father would be fifty this year.

Through the window, Brayden saw a parade of limousines passing before the wide lawns, inching down the block like black beetles, the wings of their doors opening to let out women in veils, men in dark sunglasses. A funeral.

"Who?" he asked.

Momma's hands shook on her coffee and he thought she'd scream again. But her mouth stretched from a gasp to a smile. "You're feeling better," she said. "You—talked just now."

Cadence had gone still, watching the funeralgoers in the yard. Mostly family, it looked like, all of them the same mahogany color, uniformed in black suits, distant figurines of grief. A boy, his suit draping over him like an older man's loose skin, helped a woman out of a car.

"You said—" he began. "No one's gonna die over here."

His mother breathed in as she scooped him up. "What do you mean? Can you explain a little more?" She thumbed his arm, wanting him to keep talking, but Cadence was already turning from the window, knowing what he meant.

"I know." She closed her eyes. Her hair frizzed amber at the roots, a halo of thoughts caught in the light. "But did you hear any gunshots?"

He shook his head. Slowly, his chest let out a little air.

"Okay then. So we don't need to be scared, right? We don't know what happened."

Best they could, they relaxed into making his father's cake. They baked the two brown halves. Whipped the frosting and squeezed more lemons until their fists ached. After they'd tasted the cake— more sugar next time, they decided—it was Cadence's idea to take the extra slices to the family up the street. Least they could do.

Cadence went quiet as they walked, holding the cake platter away from her body. She'd washed all the flour off her hands and changed into jeans and a checkered blouse. Cheery. But then again, he guessed the whole neighborhood was. With the funeral cars gone, he could pick up on other things now. Like the smell and curl of smoke, someone barbecuing on a backyard patio, a flagstone path winding into some distant sanctuary.

When they'd passed that house and went up the drive of another with a round entryway and two stories of windows, Brayden said, "I don't wanna go inside there." He smushed his face into the new fullness of her thigh.

"Look, there's somebody in there around my age. Who might be having a hard time right now," she said. The sun leaked over her face in red shadows. "Wouldn't you appreciate some cake if you were having a hard time?"

He breathed in. His sister wanted him to do this good thing for somebody else. The doorbell gave under his finger. The sound rang through the house, and he felt it ringing through his body too: loud, then fainter, fainter, faint.

The door parted to reveal a dark boy, thin, like his whole body had flinched. His head seemed larger than the rest of him. His black dress pants gaped around his waist, and he tugged at his shirt's stretched collar.

"She sleep," he said. He rubbed his eyes, and Brayden thought the boy had a thick smell, as if he'd been wrapped in a blanket, trapped in his own scent for hours. "What, we forget something?"

"No," Cadence said. She took a step forward and then back. "We're—from down the street. We saw the cars earlier, and we thought we'd"—she held the platter of sliced cake, arranged in the half arc of a smile—"bring you some dessert maybe."

"Oh, I thought you were from the church." The boy reached for the platter, and Brayden stared at the sheer height of him, his chin high enough to rest on Cadence's head. "'Preciate you."

Brayden looped his fingers through Cadence's shorts and tugged. *Let's go.* Whoever this boy was, he needed to close the door, close off this sliver of his life: suit jackets draped over armrests and high heels tilted on the floor and lilies reaching through the light.

"We just moved in," Cadence said, her voice trailing up.

"Oh yeah?" the boy rubbed his eyes again. "Congratulations."

"I'm Cadence." She pointed to herself, then down. "This is my brother, Brayden."

"Oh, so you're like really new. I thought you might've been someone my mom knew."

Cadence shook her head. "I don't know her, but I think I saw her this morning. I think I saw you kind of—helping her out of the car."

The boy was nodding too vigorously to really be listening. "Look, name's Nelson. I don't want to be rude or anything, but it's been a crazy long day. I'll get into this cake later, but the only thing I want right now is my bed. So can we do the meet and greet another time?"

"I get it." Cadence's fingers were so tight around Brayden's. He felt her hand's secret heat. "You're not being rude. You're handling it well, I think, whoever died."

"My older brother," Nelson said, and he really was pulling the door then. Something in Brayden screamed, screamed so loud—*People do die here!*—and when he threw his arms out and hugged Nelson's legs, he was squeezing all that sound out.

It took him a minute to hear Nelson saying, "Okay, okay, little man. Nice to meet you too," before Cadence went, "We're just down the street. If you need anything."

HEAT DRAINED TIME FROM SUMMER. Before they'd moved, Momma would wake him early to study. They practiced math and spelling and reading: cyclops and snake-headed leopards and women who shed their skin like garments in the night, their real bodies tender and red and exposed as they wandered candlelit plantations or sea island shores.

"*And through the window where he watched in secret, the lover observed the lady of the house slip off her skin. Same way somebody might take off a dress,*" Momma read, and he listened, trying to picture it. "*She unhitched the skin from her toes and forearms, then lifted it overhead and folded it into a neat square on her bed. The lady was all pink, after. Like a walking heart. A frightening thing. When she'd gone out for her stroll at the edge of the land, her lover broke in through the window. He grabbed the skin off that bed, planning to rub honey on the insides so it would stick to her for good next time. No living being can stomach anyone walking around like that. It makes you wonder about your own body, its layers.*"

"But why?" he'd asked, meaning: Why would you leave your skin behind? Who would watch it for you?

"It's a disturbing story, for sure," Momma said, lowering the pages. "Your sister used to hate anything about boo hags."

Brayden looked at Cadence. Beside them at the kitchen table, she wrote essays, one finger pushing up the flesh over her eyebrow, her concentration walling them out.

Now, she still felt distant, though there should have been nothing stealing her away. After Momma left in the mornings, the two of them lounged in the sunroom. There was a gap where the walls didn't quite meet the floor, and he brought Cadence what blew through. Green paws of sassafras and spiked seedpods of sweet gum, things she named without putting down her book. He sensed her watching him—she was *always* watching him, he knew—but maybe not as strongly as before.

When rain sprayed the windows for three days straight, he said, "I think the house is gonna break. Collapse." He studied the ceiling, as if he could see the piercing droplets.

"It's not gonna collapse," Cadence said. She wasn't looking at him, absorbed in her next book. "It's just loud, that's all."

Once, he crossed the house's nighttime dark to her room. Looking in, he thought the lump on the mattress was too small to be his sister. But then she breathed deep, like she was coming up from underwater. He needed her to wake and whisper, *There's a little monster in my room.* He needed her to crack a joke in half sleep. As he waited, thunder rolled against the house's sides. He imagined the sky dumping water into the creek, which must be filling now and carrying leaves and flailing creatures out to the Ohio and away.

"Bray?" his father said from behind him. "Let Cadence sleep, okay?"

He waited for his sister to stir. She remained still, but did her breathing let up? A part of her rising toward him?

ONE THURSDAY, SHE WOKE HIM and said, "Let's go back to Nelson's. He's still got Momma's platter."

Brayden studied her, the black dress buttoned over her body. She put her fingers in his hair, smiled. He would go anywhere if she'd give him her full attention when they got back.

Nelson answered the door again, this time in basketball shorts that hung loose around his bare torso. Brayden looked at Cadence, expecting her to look away. But his sister didn't seem to care that the boy was only half-dressed or that facial hair skimmed his mouth. "We don't want to bother you," she said. "We only came for our platter."

"Right," Nelson said. "I think I got that in the dishwasher or somewhere." He left the door open as he retreated into the house, and Brayden's whole body went: *Wait. Wait.* But Cadence was already following Nelson with the lazy air of a bee drifting toward nectar.

Momma would have said the place was only half-clean. No trash on the white-tiled counters, sure, but an overripe-fruit smell crept out from the trash can. And, yes, Nelson had dishes soaking in the sink, but when Brayden stood on his toes, he could see the flat gray water, not enough soap.

"This it?" Nelson said, pulling out a platter decorated with kittens rolling in a bed of daffodils. The look on his face pretended seriousness.

"Not quite," Cadence said. But she was laughing, and Brayden had to admit the platter was ha-ha hideous.

Nelson pulled the real platter out of the dishwasher, and thank God he hadn't run it yet, lemon cream still smearing its ridges. You couldn't put a dish that nice in the dishwasher, Brayden thought. It might crack. Even he knew that.

"Thanks," Cadence said. "Can I wash this right here?"

"Wash away. If you want, you can bring more cake too." Nelson leaned against the refrigerator, one foot pressed against his calf. "Could've had that for breakfast, lunch, and dinner."

Brayden walked deeper into the kitchen. Papers fanned across the countertop, one glossier than the others. A funeral program. Red and black and holding a boy's picture in the center. The oval face and thin mustache so closely resembled Nelson that Brayden thought this might be a joke too, a funeral for a boy still alive. But no, Nelson looked thinner than the boy pictured here. A shaving of his older brother. *Dele Brooks.*

"Don't say we look alike," Nelson said, watching. "Everybody says that."

"Put the program down, Bray," Cadence said. She dried the platter with paper towels.

"He's cool. People forget what D looked like. So when they see me, they think, 'Aw, he's pretty close.'" He crossed his arms. "At the service, I thought about pretending to be him. Just for forty-five minutes. Just like—*Psych! I'm not really dead.* Closed casket anyway. People would buy it for a little while."

"What happened?" Cadence said, her voice soft as a touch.

"Accident." Nelson's voice went low to meet hers. "On his way to basketball practice. You watch the Louisville games?"

Cadence shook her head.

"Well, he played for them. As a starter. Everybody knew him, so—" He scratched the back of his head. "Like he's easy to look up. You must not *ever* watch the news."

"So he didn't get shot?" Brayden asked. Deep in his mind, bullets fractured car windows. A boy's face shattering.

"Naw," Nelson said. "A car accident."

"He asks that a lot," Cadence said.

"Oh, word?" Nelson asked. But he didn't say anything else.

They watched Cadence drain the sink's cloudy water. She rinsed the basin and filled it again with tangerine suds. In the silence, Brayden thought Nelson might ask if they'd ever been shot at. Or he might tell Cadence that she didn't have to clean his dishes. But the boy didn't. He watched her.

"You don't—want to help?" Brayden asked. The boy looked at him, not even a little ashamed, and moved to stand beside Cadence while she handed him plates to dry.

THEY WENT OVER a few days a week after that, helping Nelson with chores, his mother a silence radiating from behind a closed door. Of course Cadence would know what needed doing, Brayden thought. He crouched beside his sister and helped her wash tile and vacuum carpets and fold laundry warm from the dryer. That was who she was, even if they could've been playing games instead.

At least Nelson joked a lot. He put his clean underwear on his head, so it folded over backward like a durag. "What? Whaat?" he went, when Brayden covered his grin with one hand and pointed with the other. He put a rubber frog in the bucket of cleaning water, and after Cadence laughed through her scream, Brayden rolled around on the floor, hysterical. When Brayden went a whole morning without speaking—his brain remembering a nightmare where Cadence took off her face—Nelson stayed silent too. Both of them communicated in a flurry of hand signals until Brayden was forced to grin and tell Nelson: "The cord. You have to plug it *in*. The vacuum."

"So you never been to a real school, like ever?" Nelson said one Friday. They sat on his bedroom floor, dents in the carpet where furniture had been moved. "That why you so quiet?"

"He talks when he wants," Cadence said. She studied the closed door across the hall, decorated with university bumper stickers arranged in a jersey number. Nelson watched her. Got up and closed his door.

"You play sports, little man?" he asked, settling back across from them.

Brayden shook his head. Said, "No."

"I got a basketball goal in the backyard if you want to shoot a little something."

He looked at Cadence for permission, but she was giving him a look that said: *Well, answer the boy.*

"We have—a creek in *our* backyard," he said finally.

"Yeah, I been over there a couple times, as a kid and whatnot."

"With your brother?"

Nelson's mouth twitched, and he picked at the carpet. "Yeah, him," he said. "Some other people too."

They usually left around early afternoon, when Nelson had to get ready for work at the Food Mart. Brayden and Cadence slipped on their shoes while Nelson got changed in his bedroom, speaking to them through the closed door.

"So you got a job or something," Nelson called, "when you're not, like, helping me out? Cleaning other folks' houses and getting paid in jokes?"

Cadence shook her head. "I watch Brayden, he's my job."

Brayden looked up at his sister. *Job?* He was not a job. They laughed and played games and danced and he loved her so much that he would help her clean a dead boy's house, even though nobody had asked them to.

"Y'all want a ride?" Nelson asked when he came out in his black uniform polo and khakis. He looked older, like he'd grown out of the boy who accepted help folding his clothes. "You might pass out walking those fifty yards."

"I think we can manage it." Cadence reached down for Brayden's hand.

Nelson nodded. "I'm gone, Ma," he called, but there was no answer.

"You go in to check on her, right?" Cadence asked.

Nelson looked back at her door. "'Course," he said. "All the time."

SOMEHOW, AFTER THEY'D LEFT NELSON'S, their afternoons went liquid with joy. They played rummy for hours, and Cadence didn't once glance out the den window. They wrestled, and she pushed him into the carpet until his voice soared out of his chest: "STOP, HA, HA, HA, OH MY GOD STOP." Once, she turned on the radio and Janet whisper-sang through the speakers and his sister danced and he became Michael beside her and the house opened around their bodies parting the air.

So why had she called him her job? Whenever they walked to Nelson's, he felt something hovering behind. Not fear or a dead boy following them. Not the wind right before a bullet makes contact. But a feeling that she wanted something that had nothing to do with playing games. It coiled below her skin, as insistent as a tendril of hair pushing over her ear.

"So what your parents do?" Nelson asked one Wednesday. He had the day off, which meant that once they finished scrubbing down his shower and sink, they could go into the backyard and eat the sweet potato sandwiches Cadence had thrown together with scraps from Nelson's fridge. They drank store-bought lemonade so sugary it pricked his tongue.

"Momma's a professor now, and Daddy works at the Ford plant," Cadence said. Brayden nodded and wrapped his hand around the basketball goal's hot metal, swinging his weight from side to side.

"Professor?" Nelson said. "You must be one of those freakishly smart homeschooled kids."

Cadence smiled. "I didn't seem smart to you already?"

"I mean, yeah, you did," Nelson said. He leaned off his chair and set his cup on the ground. "I'm just saying. That's fascinating, being in the house all the time. Dele, he had to get out. Even before college and everything, we'd go places just to ride. Hop out of the car. Run around in the middle of the road and get back in. Sometimes, we'd walk into a store and shout, 'He's getting away!' to see if anyone would run outside, thinking they'd been robbed."

"You weren't scared?" she asked.

"Of what?"

"I don't know. But—your Momma wasn't scared?"

"I mean, not really. Hard to be scared with Dele. Like—if you knew him, you'd probably want him. Lots of girls did, and I wasn't even mad. He wasn't scared of shit. He probably looked at that car coming and just thought—" Nelson flipped the basketball in his hands. He and Cadence had forgotten about him, Brayden knew.

"Well," Cadence said. "You're handling it really well. Hard to sometimes." She was looking at the boy so intently, waiting.

The silence grew uncomfortable. Nelson said, "So we playing or what, little man?" and Brayden ran and grabbed the ball.

He thought Cadence might join them, trading layups since the concrete square in the yard was too small for them to run around. But she stayed in her chair, knees tucked under her chin. A dragonfly skimmed over her shoulders. Under her gaze, he felt himself open, mimicking Nelson's plays. Lean left. Lean right. Nelson always a beat faster. He reached for the ball and felt only air, the ghost of where Nelson had been. This ease must have been something Nelson's brother had taught him. And the boy was giving it to him now.

Nelson made one basket, then another, the ball swishing through the net. "Like this," Nelson said, positioning his hands. It took Brayden eight tries to make a shot, but when he did, his whole body felt like it soared and flipped.

"Alright, I see you, MJ," Nelson said and held up his hand for a high five. Brayden slapped hard, energy pulsing between them. Nelson winced. Took a step back.

"Bray, have some lemonade or water," Cadence called. "I don't want you getting dehydrated."

He picked up the jug of lemonade. It was warm.

"I need ice," he said. His voice had never felt so light. "Right now!"

"Want me to get you some?" she asked. But she looked tired, as if anchoring herself to that chair was wearing her out.

"I'll get it myself," he said. He went into the house, which still held the dull sting of bleach. When she and Nelson had cleaned, Cadence had told him to play in the living room so he wouldn't breathe in the particles, which had felt like salt rubbing his insides. He held his breath now, dribbling an invisible ball with one hand, crossing to the fridge to press his cup against the ice maker. Then the house went quiet around him, and he knew that Nelson's mom was lying down somewhere, resting, but he couldn't feel her at all. She was sleeping, he guessed.

An ice cube dissolved on his tongue as he left the kitchen. On the other side of the sliding door, the court was empty. Nothing but concrete and high grass until he got closer and looked to the side. To the left and on the patio, Cadence sat on the chair, her hair a million braided currents. Nelson had his arms scooped around her waist, his face buried in her stomach. That glass sealed them away. Nelson's face twisted as he raised his head, eyebrows and low mustache drawing together. The boy wasn't crying, but he might. "I am handling it," Nelson said, voice muffled. "I know I am." Cadence put her arms around his shoulders. He clutched her tank so it rose over her back.

From behind, a shuffle in the kitchen. The rest of the ice went down slow as he swallowed and turned. A woman in rollers and a green nightgown was taking a roasted sweet potato. Nelson's mother. He froze. She'd turn and see him. He had a memory of Momma hollering. That energy stretching out her skin. He braced himself for the scream.

But Nelson's mother didn't. Instead, she wrapped her potato in a paper towel, peeled it open. As she ate its center, a thread of saliva stretched between her parted lips. Her eyes, sunken in pouches of dark skin, passed over him as she turned. She padded back down the hallway, soundless.

I am invisible, he thought.

Or so many things in the world were.

HE FELT SMALL for hours after, even once Cadence said they had to get going. Their mother would finish her classes soon, and she wouldn't know where they were. Nelson nodded, palmed Brayden's head. He leaned out of it.

"How should we decorate the house for Dad's birthday?" Cadence asked when they made it home. In the kitchen, she rubbed paprika into a raw chicken quarter, its leg splayed open to reveal the pink innards.

He said nothing. He rinsed the green onions, watching the water run dirt into the sink.

"What?" Cadence said. "Something happen?"

He looked at her. *What if?* his body whispered. *What if his momma had screamed at me and you didn't hear because you weren't paying attention?* His sister had bunned her braids, her face smooth as she stared back at him, curious.

He set the onions on the cutting board and went to the sunroom. Dry leaves had collected near the wall, and he pushed them out of the gap one by one, watching them drift toward the grass.

When Momma came home, the rain starting up again, he heard them talking in the kitchen. His father's birthday was the following Friday, August sneaking up on them. Momma would take him out to dinner and an evening show, and then they would have the cake, perfected this time, the extra sugar.

Brayden listened, imagining Cadence whisking them away to Nelson's while his parents were out. Why did she clean his house when the boy should know how to clean it himself? Why did she let him distract her?

He waited until he heard the oven door close on the chicken, the soft thuds of Cadence returning to her bedroom, the rinse of her shower. He found Momma seated at the kitchen table, sorting the mail into neat piles. Bills for her. Bills for his father. College brochures for Cadence. Momma pulled him against her. Her body still held the plastic smell of her slicker.

Brayden asked, "Can you make her stay home?"

"What do you mean?" She peeled away to look down at him. For once, she wasn't counting his words.

"I don't want to go to his house anymore."

"Whose?" His mother lowered her face to his, her mouth tight. "Whose house?"

THEY WAITED FOR CADENCE to return. She entered the kitchen damp from her shower, skin a little red in the part of her robe. She ruffled his afro, and he moved into her hand, wondering if their trips to Nelson's had been a bigger secret than she'd let on. Momma had said they could go out, but something about the way they'd always returned in early afternoon, even when Nelson didn't have to work, told him Cadence didn't want Momma to know about these trips.

"I didn't know you'd gotten so close to that family," Momma said. She set down the chicken, fresh out of the oven and crisping at the edges.

Cadence glanced at him and then away. "Bray and I have just been helping out. He—Nelson—lost a brother."

"That's horrible." Momma took off her mitts, slow. "I really appreciate how sweet you are. I'm sure they appreciate it too."

His sister put her hands on the back of a chair. She'd painted her nails a bright melon color.

"Maybe, instead of going over there for a few days," Momma went on, "you can help me pick up some things for Dad's party?"

"Sure," Cadence said. "That won't take all day."

"I know."

Brayden slipped out of his chair, went to his room. He could feel Cadence's eyes trailing him.

Through the door, he heard his sister say, "But it's *not* hurting him. You should've seen him today." Then: "He talks *all* the time. It's not important just because he *says* it."

Momma mumbled something, her voice low under the onion sizzling in the pan.

"We all need things," Cadence said. "We all do."

THEY DIDN'T GO TO NELSON'S the next day or the next. He thought Cadence might be mad at him, that maybe she wouldn't want to play anymore, but she went round after round, more sketches and decks of cards. Still, a ghost passed under her mouth, a dark secret to it, some part too deep to see.

"Let's go out," she announced when the rain stopped, her voice too loud. They'd been weaving streamers for their father's birthday celebration, blue strips of paper twirling into each other.

"Where?" he asked. He waited, one piece of tape suspended from his finger.

"To the creek," she said, without looking at him. She repeated it when he remained quiet, focused on the streamer trailing around his left leg.

It was less frightening than he'd imagined. They crouched over the damp soil and cupped salamanders in their palms. Cadence plucked jagged leaves of clearweed and the last of the purple columbine flowers, something new to draw when they went back in. The creek water rose high and muddy brown, like black tea with a little cream. They squatted on the bank. A short ways down, a fallen tree crossed the creek, and Cadence walked over and nudged it with the toe of her sandal. Would she cross? Leave him here alone?

"Just checking for mushrooms," she said. The tops of the trees cut shadows over her back. "Or anything else that might be growing under here."

She didn't tell him to stay away when he approached. He squatted and peered below the trunk stretched across the creek. Impossible to tell what was under there. When he stood, a petal of columbine slipped from his fingers and went downstream.

WHEN HIS FATHER'S BIRTHDAY ARRIVED, the three of them woke before the sky had time to think of daylight. Cadence and Momma had already baked the two cake halves, and they made the frosting in the early morning blue, squeezing in the fresh lemon and spreading it on. He tasted its smoothness, his job to be in charge of the sugar. When the sun tipped over the horizon, Momma put on coffee. Cadence hung the streamers they'd twirled, draping them across the living room. When his sister walked below them, she had to tilt her head to avoid brushing the paper.

Daddy couldn't have been surprised by the cake and decorations, but when he trudged in, dressed in jeans and a plaid button-down, Momma said, "Here comes the old man now." His father swelled at the sight of them, his chest rising.

"Say something," Momma said. Moments before, Brayden had watched her rub lotion over herself, the flakes of dry skin. Her body gleamed, sheathed in her white dress.

"*We're* supposed to say something," Cadence said sleepily from the couch. "We're supposed to sing him 'Happy Birthday.'"

They sang. First the regular version and then Stevie's take, his father's eyes softer than he'd ever seen them, this man who hauled spare engines off the back of his truck and protected his family in hallways. Daddy was suddenly a boy himself, as if all that skin and muscle had peeled back like a puffer coat, revealing someone amazed this day had arrived.

"You never think—that many years," he said when they sat down to a breakfast of eggs and biscuits and sausage. "A lot stands between a man and fifty."

"Well, maybe not so much between forty-nine and fifty," Momma said, and his father cupped her hand across the table, like he was passing her something sacred.

His parents decided to eat the cake once they got back from the concert, and they left for work, the delight delayed. Still in her pajamas, Cadence read on the sunroom couch, and he wanted to ask if they could trap salamanders by the creek again—or maybe frogs—but she seemed tired, her head lolling against her shoulder, rolls of fat on her neck.

When the doorbell rang, he jumped. Looked at his sister wrapped in sleep.

On all fours, he crawled to the front door and peeked through the window. Nelson, shifting his weight and holding a brown paper bag. When the boy nudged the doorbell again, Cadence approached, asking, "Who is it?" She looked through the peephole. Opened the door.

"So you just gon' leave a man to fend for himself?" Nelson said. He grinned, but there was a certain wariness to his eyes.

"It's my dad's birthday," Cadence said. She crossed her arms over her pajama top. Her grin came at the end of the statement, small as a period.

"My bad. Should I leave these then?" He looked at the groceries. Then at her.

Brayden knew what she was going to do before she said, "Come on in." He didn't know what he felt. Only—it couldn't be his sister and Nelson alone again. Not without him.

If Nelson remembered Cadence holding him, he didn't show it. He set his bag on their kitchen counter—"Couldn't stock these so they gave them to employees"—bananas only a little brown and bruised oranges and cereal boxes dented on the sides. If it hadn't been for the fact that one of those boxes was a chocolate cereal Momma never bought, Brayden wouldn't have said, "Thank you" or let Nelson tap his head with his fist. Plus, the boy was walking away from Cadence, peering at the VHS collection and the streamers dangling from the ceiling.

"So, what? Y'all just watch movies all day?"

"We draw, talk, lots of stuff." Cadence had her back to them, unloading fruit into the fridge. When he looked at Nelson, the boy was staring at him, a half grin. He felt the room shrink to their pair. Nelson would not or could not look at his sister.

"Show me what you've been working on, little man," Nelson said.

He led Nelson to the sunroom, showed him the drawings they'd made over the past few days. At the boy's careful examining, he went shy, wanting to impress. Cadence stuck her head in, said she was going to change out of her pajamas if Nelson was going to stay. She was a mess, she said. Hadn't even brushed her teeth.

"Cool," Nelson said, handing the drawings back. "I don't know about art, but these seem pretty neat."

"There's a lot to draw over there," Brayden said, pointing to the creek.

"Yeah," Nelson said. "I bet."

❋

THE BOY SEEMED FAMILIAR with the creek, passing right over the worms and salamanders nosing through the mud. When Nelson crossed the trunk, a sneaker at a time, one, two, Brayden looked back at the house, where Cadence was changing.

"You going to fall," Brayden said, and Nelson tipped back his head and laughed.

"Boy, please. We used to get into this before you were even born." He made it to the other side, the brown creek parting them. Brayden looked at the high water, rushing.

"I'll walk you over if you want," Nelson said. He crossed the trunk again, arms out beside him. There was no breeze in all this heat, nothing that might tip him over.

Brayden studied the trunk, the thickness of it, which hadn't acknowledged Nelson's weight. He imagined Cadence finding them on the other side. What could he bring back to her? Show her so, the next time, they'd cross together?

"Give it a try," Nelson said. "You and your sister act like you got all the time in the world to do what you want." Behind him, Nelson put both hands on Brayden's torso. Brayden let the older boy maneuver them up the mossy slope leading to the trunk.

When they crossed, he saw the water moving under him, slower from up here. A stray branch rode the current, easing below the trunk and reappearing on the other side. How silly to think that he would've drowned, the trunk steady under him. Soon he would be seven and then eight and ten, and eventually Nelson and Cadence's age or maybe even his father's, and things would frighten him less than they did.

"See?" Nelson said, when they'd reached the other side. No salamanders curled through the dirt, but he saw new red flowers that Cadence might know. "Scared over nothing."

Cadence came outside the house, then. A flash of a pink tee over denim.

They watched her cross the yard, then Nelson's mouth went up at the sides: "How about a little prank, man? You down?" Brayden studied his grin, Nelson looking at him completely.

When he smiled back, Nelson put a hand on his shoulder. Walked him behind the trunk of a thick tree and crouched low with him. "You don't come out until I tell you, alright?"

Brayden nodded.

He watched Nelson cross the makeshift bridge again, almost hopping this time, quick, with his toes pointed.

"Listen," Nelson began when he met Cadence at the bank. He put both hands at the sides of his head, pushing against his skull. His voice went high. "The whole thing was an accident, I swear *to God*."

"What are you talking about?" Cadence walked past him, her eyes scanning the small wood.

"I mean, he was just goofing off, right? And he wanted to go over the trunk, and he just kind of—went in and I thought I could get to him in time but—"

"Hold on. Hold on," Cadence said. Brayden understood the game now, and it *was* kind of funny, watching the confusion crease her face, playing dead without being dead. Taking away the weight.

"Bray wouldn't cross the creek by himself," she said. "He can't swim." But she looked.

"That's what I thought," Nelson said. "But—" He pointed to a ripple in the water, and Brayden chewed on his laugh because those circles did kind of look like someone had fallen in. Cadence, squinting, wasn't buying it yet. Then again, he was so good at being quiet. The earth's smell rose heavy around him. He crouched, the damp soil pushing against his sneakers.

Only—Cadence's whole body went still. Her eyes snapped toward Nelson and he didn't recognize it, the shudder in her lip.

"So your brother died and now you want to pretend mine's dead too?"

"Whoa." Nelson put his hands down. "That's not—"

"This is *so* lame. I mean—" His sister's face scrunched up, and he felt himself shrinking around the tree, farther from her look. "You think being dead's something to joke about?"

"Okay, okay. You're right. I'm just playing." He reached for her arm, and she pulled it away.

"You only want to play games," she said. "And if that's how you handle your issues, then fine. But when you've *actually* come close to dying—. When you *personally* have—." She hiccupped a little. Tucked her hands under her arms, like she was holding her skin around her.

"Whoa," Nelson said. And then softer. "Whoa. Whoa. Whoa. It was a joke, okay? A dumb joke."

Cadence didn't look at him. "Bray," she whispered, her voice smaller than he'd ever heard it.

"Come out, little man," Nelson said. "Joke's over."

The trees seemed to make space for him as he revealed himself. Warmth spread through his body, burning him from inside out. He felt every freckle on his face.

"I'm here," he said.

"That wasn't funny," Cadence said. And then she did cry, his sister who hadn't even cried when the bullet soared above his head. "I would've had to jump in there after you. I would've *had to* or Momma would've killed me. And to think you—."

Nelson pulled her against him so, for an instant, her body crumpled, her thighs and knees jutting out. Then, she rose and swung at him.

"I'm sorry," Nelson said, catching her wrists.

Brayden watched his sister from the bank, waiting for her to come get him. Or should he cross over to her himself? He felt he could do it. True, he couldn't swim like *she* could, but when Momma had taken them to the Y once a week for a summer, he'd lain on his back. Floated, while she swam beneath him in the deep end. Floating had been enough.

He'd never seen Cadence looking the way she did now. He'd never seen her folded under someone else.

"I'm sorry," Nelson said, still holding her tense arms. "Like I said, I didn't know."

❋

INSIDE, NELSON STAYED WITH THEM for a while. Cadence abandoned her muddy shoes and took the couch, her bare feet folded under her hips. Nelson peeled a banana for her, and Brayden poured her a glass of water and squeezed lemon into it with all his might.

"I'm fine," she said when they brought the fruit and water to her. Joined her on the yellow couch. "It was a stupid joke. Boys are stupid."

"Where'd the bullet come in?" Nelson asked when they were halfway through a movie. On-screen, a boy sped down a highway, lights streaming over his cheeks.

"Like this," she said. She drew a line in the air over her forehead.

Brayden listened to them, remembering his sister's heartbeat against his ear, the way her hands shook when she showed them to their mother, absent of red. He realized now there must have been blood on her somewhere. Had to have been, since she'd skidded across glass to get to him, the shards embedded into her pajamas until she changed.

On the television, the boy parked the car under a streetlight. Got out of the driver's seat and looked around, bewildered.

"What'd you do with Dele's car?" Cadence asked.

"It was totaled," Nelson said. "Nothing to *do* with it."

He thought his sister might touch Nelson the way she had before, but she didn't. She cupped her hands against her knees.

When his parents came home, all laughter and arms slung across shoulders, they stopped at the sight of them.

"Oh, hello?" Momma said. Her hair was frizzy, and she tilted her head to one side as if she'd been drinking.

Nelson crossed the room and shook Momma's hand, then Daddy's.

"He brought groceries," Cadence said. She turned down the TV's volume.

"That's thoughtful," Momma said, and Daddy said, "You went shopping or something?" and Nelson shook his head.

"Naw, I work at the Food Mart," he said. "And since y'all took care of my family." He shrugged.

"Right," Momma said.

When no one said anything, Nelson added, "Happy birthday, sir."

Brayden rose. He still could not look at his sister full on, this new person coming together in his brain.

"I think—cake now," Brayden said, hovering next to Nelson. Momma glanced at the two of them.

"Sure," Daddy said. He squeezed Nelson's shoulder. "It's about time for that."

They gathered around the kitchen table. If Nelson remembered that he'd had such a cake before, he didn't let on. They sang and the candlelight flickered over their faces. Daddy's full cheeks. Momma's slanted lipstick. Nelson on one side of the table and Cadence next to him, her eyes half-closed as if she were wishing too.

When his father blew out the candles, his mother picked them one by one and passed them down, pinched between her fingers. Across the table to Nelson, who gave them to Cadence, who turned to pass him the slender, naked candles. As Brayden reached, he saw the singed ends curling black in her palm. Alarm rose in him. "They're long cool by now, Bray," his sister said. He kept reaching. Saw orange light swallow his nails.

He wondered if this was how you managed, each person taking something small from the person beside them, one by one as the heat dwindled, until what you carried could finally be set down.

SURFACING

MEMORY SETTLES OVER THE HOUSE LIKE SALT BLOWN IN from the sea. Or softly, the way Spanish moss wilts green over the drive. For weeks, she's wanted to return, and now she relaxes in the truck's passenger seat, watching her husband cut across the yard and search the perimeter. He's all straight back and broad shoulders, his large hand swatting away deerflies. And behind him, her childhood home is a box of white paneling and sky-blue trim. Being here again is like being gently mothered, she thinks. Though she is grown, now, and the state of her marriage is a question. She may fail in so many ways, but already, the island brings relief.

It couldn't have come fast enough. She's missed this Harrington cottage where Olivia raised her. Olivia making red rice in the kitchen, a mess of sausage and chili powder staining the counter. Olivia bringing home work from her shop, threading charms from her place on the den's coral couch. Olivia disappearing around a corner, the flutter of a pastel caftan over her dark arms as she called back: "I chose you, yeah, child? So if you're crying about some dance lesson you want to take, I guess I chose your whining too. You'll have it if it's important to you."

Not that she'd known sadness then. After turning eighteen, she'd watched Olivia sink into the silence of brain tumors. She'd inherited Olivia's small savings and the house—cut fresh with death—and fled St. Simons for college in Orlando, where she danced and met Dev and buried her grief in a new life. They'd studied at the library and shared breakfast at his uncle's construction site, swapping stories. An eighteen-wheeler had crossed the median, he said, and blasted his family from the earth. Her childhood with Olivia, she confessed, had been so lovely that she didn't mind not remembering her first foster homes. She and Dev had married after graduation, two people riddled with loss.

Dev approaches the truck window. Raps it with his knuckles. She rolls it down, letting in the June smell of the Georgia coast, stickier than Central Florida's.

"You good with waiting here? While I walk around back?" he says, a weight in his lower face. He thinks so much can go wrong: wandering men squatting on the back porch, wild animals lurking at the lawn's edges. Death has always come for the people he loves.

"Yeah, alright," she says. Honest, for once. She watches him turn away, his bunned afro and cargo shorts disappearing around the house's side.

During her few weeks here, she'll make her body hers. In January, her hips went weak. Pain streaking from her raised thigh and down her legs. A fluke, she'd thought, until every movement became less precise, the pain rippling through her pelvis. Until the director's eyes measured her. Dev's too, as he watched rehearsal one evening, early to collect her from the theater.

"Why pretend it doesn't hurt?" he'd asked when they got home.

She shrugged off her coat. "Lots of people sacrifice for what they love."

"Well, you don't need to." When she froze, he added: "I mean, doctors helped the first time around, right?"

"I guess." But she crushed her coat against her belly. Went into the bedroom.

"What?" he asked, following. "What?"

The implication was too much: *Sex used to hurt too*, he meant. *And you got treatment for that.* Only she hadn't. After the doctors failed to help her during those college years, the pain striking her whenever Dev pushed in, she'd lied, loving him, and said sex felt good. It was part of the way she'd clung to him, then. And now this change in her dancing might persist too.

"I've—never taken care of it," she said. "It's never really gone away."

"Never?" he asked. He let go of her wrists. "This whole time?"

They'd both needed space. Him to deal with her lying. Her to heal herself—from dance and sex—without the pressure of his presence. Not that moving out helped. She'd traded their life for longing phone calls, for a houseful of dancing girls whose bodies obeyed them. These girls welcomed boys with shark-tooth necklaces into their beds and danced to house music thumping against her door. They slipped on tulle dresses and made an audience gasp with the slow tilt of their bodies. In their final show, the troupe mimed a clock hand, slowly turning across the face of the stage. Her dancing worsened. She'd barely survived this season. She had to get better before the fall.

As she'd cleaned out her stall, she'd known where to go. How else to get ahold of herself than to return to Olivia's, her memory of childhood lush and restorative.

Dev returns to the truck. He shields his eyes, squinting through the sunlight. She's always had to look up at him, his body like a wave suspended over her petite frame, but she feels herself rising as he approaches, as if it's her body cresting. He's given her so much. Agreed to help her move in. Even shaved for her, she'd noticed when he picked her up that morning.

"Everything's clear, far as I can tell," he says. He scratches at his chin. "Guess it's safe for you to go in alone, if that's still what you want."

AT NINE, SHE'D BEEN a polyp at Olivia's side. There's not much she remembers from the first slice of her childhood—a stain in one foster home's ceiling and a wooden banister in another—but she recalls the social worker bringing her to Olivia's. The slow ride past the white retirees walking the pier. The streets shadowed by tunnels of mossy oaks. The wood cottage smaller than the other two-story bungalows, though the fresh coat of paint suggested enough money for beauty. They'd stood on its porch, Mrs. Dawson holding her sweating hand. When Olivia opened the door and reached out, her fingers were warm on her shoulder. Olivia's dark skin, rich as bark. Her own, light as butter browned in a skillet.

The women above her exchanged looks. "You understand?" Mrs. Dawson asked.

Olivia nodded, brushing her off: "C'mon in, Grace. Leave your shoes at the door."

Over the years, Olivia would say she behaved like a toddler during those early months. She hovered outside the bathroom while Olivia bathed. She hid behind the counters at the boutique, watching Olivia explain her sweetgrass designs to her customers, detailing how her ancestors had mastered silversmithing, replicating patterns in the earth. "Making dinner was impossible, girl," Olivia said once. "Sticking your hands in everything. Calling yourself useful." All Grace remembers is the longing—the hope that this woman would keep her.

Even at twenty-four, the desire doesn't disappear. Grace enters the house, aware of Dev lingering on the porch steps. Through the layer of dust, her mind smells a sharp twinge of bay leaf. There's the pastel couch covered in plastic. The hanging woven baskets. One of Olivia's old customers, Mr. Jenkins, who'd often bought gifts for his wife, has kept an eye on the place all these years—cutting the grass, checking on the house after hurricanes, forwarding her the mail. "Anything I can do, Grace," he'd said. "Such a shame."

Upstairs, something shifts, low as wind. Irrationally, she thinks: Olivia. Then: Maybe Dev's missed something? She climbs the carpeted stairs and turns left toward her old room.

She senses someone inside even before she opens the door—a bend in the air that bristles against her skin.

A woman sleeps on her bed. Black hair covers her face.

Just in time, Grace catches her shout. Sucks it back, along with all she notices. The toenails glittering pink. The silk of flat-ironed hair. A silver charm bracelet. Not a woman, then, but a girl. If she were a dancer, she'd be a cygnet.

Grace steps deeper into the room. It's been a long time, but nothing's been touched, she thinks. Her jewelry box—empty anyway—sits familiarly askew on her turquoise dresser. A tapestry of a rabbit outrunning a fox hangs undefaced. Even a scarf, threaded gold and blue, still droops from her closet doorknob, abandoned when she left for college.

Olivia would bring the girl tea and say, "Well go on and tell your story. Some of me in you, probably." What if this girl has nowhere to go? What if, for God knows how long, Olivia's home has been hers too?

Grace eases out of the room and pads down the stairs, then steps outside. When Dev spots her, he straightens from his hunch over the porch railing. Already, sweat forms in the spots where his T-shirt brushes his back.

"There's a girl in my room," she whispers. "Asleep."

He blinks. Then he says, "You mean like a real person? *Inside* the house?" Then his hand is on her waist, guiding her from the front door.

His touch shocks her more than anything. The whole drive over, he'd only gripped the wheel.

In her surprise, she lets him pass, move into the house without her. Then she thinks: Follow him. Poor girl will be terrified to see him standing over her like that.

The thought comes too late. When the girl shouts, Grace is only on the stairs.

THEY CALM HER DOWN with a glass of water. Dev leans against the door while Grace crouches before her, murmuring, "Hey, hey, we won't hurt you." The girl's brown eyes—she really *is* a girl, fifteen, maybe sixteen—shift between them.

"I didn't take anything," the girl says. "I just fell asleep."

"How'd you get in?" Dev says. Between his fingers, he holds the girl's sandals hostage. "If you don't want the police over here, you better make something make sense." As if they will call the police.

"There," the girl says, nodding toward the bay window. Of course. Grace can remember opening it on spring mornings, curling on the window seat with a magazine splayed on her thighs, a glimpse of marshes and egrets over the neighbor's roof. "It was unlocked—"

"This is the second floor," Dev says. "What'd you do, climb?"

"There's some woodwork," Grace says. Some decorative paneling where Olivia had been planning to grow peppers. "That's how you got in?"

The girl apologizes again, takes a long sip from her glass. "No one said other renters were coming. I never would've come in if I'd thought that."

"We're not renters," Dev says. He unfolds his arms, letting the girl's shoes dangle.

"No one's been here," the girl says. "How would I know?"

Dev motions for Grace, a certain cock of his head. As she crosses, she prays the girl won't bolt out the window.

When her face is inches from his, he whispers, "You sure you don't want to call . . . somebody?" He glances over her shoulder.

"Not yet." She rests her gaze in the dip of skin at his collarbone. Not so far up that she meets his eyes. "She's so young. Who knows what she needs?"

"I'm no criminal," the girl says. She eases off the bed, her arms raised to show the pale underside of one hand, the cell phone in the other. "I just hang out here. My parents don't know I brought my phone on vacation."

Dev scoffs, "You've got to be kidding me." But the sound is lighter, almost a laugh.

The girl's eyes slide up as if searching for another explanation. But then she looks down and works her fingers over the phone. "My boyfriend," she says. "My dad will lose his cool."

She turns the phone to reveal a teenager photographing himself in a bathroom mirror. His body, slim and dark. His face shy, uncertain of his handsomeness. What appears in Grace's belly is vague and uncertain too, until she silently names it for what it is: jealousy.

"We FaceTime here," the girl repeats. "It's quiet—and like I said, the window was open, and I can see if my parents are looking for me. *And no one's been around.*"

Grace wishes she knew Dev's thoughts. Don't have a secret boyfriend, maybe. Or, Thank God Grace and I never made a kid. He's gone silent beside her, so silent she doesn't know if he feels this child's insistence, her willingness to work her body up a wall, over a porch roof, and through someone's window. It makes their own love seem small.

"Look," the girl says. She flops her arms. A burst of childlike tantrum against the curve of her waist, exposed midriff over denim. "I'm staying right there."

Through the window, she points at the neighboring house, brown and shake shingled, which Grace remembers belonging to an old couple who'd passed away within days of each other one autumn. "Hear me good," Olivia had said then, sipping coffee as she stared at the couple's grown children, dressed in black as they filed through the front door. "They'll sell it to some rich golfer, and his dream home will punish us with the property taxes." Which had sort of happened. The manor next to their cottage had been renovated, turned into a vacation rental.

"See?" the girl says, pointing outside. Below, a Black man walks toward a silver convertible parked at the curb, his keys swinging. "That's my dad. His name's Adam Wright. And me—I'm Natalie."

*

WHEN THEY LET THE GIRL out the back, Grace studies the way she leaves. Natalie takes one step into the yard, then another, peering around the corner to make sure her father's driven away from the front. Then the girl slips her phone under her bra strap, right above her heart, and jogs across the lawn with her hand over the device, keeping it close. She's quick, purposeful, her feet nearly escaping from her sandals. She came all the way over here just to call him, Grace thinks. She'll do anything for that boy.

"What's on your mind?" Dev says. When she turns, he's inches from her face again, his own soft and open.

"Nothing," she says.

The day is getting away and it's time to clean and unload.

The girl has made both of them quiet. It takes half the afternoon to get everything inside and unpacked, all her sweaters and tights and spices, things that seem oddly empty to her now, not enough to sustain a life. Aside from mentioning where to put her boxes, the rolls of clothes she's secured with twine, the conversation wilts. The whole four-hour car ride, they'd talked about the houses he was building, her hip therapy. Stress, her physical therapist had said. Too much tension. She'd tucked her feelings for Dev deep in her ribs, along with all the other questions about where he would sleep and how soon she'd be ready to be with him again.

And yet here he is, working himself into this house. Once they finish unpacking, he inspects the den window, a man so absorbed in his work that it's like she's watching him through glass.

"Latches are a little damaged," he says, leaning close enough to kiss them. "Probably weak from erosion. Girl could have gotten in this way, to be honest. You don't have much keeping these locked."

She stands, fixed, in the square of sunlight passing through the window and stamping itself onto the floor.

"Just need replacements. We can pick those up at any hardware store."

He notes the chipping paint on the front door, the tiny holes in the hardwood floors where particles of sand have dug their way in.

"Could be in worse shape, all things considered," he says, wiping his hands on his pants. "Lucky you've had no flooding the last six years."

She knows she should worry on some level, but she thinks of the girl, her ease.

As Dev bends over a box, Grace rests a finger on his spine. Having missed him so much, is she capable, now, of bringing him into her? When he touched her, she'd stored the memory of his hand.

He goes still under her finger. If this were a scene in a ballet, he would rise slowly, then lift her by the waist, and she'd straighten, prop her hands on his shoulders, feel him propel her overhead. It's a relief when he reaches around to clasp her fingers in his own. He's missed her too.

"You hungry?" she asks. She's close enough to smell his wood smell.

"Starving." And though he's not looking at her as he stands, she can trace his smile, an unwinding in his cheek.

SOMETIMES, SHE THINKS, memory lodges in the body. She's always suspected that people have been wrong about the brain, about the flashes of light and color sparking in its folds, compressed by hard skull. Memory travels down arms and legs familiar with the dance, under the arch of the spine or the foot. The body remembers.

Her first time at sex. A Thanksgiving holiday with the campus emptied, students home for roasted turkey and yams drowning in marshmallows. She and Dev had made grilled cheese, the ingredients easy to find in the picked-clean supermarket. A glob of cheddar coated his fingers as they'd stood in her kitchen, and impulsively, she'd slipped those fingers in her mouth. Up to the knuckle. He watched, and she saw herself go still, her hoodie tied around her waist like a bow. So she could do this too, hold a gaze offstage.

"You sure?" he said as he hovered over her later, face flushed. They'd both been shy, reluctant to trust someone else's body as home. "You've got this look."

She nodded, wanting his closeness. Of course, she'd been a little nervous, remembering the pressure of inserting tampons. Maybe she clenched a bit.

But she hadn't imagined this pain. Dull, then reverberating through her hips, as if he'd moved into bone instead of flesh. To be wet and closed, some dam hidden within you. She gasped, and he mistook it for pleasure. He rocked against her—*against*, not *into*—and she yelped and he sighed and flopped his head beside hers, releasing all his breath into her ear. Outside, someone drove by on a campus cart and the blue light shuddered over his closed eyes.

"Did I hurt you?" he asked.

She mumbled against his shoulder. "First time, I guess."

Only, it kept hurting. Months of pain. In her dorm and his and the spare room in his uncle's house, where they spent spring break. They tried more lube. Longer foreplay.

Then: doctors. She let her body go limp as they examined her, the cool grind of the speculum. "Spasms," they said. "Here are exercises for your pelvic floor. . . . Here is how he can slide in one finger and then three. . . . Here are plastic cones to put inside yourself. Start with the smallest and move up until you acclimate to penetration." Sitting on her toilet, she'd pushed in the thinnest penis-shaped object. Detached from him, the cone only made her body resist. Two weeks later there was still no improvement.

"How's it going in there?" Dev said through the door. "Better?"

She remembered him waiting in the clinic, his body bent awkwardly in the plastic chairs. When she'd emerged, his eyes went: *Am I going to have to live without this too?*

"Yes," she lied. "Much better."

When he said, "Thank God," she returned the cones to the paper sack. Folded down the top and placed it in the cabinet below the bathroom sink.

She pretended. Relying on his tongue for her pleasure. Wrapping her legs around his waist as he entered her. Biting her lip in a semblance of ecstasy. Closing her eyes as if the stars behind them meant she was soaring. Out of her body. Beyond the rafters. Higher. By the night of their wedding, in a coastal bed-and-breakfast, a quiet room with blackberry wallpaper, she thought: Apart from this, he makes you so happy.

She still hopes she can make her body do what she wants. As they eat dinner on Olivia's porch, she thinks, This is what we needed. They've soaped and scrubbed the chairs and floors, and the wood holds rainbowing water in places where it's uneven. She takes bites of her crab sandwich, picked up in town, and crumbs land in the tiny pools. Already Olivia's house feels lived-in again.

He studies the way she sits sideways on the chair, turning toward him so their knees touch. "That doesn't hurt your hip?"

"It's not like I've been dancing." But maybe she's making him uncomfortable. When she adjusts to face the right way, he stops her. Rests his thumb in the groove of her knee.

"I'm not saying—" he begins. "I mean—I'm glad you feel alright."

She nods. Already, this place, the space she needed, is working.

As they wipe butter from their fingers, a couple comes out of the neighboring house. The man's Hawaiian-print shirt breezes around his body. The woman carries two foil-wrapped plates, gold bracelets clinking along her wrists. Come-heres, Olivia would've called them, in contrast to the Been-heres, people who'd lived on the island for generations. Though she'd become Olivia's daughter, Grace had never known how to refer to her own manner of arrival. She'd kept the house all these years. Tacked a sign on the front door—"Don't Ask—Won't Sell"—like the other long-term residents, before leaving for Orlando. And yet.

The couple heads in their direction. In the distance behind them, Natalie pokes her head out the front door. Her expression reads: *Please, please don't tell them anything.*

There isn't time. The father, Adam, is already mounting the porch steps and introducing himself, and then she and Dev are standing, engulfed in a hug as if he's kin.

"My wife, Sheila," Adam says, gesturing. The woman clasps Grace's hand. Her blouse slips, brown shoulders gleaming with oil. When Natalie appears beside them, shy and nudging the backs of her calves with her bare toes, Grace feels on the verge of shattering with shyness. Is she jealous again, of this girl who still has parents she can keep secrets from? Of this girl who can do so much for love?

"When your truck pulled up this morning, I thought, Here we go! Two more of us on this island," Adam says. He smiles to reveal teeth friendly in their crookedness, and Grace doesn't tell him that not so long ago he wouldn't have felt the need to count the number of Black people here. Behind her father, Natalie sucks in her bottom lip. She draws close to her mother, gesturing for her to give up the plates.

"Chocolate chip," Sheila explains when Dev peels back the foil to reveal the cookies. "Natalie got the impulse to make some today, and since we've been watching you come and go all morning, we thought we'd share."

"That's sweet," Grace says. A peace offering. Sheila pulls back her braids, a sweep of wooden beads sealing the ends, to reveal cheeks harder than Natalie's. The girl mumbles a thanks, and Grace can feel Dev softening at her side, his hand gentle on the small of her back.

"Well, we try to teach her how to be polite," the father says. He steps back on the porch, peers at a trickle of soap running down one of the posts. "You know how it is with kids. Doesn't always take."

"Oh, I think it sticks to her sometimes," Sheila says. She wraps an arm around her daughter's shoulders and pulls her in. Natalie's face goes vacant, a mask over her embarrassment. "That'll be my side coming out."

They're from Atlanta, staying for the summer, Sheila explains, taking a break from practicing law, from all their devices. They've come to St. Simons because who gets to be a family the way they should when everyone is sucked into their phones or their jobs or trying to process everything going on in the news? They need a break from all that noise. Grace nods. She gets it. She's a dancer, she says, and she's hoping that this sea air, this coming home after so long, will do her some good too. Sheila nods before she's even finished speaking. Natalie's eyes flick her way, curious.

"So, like, New York?" she says. "You dance there?"

"Orlando."

"Orlando," Natalie repeats, and Sheila says, "She's thinking about colleges. Any place outside of Georgia grabs her attention."

"Yeah, well let's hope it's the education doing it," Adam says. He puts a hand on the girl's shoulder, then drops it. "No use going that far just to get in trouble."

She's surprised by the way Dev, perhaps moved by the girl's cookies and her parents' chatter, suggests they all go to the beach in the morning. His eyes are on her, asking a quieter question: *How long can I stay?*

The Wrights nod. She does too. She imagines her body floating over the waves, brushing his.

AFTER THE FAMILY'S GONE, she and Dev take their separate showers and change into their pajamas, their first night together in so long.

"I'm beat," Dev says as they make her bed, the sheets still hot from the dryer. They tug the mattress cover over the ends, and she feels the tugging in her chest too: fear and want.

He doesn't ask where he should sleep. Instead, he picks up a pillow and blanket and starts downstairs. On impulse, she presses her thumb into the bend of his arm. *Don't go.* He waits, then kisses her on the forehead, and her body loosens.

Later, she can hear him downstairs, watching something on his phone. Some sport where there is cheering and a commentator's deep voice naming men she doesn't recognize. She stands at the mirror, wrapping her hair. Then she sits on the old carpet. Spreads her legs in a stretch, pressing her head to one knee. Should she go and kiss him until his phone slides from his grasp? Maybe this time she'll settle on his lap and pull him in and pull him in with no pain, only pleasure, like her body is growing off the feeling, no limit to where it starts and ends.

She stands. Through the window, a light comes on next door, as if in response to her movement. At first, she thinks it's Sheila flinging her body across the purple bedroom and onto the bed, but no, the posture is too childish. Natalie, then. Funny how these rooms mirror each other. No wonder the girl had the idea to get some space here. The house was right there, tempting.

In the distance, Natalie turns her head toward her bedroom door. Then stands on a chair and tugs at a vent until it swings open and she retrieves something small. Her phone, which glows in her palm. She gets down from the chair and turns off her lamp, so there is only a ball of light floating in the darkness.

It's far too private, even a hint of Natalie's relationship to this boy, so Grace retreats from the window, turns out her own lamp. She imagines Dev around her, just as close as inside.

THE NEXT DAY, Grace shies near him at the beach, fifteen minutes from the cottage. Dev unrolls his towel next to hers on the gray sand, slathers sunscreen on the dark half-moons of his calves. When he notices her watching, he asks to rub in the streaks on her face, his thumb gentle. In truth, she's spent all night picturing her body accepting his. Her thoughts dotted her mind like tiny stars, bright enough to keep her awake.

Sheila and Adam have brought a cooler of drinks and cold chicken, and with both of them stripped down to their swimwear, she can't help but wonder how they spent their night, their oversized white towel spread beneath them like a bedsheet. When

Sheila leans over to retrieve a soda from the cooler, her breasts sway forward until her gold bikini catches them. Dev glances down and then away. Deep in the sand, he fumbles for Grace's fingers. His old nervousness around attractive women. After rehearsals, when he'd visit her in the theater's dressing room, he'd loiter close to her stall, the other dancers giggling as he shifted away from them, the drape of their bodies over chairs, dressers, his arms.

"Natalie!" Adam calls, squinting. Along the shoreline, the girl has her arms crossed, her jeans rolled up to the knee. She carries a Walkman, bulky and scratched like something washed ashore. "Come and eat."

The girl shakes her head, pulls back the hood of her sweatshirt to show her earbuds, the wires creeping down her front. He settles back on the towel. Puts his hand on Sheila's back.

"It's better than a phone," Sheila says. She tugs her straw hat as she turns to her husband, pearl earrings swinging. "And music's good for stress."

"Where'd she even get that thing?"

"I let her borrow it. God knows how old it is, what's the harm?"

Adam says, "Hear me on this one, Dev. If you two have a girl, putting your foot down will be like sticking it in sand every time."

At the mention of bearing children, Grace's stomach does a little flip that begins in nerves and ends in pleasure. She can feel Adam's and Sheila's smiles, heavy with knowing, on her cheeks. She gets up and says she's been craving a swim. Dev's wiping his hands on his knees, studying the sand dotting her legs.

The water is chillier than the beaches in Florida, and at the first flush of cold around her feet, she remembers an old habit of praying before she entered the ocean fully. A practice picked up from Olivia, who often murmured something in Gullah Geechee before she went in waist-deep, her eyes fixed on the islands, flat as floating backs in the distance.

"You scared to swim or something?" Natalie says coming up behind her. It's amazing, how the girl's face can be so composed, even as she twists her mouth.

"Just warming up." Behind them, a white woman jogs past with her dog, its tail swinging in rhythm with her hair. Grace wants to say, *My mother had this habit*, but she suspects this girl, dragged to the beach again, doesn't care. Natalie raises her eyebrows, an echo of the way her voice trails up at the end of her silent question: *Well?*

"Kind of a weird thing," she begins. She tells the story Olivia passed down. The Ibo brought to St. Simons in chains. Walking east into the water and singing, the memory of home lapping at their minds, until the waters closed over them. Depending on who told the story, they got to one other side or another.

"Not here specifically," she says. "Dunbar Creek. A few miles away."

Natalie shrugs, presses buttons on her Walkman. "Slave spirits. One more reason to hate this place."

"You miss him," Grace says.

Surprise washes the girl's face before she nods. "Part of me thought you'd call the police or whatever. But then I saw you and your husband together and I was like, *See? She gets it.*"

Grace says nothing, the desire to get it makes her go still.

When Dev comes up behind her, putting a hand on her waist, she feels Natalie watching them. Grace pirouettes, tapping her palms against his chest like a long-forgotten game of tag. She runs into the ocean, dives in so the water slaps her face. She doesn't have to look to know he's swimming after her, his hands inches from her ankles.

A few feet into the Atlantic, Grace rises, her toes rooting in sand and the ocean leveling at her chest. When Dev breaks the surface, she sprays the water she's been holding in her cheeks right into his face, all of it, her breath too, so much letting out that she laughs. Her mouth burns.

"You're out of your mind," he laughs back. His hair falls from his bun, sweeps his shoulders in damp coils. "If you think there's no consequence for that."

Something releases around his shoulders, his arms flying as if freed from a net. Then there is the weight of his body over hers and a wall of water at her back, easing them down. He's so light against her that she hooks her thighs around his waist, no floating away.

He lifts her, slowly, and the air breaks clear over their heads. His fingers rest on her hips, and though he squints through the sting in his eyes, she can tell he's afraid he's hurt her.

"I thought you—" he begins, and she leans into him, kisses him so the warmth of their mouths matches the warmth fanning between her legs. She will not let go. If every moment were like this, she could keep her fear at bay.

"Alright, you two!" Adam calls from the shore.

They break apart, though she laughs into his smile, willing herself to believe they've broken through to the other side.

AFTER DINNER, SHE SHOWERS ALONE. Her body feels restless, every bump of skin rising curious into the stream of water. She pictures Dev downstairs, waiting. All through swimming and the ride home and dinner in the Wrights' backyard, they'd swapped eye contact, knowing they'd soon be alone.

By the time she's scrubbed the beach from her hair and rubbed lotion into her skin, the sun has gone down. Full night, shelled creatures scuttling around outside. She goes into her bedroom and smooths her comforter. Both hands on the cotton. She hears Dev enter the room, feels his fingers on her shoulders.

"I missed you," he says. Then adds: "I mean, I *miss* you."

"Me too," she says.

His fingers press into her, as if he's steadying himself. "I've . . . apologized in my head so many times," he says. "You must think I'm blind. For not noticing for so long."

She kisses him, lets him scoop his hands under her. He settles her onto his lap. She grabs his face, her thighs hoisting her onto his torso. Test of what her body can do.

The fear comes before he's undone her robe completely. That familiar lump in her chest, a second heart trying to beat its way through the first. As he moans into her neck, she can feel the valley of her hips tightening, though he's not yet inside her. Not even close. So much coming back, all those nights of pain.

She pushes down her worry. Relaxes against the cushion of his thighs. With her hands, she guides back his head, so he's looking at the ceiling. His own hands are heavy as he eases them out of her robe, and she can't fool him now. Herself either.

"Be honest," he says.

She gets off his lap, unsteady as blood rushes to her legs. She crosses the room. Cools herself against the window, her forehead resting on the glass. Across the way, Natalie's bedroom is awash in cloudy purple light.

"Maybe," he says, voice soft, "we just need more time."

In her neck, her pulse thrums away. No amount of swallowing will still it. "I've had time."

"A different doctor, then."

"Why? They've already said there's nothing wrong." She's told them everything she remembers, listed every old dance injury. Nothing of use in her childhood, she told one doctor with square-framed glasses, who'd recommended therapy. Olivia had been wonderful, and who knew, really, what was before that?

Something unfurls in the air, an invisible ribbon loosening the knot around them. In the house next door, Natalie enters her bedroom, her hair in a towel, her shoulders a hanger for the baggy sweatshirt that sweeps her knees. Grace thinks, Oh, I have never been that young, that easy.

She jumps when she feels Dev's breath on her neck.

"It's me, isn't it?" he asks. "You don't like sex with *me*."

"Oh no," she says, so quickly the words catch on their way out. "I don't like sex *at all*."

When she allows herself to turn to him, he says nothing. He laces his fingers with hers. The warmth of his flesh and the cool glass split her in half.

They stand there, minutes widening between them, possibilities they could step through.

Please try, she thinks he's going to say when he stiffens—or worse, *I can't*—but then she realizes the waves of light on his cheeks are coming from somewhere else.

She follows his gaze to the source.

It's Adam, pacing in Natalie's bedroom, passing before her lamp and back again. He speaks to the girl, who lies on her bed with her earbuds in her ears. Her face is blank, a certain shuttering in her eyes, so that even though she gazes in their direction, Grace knows she can't see them in this darkness, her music carrying her away. Adam puts out his hands, beckoning. She shakes her head and then mouths, *I don't.*

"What's going on over there?" Dev says.

Natalie, Adam mouths, and every feature of his expression pleads too. *Natalie, please.*

Grace knows before she knows it. Her body shrinks deeper into itself a second before the father sits on the girl's bed. Before he puts his hands on her thighs and guides each leg open.

Natalie moves his hands away, gentle. He leans back on the mattress.

The girl rises. Closes the blinds.

GRACE FLOATS FOR A WHILE after that, aware of Dev leading her from the window, of him repeating, "He didn't. He couldn't," of her mattress firm under her, of Dev disappearing and returning again. Imaginings flood her mind: Dev opening her window and shouting; Dev pummeling Adam's face into disfigurement; a body she recognizes as her own running down a dark green hallway and sweeping the girl into her arms. She would take her . . . where? The only safe place she can think of is the theater, all those women in control of their bodies—and, even then, not always.

She breathes. What would Olivia do? She remembers the last time emotion exploded over her like this, when she'd found Olivia in the front yard in the middle of the night, dazed, her purse on the grass, her coat half-unbuttoned, one hand balled against her skull like a growth. "My head," she'd said, wincing. "I can't." Hands shaking, Grace had fished Olivia's phone out of her purse and dialed 911 three times, confused as to why it wasn't working, until Olivia, eyes dim, eased herself up and pointed at the green button for CALL.

"Dev," she says. His slouching body is a hook in the darkness. "We have to tell somebody."

"Who?"

"The police. Social services. Someone."

For a long time, he remains silent. Then he flicks a switch and shocks the room with light.

"I don't know," he begins. "What if we didn't see what we thought?"

"What *else* could we have seen?"

"I don't know. Only—" He stops. "We were both thinking about sex, anyway."

She pushes past the unease in her legs and goes to the window again. Maybe this strength is Olivia too, a small awareness her body imitates. The thought fades. The blinds close them out. Pure darkness through the cracks.

"I can't see anything," Dev says. And then, relieved: "See? There's nothing."

NEITHER OF THEM RESTS. The images drift through her sleep, a sleep so thin that the sounds of Dev tossing on the couch disturb her. She imagines the rental house, the quartz kitchen, the table where Natalie eats across from her father. She imagines Sheila asleep in the master bedroom, past the green hallway, unaware.

Somehow, the sun reaches into her room and touches her, and then she really is awake. Her eyes trace faint cracks in the ceiling. Downstairs, there is stillness.

Who knows what Olivia would do? A memory floats to the

surface of her mind. A weekend watching romantic movies, love scenes with actors crumpling against mattresses, walls, rugs. Olivia beside her on the couch, studying her. "If you want to talk about sex, we can," she'd said. But the question chilled her. Weird, maybe, to imagine Olivia at it. Or maybe something else unsettling.

We have to call someone, she thinks, heading downstairs. But when she enters the living room, Dev is gone. She sees the note taped to the back of the front door. He's left, she thinks, inhaling. Then she reads it: *Doughnuts. Coffee. Be back soon and we'll talk. Everything's going to be okay.*

Talk. She wants to, but what is there to talk about until they know?

HER EXCUSE IS FLIMSY—those cookies, so good, she'd like to try the recipe today—but she composes her face as she rings the doorbell. When she looks over her shoulder, Dev's truck is still gone. Would he talk her out of it, if he were here?

Sheila answers in a red terry-cloth robe, and Grace smiles for too long, auditioning. She doesn't know what to say. If she'll be able to say anything if Adam appears.

"Forget something last night?" Sheila asks.

So sorry, Grace hears herself say, she thinks she did, some jewelry Natalie was admiring that she'd forgotten to get back, so silly.

"Go on up." Sheila shakes her head as if trying to jostle her thoughts into place. It's so early, no one seems to be thinking clearly. "Can't promise you she's awake, though."

The chill shoots straight through Grace's knees as she enters. If she runs into Adam, she'll shudder—or worse—and how foolish has she been to come here without Dev? Why isn't he panicking and here *this time*?

The house's design is modern, and upstairs, the walls are so bright it hurts—not green like she could've sworn, but white.

The hallway's monochrome photographs of half-submerged shells look dark, as if captured at night.

Natalie's bedroom door stands ajar. Grace knocks lightly, and it gives. In person, the walls in here are more mauve than purple. Natalie sits at her desk, staring back. She looks older, her cheekbones, Grace notices, are more prominent than she'd realized.

"Heard you talking to my mom," she says. "I don't have anything."

Grace slowly crosses the threshold. Natalie's hair touches her collarbone and smells faintly of flat iron.

"No, I know," she says. "It's not about that." She looks around, the carpet lined with vacuum tracks. The walls' color makes it seem as if she's standing in someone's throat. Books form a small pile on Natalie's nightstand: *French for Beginners*, tattered romance novels, *New York by Skyline*. She can't tell if this is how teenagers entertain themselves when they aren't supposed to have a phone or if the girl is throwing herself into everything she can.

"What then?" Natalie says. "Are you just now upset about—?" She lifts her eyebrows and lowers them again, a silent signaling.

Grace studies Natalie's bed, the neat tuck of her sheets. How can she leave without saying anything, without knowing if what she remembers is true?

"So," Grace begins. Her voice quivers, and Natalie's eyes sharpen. "Sometimes you don't have to get upset about things that have already happened. Sometimes—you see something else and that makes you more upset than the first thing."

Downstairs, bacon hisses in grease. Natalie's eyes slip toward the door, then back. "What'd I do?"

"Not you. Your father," Grace says. When Natalie doesn't move, she adds, "In here. Last night."

"So you see through blinds?" Natalie says.

Then her eyes widen, the dark of them shining, and Grace can see everything as she rises out of her own body. She sees Natalie's fingers digging into her thighs, sees the collapse of her chest. She sees herself, too, small as the child she must have been once, and Natalie grows large now, standing, one hand gripping her chair.

"You didn't see anything," the girl says, her voice low.

"I didn't see everything but—"

"Wasn't anything to see at *all*. I was rude, and he wanted to lecture me. That was it. Whatever else—" She opens and closes her mouth. "I mean, he's my *dad*."

"That's what I'm saying," Grace whispers. Below them, someone bangs a coffee mug.

"If that happened, that'd be so . . . messed up. Gross. I'd be—" Her eyes close. She wraps her arms around her waist. "Please get out."

"Listen," Grace says. She spins, finds a scrap of paper on the desk, scribbles down her number, though her hand shakes and she has to start again. "Listen, I know you still have your phone. I want you to—"

"Don't touch my stuff," Natalie says, too loud. Downstairs, silence.

"Okay," Grace says. "Okay." She drops the pen, shoves the paper into the girl's hand. It slips out, shudders to the carpet. What can she do?

"Get out," Natalie says. Louder now. "I have a boyfriend. College in two years. My *mom*." The girl's eyes line with tears, and Grace knows her own will make it worse. "Get out. *Now*."

"I'm getting out, I'm getting out," Grace says, walking backward to the door. Natalie stoops to snatch the paper from the floor. Crushes it in her palm. All Grace can do is repeat: "It's okay. It's going to be okay."

Grace wipes her eyes so furiously, stumbles down the stairs so quickly, that she nearly runs into Sheila at the bottom landing.

Sheila steps back, coffee splattering the breast of her robe. "What in the world?"

Behind her, Adam crosses into view, and it's too much, how normal he looks in a band T-shirt and loose jeans.

"Did you know?" Grace asks. She blinks, and Adam's face has begun to twist.

"Know what?" Sheila says, and catches her hand.

Grace's eyes dart between their faces. What can she say with him watching? "Your daughter. Talk to her."

She slips out of Sheila's grip, slips out of herself, to see her body crossing the yard, away from Adam's pinching eyes, from Sheila turning to face him, from the girl waiting on the stairs.

DEV IS STILL NOT BACK, and she takes every second of his absence to return to herself. In the kitchen, she splashes water on her face. Stretches her hip, suddenly tight. Would Olivia go back? Leave a letter? Ask the girl more?

Something familiar taps her brain. That quiet slide into herself that accompanies memory. Like an old routine her body remembers when she is alone in her room, practicing before the mirror. Or like Olivia called up from the scent of a stranger's perfume, or a throaty laugh, or a pair of eyes lost in thought.

Grace climbs the stairs, opens the door to Olivia's room. It's empty, painfully so, stripped down to white walls and a single wooden bed. A mattress holding the folds of an invisible weight. There's something she needs to find, but everything's been cleared out long ago. Everything but the images fighting their way to her brain's ceiling. She closes her eyes. Lets them come.

A hallway. Green. She's *small*. She walks into a room and lies next to a girl her age, a slash of mouth in the dark, a heated body with hair that fluffs out and tickles her ears. The girl's hand is sweaty around hers, and it tightens when a man's voice mumbles, "Quiet, both of you." A jaw framed within a moonlit window, the shine catching a belt buckle. Something wet on her knees. A dark smear on her thighs. Then nothing.

When Grace opens her eyes, dust particles spiral in the sun, flailing over Olivia's bed.

Noises rise from downstairs. A turn of a key in the lock. The rustle of paper bags. "Grace?" Dev calls.

She thinks she responds. She's not sure. Questions for Olivia fill her body: *What happened before? Did we ever talk about it?*

"Listen," he says. "I went for a drive. To think." She hears him coming up the stairs. "And—I want to say maybe I can take some time off work. Maybe stay here, so we can figure this out together. However you want. You hear me?"

He pauses at the top of the landing.

"Oh hey," he says. When he sees her, he lowers two paper cups. "What happened?"

Something is growing in her, taking shape as it lifts. A light focuses on its figure.

"Grace?" Dev repeats.

She turns at her name. How intense, the remembering. It causes so many ripples through time, joining these other segments of her life, each portion a wave coming to meet another. There is no stopping it: the past, swelling in her, awful, threatening to sweep away what peace she has. Yet she wills herself closer to it. The same way she would go toward any child still submerged, still fearful of the break, before the air.

MORNING BY MORNING

SOMETIMES, SHE CAUGHT GOD MID-BLINK. AT BEST, SHE felt His gaze as a fullness in her chest, a gold column of light that pushed out everything else. But during some prayers, she felt not absence but thinness. Like He was there, but not looking at her completely. No answers for it. Even though she was changed now. Twenty-eight and living again in New Orleans, the city of her birth. So maybe she had to try harder—be better—to keep His attention.

Those were her thoughts, anyway, before her phone rang, interrupting her from rereading baptism procedures at her kitchen table. This warm December Saturday, sunlight combed the mess of her Tremé studio. The yellow patchwork quilt wrinkled over the bed. The flats and sandals jumbled in a heap by the door. At least messiness gives me an excuse not to let him up here, she thought as she found her phone beneath a jacket on the floor. But it wasn't Jay. Instead: Helene, from church.

"You free, Sariah?" Helene asked, her voice calm, measured.

"Today?" She couldn't imagine Helene—with her square-jawed fiancé and ivory dresses and river-black hair pinned with a floral hair comb each Sunday—wanting to hang out with her. Usually, Helene called to guide her into being a deaconess. To discuss Communion duties. To warn her not to wear dresses too tight around the swell of her breasts and stomach. To remind her to wear white heels, not black. "Sure—what do you need?"

"A break, to be honest," Helene said, laughing, her alto warm. "My family owns this property down in Lafourche. My grandmother's before she passed. We rent it out, but it's free this weekend and since there's the bayou baptism tomorrow anyway, I thought it'd be a nice getaway."

A getaway. She could spend all night communing with Helene, who knew God so well the light spilling into the sanctuary always fell over the back of her head. Once, the woman had led a prayer during service that had made Sariah shudder and feel God like a gold pressure in her chest again, a feeling so hard to come by on command. Though Helene could do it.

"You're not spending New Year's with Kevin?" she asked, right as Helene went, "Tomorrow's service will be easier if we wake up there. I know you're nervous."

True. All week—when she wasn't fretting over Jay, the effect the two of them were having on each other—she'd been visualizing what the other deaconesses had asked of her. In lieu of a watch night service, the church would honor the Lord on New Year's Day, holding baptisms on the bayou instead of at their North Villere property. The first day of the year a Sunday for once. And she, the youngest deaconess, would hand towels to the baptized emerging from the water, draping the white plush around their shoulders like wings waiting to unfurl. Other than Pastor Marlon, she'd be the first to greet the saved. She wanted them to see God in her, to feel His closeness as they stepped into new life. So He had to inhabit her fully. Her spirit had to be right.

"That'd be sweet," she said finally. "I could use a break too."

A relief in more ways than one. She hung up, blinking at her phone, grateful for what could be called divine intervention.

"Lord?" she asked, seeking Him. She felt Him appear in her chest, pushing her lungs.

So she was right. Getting out of her apartment, out of Tremé this New Year's Eve, would remind her who she was to Jay. His assigned deaconess, his welcomer into their small church, his guide when he needed praying for, his cheerleader during tomorrow's baptism. She wasn't supposed to flush and imagine him calling her up tonight. She wasn't supposed to want.

HOW FULL OF GOD'S LIGHT she'd been the night she met Jay. For once, feeling His presence against her ribs had been as simple as turning toward another body in bed, feeling a warmth without even opening her eyes.

It was early October, then, and Pastor Marlon had tapped her to help lead evening prayer group. "You've got that personable thing going for you," Pastor Marlon whispered as they set up in the chapel, his cuffs not yet buttoned over his dark wrists. They arranged pink boxes of doughnut holes on the table. Set out miniature bottles of lukewarm water. "Folks'll say what's really on their hearts if they feel they won't be judged for it."

Perhaps he was right. In the prayer circle, that half-moon of folding chairs set up between the front pew and the pulpit, she held the hands of the black-bloused woman sitting on her left, the plaid-shirted man on her right, and tried to shrink her body in her mind. To become a vessel for God instead of a house for her own longings. Her nightly prayers had served as practice: *Lord, forgive me for buying that dress that was too short, forgive me for grinning when that man at the coffee shop said he loved a woman with real thighs.* But she'd already gotten all that cleaned out. Maybe that was why God felt so close now.

Around her, so many asked for prayers. The Johnsons, whose daughter had moved to Seattle and stopped calling. Christine, with her gold nose piercings, returning to college at forty. As the attendees lifted their voices—"Please Lord, let my wife's biopsy come back clean" and "Fix it, Jesus. Fix this addiction tearing up my family"—she echoed, "Amen" and "Please, Father." She kept her eyes so tightly shut that other people's desires pulsed blue behind her eyelids. Her palms tingled from gripping hands, like God had fused them together with sweat and the oil of skin.

She opened her eyes only because she felt the break. A man grabbing her left hand, severing her connection with the black-bloused woman who'd been speaking: Louise, praying for God's discernment when it came to loving a woman and not a man. She'd been trying to squeeze Louise's fingers so tightly, wanting to push love through—and now this man with his dreadlocks woven back, a red birthmark staining the corner of an eye, had her hand.

Welcome, she nodded at him, hoping her body could speak. She didn't want to disrupt the others still bowed in prayer.

He raised an eyebrow: *Like this?* His hand adjusted its grip on hers. Leaning forward, he'd taken a seat on the pew behind their folding chairs. Guilt unlocked in her chest: Whatever he had to pray for, she wanted him drawn in fully, not simply sitting behind them.

She nodded again, tugging him closer. She didn't know her plan, maybe she could scoot over and they could share the seat and he could—

Thank you, no, he said with the flash of his smile, the pinch around his dark eyes. She thought he'd relax his grip but he didn't. His fingers rowed her back from her prayer's gold light, back to the chapel that held her body and his and the others.

After, when the prayer circle ended and the attendees sipped water, taking their time in the chapel brighter than the outside dark, she found him studying the crystal windowpanes, the amber-stained crosses etched into their centers.

"The ones in the sanctuary are nicer," she said. The top of her head, the spaces between her short curls, felt hot. "You seen them?"

"Once or twice." He pressed a finger into a cross's center, where its heart would be if it were a figure with outstretched arms. "Can't come on Sundays, but I've met Marlon here a few times. Or excuse me." He laughed, some private joke his eyes couldn't fully transmit. "*Pastor* Marlon. Whatever he goes by here."

"Either works," she said. And then: "You know him?"

"He invited me to join." He withdrew his finger. "He keeps telling me it's time to come home. What do you think about that?"

"About what?"

He wasn't standing close to her, but his direct gaze closed the gap between them. It was like an electric net tightened around her hips and stomach. "Yeah, you look like you know how to pray, alright," a man in a Saints jersey had told her earlier that night. She thought he meant she looked solid, rooted. Though she wasn't really.

"Is there?" He smiled softly. "A time to come back to church? If you believe in God?"

"You came," Pastor said, coming up to them, clapping his large hands on the man's back. He suddenly seemed younger than forty-something, his laughter vaulting over his teeth. "Late's better than never."

"Told you I'd try," he said, and then Pastor was introducing him as "Jay" and calling him his "little brother." Man, they went way back, Pastor said. He used to watch him wobble down their block on his trike.

"That's the memory you're going with?" Jay said, raising an eyebrow. But the hollow of his collarbone still studied her. "Hasn't been me for a long time."

"Well, here we are," Pastor said, and then they were both looking at her, as if afraid she'd seen too much of them. Curiosity spiked in her, then trailed across her forehead. She wanted to *know* this man, whatever he couldn't say.

"Good the two of you met," Pastor went on, clearing his throat. "Jay, Sariah's your assigned deaconess. Last names T through Z. She'll help you get settled. You just—. Excuse me." Another attendee, a broad-shouldered man who'd prayed for his ceramics shop, tapped him. Drew him away.

"Under your care, huh?" Jay said. He fingered the glass again. "Must be a lot of folks with names in that range."

"Only you," she said, and when he tilted his head, she added: "I just finished qualifying in July. To be a deaconess, I mean."

"Congrats," he said, though she couldn't tell if he was serious. But no—he was.

"I'll help you any way I can," she said. She hadn't wanted to admit how new to this she was. With her nerves so alive, prickling her skin with heat, she couldn't feel God hovering near.

She hoisted her purse over her shoulder, like she was older, a church mother, immune to him. "I'll pray for peace around your joining, if you want."

"If *you* want," he said. He was touching her now, his fingertips at her elbow as he eased her against the wall, letting people pass. "Me—I have a hard time praying. I don't like to admit what I want in case I don't get it."

SHE AND HELENE DROVE into the bayou's muted wilderness, leaving behind Tremé's Creole cottages, their white posts like slender bodies forbidden to touch. US 90 skimmed the brown waters, glided past the tupelo trees sighing as their roots sipped. She'd chosen to drive, wanting to give Helene *something*. When she'd pulled up in front of Helene's duplex east of the Garden District, she'd been expecting Kevin to join them. But no, there'd only been Helene stepping off her porch, a Louis Vuitton duffel nestling against her body. She'd never seen Helene in jeans and a ponytail, her hair's shorter edges lifting like feathers.

"Everything alright?" Sariah asked, now that they were down the road. Helene still hadn't mentioned her fiancé, why she wasn't with him.

"Fine." Helene closed her eyes. Her hand rested atop the button of her jeans, the sapphire on her ring finger passing from black to blue and back. "I thought this might be nice. God told me we both might need it."

Wasn't that the truth. And how amazing that God spoke to Helene so easily, so consistently. He's not like that with me, Sariah thought. Instead, He came when she was repenting for something. For hesitating before putting her check in the tithe envelope. For asking forgiveness for letting her thoughts drift again toward Jay, his arms, his mouth. Only then did she feel Him again, that gold swell. She hadn't figured out how to sense

Him when she was just—being. Though maybe that was because she struggled to control herself.

She returned her eyes to the road, noting the clusters of ibis on the waters, their tails blushing pink. If she were back home, Jay would call from his apartment, fixing himself coffee or pan-dipped French toast. "I'm nervous about tomorrow," he'd joke. "Explain again why I'm doing this." And, somehow, she'd end up at the bar where he worked, laughing like nothing about her had changed since she'd returned to her parents' God.

As if her thoughts summoned him, her phone rang from the cup holder. She knew before her glance made out his name, before Helene's eyes fluttered open.

"Who's that?" she asked. "Want me to answer?"

"That's alright." And then—because the omission felt like an admission: "It's Jay. My candidate for tomorrow's baptism."

She could feel Helene studying her as she drove, but she kept her eyes on the road, on the winter sunlight spreading over the wetlands. Once, in their church pew, she'd seen Kevin trace the hem of Helene's skirt in the middle of service. Helene had clamped her hand around his fingers, pressing into them some private message or keeping them from sliding up. She wanted to know, too, how Helene had figured that out. How she could have sex with Kevin but not be ruled by it, and still have enough room in her body for God to dwell there permanently.

"Don't let him get too comfortable with you," Helene said. Her voice was tight, snug in its own truth. "Some men live their lives to different standards. Baptized or no."

JESUS WAS BETTER AT IT. Treating the body like all bone, a mere gate for the soul to slip through. She couldn't talk to Jay on the phone without feeling like everything she learned of him made her more aware of what he withheld. How he'd made his way back to church because life—the constant outflow of money, the ever-hotter summers, news of the president—wasn't any simpler without God. How he thought a long sermon was a wrong sermon. How his bartending meant every woman thought he should fix her life or let her fix his.

"What do I care who these women sleep with?" he said once in late October. She'd returned from a run, was standing in her kitchen with her phone pressed so close to her ear his voice slipped into its pink. "Explain that one to me."

"Maybe you'd care if you knew them," she said, pulling at the elastic of her shorts to let in air over her hips. In his silence, she wondered if he was thinking about the two of them. When he'd asked, she'd told him she'd been abstaining from sex for eight years, since she was twenty. Which limited her choice of boyfriends.

"Maybe I would," he said. And then they moved on, the rhythms of his voice telling her what he didn't say aloud.

A laugh slipping out when she told him, "Yes, Jay, a tithe is a *full* ten percent."

A sudden pause when she said God had sent her a dream, a vision of him being baptized in yellow waters.

"What does that mean?" he'd asked, and she said she didn't know. She'd only even known it was from God because she had that gold fullness in her chest.

"See?" Jay said, laughing again. "You get on me for asking questions. But seems to me like you don't ask enough."

Perhaps she didn't. By that point in the conversation, she'd sat down in her kitchen chair, her thighs and upper back still sticky with sweat. She asked God, *Are You here? Have I done something to make You go away again?* Even then, she felt Him near the ceiling, not in her, though she'd been good and had never invited Jay over to her apartment or been to his.

In mid-November, he'd invited her to his bar, least he could do since she'd put up with his questions about God and the church and the difference between. She'd made herself wait a week, and when she arrived at the bar's brown-brick front, she stared through its glass doors. Exposed brick walls holding gilt mirrors. Plastic candles haloing orange. Already it was half-full, locals in sheer dresses and bright tops tracing cocktail glasses or picking delicately at oysters. That was alright. Maybe the place getting full as Friday crept toward Saturday would give her an excuse to leave—if God punished her by pulling away completely.

"So you're not drinking 'cause you're here on church business?" Jay said when she was seated at the polished cherrywood bar.

Her fork parted the waves of her salad. "No . . . Because it's early. It's not even seven."

He laughed. "Late by most standards." Dressed in black, he looked smaller. Or maybe it was because the bar hid his lower half, leaving her to imagine it. "So you don't believe in happy hour, I guess."

"It's not that I *don't* drink." Though she only sometimes had a glass of wine before bed on particularly difficult days, like when the attorneys at her office were too busy to be polite in their emails to her and the other paralegals. Or when her father called from Houston, warning about late-summer storms, asking if she was ready to move, God sent only so many warnings before He left you to yourself.

She watched Jay as he mixed Sazeracs and brandies, his tongue peeking from his mouth in concentration. He set out the glasses for the waitresses, who carried them off to women in chiffon dresses, their eyes flickering toward her, studying her body with the same expression as runners in City Park: *Would I call her thick or just fat?* Though it was only God's opinion she cared about. So much of her body, so much He'd fearfully and wonderfully made. Hard to hide it with closed-toe heels and high-waisted jeans and a scarf lowered over her cleavage. Still—she could feel Him watching without pouring Himself into her. He was deciding. Or maybe He'd spoken and she'd missed it: *Your body is a temple. Who are you preparing it for?*

"You still praying for me?" Jay said during a lull. He poured her another glass of water. Behind him, the rise and fall of liquor bottles resembled organ pipes.

"Always," she said. "When you're baptized—it's a big life change. I think feeling Him like a real presence, like you might feel someone else beside you, is the difference between people who stay connected to their faith and people who don't. Which is, you know, the real hell."

"What is?" he said, easing the glass toward her. A bead of water slipped down its side, and he caught it with his finger.

"Distance from God," she said. "I've been there, and—I don't want that for you."

IN THE BAYOU, Helene's ranch house was flat with peeling wood paneling, like the place was an eye halfway closed. Easy to imagine out-of-towners wanting to escape into the quiet swamps. Boats resting solemn in the neighboring yards. Nets hanging like textiles from garage doors. Insects humming, plenty for larger creatures to eat, no need to worry about holding back.

"At least gators aren't out this time of year," Helene said as she unlocked the screen door. "For the baptism tomorrow," she added when she saw Sariah's face. "In all the years my grandparents lived here, I don't think they ever saw one in the house. In the yard once or twice, but not *inside*."

Sariah tried to imagine what such a thing might look like—a scaled creature with its jaws open wide, sitting on the living room rug—but, once they'd entered, the house looked modern, renovated for guests browsing online photos from afar. Cream quartz countertops and a red paisley rug smooth with vacuum tracks and hardwood holding the sharpness of pine cleaner.

"Thanks for coming," Helene said, dropping her bag on the navy leather couch.

She'd abandoned her sandals at the door and now she plopped down, massaging the pale undersides of her feet. "I like to come here every so often—check if the cleaning crew is doing their job—but I hate the drive. Kevin usually takes me."

Sariah was still studying the place's spotlessness, which reminded her of her own apartment's mess, of what she was avoiding. "You and Kevin spend weekends here?"

"Sometimes," Helene said. She seemed younger, spreading her toes into the rug like an exasperated teenage girl. "He's big on fishing, anyway."

On their way in, they'd picked up shrimp po' boys from a roadside shop, and they ate them at the vinyl kitchen table, on clear plates still damp from rinsing. Their conversation flickered like a cloud of lightning bugs fading in and out. Yes, Helene had lived in New Orleans all her life. No, she didn't suppose she'd ever leave for good, even if the storms spiraling through would eventually worsen.

"What about you?" Helene asked, nudging a tomato back into place with a French-tipped fingernail. "When you first joined, I thought you'd just moved here."

"I had," she said, sipping her lemonade. She felt the tartness long after she pulled her lips from the straw. "From Houston, where I grew up and went to college. But before Katrina, my family lived in Carrollton."

"Really? I didn't think that area got hit too hard."

"Not compared to others." How to explain. How quickly her father had packed her and her mother and brothers into their Buick. How quickly he'd driven them to their grandparents. From Houston, tucked on Grandma Lillian's floral couch, they watched the waters licking the rafters of square houses, people waiting on shingled rooftops—until the news outlets cut to aerial shots of the Superdome. "Well, guess they're safer in there, right?" her older brother said, though to her it looked like someone— not God necessarily, though it wouldn't have been unlike her to think that then—had put a lid over all those people so the rest of the world wouldn't have to see or think about them.

When Helene excused herself to take an aspirin—she apologized, she had a headache, part of the reason she needed a getaway—Sariah stepped outside, hoping too much time hadn't passed since Jay's call. She needed to show him she was here for him in the right way, to get him through tomorrow's baptism. Then, she'd know she hadn't gotten in the way of God's plan for his life.

"You haven't stopped by all week," he said when he picked up. Behind his voice was a little cloud of chatter. She imagined him out, in a grocery store most likely, buying champagne or beer or whatever he drank for New Year's. "I missed you—if it's alright to say that."

"Why wouldn't it be alright?" she said. Though she was alone on the wood porch, only a maroon car driving along the main road, she smoothed down her short coils.

"Oh, I don't know," he said. "You're funny that way. All your commitments and everything. I wouldn't want to go and offend you."

"You didn't." And then she allowed herself: "I missed you too."

"Where are you anyway? You don't sound like you're at home."

"On a trip with Helene. We're down in Lafourche—only a few minutes from where we'll all be tomorrow. She figured it'd be easier if we woke up here."

"So I won't be seeing you tonight."

A spider the same brown color as the winter-leeched yard crawled up a post, inches from where she leaned. "I mean, I'll see you tomorrow morning. The big day."

"Yes—but New Year's Eve's not the kind of night you spend with just anybody."

"Oh yeah?" She looked over her shoulder, through the glass cut into the front door. Helene still hadn't returned to the kitchen. "Who are you supposed to spend it with?"

"I think you know."

"Not quite. Not like I can read your mind."

"I think you can," he said. "At least—the parts you want to."

She breathed in. Grateful she'd called or grateful she'd come away with Helene. She searched for that bright feeling of God in her chest and felt only her own heartbeat. More than once, she'd wanted to tell Jay: *God will leave me, leave you, too, if we push Him.*

"So anyway," he was saying, his voice louder. He'd left the store, wherever he was. "You know if anyone's bringing any greens or black-eyed peas tomorrow? Need me some money and luck next year."

"I'll cook some if you want," she said. "Consider it a baptism present."

"Oh, yours can't be better than mine," he said, laughing. "But I'll take you up on it."

When she stepped back in, Helene had untied her hair, was pouring red wine into a glass.

"I was thinking this is supposed to be a celebration," Helene said. "It's New Year's Eve and tomorrow we've got people joining the kingdom of God."

"Right." Sariah slipped her phone into her back pocket, closing the front door behind her. She'd never seen Helene drink anything other than water or Communion grape juice.

"Sariah," Helene said, shaking her head. She draped her fingers around her wineglass, her engagement ring quietly blue. "I'm thirty-four this year. The oldest I've been in my *life*. And—how old are you? Twenty-seven?"

"Eight," she corrected.

"So you're going to make me turn this into a party on my own? What would you be doing if I hadn't dragged you away?"

It was three o'clock. She would not be inviting Jay over. She would not be picking out lipstick to wear at midnight. She would not be—

"I'd be having friends over," she said. "Watching a movie. Dancing to the countdown."

"Great, let's do all of it," Helene said, putting down her glass, emptied. The woman's eyebrows were set so firm, so determined, like she was calculating a setup for the church picnic.

Sariah couldn't help but laugh. "Why? What would you and Kevin be doing?"

Helene was already pouring herself another, watching the level rise to the brim.

"Kevin's doing what he wants," she said. "So now I'm doing me."

Sariah didn't push, didn't ask what made Helene lift her glass to her lips so quickly. Helene would share if she wanted. Sariah poured her own wine, but then—the bottle was empty. Not enough to last the night.

"Let's walk." Helene laughed, slipped on her jacket. "There's a little grocery close by."

It was getting colder, but the sun shone, still there though they couldn't feel its warmth. She felt lucky to be beside Helene, this woman she admired, who she hadn't realized considered her a friend. It had been so long since she'd been out to the bayou, not since she was a girl and her family went fishing, their lines bobbing up and down. Her brothers hollered that they didn't believe anything swam under the brown waters. Her father insisted they wait. Her mother rubbed sunscreen into their arms until their skin grayed. And then—one bit her line. She hauled the fish onto the dock, its silver so much brighter than imagined. "Throw him back," her mother said. "God wouldn't want us to kill him if we're not going to eat him." Though she hadn't wanted to, so reluctant to give him up that she let him flop on the dock until he went still. "Well, that's between you and the Lord now," her mother said, shaking her head.

How quickly all of that came back. She'd been so much younger, an entirely different person.

"Can we grab some collards and black-eyed peas?" she asked Helene. They were walking along the road, Helene's fingers stroking the brilliant white-doves camellias.

"You believe in that?" Helene said, though she was smiling, her eyes aglow with wine. "Money and luck and cooking your own fortune?"

"Let me make some for you and we'll see how this year turns

out. If I were planning a wedding, I'd want all the luck and money God had to hand out."

Helene stiffened as they approached the wooden grocery at the road's end, beside a gas station and fishing shop. She stayed that way as they wandered down the speckled linoleum aisles, picking up wine and black-eyed peas and collards and a frozen pizza, Helene's craving. She wanted to do what she never did, Helene said, which was just to do what she wanted.

They didn't say much else until they were walking back to the house, the air growing colder, the plastic bags weighing on their shoulders and fingertips.

"You know what he said about me?" Helene said suddenly, tilting her chin as if she were reeling herself out of her thoughts.

"What?" In the quiet, Sariah had been thinking of tomorrow morning, the approaching baptism.

"That I didn't know how to have fun, that I couldn't love him through all my rules." Helene held the wine to her chest, thumbing its green stem. "I bet no one's ever said that to you."

They hadn't. When she'd been younger, boys called her lots of fun—*too* much.

"See?" Helene said. She was blinking too quickly, like the wind had blown a bit of wilderness into her eye. "I knew it, the way you are. Like when you were dancing at the church picnic that time. Or when you led that karaoke contest at the carnival. I'd thought it was all too secular but you—you knew people would like that. And that's why the deaconess board nominated you. Whereas me, they knew I'd be efficient."

Sariah didn't know what to say. She should humble herself: *Well, I'm not so great.*

"You're not only efficient," she said, "but I think it's amazing how determined you are, how seriously you take your faith."

Helene said nothing. They were coming back up on the house, Sariah's car parked in the driveway, its orange bright against the house's gray.

"I do take it seriously," Helene said finally. She shifted the bottle against her chest. "Even though Kevin can't see it. Or—maybe he does and he thinks other things are important. Last night he said, 'Helene, I just can't see marrying someone I've never had sex with. Who's never had sex.' Like he wasn't the one who proposed. Like we haven't been going to church together all this time."

"So—you mean you've *never*?" she asked.

What was that feeling passing over her, a chill beyond the shadows of tree branches? In all the times she'd seen Helene and Kevin together—pulling up to the church parking lot in his black truck, settling fingers on each other's arms during barbecues, rising in the pews as Pastor announced their engagement—she'd never thought Helene had never touched or *been* touched. Not at thirty-four years old.

"Not even once," Helene said, coughing a little as she stepped over the driveway's ledge. "And with Kevin—I didn't wait this long, give up all that, to throw God away now."

Sariah's feet stopped. Just shy of the yard. Helene grew smaller, continuing up the driveway.

"What do you mean?" Sariah said. "Throw God away?" She felt stinging in her fingers, a nudge in her chest. God—no. Fear—no. *Dread.*

"By sinning," Helene said, unlocking the screen door. She turned around, her eyebrows twisting. "You think He'd answer my prayers, take care of me, if I'd been out there running around like everybody else? You think He'd let me off the hook?"

AS FALL TURNED into early winter, she'd returned to Jay's bar again and again. Talking to him resembled following a guide through a museum, entranced not only by the way you understood the brushstrokes on each painting, but by the way he did too.

"You think . . . who you were as a kid would be surprised by who you are now?" she asked one November night, leaning on the bar with her chin on her knuckles. "Teenage me never would've thought I'd be a deaconess."

"Oh, really?" he said, spraying amber beer into a glass. "Little Jay would be shocked I grew out my hair long as my father's."

Another time, she asked if he thought David in 2 Samuel really loved Bathsheba. After he'd impregnated her, did he only kill her husband out of fear?

"Well he *cared*," Jay said, the bar's light turning his teeth red. "Not saying the guy was right, but he kept her from being stoned. Or whatever they did to side chicks back then."

And later: Would God really let New Orleans be lost to floodwaters forever? Climate change or no?

"Believing in Him makes things easier," he said. It was the week before Christmas, and he'd walked her home from the bar. They stood at the gate to her little triplex, its iron pressing into her back. "But it's not like He hasn't let things happen since Noah's flood."

He'd been sixteen, he said, on his way to grown. When the storm came, his father believed they'd been in their Gentilly home for so long that they'd just hunker down. He'd felt a snap of fear even then, worsened by his mother praying as they boarded up the windows, by his father laughing and calling God "that old hobby of hers." And then—the water yawned in, devouring the family's tan couch and the end table his brother carved in woodshop and the wrinkled shoes left near the back door, his mother determined to keep her floors clean. The water lapped it all up, whetting its appetite for them, too, until they'd fled upstairs, the blackness groaning behind, chasing them to the roof. They'd waited there for days without food or water, his mother praying and his father gripping her hand and his older brother trying to sleep it off. He tried sleep, too, hoping to wake and see helicopters. Hoping one day this could be forgotten, as easily as his father had forgotten God.

"I'm sorry," she said. She wrapped her arm around her back, felt the fence cool against her knuckles. "I can't even imagine."

"You can," he said, giving a little crescent smile. "You're from here, aren't you?"

She shook her head, then nodded. Yes, yes she was but—"We left for Houston when the warnings came. We got a house and went to school and we were—"

She'd been about to say "fine." But that wasn't true. It wasn't only the storm, everything lost. There had also been her parents' interpretations. After the waters had drained, her family had gone to clear out their things from the flooded storage shed, and she'd found her favorite yellow dress, ruined. Its straps had once slipped down her shoulders and made her feel like the wind was saying her body deserved to be soothed, seen, touched. She hadn't even known it was there. It had been missing from her closet for months. "Don't get bent out of shape about it," her mother had said. "Maybe this is God's way of punishing you for not setting your sights on heavenly things."

"You feel guilty about leaving," Jay observed. He tucked his hands into the black puff of his coat, his eyes so warm and brown it was hard to believe he was cold. "Don't."

"That's not what I was thinking." She tightened her scarf. "I always knew—one way or another—I'd come back to this city. I couldn't abandon it."

He waited. She did too. He'd already told her what he rarely spoke about: his reluctance about openly claiming a God who'd once—in his mind—left him vulnerable.

"It was good for me, to start over here," she went on. A red Eldorado drove by, neo soul trickling through its speakers. Jay stepped closer to hear her. "I wasn't—very good before."

She told it all, trying to explain how wrong she'd been for delighting in her body. Even though her brothers teased her about being bigger, calling her Madea, calling her braid her "oxtail." Even though loving herself was looking after herself. But there was no denying that God left her when she started taking pride in dresses or the push of her breasts or the sway of her ass when she walked. She'd felt nothing in church, then. Though her mother said it was her own self-absorption, the way she bought cherry lipstick or wore leggings as pants.

But her *body*, what it could do. In secret, she slept with boys at her new school. Boys who went to church on Sundays, who spent weekdays flipping through auto magazines or playing basketball on cement courts or getting older sisters to drop them at the Galleria, where they'd slip their palms into her back pocket while walking. Sex came easy. In her bedroom with her mother out at Bible study, her father at her brothers' soccer games. At her friends' houses during sleepovers, their parents asleep upstairs. And, once, in the church basement, the damp swallowing their bodies as her then-boyfriend, Terrence, bit her neck, his braces cool. Maybe she'd believed enough in God then to know she was wrong. But God did not have a face, a body, a mouth. A commandment didn't have the warmth of a whisper in the dark.

"But I was ignorant," she said, holding herself. "The commandments bring you close to Him."

"Close to Him," Jay repeated, his eyes lowered.

"I have to get in," she said. Maybe she'd shared too much. "Back up to my place. I have some work things to finish."

"Wait," he said, pushing open the gate. "What you said—"

"I'm fine." She stepped onto the concrete pathway and closed the gate between them. "But maybe we'll talk later. If you need something before the baptism?"

She wasn't sure he'd call again. But he did. Christmas Eve, when she stood in her parents' subway-tiled Houston kitchen, making a cranberry coffee cake. Her mother sliced fresh pineapple for the ham at the table. Her father and brothers argued in the living room about whether to go to services or the movies. "The movies?" her father was saying. "On Jesus' birthday?"

"You'll never guess who came by tonight," Jay said. "Louise from prayer group? On a date at the bar. She and this chick were saying grace."

"That's great," she said. "I'm happy for her."

And then Jay was asking if he was a jerk for getting his family alcohol for Christmas. He'd bought bottles off his boss because he didn't have the patience to guess what anyone in his family might want. She listened, stirring the yellow batter, smoothing the pecans and cranberries to keep them from settling.

"I been praying for you," he said finally. "You know, what we talked about."

"Thank you," she whispered. Behind her, her mother cleared her throat.

IN THE BAYOU RANCH'S KITCHEN, she could see Helene straining, a slight tug on her laughter. The woman had drunk most of the wine while they set the peas and collards to boiling, slid the pizza in the oven. Now Helene sang along to the year-end music videos replaying on the house's flat-screen. As Sariah stirred the pots' contents, she couldn't tell if Helene listened to this music on her own or with girlfriends or if she learned the choruses as they repeated. Helene was singing Lizzo now, ecstatic, shifting her hips from side to side.

Sariah hadn't had much to drink herself. Only a few sips from the glass beside her on the counter. Helene's words still buzzed in her brain: *You think God would let you off the hook?*

"Oh, so you don't need wine to loosen up," Helene said, wiping her eyes, a little red rimmed. "That's fine. But come dance."

And then Helene was tying her T-shirt at her ribs and grabbing Sariah's hands so the two of them could dance barefoot on the living room rug. Sariah tried to set the spoon on the counter, but it missed, hit the floor, hot peas splashing her toes.

"There you go," Helene said, watching her sway her hips, loosen the tension in her stomach. "Knew I was right to invite you."

Her thoughts twirled, faster than her arms or feet. Faster than she could control her laughter—verging on hysterical—when Helene asked if she would teach her how to twerk.

Her thoughts didn't settle until Helene, around nine, wore herself out and asked if they could watch a movie. *The Preacher's Wife*, her favorite holiday film, which she hadn't seen this year given the foolishness with Kevin. Sariah sat on the floor, her plate empty, save for mixed pea and collard juices, pizza crumbs coasting on the green puddle. On the couch, Helene sat above her in satin pajamas and a zebra hair bonnet, her cheek leaning against the armrest, the movie's grainy light softening her face.

How could she make sense of it? That rupture in her chest when Helene had said, "If I'd been out there running around like everyone else?" Was this lifelong self-sacrifice why—in all the times she'd felt God radiating from Helene beside her in the pew, from Helene's powerful prayers—God filled the woman so fully? Would her own body only ever have half of God because she'd loved Him only half her life?

"What's it like?" Helene said drowsily when the movie had been on for some time. Whitney Houston was singing in a yellow choir robe. "Sex, I mean."

"Oh, I don't know." She drew her knees into her chest. "Been so long since I've had it."

"Yeah, but you miss it, right?" Helene said, her voice so soft you could stroke it. "Once you have it, you always miss it. That's what Kevin says anyway."

"Same could be said about God."

Helene hiccupped before laughing. "Yeah, girl. But that's not what I asked."

"I don't know how to explain it to you." She'd felt seen. She'd trusted in her own breath and skin and fingertips. But she'd thought she'd gotten away from that—before Jay.

"Part of me wants to," Helene said, her voice too worn out and wine-drunk to travel the length of her throat. "Sometimes, when Kevin touches me—it's like this whole other part of me wakes up. But then I think—God'll hate me. Or maybe not hate. He doesn't hate anybody. But He'd be disappointed, distant from me."

"Distant," she echoed quietly. Outside, miles away at full volume or just next door at half, someone set off a firework, a lone snap.

"Right," Helene said. When Sariah turned, the woman's eyes were slits, shadowed by her eyelashes. "'Cause some things, even if you get baptized or ask for forgiveness, can't be taken. Taken back. Like not being a virgin anymore. Or getting a disease. Or getting pregnant."

"So that's it." She couldn't feel her body, her voice merely hovering. "No taking it back?"

"Well, even the Bible says some things are unforgivable." Helene yawned, folded her right toes in the wrinkled arch of her left foot. "Taking the Lord's name in vain, blaspheming, murder. And other things, too, probably. Or—if not unforgivable, exactly, then God wouldn't forget. I mean, He has to have some way of separating the real believers from the imitators. How else would He measure our lives in the final book?"

They sat in the dimness, the TV's volume low. The wideness of Whitney's singing mouth didn't match the quiet. Their own breathing. The soft hiss of insects clinging to cypresses.

"See?" Helene said. When Sariah blinked, the woman was standing above her, shaking her head, her shadow wobbling on the coffee table. "I knew talking to you would help. Because I'm right. I know I'm right not to. And that's what I'll tell Kevin now I've had a chance to think."

Helene turned off the TV. Mumbled, "Only ten thirty, really? God, I'm tired. And we've got an early start tomorrow. Unless you want to stay up? You look like you want to."

"You go to bed," she said, still on the rug, slowly returning to her body. In the new darkness, without the TV's glare giving them the illusion of length, her toes looked smaller than the rest of her, her nails like little shells soon to be lost to her skin.

"The kitchen," Helene said in half sleep, though she'd started down the hallway, toward the bedrooms. "I don't want you to have to clean it all."

"I'll get it. Not much anyway."

It took her a minute to pull herself off the rug. To walk into the kitchen. Its tile shocked her feet with ice, her soles so much colder than the spiral of heat between her lungs. She ladled the collards and peas into Ziploc bags. Washed each pot with a fresh sponge and then wiped down the counters and the sink and the sill of the window looking over the backyard. Moonless night. The grass could've been water surrounding them. She prayed quietly, but felt nothing, no fullness in her chest—though maybe now she knew why.

When she finished, it was after eleven. She slipped down the hall to Helene's room, the door open, the woman so caught in sleep's undertow that she hadn't closed it. A series of slivers in the darkness: the plane of a cheek submerged in a pillow, the thin slope of calves. The only full part of her was her fist clenching before her nose. Hard to tell if she still wore her sapphire or if, resolved now, she'd removed it. Like she could hurt, yes, but she knew who had her. God. She needed no one else.

SHE LEFT A NOTE. In case Helene woke. She was going for a drive because she couldn't go for a run, which was what she needed to get her head together. She'd be back. She left two aspirin on the kitchen island, atop a slip of legal paper.

She drove. The swamp looming, tupelo trees leaning away from her car, the metal streetlights like arched fingers ready to press down. Or merely pointing.

She didn't worry about the road melting to water—so much of it everywhere, it'd be so easy to drive into it blind—until her odometer told her she'd been driving for thirty miles, until the streetlights faded. Above her, there were only the spindly tops of trees and a multitude of stars through the windshield, light flung and scattered at random.

She eased the car to the road's shoulder. Stopped. Because she wanted to keep going, which scared her. Always had. Her body had long been sure of what couldn't be good. By contrast, the things that made sense logically, that conformed to the rules she'd been taught, she had to fight to grasp.

She breathed in and out. Saw something white and feathered flutter in the trees' dark hollows. There *must* be water, impossibly close. She thought of praying. Or even asking God to say once and for all how He felt about her, if He was what Jay once called "wishy-washy" because she herself had once been. She didn't pray. Didn't want Him to see her just then. She cut the headlights, as if that would help. As if the absence of light could sweep her from His view.

She could sit with it that way. Let herself emerge.

She'd been twenty when she'd gotten pregnant. It'd seemed impossible, after all the times she'd merely enjoyed her body. She'd taken her little pill most days, mostly on time. She'd felt semen empty from her as she rolled toward the boy in her dorm room's bed, thinking nothing of it. She'd never believed sperm could meet one of her eggs because she'd never seen such tiny cells in action. So aside from the look on her gynecologist's face, how could she know it was real?

She'd taken the train. In the clinic ten miles from campus—where it had still been possible to end a pregnancy, then—she looked at the sonogram, her womb a gray cave streaked white, a tunnel with wind roaring through. "Yes," she'd said when the doctor instructed her to read the forms, to look at the baby again. "Fetus," he corrected, palming his stubble, his mouth twisting. But she repeated, "Yes." Dug her heels into the stir-rups. She was sure.

She sat up on the paper covering the beige recliner. Swallowed her first pill and then slipped the second into her backpack. Then she took the train to her parents' house and watched cartoons on the television, feeling, for the most part, like she'd simply been gone a long time.

She thought again: It had all been easy. The doctor had looked at her so urgently from behind his spectacles, like she was doing something serious. Only—she didn't feel guilty. She was supposed to go with her parents to Bible study that night, and she felt no hesitation about stepping into church with that second pill in her backpack. Anyway, didn't every commandment come down to not being bound by your body?

She'd felt that was true more than anything. Then, after daydreaming through the church's discussions of Job and eating spaghetti with her family and deciding she'd head back to campus in the morning, she'd gone up to her childhood bedroom and taken the second pill. Soon after—her stomach unfurled, withdrawing from some heavy presence. Her own groans escaped her, barely muffled by her pillow. "Well, I suppose God didn't call it a curse for nothing," her mother said when she handed her a pad, believing she was cramping because of her period. "Eve certainly made the rest of us pay."

She knew if she told her mother what was really happening, her mother would say any number of things—all of which came down to punishment. Because she hurt now. Hurt right through the hot clotting between her legs—nothing easy about it, and, according to her mother, things that were uncomfortable, things that were difficult, were always linked to sin, somehow. Though Sariah would've sworn otherwise, before. "Don't leave me to it," she moaned into the empty dark of her room. "Please."

And then, right when she hurt the most, God came as a fullness in her chest, a gold light carrying her into sleep.

She'd never felt it at any other time in her life. That intense cleansing. But God's sureness, the way He'd finally appeared when she was mid-apology, maybe she could use that to bridge herself back to Him again and again. Maybe this was what being Christian meant, needing to be reminded of when you'd hurt, using every difficult moment of your life to bring you back to God. Maybe God only saw you when you suffered or when you had chosen some sort of loss.

Only—now Helene was saying it was too late, she'd never have Him completely, despite her sacrifices. She'd already soiled herself in His sight, whether from sex or unwanted pregnancy or her choices for her body or whatever Helene decided made a person unworthy. It was as if God could always see you, yes, but your decisions nevertheless cast a fog. For some people, it was too late. It would always be difficult to reach Him.

She drove back the way she came, felt her body inside the car, so full, so sure of how it had led her there. That bend in the road. That crushed metal railing. Those streetlights coming back.

She knew to drive to Helene's, dark inside, the driveway illuminated by floodlights. Knew to park quietly, cutting the engine at the curb. Knew to slip in and grab the food she'd prepared and slip out again. She texted Jay: *Heading back, if you want to meet up. Maybe peas and collards work twice as good if you eat them first thing.*

She wanted what she wanted. And if her old self had never gone away, hadn't been lost to healing waters, then what was the point in ignoring her?

IT TOOK HER OVER two hours to get home, the drive extended because of New Year's traffic and roadblocks, and a stop at a gas station, where she could see the attendant inside watching the postmidnight performances on a small flat-screen. Where had she been during the turn of the year, the exact tipping point?

In her apartment, she showered. Washed the sweat smells from her body, let water rinse between her curls. It was after three by the time she finished, celebratory gunshots and fireworks still splintering the night's quiet. Moonlight pulled itself over the broad leaves of her calatheas, softening the plants' purple undersides.

She prayed, testing. Something twinged in her chest, not as if God had spoken, but as if He'd turned His head a little.

She was dozing when her phone buzzed against her hip. In waiting for him to get off work, she'd folded her comforter over her body and let the heat put her to sleep. She'd meant to clean. To throw the dirty clothes in the hamper. To stack her books beside the TV so it was clear what parts of the apartment belonged where, no rooms blurring together.

"I'm downstairs," Jay said when she answered. "Still want me to come up? I got fish to go with the sides."

Funny, him being in her apartment. If he'd seemed smaller in the bar, he stretched taller here, his head nearing the tops of her white-painted cabinets. As he set the plastic bag on the counter, his hips askew in his pale jeans, she realized he'd been home and showered, his spiced rum smell filling her kitchen. Both of them had prepared their bodies, though they hadn't yet admitted what they'd come together to do.

"Thanks," she said when he opened the takeout box for her, his fingers deliberate. "I've eaten, but I always get hungry this time of night. If I'm up."

"Up late often, huh?" he asked, sitting across from her. Above the brown circle of her kitchen table, her light fixture swung back and forth. He must've brushed it on accident.

After his initial remarks on the food—"not bad, not bad"—they ate in silence.

Then their plates sat empty, but he wasn't leaving. His eyes traced her apartment walls: college photographs and framed Scriptures and pastel ceramic birds collected since girlhood.

"You're a lot messier than I imagined," he said. "Though—I guess I shouldn't be all that surprised, with how you invited me up."

"You're right." She folded her legs under her hips. She didn't even have nice pajamas, just an oversize T-shirt with no bra underneath. "It's not the sort of thing I—did."

"Want to talk about what happened?" he said. "Didn't think I'd see you until tomorrow."

"Not really. I think I've gone without for a long time. A really long time." So long the sacrificing knotted around her—and apparently it wasn't even enough.

He laughed, which she hadn't expected. Was it relief? Or had she been misreading him, assuming he wanted her too? She grabbed her knees. Said, "Don't laugh."

"I'm not. I don't." His laughter slowed and he pulled at his jaw. "Look, I've never given anything up the way you have. Can't even say that's the sort of promise I'd even think about making. But I can't pretend things haven't been nice the way they are."

His eyes met hers, hesitant. The darkness in them was slipping back, as if he wanted to see her better or show her something. "Look, I might not stay the night, alright?" he went on. "I don't do this often because—women tend to think I'm dogging them out. I'm not. It's the nightmares. I don't sleep well, and you don't want to carry on like that in front of anyone."

"That's alright," she said. Neither one of them was blinking. "You don't have to stay."

"I said, 'I *might* not.'" He paused. "Seven years for you?"

"Eight." She could feel herself breathing all over, even the parts of her body her lungs didn't reach. Her belly. Thighs. Hands.

"Long time," he said, but he was biting down on his back teeth to keep from smiling.

"You're not going to try to talk me out of it?"

"Nope. You're grown, aren't you? Sober. You should know what you want." He laughed again. "And you're not going to try to get me to marry you? You're not going to roll over and go, 'We're committed now, in the eyes of God'?"

"I won't," she said. "To be honest, right now I don't even know what that means."

HE HAD HIS FINGERS in the small of her back, hooked into the dip of her bones. He was a shier kisser than she expected, his tongue hesitant before it slid in and offered his taste. Salt and then the memory of dinner and then a sweet blue black.

They were on her couch. He pulled her thighs around his waist, and when she groaned at the armrest prodding her spine, he slid her down. Lifted her shirt up and over. She saw him stare, slide his hand over each curve of her body. He was seeing her, but he wasn't here anymore. He'd gone inside himself. When she unbuttoned his shirt and flung it, he worked at her underwear.

"I have a condom," he said, speaking to her navel. "Want me to use it?"

She nodded. He stood up, let his jeans ripple around his ankles. She thought of Helene still in the bayou, the way she'd say, *You can't take this back*—even though she didn't want to. She thought of God too. Looking away or perhaps not.

She closed her eyes until the thoughts vanished. When she opened them again, Jay was stooping and fumbling through his pants pockets to find the metallic wrapping. He kicked off his socks and stood awkwardly again. Not looking at her, he slid the rubber over himself.

"You have to say," she said. Despite herself, she was wet. Maybe had been for longer than she'd realized. "You have to say it's not just me. You have to look at me."

"What do you mean?" He looked up, eyes squinting. Then he saw her face. Softened.

"Oh," he said, lowering onto her. "I do. I want this. I want you." Then his hands parted her thighs.

She couldn't feel him when he slid in. She knew they were together only by his rocking, the way he murmured into the private center of her ear.

"You're perfect," he said, lifting himself to look at her. In the yellow of her apartment, the stove light reaching them, she saw him tunnel into her slow. Saw before she felt him reaching deep, catching her. And then she let herself do what she wanted, move, too, rock her body into the pleasure she'd kept at a distance.

She felt herself moving beyond him, even as she tried to stay.

"Come now," he said, breathless. "Please, I can see you want to."

She tried to hold on to his face as she rose. But she couldn't, her eyes were closing—*had* to close—and then there was nothing but her own bright dark. And, too—something beyond, hovering with her. Though it sparked and shattered when she reached it.

✻

SHE THOUGHT HE MIGHT LEAVE, but he didn't, not right away. When she uncurled from her side of the bed, her feet brushed his, and then she slept again. When light filled her sheer curtains, she stretched and found him gone. Who knew if he'd still go to the baptism, if he'd take the bus or drive with her. But she needed caffeine first, needed to find that feeling in her body. How high she'd been. There'd been her and light and *something*.

She prayed for the feeling to stay as she stepped over the mess of her apartment. As she brushed her teeth and put their leftovers into the fridge and poured tea into a thermos.

It's nearly seven, God said in her chest. *You don't have too much time.*

Below her hand, the trickle of tea wobbled. He'd surprised her. She'd thought—

Hurry, God said, and His voice was so loud it took up residence within her. Filled her to the brim.

She stepped outside, her skin humming. When she got into her car, God said, *Wait. A minute please.* She obeyed.

By the time her tea was cool enough to sip, Jay was knocking on her car window, dressed in white pants and a white button-down.

"Hoped I'd catch you," he said, climbing into the passenger seat. "Didn't want you thinking I'd bailed just because I wasn't there when you woke up."

She nodded, trying to grasp where she'd been hours before, when she'd felt like morning breaking. Tried to hold on, too, to God's voice in her chest, its gentle magnificence, how it covered over everything else.

She held on to it as they drove through the bayou, the car quiet except for the gospel station, the shifting of Jay's hands against his trousers. She held on to it when they stopped at Helene's, when Helene said, "I saw your note and I was worried, even though God told me you were alright," when she changed into her white deaconess dress, when Helene got into the back seat of her car because Jay was still in front. She held on to it when, in the rear-view mirror, she saw Helene's tired eyes flicker between the two of them. Of course the woman was unsure. Everything Helene said about God came from her own voice.

The high would pass, Sariah knew. Was fading already as she sat with the other congregation members in the wooden chairs along the water's edge. Wetland grasses stretched up the side of her chair. Before them, the waters were churning, and the sun dipped its beams into the brown and turned it to gold. Rapture passed over Pastor Marlon's dark face as he spoke of what they, the candidates with their white towels swirled around their heads, were about to enter into. Jay's eyes were half-closed, maybe in half sleep, maybe in prayer. His fingers pressed into her palms. Perhaps that feeling, that star launched from her body, would return, was merely resting. And maybe God would return, too, if she didn't blame herself whenever she couldn't feel Him. He was God. He would go without going.

The wind brushed her cheeks as she watched the bodies wade in after Pastor. She stood at the meeting of land and water. Behind her, Helene said, "Here you go." The woman was smiling, dabbing at her eyes with her bare fingers, the sapphire ring hanging from a chain around her neck, swaying forward as she handed off the towels.

But God. Those bodies dipping back, their white clothes floating, a trembling weight that spread over the water. Pastor Marlon's hands on the smalls of their backs before he released them and they came toward her one by one, blinking, reaching out for her like they could see all of her through the sting. Or like they were trusting their bodies to find her.

Here, said the brightness in her chest, rising up through her mouth. She handed them the towels' softness. *And this. And this.*

GATHER HERE AGAIN

HER GRANDBABIES SHOULD BE ASLEEP, YET HERE THEY are, restless as everyone else tonight.

By the time they tiptoe down the central stairs, the creaking giving them away, she's long lost the sun. The sky is a sweep of black. Only the backyard porch lights keep her eyes from working too hard as she kneels into the garden. Clusters of chickweeds, their white tufts masquerading as flowers, have sprung up between the chrysanthemums and squash, whose vines circle each other loop after loop. She yanks the weeds and stuffs them into a brown plastic bag.

"Mmhmm," Damonia says. She's kept open one half of the sliding door and can sense the children inside listening. They don't move from the stairs. Maybe her voice doesn't carry far enough. "We'll just take care of this, right quick," she says. "Before we go back to bed like we're *supposed* to."

Quick or no, someone's got to take care of what grows around the house. Earlier that day, her daughter peered over the kitchen windowsill, stared straight down into the garden, and said, "Oh, look at these little things." As if weeds were anything to be grateful for. Go figure that's how Stella would think of it, standing there tugging on the sleeves of a silk blazer glossy as her hair. What on earth did she do to that hair to give it that shine? And in all the days of her life, has the girl spent so little time outside that she'll see a weed and not know to yank it up?

"Grandma?" Nemy calls, her voice loud and clear through the screen. "Grandma, is that you outside?"

Damonia says nothing, studies the dirt she's disturbed. Maybe she shouldn't have spoken. If she'd stayed quiet, the grandbabies could've gone back to bed, instead of continuing down into the kitchen. Something turns in her stomach, and she massages her side, feels her flesh give under her hand. Beside her, a breeze lifts a corner of the plastic bag and lowers it again.

"She ain't outside," Howie whispers. "She's not allowed." His voice fades as they head back up the stairs, pausing somewhere near the top.

At least she's keeping this one promise to Stella—being a stickler about bedtime, instead of letting the children tire themselves out on the trampoline or the oak's rope swing. But her daughter can't tell *her* when to go to bed, or where she is and isn't allowed to go—though no one has forgotten her accident on the stairs last June, how she'd fallen and ended up on the foyer's hardwood floor, head twisted toward the front door for what seemed like hours. She'd lain there, feeling the rise and fall of her chest, staring at that door until it opened and her son-in-law's upside-down face—confused, then quickly terrified—entered her vision.

She'll do what she can while she can, especially during autumn. No summer heat to press headaches against her skull, no winter chill to keep her at the fireplace. Autumn has even given her this time alone: Stella and Derek have gone to a costume party at the new neighbors' a few doors down and are not there to argue that she needs "looking after," like the children. If it wasn't for the regular babysitter—a short, light-skinned girl named Diamond or Ruby or some other gemstone of a name—canceling, Damonia wouldn't be in charge. But her body isn't as withered as Stella thinks. Dropping a teacup now and then doesn't mean she can't take care of her grandbabies—not yet.

Her fingers dig like spades through the dirt, under the weeds. "There you go," she says. "Give a little." And with the right pressure, the weeds give easy, or easy enough.

Depending on what the Lord sees fit to do with her this time next year, how thoroughly he will unravel her body, this may be one of the last times she can clean up the garden, pull the weeds and cut the squash, brush the caterpillars from the flowering cabbages' undersides, which can look deceivingly healthy from above.

She leans forward. The soil has soaked her pajama bottoms at the knee. She'll have to change before Stella gets home. Otherwise, her daughter will give her that look: *What have you been doing? You went outside when the kids were asleep? With all that's going on around here?*

It's a damp Saturday night, and either her ears are failing or the neighborhood really is this silent. Everybody in Starr Hill—the few remaining Black residents and the new white ones—must be studying their phones the way Stella has been all week: pictures from the summer, men carrying torches through the darkened campus, students surrounded at the foot of Jefferson, smoke and stone angels, the flags waving in the white of early afternoon, protestors rushing toward one another with shields and placards, bodies swirling together among gas and guns and the spray of saliva, the slow dispersal, the car smashing into the crowd, people flying or crushed. Or maybe everyone is looking at the post that's popped up since, the lone black graphic with white lettering: *Return the Right 10.28.* No one in charge, apparently. Just some picture going round and round the drain of the internet and refusing to vanish. Despite all the speeches condemning violence, the idea of another rally tonight has everybody on edge, trying to figure out what's real. Are the men from summer—or their kind—coming back, or is this some sort of early Halloween prank? Who knows what to believe. Or how to prepare for the worst when it comes.

Earlier that night, Stella and Derek had taken their time getting ready to leave the house, making a show of putting Howie and Nemy to bed—the teeth-brushing and singing and tucking in—as if she, Damonia, in all her years, were incapable of minding the children in a practical way.

"What time's the party start?" Damonia asked when they'd finished. She was at the kitchen table, nursing her decaf. Stella and Derek bent over the marble island, their attention absorbed in his phone's band of light.

"Eight," Stella said. She stopped scrolling to look up. "Haven't I been saying eight all week?"

"Well then why haven't you left?"

"I'm trying to figure out if anybody knows anything, Ma. What's wrong with that?"

Outside, now, in the dark, Damonia pulls another cluster of weeds and hears faint conversation as strangers walk up the street, their voices lifting on the other side of the fence. Two girls. Teen-agers, she guesses.

"So Tavis offered to walk with us as far as the Johnsons', but I was like, nah—"

"Why not? What's he got to do otherwise?"

"Who knows. Wait, you saying we should call him?"

There's a pause, and in that silence a clacking sound: beads or shells colliding with each other at the ends of one girl's braids. "Nah, we don't need him. They got the new streetlights on that end, anyway. And I wish somebody *would* try me tonight."

The girls move on past the house, past the other faux colonials. Damonia wonders if they might be headed to some counterprotest or just a party, if they are dressed as angels or witches or, from what she's noticed on the screens appearing throughout the house, kittens. Had she been young in this time, she would have gone as the former First Lady, with her hair tucked around her dark face, her toned arms inherited from generations of people who worked with their hands. She would have dressed as that woman every year, if given a new adult life, her age forty-eight instead of eighty-four as she paraded through costume parties, that First Lady always and forever. Who would've believed it.

She can sense her grandbabies easing down the staircase again, can almost *feel* their small toes pressing against the wooden steps, tentative. Descending the stairs with real purpose now, to make sure she's still there. She knows them like she knows her body's own rhythms: the way her heart slows when she wades through the guest room's nighttime dark, her flaking skin chilled by the house's stillness. The way it speeds toward panic when she wakes and doesn't recognize the open air of a room bigger than the one she shared with Beauford for fifty years. Sometimes, her heartbeat is gone entirely when she realizes he no longer sleeps beside her, his massive, steelworker's body a missing heat, his gentle fingers absent from the small of her back. It's hard to believe she, too, will be gone soon, vanished from this house, this life. Sometimes, Beauford feels so close, it's like he's just hidden in some corner of a room. Perhaps waiting to collect her.

The children are in the kitchen now. Damonia thumps the side of a gourd, pretending to garden when really she's letting them know she's outside, right below the porch, along the kitchen's outer wall. Their footsteps are slow, hesitant, not the usual pattering around. And how could they not be uncertain, given the nonsense Stella and Derek told them?

Her daughter and son-in-law almost hadn't gone to the party. Damonia remembers Derek rubbing Stella's shoulders with both knuckles, his lips pressed against her hair. "It'll be alright," he'd said. "The kids'll be alright. Just something on the internet, for now. And if anything happens, we'll be close by. Walking distance. We deserve a break."

"You do," Damonia said, then sipped her coffee. "Considering the way you two work."

Derek gave a weak smile. A wrinkle spread across Stella's forehead. When neither of them said anything, Damonia stared into her coffee. How odd: The kind Stella brewed left no powder swirling in her mug.

"You don't stop living," Damonia went on. "You don't stop living because a few knuckleheads feel emboldened. Even if that maniac did run over that poor girl."

"God, Mom," Stella said, looking upstairs, toward the children's bedroom. Derek sighed and pressed a button on the phone until it went black. "Do you have to say that so loud? Nemy's four. *Four.*"

"I know. But, to be honest, I was four once. And she can't live in this town and not know such things."

"Will you just promise me you won't say anything?"

"Why? What did you tell them?"

"Mom," Derek warned quietly, and she should've known then it would be something stupid, given how Stella squeezed his arm.

"I told them they had to stay in bed because it was almost Halloween," Stella said. And then when Damonia stared at her, struck dumb, she went: "Please, Ma. Promise you won't say anything more?"

"Fine," she said. "I won't." Just so her daughter would feel safe enough to go.

DAMONIA CAN'T FEEL HER KNEES by the time the children press their faces against the porch's screen door. They stand above her, their bodies all curve and cylinder. Nemy pokes her fingers into the screen to watch it stretch. Her daughter's children, so hard to come by. There had been rounds of tubes and treatments that Stella had explained to her again and again.

"Grandma," says Howie. He is in the third grade, and is she imagining that his voice is already deeper? "Grandma, you left the glass part open."

"That door's got a screen on it, Howie. It's not all the way open." She shifts her weight to her thighs, feels it now, the locking in her knees. "Why? You seen a few gnats flying around in the kitchen?"

"No," Nemy says. "We didn't see nothing."

"Ha! I got you." Damonia forces out the laugh, leans to one side and palms the damp earth. "I got the *both* of you. How long you been sneaking around?"

"We were looking for you," Howie says. His body is still, his flat gaze on her hands grimy with dirt. "You left the TV on in your room. We could hear it all the way upstairs."

"You tricked us!" Nemy says, laughing. The gap in her teeth is like a window in a white-brick house. "You tricked us! You tricked us!"

"I'm not in the business of tricking you," Damonia says, and Howie's eyebrows draw together how Beauford's used to. Or maybe it's that he's looking down at her. "Have I tricked you before, chile? Is that why you keep coming downstairs, late as it is? You think I got something to trick you about?"

Her grandchildren look at each other. Howie sideways at Nemy and Nemy up at her brother, one puffy ponytail covering the side of her face. They wear identical plaid pajamas, red and blue with high-water bottoms. Howie slumps, and Damonia resists the urge to correct his posture, the curve in his back exaggerated by his hands, balled in his pockets. She thinks of the two teenaged girls, how they must have walked with their backs straight as they passed through the streetlamp light. A good thing, for young people to feel so brave. She'd witnessed it up close, once.

"They gon' get you, you keep staying out there," Howie says, and with the way his voice has gone quiet, he does not seem eight, but much, much older, as if someone from another century has loaned him a voice.

"Who will?"

"You know," Nemy whispers, and she takes one step back from the screen door. "The bad things. The ghosts coming out tonight."

"Ghosts?"

"Yeah," Nemy says. She plays with her bottom lip, an ugly habit.

A man's laughter reaches them from the street, from the front of the house. Nemy yelps. Howie slides open the screen door, as if to usher Damonia in. "Yeah, bro, I'm on the way," the man says, his baritone bobbing through the dark. Then silence.

Howie's shoulders relax as he closes the door again. Nemy pulls her pajama top down and over her knees. Damonia feels silly as she smooths the hairs that rose along her neck. The scariest things in her life have always come slow.

"You've got to get inside, Grandma," Howie says. His gaze burrows into hers. "You remember what's going on?"

Because they are watching her and she does not want them to see what standing requires, much less making it up the stairs, she pulls another set of weeds. God, Stella, putting her in this position, having to go along with this silliness rather than telling them the truth. "No ghosts are going to get me out here," Damonia says. "You know, me and your granddaddy, we've beat ghosts two, three times over. They've got more to be scared of with us."

"You really have?" Nemy says.

Damonia nods. Still, there are far too many stories that could keep that belief from sinking all the way into a person, child or no. When Beauford was alive, he'd once whispered to her in the dark, "We ought to tell them, you know. We ought to tell them about my brother." Though they thought they'd have more time before Beauford's stroke, time to tell more stories about Simon, how he could run faster than any other teenager and draw somebody's likeness in five minutes flat, how he kept a two-dollar bill in his wallet for luck. All those stories to be told before the final one of him being strung up in a bur oak. She's still tempted to tell them herself. Sometimes, she senses Beauford wanting her to.

"Yes," Damonia says, though maybe she's taken too long to answer. "We've really done it before."

Nemy's mouth parts. Howie raises an eyebrow. "Prove it," he says.

Oh, Lord. Where can she begin? With her own grandmother in Milledgeville, who'd seen the night riders on their long procession through the pines, their horses moving so slowly that the raised torches looked like an orange snake gliding up from hell? With her momma, who'd seen the horns and red-painted faces leering at her from the edges of the field?

She does not even know how to tell her grandbabies about her own encounter with the men who were not ghosts. First, she'd have to tell them about how she and her four siblings had been racing through the town square that afternoon, seeing who could tag the oak outside the drugstore the fastest, and how they'd caused Miss Julie to swing out her bike and dump herself into the road—her lace dress smeared with clay, her wobbling face all scratched up. They'd run home, but her oldest brother, Willie, knew the night riders would be coming for them, the same way they'd come for other families. Once, their mother had even told them that, almost two decades before, a mob had kidnapped a Jewish man from prison and brought him to Marietta to be killed.

Back at home, Willie unlaced the vines from the fence at the edge of their small plot of land. "You seen Mr. Abel looking at us?" Willie said as he pulled the vines across the ground, careful not to break them. "You saw how he grabbed Miss Julie?" He told them his plan, how they'd pull those vines across the yard, through the gap in the cabin wood so that anybody coming at them would trip.

Their mother, who'd left the hog house at their hollering, watched them from the cabin door. "What did y'all get into now?" she said, and when Willie told her, it looked like her anger made her bigger. One of her chapped hands gripped the doorframe, and Damonia could see those awful words rising in her: *Go on outside and pick a switch—and don't make it a small one.* Then Momma let go. She looked out at the yard, where they'd been growing their own watermelon, corn, and cantaloupes, where, only the summer before, their father had been swinging the littlest, Ann, round and round until he made a noise like "Nnn" and set her down, half of his face sagging before the rest of him went too. "You might not have ruined it for us," Momma said. "They might leave us alone." Then she pursed her lips and left them. But while Howie and the others finished the vine trap, Damonia wandered to the back room, her heart one long, drawn-out shudder. Momma was kneeling on the floor, a suitcase open against her thighs, her hands lowering Papa's cologne bottle into the clothes folded in neat squares.

"If you can imagine a house half the size of this one," Damonia tells her grandchildren, "imagine it made all of wood, with gaps so wide you could see out of them. And one night you look out and you see a ghost."

As the grandbabies listen, she knows they are picturing a floating blob with black holes for eyes, not so different from what she's really talking about, the sheet-draped figure stalking the cabin, fire in his hand. His boots had smushed the soft earth as he walked round and round their property. When she says, "Now picture me as small as you," they squint.

She was eight, her body a hard board beneath her nightgown. She'd crouched beside her brothers and sisters, all of them peering through the gaps in the walls and out into the night, hazed with flame. Even after what Willie and Momma had said might happen, Damonia hadn't really understood. She had not expected the night rider to look like this.

"Come on out of there," the figure said. "One way or another y'all are comin' out."

The ghost laughed, a wheezing sound thick as smoke.

Damonia does not tell her grandbabies that the figure had turned back to laugh at the other men, who'd been waiting on the dirt path in the distance. "You want 'em out, just burn it down already," one of them called out. "Get on with it." But the ghost waved them off. "You wait," he said. "I've got my business too."

"Momma was telling us to hush," she says to Howie and Nemy, because one of her siblings had started to whimper—Ann, maybe, or her brother Joe, who, at nine, didn't talk as much as he should've. Or maybe the sound was her own.

Momma cupped her hands over their mouths two by two and guided them from the walls. When she came back for Damonia, her palms carried the smell of pork and salt. Damonia turned, and her siblings were all touching some part of their mother:

Willie gripped her bicep and pretty Shirley her elbow and Joe and Ann her nightgown. Momma wasn't holding any of them anymore; she'd grabbed the hunting rifle off the wall.

The figure rapped on the cabin, still circling, the orange flame disappearing and then reappearing again through the gaps in the wood: "I know you're in there, and I'm gonna burn you alive. You know who I am? You know what I'm prepared to do?" He said things she didn't quite understand—something about his return from hell, about armies at Chickamauga, how the war wasn't over and this ghost would have his revenge. She didn't quite understand him then, even as her flesh peeled from the inside. She wouldn't understand until her momma explained it after they'd fled.

A ghost, Damonia tells her grandchildren, not a man pretending to be one. But the ghost is not the most important part of the story. What's important is how Willie scurried away from Momma and grabbed the vines twined with rope they'd worked through the house. They all grabbed a piece. "Get ready to run," Willie said. And they pulled.

When the figure tripped, the fire flared up—a rush of sound. His cursing flowered into shouts, and Damonia watched Willie's eyes startle in the dark. He backed away, and their father's knife fell out of his pocket.

"Shit," Momma said, and leaned the gun against her shoulder, barrel up. "We've done it now."

She yanked a quilt off the sofa and pushed open the front door. Yellow light cut in, and after she threw the quilt, the hollering muffled. "Come on now," she said, and urged them out the back door, out to their father's old truck. "In the cab, all of you," she said, keys in hand. They obeyed: Willie by the window with Joe on his lap, Damonia in the middle with Shirley on hers, and Momma behind the wheel with Ann. All their shoulders pushed against one another, and the gun sticking out the open driver's window. When Momma pulled off, Damonia twisted to look back, ignoring Shirley's whining. Their house, slowly being erased within yellow light, shrinking and shrinking until you couldn't see the glow anymore. "Breathe, everybody," Momma said. "Willie, you can get in the back soon enough." They would not stop for longer than it took to get gas, who knows how long, seemed like forever, until some sign on the road told them they were in Virginia.

They'd been lucky, though she doesn't tell her grandbabies this, either. The hooded men had rushed toward that figure writhing on the ground, rather than after them. They'd been lucky too, that the men, in choosing to perform the past, had chosen horses, which slowed them down even after they'd noticed her family was gone.

"I don't believe a ghost could trip," Howie says. His eyes pinch at her. "I think they'd, like, try and move through it or something. Float."

Damonia sighs and massages her knees. There's some feeling back in them. A little nerve tingling. "Any floating ghost is one you don't need to be scared of."

"I saw a ghost floating outside my window once," Nemy says. Her brown eyes widen in her chubby face.

"Oh yeah?" Howie leans into the screen door. "What it do to you, then?"

"Nothing. Just lookin' in at me and stuff."

"You dummy." He sucks his teeth and swats the air. "You talking about the moon. Ain't no ghost just going to sit there and look at you."

"Hey," Nemy says, and her face is the bottom of a squash, wrinkling.

"Howard," Damonia warns.

Howie shuts his eyes, and because Damonia knows that neither of her grandbabies is focused on her, she pushes off the ground, her knees creaking, her hand squeezing the weeds in her fist, her eyes watering behind her glasses. The pain slows her down. She cannot make even this simple grandmotherly gesture: reaching out to wipe Nemy's tears before they really get started.

Or to pop Howie upside the head for causing them. She can only manage one stair.

"Alright now," she says, and she has to settle for putting one hand on her hip, the other in a fist around the weeds. "Y'all stop messing with each other. Don't let fear make you mean."

Howie mumbles something as Nemy rubs her eyes.

"What was that?" Damonia says. "You got something to say?"

"I said, you can't beat no ghost. And everyone knows it." He opens his eyes again. His brows draw together, and something in her contracts. Only at this moment does he really look like Beauford. "How come we can't stay up tonight when we been fine every other Saturday?" She takes another stair: Are his eyes watering now, or is it just the light? "And that lady in the pictures on the phone wasn't even out at night and she wasn't even alone."

"Stop it!" Nemy says, and pulls her pigtail.

"You can, Howard," Damonia says. "You can beat a ghost. I've seen it before."

Howard says nothing, and in the silence, a car passes on the street, a hum that keeps on going.

"I think," Howard says finally, gliding his hands into his pockets again, "I think you're making that part up."

It must be the chill, that cold thing nudging her back. "The way I was raised," she says, "we don't accuse adults of telling lies."

"I wasn't calling you a liar! I just said—"

"You just said what?" She feels the glare on her face like a mask. What is it Stella is always saying about parenting: Asking him what he means? Act don't react? Ridiculous. Her own mother never lied. Even in the truck, breezing through the forests none of them would ever run through again, she put them in their place. "You think the ghost's gonna follow us?" Damonia had asked, shouting, the wind beating her face senseless. Momma breathed in quick. "I don't want to hear that foolishness," she'd said. "That was Mr. Abel, and you know it."

"You just said what?" Damonia repeats, because Howard isn't looking at her. "You backtalking?"

The boy mumbles again. And she reaches forward. Opens the screen door. Squeezes his shoulder. You have to let a child know you've got things under control. Let them know the only thing they have to fear right now is you. Howard's eyes slowly rise to her face.

"'No, ma'am," he says. "I didn't say anything."

She stares at his expression, how it folds in on itself. He looks, suddenly, eight again. Beside him, Nemy pokes out her upper lip, as if she's unsure whether she should cry.

"You two," Damonia says, "ought to be kinder to each other. You ought to act better."

Thank God Howard is looking at his feet, missing the way she grips the railing. Squeezing him has worn her out. A siren hollers in the distance.

"Sorry," he says. "I just don't think . . . it's ghosts."

Nemy whines and rubs one of her feet on the kitchen tile. Damonia bends and unbends one knee, the pain familiar now, though not deadened.

"Howard," she says.

"Yes?" He takes a step back from her, into the white light the television casts into the kitchen. "Yes?"

"You're scaring your sister."

Howard looks at Nemy. The old thing looking out of him is its own sort of ghost, insistent on passing through. "I'm sorry," he says. Nemy sniffles, then raises her arms, asking to be lifted, though it's been a long time since Damonia could bear her weight. So she hugs her against her thigh, feels the throbbing heat of this small body and realizes how cool her own has become, out there in the garden. She rubs Nemy's back in deliberate, perfect circles.

Nemy turns up her face and asks, "When's Mommy coming home?"

"Soon," Damonia says. "She'll be on soon. Should we have a little treat before we get to bed? Something sweet?"

"Yes!" Nemy shouts, the sound echoing through the house. Howie's mouth twitches, a reach toward a smile. Still, he keeps his gaze down, and Damonia gets the sense that this is not because of shame but because he's afraid of her. The same way she avoids looking in the mirror, to avoid that reflection of a person she never thought she'd be.

She leads them into the kitchen, washes her hands at the sink. She will get in trouble for this, she knows. When Stella returns, she'll notice that the three bat-shaped cookies, brought home from the pharmacy where she works, are missing from the pantry. She will turn to Derek and say, "We didn't give them those, did we?" She'll hear Damonia in the bath—much later than she should—and know that the children did not stay in bed after all. And then Stella will give her that low and level stare, not a little put out over the fact that, no matter how much work she's put in, her house still doesn't reflect the fruits of her labor.

Damonia sits across from the children, three bodies tense in the overhead light. Nemy nibbles her cookie and fights off the sleep her milk lulls her toward, her head bobbing out of her palm and back down again. Howie leans back in his chair, his eyes fixed on the sky outside the back window, the streetlamps washing the porches in amber. She studies her grandbabies. *Oh Beauford, if ever I was ready to go.*

"You slowing down?" she asks Howie. He's set pieces of wet cookie on the napkin. Nemy's eyes are closing, her cheek flat against her palm.

"Nah," Howie says. "I was just thinking."

She watches his face, how it is new and his own. She wonders what it would be like to believe in ghosts, in returning from the dead or never being dead at all. If it were her, for instance, would she hover over the neat lawn, float up the steps? Her body would be nothing, finally, free to glide through the doors, sail upstairs (no need to rest), wrap her arms around Stella and Derek and the grandbabies, babies no longer by then. But so much in her life has revisited her. The weeds. Her men and their strokes. The figures outside her cabin and the figures marching into her town. Too painful, allowing herself any fantasy of hovering near her family, despite the love. What she knows of the world has tarnished even the idea of coming back.

"Here," she says to Howie. "You'll be alright." She breaks her own cookie and offers him a piece. Watches him bathe it in milk.

IN THE SWIRL

THAT SUMMER, VERMIN FLED THE ALABAMA HEAT,
scrambled into the pool, and drowned. They must've been com-
pelled by the pumps churning the water, the waves cresting teal
blue from the pool's sides before flattening in the middle. The
pool carried so much from the shallow end to the deep and back.
Dry leaves curling like upturned palms. Black hair ties looping
toward the bottom. And mice, roaches, and infant snakes.

You discovered them your fifth day working as a lifeguard.
The county pool lay hidden at the base of a concrete hill, and you
eased your father's old green Camry downward, past the oaks and
maples that kept the place out of sight of the main road. The job
was your father's idea, a way to maintain the swim techniques
he'd taught you in case of emergency, what better way to spend
your first summer home from college. "Call me when you get
to work," he'd said when you left the house that morning. He'd
heard on the radio about a string of assaults in the area. "You
lock yourself in and keep quiet until the other guards arrive. They
need to start being on time anyway." His Big Al bobblehead nodded on the dash as you parked, the flopping elephant ears sillier
than your father's warning.

Not that you were worried. Sure, someone might have seen
you slip out of the car in your red swimsuit and guard shorts.
Sure, you'd dyed the ends of your afro light pink, what your
father called "loud as your mother." But you locked the gate
behind you and doubted anyone could scale the twelve-foot fence

surrounding the entire complex: the lifeguard office's wooden hut, the adjoining cinder-block bathrooms, the pool stretching twenty-five yards behind both.

And anyway, what you cared about was endearing yourself to the other guards. Jacob, Simon, and Renee—who'd worked summers here for years—had told you to check the skimmers, those white boxes stamped into the pool's concrete deck, recently renovated and repaved, each morning. The skimmers collected whatever had fallen into the water during the night, whatever the pumps had pushed out. Critters, they warned you. Millipedes. Rats. All trapped in mini cyclones in the skimmers' baskets. You were the newbie—your job was to clean them out.

You'd been lucky your first few days. No one had come swimming, and when you lifted the skimmers' lids, you'd found them empty. But that day, before the others arrived, you found a mouse. Terrifying, that white-furred body, bulbous with drowning. You hollered.

Jacob heard you. He shouted your name from outside the entrance. You ran, stumbling over the half door separating the pool deck from the guard office, nearly colliding with the front gate.

"What's up?" he said as you removed the padlock and let him in. "Why'd you scream?"

You couldn't speak, so you led him onto the deck, your legs wobbling. Sunlight fell over his shoulders, the stretch marks above his biceps. Like something had clawed him and he'd survived. He was completing a third year at Jefferson State Community, and, in a brief moment of trust your second day, he'd stroked your wrist and told you that his biggest stress was trying to figure out what he wanted to do with his life.

"I got you," he said, crouching down, chuckling. He snapped on plastic gloves from the first aid kit. Past the pulsing in your chest, you saw every loop of his dark hair, every individual curl.

Was it a pretense, a kind of show, this response to how overwhelmed you felt? You backed against the fence, pushing yourself against the wire until it pressed diamonds into your shoulders. You could see the mouse so clearly, its thin hairs lifting as Jacob scooped it from the water, its bones slipping under patches of bare flesh. Its skin was pink, as if the creature were embarrassed.

Jacob laughed at the sight of you. "Book smarts aren't everything," he said. Then he leaned back and flung the mouse over the fence.

AN ODD THING TO SAY, really. Given the cleverness of the other guards. The four of you spent hours chatting in the office, lounging around the gray folding table, knowing each other more quickly, more intimately with all the lazy time. Your pool was so secluded, so hard to find, that it was the least crowded in the county. Had been, Renee said, for years.

In early June, you learned that she wanted to be a marine biologist, that working as a guard kept up her athleticism between semesters at UA. Every now and then, when the office's whirring fan wasn't enough to keep her cool, she'd vault over the half door, dive into the pool, and swim a few laps, a red nylon streak that vanished at the far end before reappearing.

"Might as well work on myself while I've got the chance," she said once, after she'd finished rinsing off in the outdoor shower and begun retwisting the puffy sections of her hair. "Next summer, I'll probably be working in a lab somewhere. Doing something else."

"You won't be the only one," said Simon, his chin resting on the office table. Headphones bracketed his ears, the tinny speakers playing that summer's Usher hit. Practice, he said, for when he'd start working at his uncle's radio station.

"You a listener?" he asked you, wincing as Renee's twists flung droplets his way. He had a dark, narrow face, thin facial hair lining his lips. "You tune in?"

"Not really," you said, as Jacob rolled his eyes and said, "Not everyone's a listener, man."

"Well, actually, I heard it one time," you said, then shared the memory of your father playing the station one morning before he left for his job as a warehouse manager. Men had laughed through the speakers, claiming that Obama was "chickening out" as he ran for reelection. "All of a sudden, the man believes in gay marriage," said the host's baritone. "Holding office for four years must've made him soft."

"Or he's learned to care about other people," your father had said, and you agreed.

"I mean, my uncle's no bigot," Simon said in response, tugging his headphones around his slender neck. "He's not saying . . . gay people *shouldn't* get married. He's just saying Obama's too scared to say what he really thinks. That homophobia shit's not too popular right now."

You thought: It could be the other way around, like he was too scared to come out in support of love, before. Though this you didn't say aloud. You were earning a painting degree at your little liberal arts college in upstate New York, the sort of place where pink-colored hair wasn't out of the norm. When the guards asked how you spent your school year, you talked about camping on the quad with spiced cider or volunteering at the co-op or writing letters to university deans about the de facto segregation of your dorms.

"Damn, that's a lot," Jacob said, yawning, his square jaw elongated. "Don't you ever just, I don't know, study?"

"Well, there are so many things to care about," you said, though you didn't add that, while standing on platforms at campus rallies, you were good at getting the rest of the crowd to care too. More petitions signed, more emails added to listservs.

Maybe because the other guards were two years older than you—and didn't feel the need to express themselves in funky afro colors and fake gold tattoos—you wanted to impress them. You'd be the first to volunteer to clean the toilets or pour Pine-Sol on the bathroom's tiled floor or climb into the guard chair if and when somebody finally came swimming.

During your third week, a white couple showed up in matching black suits. They paid their five dollars to swim, though the woman mostly lounged in one of the deck chairs and read, peeking up at your place in the chair from beneath the brim of her sun hat. Her husband swam laps, ignoring you both.

"I've never seen that," she said, nodding at your hair. "Young people are so creative."

"Try it out," you said. It was hard to tell her age with her hat and sunglasses. The brown hair plastered to her neck showed no signs of graying. "Doesn't have to be a young thing."

"Oh no," she said, laughing. "Some things you let go when you get older."

After forty-five minutes, the couple left, their shoulders shiny and pink. You returned to the shelter of the office, where the other guards played cards.

"What'd she say to you?" Renee asked, tossing a water bottle to your place on the half door. You loved to sit there, one leg dangling inside the office and one leg out, the ledge wide under your hips. Jacob sat beneath you at the office table, his eyes tracing the metallic swan tattoo you'd pressed onto your skinny calf.

"Nothing much," you said, unscrewing the cap. "That my hair looked nice."

"It's cool," Renee said. "Like someone blew a giant chewing gum bubble around your head."

"Thanks." You smiled, too hard, and Renee smiled back. This was the first time any of them had paid you a compliment.

Not that the moment lasted. Right then, a large black beetle waddled onto the ledge, inches from your knee. You squealed, slid off the ledge, right into Jacob's lap.

"*Damn*, clumsy," he said, his cell phone clattering to the floor. But he didn't move to pick it up, not yet. His fingers pressed into your thighs, where he'd sort of caught you.

Across the card table, Renee and Simon laughed.

"Girl," Renee said, shaking her head, "you are *too* much."

"What do you mean?" you said, though that only made Simon laugh harder.

"And now—" Simon said, gasping for breath. "She got the *nerve* to pretend we can't see what's going on. You two need to admit it."

You looked back at Jacob, at the way his eyes suddenly lowered. Everyone could see it, your crush, though you hadn't fallen into his lap on purpose. He'd simply been there and you'd trusted him to catch.

"What do you think a little bug's going to do to you?" he said, reaching around your shoulders. He flicked the beetle away, its shiny body sailing out and over the deck.

"Who cares what it can *do*?" you said, slowly getting up. "They're gross."

Jacob looked at you, one eyebrow raised. Then he looked down at his fingers. Nodded. Said, "Okay, yeah, but it ain't all that. You don't have to let yourself get worked up."

YEARS LATER, WHEN YOU WERE twenty-four and interning at your second New York gallery, you looked through the glass doors and saw a pigeon lying on its side on the pavement, one wing bent at a funny angle as it kicked itself in circles. It was trying, you guessed, to fly.

"Not today, of all days," your boss said, her bun stiff and immune to the shaking of her head. She stepped away from the watercolor figures hanging from the walls, bodies her client had painted in fragments, a back hunching along the Brooklyn Bridge, two red-sneakered feet dangling over the Hudson. "Clean that up. I can't have people seeing that out front."

You were still blinking at it, the gray diagonal of its extended wing. You couldn't make out a beak. There was only mush where its face should've been.

"It must've flown into the glass," you said. "And fell. From somewhere way up." On the sidewalk, a few pedestrians stepped around it, their bodies a cluster of peacoats and combat boots and slouchy canvas totes.

"I don't care *how* it got there," your boss said. In her reflection in the glass, you could see her scratching her nose with acrylic fingernails. "Get it."

You went out with a dirty towel, which you placed over the pigeon, gone still by the time you reached it. The towel covered the bird, a lump under the red, dust-stained cloth.

"You're going to pick it up, right?" said a man who'd stopped to watch, heavyset in a khaki puffer coat. He was squinting at your hair, dyed a quieter indigo by then. "Or you planning on leaving it there?"

You wrapped the towel under the bird. Because you couldn't quite bring yourself to toss it in one of the metal trash cans, you placed it in one of the alley's cardboard boxes. Your hands shook, remembering the bird's soft crush against your palms.

It wasn't until you washed your hands in the gallery's bathroom that you realized: You hadn't shouted. Not outwardly, anyway. You dried your hands, no longer shaking, your mind searching inside yourself for any trace of the girl who would have screamed aloud at the sight of the pigeon, who wouldn't have been able to bring herself to touch its corpse, who was never the one to move on first.

FOR INSTANCE, YOU'VE NEVER FORGOTTEN that Wednesday in late June when you, Renee, Jacob, and Simon were locking up. Closing time, and you'd only had to guard a grandmother and two children with neon water wings, as well as the same white woman in the sun hat, who'd read poolside until she'd fallen asleep. When she'd woken, her skin glowed maraschino red.

"Can't believe she didn't even swim," Renee said, slinging her backpack over one shoulder. She'd changed into jeans and a white tee that exposed her midriff, and you stared at the scar trailing her torso. You'd never noticed it before, thin and pale pink against her dark skin. "If I wanted to sit in the sun, I could do that in my front yard for free."

You waited for Simon or Jacob to ask about the scar as you walked across the parking lot, your sandals slapping the fading lines and lumped concrete. But neither one of them did, lost in their own conversation. You heard Simon say to Jacob, "Can't today, man. Not heading that way."

"Renee," you said finally, when she was nearing her black compact. You pointed at the scar. "What happened? You look like you've been cut in half."

"Oh, that's so old," she said, not quite laughing, rubbing a thumb over her belly. "From a car accident two years ago, when I was a sophomore."

Her ex had been drunk, she went on, her dumb idea to get in the car with him. And of course he was driving too fast and flipped his Ford miles from campus. He split his head open, needed surgery on his left eye. And she? Well, the seat belt saved her life and left behind its handiwork.

You reached out and thumbed the scar's swell, still soft. "Renee, I can't even—"

"It's not so bad," she said. She stepped away from you and folded her body into her car. Her smile twisted before she closed the door and said through the rolled-down window, "Really. These guys saw it when it was worse."

You felt Simon and Jacob behind you, only vaguely listening. Simon had gotten into his own car and was playing a song you'd never heard, all bass. Jacob stood at your shoulder, texting someone on his flip phone. But you thought about it long after Renee and Simon had driven away.

"What does she mean it's not so bad?" you said to Jacob, who stood with you. "He could've killed her."

"Yeah, but he didn't." Jacob was still texting, and only then did you notice that your car was the last in the lot, his brown sedan nowhere to be seen.

"My brother needed the car today," he said when you asked, though he was looking at the pines encircling the lot. Leg hairs curled up his calves, thick and dark and making their own way, and he scratched them, nervous. "So I'm going to take the bus."

"I can drive you," you said, and he shook his head once, his gaze retreating. But you insisted and he went, "Well, if you want to."

"Awesome," you said, so giddy that he laughed. When he climbed into your passenger seat, his legs bent against the glove compartment until he eased the seat back.

You drove, going on and on about Renee and her boyfriend and how she *had* to still be upset. "Did he apologize?" you asked. "Or has she talked to anyone about it? Her dad? Her mom? I *know* they didn't let that slide. I don't believe she's let it slide."

"Yeah, I mean, I guess," Jacob said. He looked up from his phone for once, watching you. "I'm sure her ex feels bad about it."

Beneath your voices, the stereo played a Mariah Carey album, which had been your mother's before she'd felt in her spirit the need to move to Atlanta for her art, soon after your younger sister stopped breastfeeding. She'd given it to you and told you to play it when too much time passed between visits. She was still your mother, even from afar, she said, and one day you'd understand what it meant to be hungry for your own life.

"What *is* this?" Jacob laughed, turning down the volume on the ballad. Aside from giving you directions down several side streets, he hadn't spoken. "Do you listen to anything less sappy? Something that might be on the radio?"

"She *is* on the radio," you said. But when you glanced at him, he was smiling. "And, come on, you have to show some respect. Imagine writing down everything you're going through, and then singing it. Like this."

"I don't know," he said. His large hands rested on his lap, pulling at his guard shorts. "She's not what I listen to."

You wanted to ask him what he would've preferred, but your phone buzzed, your father calling. You hit ignore, then silenced your cell. When you glanced at the passenger seat, Jacob was eyeing your swim uniform.

"How come you don't change clothes after work?" he asked.

"Because I'm going home anyway," you said, steering the car. "And *you* don't change."

"Well, I'm a guy," he said. "Nothing's going to happen to me."

You didn't admit it, but you knew what he meant. Once, you'd driven out to Riverchase before heading to work, needing to kill time after dropping your sister at science camp. You'd stood outside the mall's Forever 21 in your swimsuit and guard shorts, studying the chevron patterns on the sundresses, wondering if you could work that textiled look into your paintings. Your paintings were all over the place, your professor had remarked the previous semester, and you wondered if using a technique with deliberate organization—cross-hatching, dots, stripes—would prevent you from going wild on the canvas. As you studied the fabrics, a gray-sideburned man came up behind you and with sweaty fingers pinched the inner flesh of your thigh. You turned, startled, your fist faltering as it raised. He only grinned, his chapped lips splitting. He kept walking, looking back at you over his hunched shoulders before he disappeared into the crowd, but you didn't forget it. Nor did your thigh, burning. Nor your mouth, for once too startled to scream. In the distance, the carousel chimed again and again over your silence.

You didn't tell Jacob this, already aware that he saw you as the girl who always overreacted. But he was becoming a different person beside you, stiffening as the sun went down, as the manors on the street turned to peeling bungalows with cars parked on the lawns, as you passed liquor store after liquor store.

"This is me," he said, when you pulled into a cracked driveway. "Appreciate you."

And then he was out of the car, jogging up the front steps, not looking back. The porch dipped under his weight. Moths fluttered around the dusty light bulb before he passed under them, disappearing into the house, into a life closed off to you. You drove, heading toward your family's four-bedroom home in Pleasant Grove. He'd gotten out of your car so quickly, and there were things, you felt, he wasn't telling you. Two weeks prior, when the county clerk had been a day late in dropping off your paychecks, he'd cussed under his breath and swum laps for the better part of an hour.

When you got home, your father greeted you at the side door before the garage door had a chance to fully lower. The round stone of his body filled the doorframe, both blocking the light and part of it.

"Where were you?" he asked, still wearing his navy-blue work uniform. He pulled you against him. Over his shoulder, your sister sat at the kitchen table, awkwardly carving her spoon into his string-bean casserole.

"Dropping off Jacob," you said. "From work."

"You couldn't answer your phone?" your father said, pulling back. He ran a palm over his stubbled chin and explained that he'd heard more about the assaults, that a man was following women home from your neighborhood grocery store and raping them in their garages. He was still out there, eluding police, and when you were late, when you hadn't picked up—

"But I was with Jacob," you pointed out. "And I wasn't even at a grocery store." Behind your father, your sister rolled her eyes and shook her head, her ponytail swinging, her hoop earrings too. *Don't get him started*, her expression said. Behind her, a large roach shimmied up the wall, right legs, left legs. You held your breath, your scream, though you knew you'd have to let it out eventually.

"Well, that's alright," your father went on. "But I didn't know where you were."

THE NEXT MORNING, you joined your family at the kitchen table. Your father had made blueberry pancakes, which he'd stacked on a cream plate, and your sister was already helping herself. Perhaps, given the way your father leaned forward, his chin resting in his large palms, his wide fingernails pressing the bags of his fifty-something eyes, you should've known what was coming. It was the same look he'd had when your mother wanted to take you and your sister on a road trip through the South. "Absolutely not," he'd said to her. "Just the three of y'all in that finnicky car of yours? And driving in the dark?"

"I know college has you thinking you're all grown up," he said now, thumbing the side of his mug. He exhaled, and from his breath came the sharpness of hickory coffee. "But with everything that's going on around here, I need you to stop all this riding around. After you take your sister to camp, you go straight to work and then you come on back. Nowhere else, not unless you've got me with you."

"What do you mean? You're going to follow us *everywhere*?" you said. You glanced at your sister, who stared at him, open-mouthed.

"If that's what I have to do," your father said, and beneath the fear darkening his eyes, you saw the clench of his whole body, his tight arms and his stomach pushing out the front of his navy button-down. This was who he was, who he'd always been. Even insisting you learn to swim had been a response to his own childhood in the sixties, when the city had decided to close its pools instead of allowing Black and white folk to swim together. "You've got to do everything you can to keep yourself safe," he'd told you during those first lessons. "You're going to learn now what I had to learn later."

Your sister stabbed her pancakes with her fork. "Mom would hate this," she murmured, and though you knew she was right, you pressed your foot on top of hers in warning. "She'd never want you breathing down our necks."

"Maybe," your father said, shrugging. Then he nudged the pancakes closer to you. "But I learned a long time ago I can't help how she feels."

THE EVENINGS YOU and your sister had spent driving to the park or mall or local Publix were over. Or changed, at least. True to his word, your father trailed you from aisle to fluorescent aisle, eyes scanning from left to right as he hummed Marvin Gaye.

"Please keep your cell where you can hear it," he said two Sundays after you'd driven Jacob home. You and your sister had wanted to go to Target—you for sundresses to throw over your swimsuit after work, your sister for underwear, believing she'd outgrown the cotton multipacks your father usually bought. "You call me when you're ready to leave, and then we can all go out and get dinner. Your pick."

Unclear why, exactly, you needed to call him when he was five feet behind. You and your sister walked down the bronze-lit aisles and touched everything: natural hair shampoos and pastel sweatshirts and stringy swimsuits. Your father peeled away only when you finally stopped near the underwear racks, when your sister turned and said, "Dad, can we have some privacy, please? We'll stay right here."

"So unnecessary," she muttered once he'd left, saying he needed to pick up a few things in the men's department anyway. "I mean, I'm fourteen. And you're an adult."

As she shook her head, her flat-ironed hair brushed the blue straps of her bra. You shifted your weight, your feet squelching in your flip-flops. She looked older than you as she examined a pair of pink leopard-print panties, similar to the zebra ones your mother had once mailed the two of you for Valentine's Day. You both had worn them to the zoo, making the gift into a joke, not yet thinking of other occasions to wear them. You'd walked past the gated animals, entranced by the elephants' graceful lumbering, horrified by the hissing cockroaches twitching in their tanks. "Damn," a man in a black baseball cap said as your sister leaned against the glass, the striped underwear peeking over her jeans. "Thicker than honey out the comb." She'd rolled her eyes, ignoring him. His friend, green eyes landing on you, said, "Or no, man. Look at baby girl over here. Legs so long I want her to crawl over my face." None of that happened nowadays, with your father nearby.

"Tell me what's going on with you and that guy at work," your sister said, dropping the leopard underwear into her red basket. "Before Dad comes back."

"We're good," you said, though you made a show of rearranging the bras by size. "Since I drove him home, we've been talking."

You didn't add the details: That he'd brought in Eminem albums for Simon to play, asking what you thought of lyrics about getting jinxed, relationships always bringing out the worst. That he'd brought you a scone from a coffee shop. "Look at you," Simon had said. "Bringing wifey breakfast." And Jacob had said, "Shut the fuck up."

"Whatever you say," your sister said. The store's overheads lit up the blush she'd applied too heavily. "You think you'd ever bring him around Dad?"

"If he ever asked me out," you said, before taking her arm and leading her to the sundresses, ignoring her when she said, "You could ask *him*, you know."

YOU WEREN'T AFRAID to ask him out, but you wanted him to admit he cared, to say aloud what he hinted at when Renee and Simon weren't around.

On a mid-July Wednesday, when the reading woman had left and Renee and Simon were napping in the office, you and Jacob dove to the pool's bottom. You swam toward the leaves clustered in the drains, grasping them and rising to dump them on the deck's concrete sides. Jacob followed, the two of you brown blurs spiraling beneath the depths. He held his breath longer than you, his body hovering below yours for minutes after you surfaced. His fingers traced circles around your ankle, teasing, and aloud you said, "That's—*nice*," though maybe he couldn't hear, with the water between you.

When he finally surfaced, a giant mosquito landed on the waves. You scrambled back.

"It's a mosquito *eater*," he corrected. It balanced on the ripples you made, rocking. "It *eats* the mosquitoes."

"That's more terrifying," you said. He slapped the water, droplets splattering your face, the mosquito eater flying away over the crystal wave.

"Calm down," he said, laughing. Then, as if some drawbridge between the two of you had lowered, he said, "Hey, you want to go out with me? Maybe Friday?"

OF COURSE, YOU WOULD HAVE other dates over the years. At twenty-six, with the Harlem bank manager who admitted that, yes, he loved acting but he had to get practical about his life choices. At twenty-nine, with the condo agent you'd met online, who joked that he couldn't *believe* you'd once dyed your hair pink or green or orange. At thirty-one, with one of your colleagues at the school where you'd taken a teaching position. Benjamin, who worked in the math department and brought you daisies.

You'd moved back to Birmingham by then, back to your city of skyscrapers encased in emerald hills. Though it wasn't the same place you'd grown up. Black people had scattered across the freeway, mixing into the suburbs your father had once felt radical moving into. New farm-to-table restaurants and tourists renting bicycles. The economy was still reeling from the pandemic and recession and political chaos, all of which had left you shaky, unable to paint. And maybe, too, you were unsure of what you were supposed to be making. You'd had a few successful exhibitions by then, articles in New York publications praising your grayscale figures contained in tight spaces: doorways, windows, prison cells. Still, you'd felt lucky to snag a teaching job at the high school you'd graduated from. Lucky too, to find an east-facing apartment in the changed Avondale area.

"Our students are going to talk," Benjamin said, twirling noodles around his fork.

You shrugged. He'd chosen an Italian restaurant far from campus, and you'd had to drive forty-five minutes, the absurdity of the distance dawning on you as you sat in traffic.

"I can't remember the last time I was on a date," he said. "I'm bursting with excitement."

The restaurant's yellow light settled over his bald head, his closed mouth as he chewed.

"Really?" you asked. You spooned your soup into your mouth, trying to recall the last time you'd seen a man blush—or that you yourself had. Sometimes it felt like you'd forgotten how.

"Of course," he said, smiling at you. He wiped his mouth. "Can't you tell?"

YOU AND JACOB HADN'T GONE to a sit-down restaurant. On your date, after he'd picked you up from your father's and swore to bring you back by eleven, he took you to the movies. A film where a blonde actress needed two brothers to rescue her from a kidnapping. You'd bought your own ticket—"Sorry, looks like my funds are low," Jacob had said shyly after stopping by an ATM on the way—but you hadn't cared as you sat beside him in the darkened theater. His heat radiated toward you, this boy who'd spent all summer warding tiny creatures away from your body. He felt different in the blue darkness, fully dressed in an ironed polo and khakis. He kept his eyes on the movie, where one of the brothers was saying he'd pay anything to get the girl back. Under the armrest, he took your hand gingerly. You gripped his fingers and squeezed, and he ran a thumb across your palm.

When the end credits rolled, he leaned in slow and kissed you, his fingers faint as they lifted your chin. How soft they were as they slid along your jawbone. How separate your bodies, before the melt of your tongues meeting, the lines vanishing. After, he pulled back and said, "I don't really want to take you home yet. If that's cool."

Neither of you had eaten before the movie, though you'd spent a full day working and tiptoeing around Simon and Renee, not telling them what you were up to. He drove you to a fast-food joint off I-20, and you sat in his car, laughing over fries and Oreo shakes. He'd paid this time, and you didn't know what that meant.

"I thought you were going to scream," he said, "when they tied her up in that basement."

"Why would I scream about that?" you asked and slipped the tip of a fry between your lips.

"'Cause you scream at everything. Half the time, you're not all that scared. I can tell."

"Maybe," you said, your voice trailing. Was that the point? Did you have to be out-of-your-mind-terrified to scream? Or could you let out whatever you felt, turn up its volume, even if you were only a little unsettled? You looked out at the red and blue of the burger stand, kids your age smoking on concrete tables and leaning back on their elbows, baring their chests to the night.

"But I know you'll handle it," you said. "Like that first time with the mouse."

"I hate touching mice too, you know," he said. "What would you do if I started screaming about it?"

You turned to him, slipping your feet out of your sandals, your burger wrapper empty in your lap. He looked sheepish, the streetlights pouring in behind him, pink stubbing his cheeks. Or maybe it was the pockmarked pattern of his acne scars, there from long before you'd met.

"I'd love if you screamed," you said. "I've never heard you get that loud before."

He kissed you again, though your bodies weren't quite hidden, the whole front windshield lit up by the restaurant and streetlights. Anyone could've seen you. You wanted him to put his hands on your breasts, on your backside, and when you said as much, he went, "Let's move to the back. Where I can get to you." And you did, where you kept kissing, your bodies turning over and over against the seats until his car windows fogged.

"Like I got my windows tinted," he joked, pulling back and laughing again. Silently, you disagreed. You thought the steam meant that the two of you had announced your feelings to the world. Even your breath couldn't contain itself.

"Hold me?" you asked, nestling into him. During your kissing, you'd pulled off his shirt, and now you pressed your cheek to the bright yellow of his chest. You didn't bother trying to pull up your dress or tease out your afro, flattened in the back. Two unruly coils jutted over your forehead.

"Alright," he said. He was slow to put his arms around you, though you could feel his heart hammering in your ear. It slipped into you, rang through the entire pulse of your body, alive and bright with want. "Five minutes, okay? We're not trying to—. It's just making out."

YOU THOUGHT THE DATE had gone well. To your father's pleasure, Jacob had you home at ten thirty and your younger sister said she'd seen him waiting in his car until you fit your keys into the front lock and stepped back into the safety of your home. You spent the night in the lavender of your bed, remembering the shape of his body, your intertwined heat, the way he'd held you for fifteen minutes before he'd said he'd better get you back.

But the next day at work, Jacob came into the office and slung his backpack over a chair and walked out without saying hello. From the half door, you watched him spring from the diving board once, then twice, then continuously, his body cutting into the water's surface. When you came over and said, "Last night—" he spit water before you could finish. Then he swam away.

Never before or since have you met someone who suddenly wasn't there anymore. Even your mother was only a handful of hours down I-20, always insisting you visit, always wanting closeness. Yet aside from figuring out shifts in the chair or bathroom cleaning, Jacob didn't speak to you. Not that day or the next or the next. Instead, he and Simon spent long hours in the water, shooting a palm-sized basketball into a goal Jacob had brought in and parked poolside. The few times you bumped knees under the office table, he pulled away. The texts you sent at night went unanswered. When, four days after your date, you worked up the nerve to ask if he wanted to hang out again, he said, "Dunno. I've got a lot going on." You learned to sit still on the office's half door, your knees folded against your chest to hide the flurry of your heart.

That night of your date, how he eventually squeezed you tighter than you thought possible, played around and around in your head. But you kept quiet, ironing your face from the inside, as the other guards talked about what they were going to do come August, how this was the time in their lives to party and be free and irreverent. Renee and Simon, who still knew nothing about you and Jacob going out, were determined to enjoy the remains of summer, playing loud music and cajoling the reading woman into ordering them a pizza, since she came to the pool only to lounge and, technically, you still had to guard her.

"I'll have to convince my husband to come back," she said, smiling wistfully as the other guards held slices of pepperoni between their fingers. "Make it worth your while from now on."

You weren't eating. Instead, you stared at the brown freckles coating her shoulders, a hardening of her sunburn. "Convince him?" you asked. "Why should you have to?"

"Oh, I'm making it sound more serious than it is," the woman said, waving her hand, though the gesture didn't match the sheen in her eyes. "He just gets busy sometimes."

And then—a week after your date with Jacob, when you dreaded going to work, when you dragged your sketchbook onto the deck to copy the dull patterns of floating leaves—the camp-ers came.

Their yellow school bus descended the hill, heading toward the pool that had belonged to the four of you all summer. The children squealed from the windows. You could hear them from where you sat cross-legged on your towel. Their hollering pulled you out of the fugue of your sketchbook.

When you got to the office, the children were bounding down the bus steps—seven, no twelve, no *fifteen* in number. Renee shouted at them to line up, her hair half-twisted from when she'd been interrupted. The children peered over her shoulders at the water, their bodies striped with sunscreen.

"Tell them someone peed in the pool," Simon groaned, don-ning his sunglasses. "Tell them they can't swim for forty-five minutes. An hour. However long they were planning on staying."

"No," you said, quietly. "They'll be devastated." From where he was helping Renee get the kids in line, Jacob opened his mouth to say something to you. Then didn't.

As the other guards tried to get the kids to settle, their coun-selor, sweating in a camp T-shirt and jean shorts, came up to you. She must've been in her mid-twenties, or maybe closer to your age, but her eyes were dark and baggy under her visor's orange plastic.

"Please," she said. "Please, don't make us find someplace else. Our usual pool was closed—some nut put in too much chlorine—and so the county told us to come here, said you guys were always empty. I think these kids'll actually *cry* if they can't get in."

You put a hand on the hot blaze of her shoulder. "We got you," you said. So easy to remember your own childhood, pools like this one with your father teaching you to swim. All the days your reedy body cannonballed into the deep, exhilarated, with him applauding from the sidelines. Even now, children move you. How they let themselves feel everything, how they're not afraid to make noise about it.

After a while, you got the kids to calm down, to spin three times in the shower before sitting cross-legged on the deck and awaiting the swim test. In order to jump from the diving boards or free swim in the deep end, they would have to freestyle from one side of the pool to the other and back. Without stopping.

"That sounds easy," said one girl with green goggles bubbling from her forehead. She looked older than the others—or at least taller—though she eyed the water warily.

"Well, we'll see," Renee said, though you were already walking away, heading to the guard chair at the deep end, trying not to look at Jacob climbing into the chair at the shallow. Behind him, Simon stood in the office with the camp counselor, counting out bills.

Nothing's as easy as it looks, you thought, starting up the ladder. A mouse, who should have known better, who could tread water for three days, could surprise himself by drowning.

You almost missed him. The boy, seven maybe, sneaking out from the group. But there he was running toward the deep end. Jumping in.

Maybe he did it for the laughs erupting from some of his peers. Maybe he wanted to prove something to the others, rolling their eyes. Either way, when he surfaced, his reasons for going in had become unclear to him too.

He rose. Looked around at the water disturbed by the tiny island of his body, by the pumps too, cleared and chugging at full force. Renee was turning away, telling the other children not to follow his example. From the opposite end of the pool, Jacob echoed her, shouting that everyone needed to follow instructions.

And then you. Standing on the deck. Seeing the boy claw at the water, his buzzed head bobbing, his mouth opening and closing, a slippery pink.

You dove in. Scooped him against you, one arm hooked under the swell of his belly. You frogged out your legs. Propelled you both to the pool's edge.

The boy spluttered at its edge. Mostly saliva, he hadn't had time to swallow much water. *Oooh*, went the other kids when you pushed yourself up and over the pool's side without using the ladder. When you lifted the boy up and out too.

"Let's stay in the shallow end, okay?" you said, leading him to Jacob, who was looking down on you from his high place in the chair, one hairy leg extended like he'd been about to jump in but hadn't. "He'll take care of you."

"Mmkay," the boy said. Then he looked up at you, your dripping hair. "You're pink."

The kids didn't stay long. Only an hour, where you watched them doggy paddle across the blue, spray water into each other's faces, or start games of chicken your whistle shrilly ended. It shocked you, how easily the boy who'd nearly drowned got over it. How he swam in the shallow end with his buddies in shark and goldfish trunks. How, after only twenty minutes, he came over to your chair.

"Can I try the swim test again?" he said, standing with one foot on top of the other, wobbling. "I think I know how to swim now."

"Maybe next time," you said, pushing your sunglasses back over your eyes. For the first time in your life, you decided it was better to be neutral, to make no promises, to show neither excitement at his confidence nor fear for his failure.

THE END OF SUMMER came fast. Soon, there was only a week until the pool closed for the season, and you'd head back to New York, Renee to UA, Simon to his uncle's radio station, and Jacob to Jefferson. You never found out if he transferred. You never worked at the pool again, and by the next summer the police had caught the grocery store rapist, and you relished the solitude of going places alone.

That entire week at the pool, as the four of you scrubbed the bathrooms and dragged the deck chairs to the storage shed and checked the skimmers for the last time—ants and centipedes and *one* mouse you dumped without complaint—Jacob played music. Elusive dubstep beats with wailing, songs where the words were indecipherable and beside the point. Once when you all played spades around the table, he put on a Mariah Carey album, her latest one, casual and more up-tempo than her earlier ballads.

"Fuck is wrong with you, man?" Simon said, pausing the disc. "You in love or something?" At the table, you examined your hand. You didn't look up at Jacob, at whatever his face was doing in the silence.

"My turn then," Renee said and put on Drake, a track where he couldn't make up his mind whether he was rapping or singing.

Renee sighed as she sat on the half door, gesturing for someone to turn up the volume. "Drake," she said. "I'm telling you. He's hard and soft at once." For years, you would hear a Drake song and think of her, wonder if she'd realized that even his music had changed.

On your last day, the pool empty in the dusk, you locked the gate, aware of Simon and Renee shouting, "Y'all take care!" from their cars, their engines revving as they flew up the hill and out of sight. It was Jacob who walked you across the parking lot, who touched your arm as you opened your car door.

"Hey," he said, his thumb light against your bicep. His eyebrows were furrowed, as if his thoughts were similarly wrinkled. "When are you going back? To New York, I mean."

"My flight's tomorrow," you said. You leaned away from his touch. "First thing."

"Oh, okay," he said. "Well, I hope you have a good time."

He stepped back and let you get into your car. Let you drive away without looking back.

YOU GREW OLDER, adjusting to muted adulthood. You stood indifferently beside your father while he remarried, a woman from his church tall in her orange taffeta. You walked through the local library with your mother, merely listening as she gushed over your framed paintings, how *good* you'd gotten when, because you could think of no other way to begin again, you'd returned to using color and filling up the canvas. You sipped coffee and watched your sister's children build forts, hauling blue pillows off your couch and belly flopping onto them. "We're swimming!" they shouted, when you shushed them. "This is the pool attached to our space*ship*!"

One day, the summer of your thirty-sixth year, you took them to Railroad Park, your sister out on a date with her husband. They'd wanted to feed the geese, though they'd gone skittish, picking at their cotton leggings and making you go first. Then throwing the crumbs onto the grass and backing away as the geese scrambled toward them. Behind you, the park expanded, wide and neatly trimmed and running right up to the distant tracks. Your niece and nephew had all the room in the world to escape.

"You're not supposed to feed them, you know," a man said, approaching the three of you. He slid his hat back from his forehead. He could've been anywhere from twenty-five to forty. "Can't imagine a meaner animal."

"At least they eat mice," you said, smiling politely at him. "Or chase them." Your niece and nephew squealed and gripped your legs as a goose spread its wings and sent water scattering.

You thought the man would continue his walk up the gravel path, but he stuck out his reddened fingers and you gave him bread. He let one of the geese waddle up to him and take it, its beak nearly catching his finger.

"Close one," he said, relief sweeping his face. And then he wiped his fingers on his trousers and walked away.

"Auntie, auntie!" your niece said. "What's this?" And when you turned to her, she held up a giant cicada, its body green and large and nauseating. It buzzed.

You screamed, knocked it out of her hand. It landed on the ground with a dull thud, and you flung a piece of white bread over it. You couldn't kill the cicada, but at least you could bury it.

"Auntie's scared," your nephew said, laughing. The sound contagious, catching your niece, who giggled and pointed. It caught you too, and you laughed through the air in your lungs, the space the scream had made. Where had she gone, this girl who screamed at any and everything? You clutched the hands of your sister's children, remembering how easy it had been for you once, to release whatever you felt.

WHAT REMAINS OF your eighteenth summer: The moment Jacob arrived at your house to pick you up for your date. He, your father, you on the front lawn. The roof's shadow rising over the grass, over the chirping of crickets and squirrels scrambling up the gutters. You wore a yellow dress from Target and felt more naked than you had all summer, the cotton brushing your skin. You'd wondered if it was too short, but your sister had rolled her eyes: *Who cares? Show it all.* Jacob had stammered, "Hey" when he'd seen you in it.

You expected your father to greet him the way he'd always talked about greeting boys you might bring home. Shaking their hands and squeezing until knuckles popped. You hovered at Jacob's side. Who cared about the mosquitoes stinging your arms, the dusk stirring into night. You were ready for your father's bullying.

But instead your father drew closer to Jacob. Gripped his shoulder.

"Be careful with this one," he said. "She'll get you in ways you don't expect."

They looked at you, their faces unknowable, except for the slight pink swirling in Jacob's cheeks. Great, Dad, you thought then. You're making me sound like a crazy person.

Jacob said only, "Okay, sir." He unlocked his car for you to get in.

This strange, strange moment, which you've only just now understood.

You, another sort of dangerous thing, in how easy you were to love. You could spook anyone with how close you were willing to get, with how you opened yourself up to the world and opened others too. Now, the hardest thing is getting back. She is waiting, the girl of you, shouting from a distance for your return.

NATURALE

FOR A LONG TIME AFTER, I SOFTENED. EVEN MORE THAN I had during my life up until then: daughter, niece, hairdresser, wife. All that time practicing being warm and willing to carry just about anything.

I carried Oriah too that April. Took in his apologies for not being the husband he should've been, for falling in love with someone else that winter. He let it spill out right around his spring break, his body leaning against the kitchen countertop, his fingertips pressing from brown to white against the granite: "It was just the one time. At the dig. I knew it was a mistake as soon as it was over and all that wind started flapping through the tent." It was the first time I'd ever seen him cry, and when he said, "*Please*, tell me what I can do," I swallowed and said only, "Alright. Can I have a minute to myself?"

I canceled my clients so we could spend a week inside our pollen-dusted town house, trying to piece our marriage back together. We sat cross-legged on our cream carpet, taking turns playing his archaeology podcasts and my neo soul records, songs about letting your hair down. We ate tart plums on our back patio, as if eating with our hands could return us to those early nights when I slept in his crummy grad-student housing, his tenure-track job nowhere in sight. In the few moments I left his side to relieve myself or to breathe, I wandered barefoot through our hallway's cedar light, stepping in the footprints he'd left in the rug, like I was warming myself up to touching him again.

In truth, the pollen smearing the sash windows was a relief. No woman who might've been watching from the sidewalk could peer in and measure herself against me.

With the way Oriah was determined to give me space, it took us until the end of that week to get naked with each other again. Bathing together was my idea. A way for us to take back everything that came with being married, because it already felt like that woman was keeping his body away from me. We soaked on opposite sides of our claw-foot tub, and through the bathroom window, Charleston light fell violet and nervous over the bathwater. I'd started wearing my hair down from its usual high puff, and it worked itself into tight knots as it floated between us.

"But do you really get what I mean?" he said. He wasn't touching me, his large hands wrapped around his dark legs. "About being two people at once? That's how it was. Like I wasn't even me. Like I wasn't—"

"I know," I said, and I made myself reach for his hand. "Really, please don't explain it again."

Who cared if he was shy to wrap his fingers around mine? Anything was better than him talking about it. I'd asked him not to tell me her name, since even just knowing they'd worked together had given me visions. A woman with hair flowing in loose waves over her back, over his arms as he held her against him. When she emerged from the tent and went back to crouching over rusted pottery shards, its neat ends would sweep the earth. No kinks like mine.

"Tell me something else," I said. "Like what you want to do tomorrow. Or I can tell you about this new idea I have for the salon. Or you can tell me about how your work's going otherwise."

"That's what you want to talk about?" He pulled his hand back. Let it slip underwater. "It's my fault, and you're acting like it's that easy. *Gone.* Over and done with."

"Not easy," I said, scooping water over my knees. "Just alright."

Carefully, his shy fingers pinching the ends of my hair, he let himself talk about the colonoware his team was unearthing, the site an hour north of Charleston. I'd been there a few times before. That plantation ground littered with ceramic fragments, traces of vessels enslaved women had spent hours coiling from clay, wall after thick wall to hold water, rice, whatever needed containing. I watched the brown in his eyes lighten as he talked, and I tried to make mine light too, attentive—as if he were taking me with him into that life. That wet sun and those flashes of tan in the soil and his hands brushing away the past. He couldn't get enough of it. Not with how he already spent so much time at the university behind a classroom podium or in meetings with full professors who hadn't visited a dig in years, the sort of academic he was afraid of becoming.

"Doesn't have to be you when you get tenure," I said. "You love it too much."

He looked at me. Then he all at once leaned forward and slipped his hands around the backs of my knees. "I don't work with her anymore, you know," he said. As he sweated in the warm water, he seemed to be emerging from something, his body shiny everywhere except the center of his brown face. "I told her—we'd reached the end of things. It was going to be you from now on."

"I know," I said. "I believe you."

Making love took me saying it twice. He was hesitant at first, lifting me out of the water, carrying me not to our bed—not yet—but downstairs to the couch where he'd been sleeping. "Cherie," he murmured, his chin cushioned in my tangled hair. I said his name back, drawing him in, tucking my head into his neck. We moved our hips slow, and I could feel him probing, wanting to know what was hidden in me. Another sort of woman, maybe, one who was waiting for her chance to slap him across the face.

I stayed downstairs after he went up, back to his usual sprawl across our bed. I turned on the television, where every woman on-screen was shouting. They pointed past the camera, wigs snatched off, and I watched, quiet, the television blaring yellow against my knees. I couldn't remember ever shouting that loud in my life. Too expected of me, even now.

A FEW DAYS LATER, when I was sanitizing combs at the salon, my mother called from prison. At first, I ignored that number popping up on my phone—probably my uncle let slip the vow renewal ceremony Oriah and I were planning—and the salon, bright and orange and fuchsia, wasn't the time or place for her to start asking me questions. It was hard enough to keep my hands busy, to stop standing in front of my mirror and mussing with my hair, black coils pushing out from some heat at my scalp like a million tornadoes. While waiting for my first client, I'd already swept broken strands from the concrete floor and refilled the tea station's kettle and wiped dust from Nya's framed art, prints of Black women smiling, their hair covering their eyes. At the surrounding booths, the other stylists knew to push down their own problems, to bend tender as peace lilies over their clients. But my phone wouldn't let up.

"What you renewing your vows for?" my mother asked right when I answered. "What'd he do?"

"Nothing," I said, though I'd raised my voice and had to lower it again. "People do it all the time. Especially if they're in love."

"Y'all *just* got married three years ago," she said. "Hell, even your father and I made it to seven before we talked about that sort of thing."

I said nothing, at first. Across the salon, past the tangle of crossed female legs, Nya was braiding up a little tender-headed girl in purple sneakers, her face red. "It hurts," the girl kept saying, until her father told her from a side chair, "Stop all that. Fix your face."

"Kind of a weird example, don't you think?" I finally told my mother. After all, she'd stabbed my father for leaving one too many bruises on her body, and he'd bled out three months before I was born, before my uncle took me to raise.

"Guess carrying you gave me the strength I needed," she'd joked once, though it wasn't funny. Her thinking I had violence in me like that.

"It is what it is," she said. "It's the plain truth."

ORIAH AND I had our second ceremony in July, summer obliterating spring in a white blaze you had to squint through. I'd asked Nya to dye my hair a honey brown, and the color lit up on video. On my left, the other stylists stood in a sun-drenched park along the Battery.

"I'm promising I'll be faithful," Oriah said, gripping my fingers as if they were strings and I was a hot-air balloon, escaping. Even the new, sculpted beard he'd grown, that he'd keep for years after, couldn't hide his nerves. "I swear it, you and me? It's kind of its own adventure, isn't it?"

I smiled hard as I could. Repeated mostly what I'd said the first time. Because I'd done what I said I would: planned summer road trips and cooked international dishes alongside him and made a home where we both could relax. Him, from colleagues undermining his work. Me, from fingers gone stiff from nurturing other women.

If not for the recording, most of that day would have flown right on by me. In the video, my uncle leans against the seawall railing, a cigarette crushed between his teeth.

"You've got me to thank for raising a woman you'd want to marry twice," he jokes to Oriah. "I'll tell you, some of them out here? A real handful." Oriah laughs, looking younger than can be believed. When he turns to see if I'm laughing too, his mouth parts wide, like he's drawing his first breath, unsure if it'll work.

I look pensive as I hold my bouquet of lilies, the wind catching my hair. There's a moment when Nya hugs me tight, as if she senses something knotting beneath the beading of my dress, even though I hadn't told anyone about the other woman then. I let her go after a while. Look over my shoulder, my smile slightly fading in its peach lipstick. I'm maybe thinking about my childhood. Dark-skinned dolls with their forever smiles. Hopscotch with the neighborhood girls, our rhymes whispered so we didn't disturb the suburb. Afternoons spent in my uncle's King Street restaurant, folding napkins to cushion the edges of the steak knives. Or maybe I'm thinking of pleasure, of being chosen twice.

Either way, my face holds a kind of watchfulness. Like I'm looking past the camera for someone to make her way toward me.

EVERY WOMAN HAD some hidden part of her. Our customers came sighing out of the early autumn and into our chairs, revealing a smattering of neck freckles as they slid out of their jackets or a lone bald patch when they removed their hats. Nya said that our real job was to tease out their troubles from the knots in their hair. Grandchildren they now had to raise full-time or hips that never stopped aching or—so often it seemed like—men who whittled them down until they went thin in places they'd never imagined. "Just wore out," my uncle would've called them. "Not even trying to keep themselves up." But not by the time we were through with them: our job to make a body light again.

By early October, clients wanted their summer box braids or havana twists taken out, no need for styles that let them travel and swim without thinking too hard about it. The ropes of synthetic tresses took hours to unwind, and having your fingers in another woman's hair for that long told you how much she could tolerate. Like if she picked at her attachments. Or if she was losing her edges, unable to sleep through her bonnet's nighttime heat.

As a walk-in, one woman in heeled boots plopped down in my chair and complained that something was eating her scalp alive. She was younger than I was, in her mid-twenties maybe, and her braids fuzzed old at the roots. Across the salon, where she was watering our zz plants, Nya gave me a look, her own hair cut into a bob: *That girl's a mess, but if anyone can take care of her, it's you.*

"You've been scratching," I said. White flakes crested above her scalp.

"Well, it's itching something fierce up there." The woman crossed her legs and jiggled her foot up and down. "You'd be scratching too if you were me."

I bit my lip. Chewed down what rose in me: *Girl, if I'm doing your head, I'll call it like I see it.* But I breathed through the feeling until it went quiet.

"We'll give you something for the itching," Nya said. "In the meantime, Cherie'll take care of you."

After the first hour of unraveling her braids, the problem blushed up at me from her scalp. The fake hair, the inches and inches of it, fell around the chair, and as the egg of the woman's head emerged, so did the red patches. It wasn't unheard of, a woman being allergic to synthetics. She'd probably spent weeks sweeping her braids into a bun, going on with her life, ignoring the burn.

"You'll need to leave your braids out for a while," I said.

"My hair's too short for that." Her glossed lips pursed as she studied herself in the mirror.

"Nothing wrong with short hair," Nya said. By this time, she was rinsing one of her clients in the sink, a woman who came in every few weeks to touch up her gray. "I tell you, it's liberating."

"Exactly. My man would lose his mind if I went around looking like a little bald-headed boy. Then I'd be liberated for real."

"Or you'll look chic," I said, and the woman pulled out her cell phone, silencing the conversation. Maybe the woman Oriah loved hadn't had loose waves, but short hair. Hair her pillow couldn't even mess up. Hair that didn't tangle during sex.

But after I'd gotten my client washed and rubbed balm into the sores on her head, the woman took one look at herself in the mirror and burst into tears. Here we go, I thought and already my fingers were reaching for tissues. Women had cried in the shop before, nervous about losing a few inches or tender headed from weaves sewn too tight. But this woman's whole face went red, the whites around her pupils too, and when her eyes caught mine in the mirror, I could see her scowling at my hair: full and sun lightened from a second honeymoon with Oriah on the Outer Banks.

In the time it took me to calm her down, she didn't look at me again. Not even during the hour I spent shaping the short curls to cover the inflamed skin.

"Everyone's got their own shit," my mother said once, when I'd been in the eighth grade. A boy had started a rumor that I let him take off my underwear on the school bus, let him keep it in his jeans pocket all day. I hadn't told anyone, not my uncle or my teachers or friends who asked me what was up. Only my mother. "Whatever somebody does, it's never about you."

THAT COULD'VE BEEN ONE THING my mother was right about.

Because whatever the client thought she saw in me was wrong anyway. No matter how my hair looked in the salon light, it had started falling out. Soft clouds that clung to my jacket when I hung it in our closet. Wisps that spun across our hardwood floors, propelled by air-conditioning.

Maybe I needed some vitamins, and since it was my turn to make dinner that night, I baked salmon and pan-fried sweet potatoes and sautéed spinach, while simultaneously reading blog posts on my phone. GROW UR HAIR TEN INCHES IN TEN MONTHS. And: HOW OMEGA-3 STOPPED MY SHEDDING!!!

When Oriah came in, I smelled the dig on him even before I turned. Sweat and sweet dirt. When I finally glanced over my shoulder, he was staring at the mail, a little cream envelope sticking out between yellow coupons.

"Small thing, the department's harvest party is coming up," he said, and I thought, She'll be there. He held the envelope delicately between his fingers, thinking. Then he threw it in the trash and went, "Eh, I've impressed the department enough this year. And we're going to be busy anyway."

"Busy with what?" I asked. But he was already turning off the oven and putting a lid over the spinach before saying the food would finish itself. He put his fingers between my thighs and asked if he was my husband, if he'd been good to me, and if not, could he show me?

After, we ate in bed, the plates balancing on our laps, the salmon only a little dry. He put on a Ranky Tanky song we loved, the lead vocalist singing about an old woman losing her appetite, no longer the person she used to be. I stood on our mattress and swayed and sang along, grinning even as I got pitchy with the low notes. He smiled up at me, his dark torso a relief against the white sheets. She's probably fuming somewhere, I thought. Bitter. Off in some one-bedroom apartment, combing out her hair 'til it breaks off.

A clump of my own floated down between us, jostled free from my dancing, maybe even tugged loose during sex. Oriah twisted to pick it up, an amber ball fuzzing against his palm.

"Normal shedding," I said. I didn't look at it too long. "And smushing me into the pillow didn't help."

He clasped his fingers around it. "I only want to make sure you're okay," he said, his beard lopsided.

"I'm fine," I said and kept dancing. "We're fine. It's probably the dye."

ONE THING WOMEN LOVED to talk about was sex. My mother's cellmates, thinking about what they'd do when they got out or how it would be different from the way it was inside. The women who stopped by my uncle's restaurant, drinking syrupy cocktails at the bar. And, definitely, women in the salon, who worried about how their hair would hold up during. If you'd sweat it out. If your man could touch it.

"Well, I won't lie to you," Nya said to a woman getting a flat iron. From where I stood taking inventory of the bottles in the glass display cases, I could see her parting the woman's hair over one eye, sultry. "You might need to wrap it when you're lounging around. But really there's no reason you can't touch it up. Give your edges another pass."

"You don't think too much heat'll damage it?" her client asked. She pulled at the collar of her lime suit.

"Not if you keep the heat on low," Nya said. "You won't hurt it long as you keep that temperature right where it's supposed to be."

That might've been true, but nothing beat letting your hair grow how it wanted. Easy to see in the pictures of my mother before she went to prison, her hair thin and hot-combed out. She couldn't put heat on it behind bars, and even with products being hard to come by, it thickened. During visits, only her face looked fatigued. Her hair was spikier and fuller than in any photos from before.

"Maybe one of these days I'll get the nerve to rock hair like hers," the woman said, nodding at me. "You know, get some like these natural hair girls. In the shower or something. Just one good time."

"That true, Cherie?" said Nya, and when she looked at me, her grin had a funny wrinkle in it. "Go on and set her straight. Because you and Oriah in the shower or pool or whatever is *no* work, huh?"

I winked and said, "Oh, being natural has its benefits" and watched them laugh. The client, shaking her head. Nya, letting her grin spread, even though she knew better. More than once, she'd seen me come in late and gone, "*Girl*," before she teased out my hair, flattened in the back. And that was from regular mattress sex. But who cared about the reality? We could all live in that fantasy of being carefree.

And anyway, Oriah and I *had* been devouring each other since renewing our vows. Bodies folded against the cool of the refrigerator, or in the carriage driveway with our groceries on the car's floorboards, or even in the armchair of his study, his research hastily forgotten. His shoulders were a wall over my body. My breasts whole worlds in his mouth.

Nya and the client moved on to talking about how they could style her hair for the holidays, but talking about sex like that left something scratching at my brain. I jotted down the final count of shampoo bottles and crossed the salon and sat in my chair, watching the door for my next client. Through the glass, the sun licked every corner of the street, warming that cool gray to brown.

So much sex. So much uninterrupted sex. It was late October, and for two months now, the usual flow of my period hadn't gotten in the way. As if a small, pulsing thing inside me held it back, urging Oriah and me to come together again and again.

THE LUCK OF IT. My IUD had failed—"That makes you the third woman I know," Nya joked—but to Oriah and me, it felt miraculous, the baby insisting on making her way here.

The first weekend after my doctor confirmed the apparent twelfth week of my pregnancy, Oriah cooked with enthusiasm, having walked to the grocery store and come back with paper bags clutched to his chest. The butter smells of glazed ham and pecan pancakes drifted from the kitchen to the couch, where I reclined and sipped prenatal tea, trying to keep nausea from fluttering up my throat.

"So you think it's a girl?" he called out. I could hear his grin in his voice. "I think my grad students would eat up a little girl. They'd lose their *minds* if I brought her to the dig."

"Who's to say she'll want to go with you?" I said, leaning back against the armrest. Already, I could tell the baby was pushy and particular. Like how she hated the tea's bitter smell but liked the taste, my stomach calming the more I sipped. "She might not care about that."

"Bet she will. She'll have to."

A few minutes later, I heard him calling his family as he flipped pancakes. "Yeah, you heard me right," he said. "Guess you have to call me a family man now." Their squeals exploded through the receiver. A better response than I'd gotten from my mother days before. She'd only gone quiet before saying, "Congratulations. If you can help it, try not to stab the man. At least not yet."

I waited for him to finish, peering at my belly, still flat. I wanted to look through my skin, to see the small hairs blanketing the baby as she grew, warming her in utero. When Oriah came back into the room, easing beside me to turn on the television, I looked at him and thought only, Mine. A whisper that lost its edge because of what followed: Please.

"I got your uncle on the line while I was in there," Oriah said, setting a plate in front of me. He laughed, scratched his chin. "You know what he said?"

"What?" I asked.

"Well, two things really. One, that he guessed I couldn't keep my hands off you, and two, that he was a little surprised you didn't tell him yourself."

Oriah looked at me, his grin sort of falling over his teeth.

I shrugged. Filled my mouth with sweet pancake, even as my molars stung and my stomach turned.

"Didn't get the chance," I said, after I swallowed. I placed my hand over my navel at the thought of my uncle holding her, telling her—what? That she should be more like me?

BUT IT COULD'VE BEEN that my uncle had only wanted to feel roped into the spotlight of what was happening, a place Oriah liked to linger too. On an early November Sunday, Oriah woke me and said, "Come with me to the dig? See what I've been up to?" At the time, I thought he was offering another way for us to be closer.

As he blanketed me in his truck's front seat, the morning made me shudder with chill. "You have to tell me if you get even a little tired," he said. "We'll come right on back."

"I'll be fine," I said, crossing the blanket over my stomach and trying not to let its wool brush the dust on his floor mats.

"I know," he breathed out. "You're always fine."

We drove. Out of our neighborhood with its renovated duplexes. Out of downtown with its gray-brown storefronts. Out onto the highway with its bridge leading over the water and up and up. See? I thought, holding my thermos. You've never been so light in your life.

Then, on our way down, I remembered the woman and something in my stomach twisted. I'd already spent months imagining their bodies together, the hairs slick with moisture at the meeting of their hips. What had they murmured about me in that tent? *She thinks her romance novels are real books*, I imagined Oriah saying. *She thinks working a booth in a salon makes her a business owner.* And the woman would laugh and turn over and adjust her tortoiseshell glasses—and maybe her hair would be loose or maybe short or maybe a style I hadn't even imagined yet. Elegant dreadlocks, maybe, the kind so many of Oriah's colleagues wore to campus in intricate updos.

The feeling worsened as the bridge turned to road, then dirt path. We trailed the backs of the plantations, oak trees dropping shadows over us, until we reached the site.

I hadn't been there in months, though it felt familiar: the cypress swamp with its melt of green, the restored main house that rose above the slave cabins, wood planked and smaller than the neighboring tents. What if there was something I could learn about her here, something to put my mind at rest?

He parked the car beside the outermost slave cabin and got out first, the way he'd been doing now that he'd developed a habit of opening doors for me. Students in dark jeans and sweatshirts greeted him before he could come around. A boy in a backward baseball cap. A girl with her ponytail pulled too tight, her hair's thin edges raked through. I could have stood it, seeing the woman, if she had hair weak as that.

I opened my own door, my fingers fumbling on the handle. Wind tunneled through the site, and I tightened the blanket around me and my daughter, though mostly my skin flushed warm. When your heart's beating fast like that, you think it's fear, at first.

"Hey-o!" said one of the graduate students, the boy, waving. "Watch where you step alright? Follow the tape."

I nodded, grinning, though I wonder now if it looked right on my face. Passing the tents, mostly zipped closed, I took my time, aware of dirt shifting under my flats. A few feet from Oriah and the grad students, I stopped at a table, spread with plastic so someone could keep assembling fragments of what looked like a vase. The thing bulged wide at its base, as if it had once been able to hold anything. I pictured the woman's hands touching it, arranging each piece just so. All I saw: how so much of Oriah's world was closed off to me. What had he seen in her, besides any lightness I might have imagined? What did she know that I didn't? I'd been raised to be amiable rather than booksmart. I'd read salon magazines more than anything else. I'd only met Oriah by chance downtown—not in the halls of some university.

"All this old stuff," I whispered to my daughter. I'd begun speaking to her, as if that could keep her from getting unsettled. But I had to keep rubbing my belly, the hairs on the back of my neck rising. I realized what that churning feeling was only when it flattened: I'd *wanted* to see the woman here, to stop my mind from imagining.

"We've been working on this one for months," Oriah said, coming up behind me. He wore a big grin on his face, and I saw how he was nearly love-drunk in this place.

I went, "She's not going to be here, is she?"

"Who?" he asked. Then his eyebrows pinched. "No, Simone's got a different shift. Told you we don't work together like that."

Simone. There it was, her name, and in my mind, below the hair that was long and loose again, she grew a face. A full red mouth. I said nothing, like my body no longer had room for my voice. When I tried to step back, his fingers caught my wrist.

"So this whole time," he said, "you thought I was lying to you?"

Something in my face must've said what I wouldn't: *You lied the first time, right?* He let go of me. Rubbed his nose between his thumb and forefinger.

"What were you trying to do?" he said, his voice low. "I come out here to—"

"I know." I crossed my arms over my stomach. "I know how good I've got it. There's no need for you to show me."

I could see how right I was, even as he tried to keep his face still. How, even with his pleasure at our baby, he wanted to bring me here to prove his world wasn't shrinking with fatherhood closing in.

"I'm the one who has it good," he whispered, his face turned toward the grad students chatting a few feet away. "But sometimes, I—don't know what to do about all this. With you."

We stayed at the site about an hour, avoiding each other. He disappeared into one of the tents, and I stood at the edge of the dig, watching the unkempt grasses tumble over each other. The week before, close to closing, I'd asked Nya for a trim, and she'd blow-dried my hair to better see the gnarled ends. "Be sure to clean that up afterward," said a customer who'd gotten a spider-black weave. She nodded at the strands on the floor. "Leave those lying around and a bird'll get 'em." Nya had laughed, said she wasn't worried about a bird getting inside, but the woman shook her head and went, "Make fun of me if you want to. But my grandma doesn't play about stuff like that. Let a bird make a nest of your hair and you'll have a headache for life. *No* peace of mind."

More than anything, that was what I wanted. Peace of mind.

"You and Professor Robinson coming to the harvest party?" said one of the graduate students, bringing me a paper cup of water. She smiled at me, and I saw she still had braces, silver with orange bands.

I looked over at him, his back long beneath his red sweater as he bent over a table. He was absorbed in his work, not looking in my direction. Hard to tell if he was still fuming.

"Yes," I whispered. "We'll be there. Everyone goes, right?"

WE BICKERED ABOUT THE PARTY like we bickered about so many things in early November: how to prepare food in a way that didn't upset my stomach, when I should eventually stop spending so much time standing in the salon, whether the uptick in my mother's calling was causing me stress. "When I get out," she'd started saying, her voice shaky. I could hear it, her fear that I'd keep the baby from her. "I'll make some corn bread. Something for the little one to gum on." Or: "Send me a copy of the sonogram as soon as she looks like something. *As soon.*" But Oriah and I kept going back to fighting about the party, all the way up to the Tuesday before.

"Cher," he said, standing before me in the living room. "If we go, I can't guarantee—who will be there."

"I know," I said. I made my voice go calm, like I really was unfazed. I was on the couch again, curled on my side with a book balanced on my hip. A Toni Morrison novel one of my clients had given me when I told her I wanted recommendations. "But you're up for tenure next year. Don't you think we should make a good impression?"

"I mean . . ." His eyes traced the ceiling as he pulled at his beard. "I've had time to think about what's important. I don't believe things'll be alright if we all end up there."

"Why? You chose me, right?"

"I did but—"

"Does she know I know?"

He stopped tugging at his facial hair. "I don't think so. I didn't tell her that when we ended things."

"Then don't worry."

He rolled his eyes.

"I'm serious." I sat up. I was barely showing, but every time I moved, Oriah's eyes went to my stomach. "It'll be fine. Do what's right for your career. Remind your colleagues who you are outside the dig and classroom."

I felt him watching me even after I turned back to the book. Flipped the page. A ghost-child was haunting her mother, absorbing her life.

"Alright," he said. "If you're sure, I think it could help when I'm up for review."

"Right." I rubbed my belly again. "Let's focus on what's helpful."

THE ARCHAEOLOGY DEPARTMENT THREW the party in the humanities house, a cozy building perched on the campus' edge. The place had white paneling and long glass windows we could see through as we approached. Professors drinking wine and holding kebabs over orange napkins. As we got closer, I saw myself among them, my reflection on the glass mingling with their bodies. My hair's honey color Nya had refreshed that morning, my afro healthy enough to take it with those dead ends gone. The burgundy lace dress I'd worn on our first honeymoon, the one night we'd taken a break from touring Jamaican plantations. I could still fit into it, my stomach not yet tight, though the baby inside gave me my own shine.

"We don't have to stay forever," Oriah said. Under his navy button-down, he was sweating. The cologne wasn't disguising it. "Maybe—let's make an impression and then get out. I'd much rather be home with you." When I looked at him, his eyes were so serious that I paused on the sidewalk, burning in the yellow gaslight. What if we should go back? What if Simone was getting the best of me after all?

But no, someone was already waving at him through the window. A large Black man with a graying mustache. He'd sat in our living room once after we'd first moved in, and I'd had to take my mother's call upstairs, afraid, suddenly, that Oriah's colleague would hear me asking if she needed money for the commissary, for socks or deodorant or anything else she might want to buy.

"Charles," Oriah said after we'd gone in and glided past the professors in black dresses and khaki corduroys. When he slipped his hand through mine, I thought, Stay by his side, and if you notice anyone who might be her, you say nothing, you do nothing, you glance in her direction once.

There were too many women anyway. Women with their hair in buns or sheets down their backs. Women who probably didn't have mothers in prison. But also—women in sweater dresses and baggy pantsuits, who studied the wine red of my dress and gave me embarrassed smiles as they picked lint from their hems. I tried not to look at them too long, staring instead at the house's decorations. No hanging paper turkeys or cornucopia cutouts, the sorts of things we'd hung in the salon. Instead, someone had arranged bouquets of green tissue-wrapped maize and squash on the hors d'oeuvre tables. Along the bookshelves, I lingered before framed photographs of men and women with their families, some smiling in mid-embrace and some absorbed in private conversations over coffee and others staring right into the lens, some in T-shirts and some in dresses and others in beaded necklaces over silk blouses. When the men saw me looking, Charles said, "Wampanoag. Though I sense I'm the only person who finds it important to think of their tribes every Thanksgiving. I don't see how you can stand around and stuff yourself and pretend."

"Well," Oriah said, "it's not pretending. It's—celebrating other things. Like family."

Charles slapped my arm, like he was trying to bounce his laughter into me. "This is who you married, Cher. Ever the optimist."

I couldn't tell if he'd meant it as a compliment, but Oriah smiled at me, and right then it was like I was seeing the two of us at the center of that party: Charles' body angled toward us and Oriah's body angled toward me and the child below my navel looking up at me too, as if to say, *Oh Momma, if you have to smile, go on.*

I kissed him. His mouth warm and soft and mine. Charles said, "So both of you are romantics," and though I smiled, I felt right then certain that he hadn't meant it nicely.

I probably wouldn't have known it was her if not for the way Oriah stiffened. She appeared beside Charles, making a little rip in the cluster of grad students behind him. Her smile hovered curious over her flat champagne. Thin lines pressed deep around her eyes, which were startlingly luminous or else absorbing the reflection on her glasses. Her hair wasn't short or long but—average. She'd done a bad job of pressing it out, and now it wasn't straight or curly. Just frizzy. Like she could come to this event comfortable, among her people, knowing how she looked wouldn't matter.

"Professor Cameron," Charles said, making space for her. "Finally someone on my side."

"Side of what?" She held her glass in both hands, and I thought, You're so unlike what I imagined. Her paisley dress trailed the floor, too long, covering her shoes. She glanced at me, a little longer than necessary, and I thought, See, Cher, she's only a person. And she's looking at you too.

"Nothing," Oriah said. He moved his hand to the small of my back and her gaze followed it. He'd done it on purpose, I felt. "I'm not getting into it with this man outside of a meeting."

"Why not?" she said. "Outside the department is as good a time as any."

I draped my arm across Oriah's and said, "Get some water with me?" He looked at me, grateful, and said of course and would they excuse us, and then he was leading me to the other side of the room, and I could feel her gaze as Oriah handed me a cup of water, as he watched me drink and never once looked back.

We stayed at the party for the better part of an hour, and I let Simone fade from the corner of my eye. I laughed at their colleagues' jokes, especially the ones that weren't funny. I shook hands and nibbled on hors d'oeuvres and stood like the type of woman who'd never shouted a day in her life, the type of woman whose waist Oriah rubbed his thumb over again and again, as if convincing himself this ease was real, the miracle of it. His thumb kept covering my skin, burying his mistake deep below this moment, below our marriage, below the trace of our daughter, still growing.

After a while, I saw light flickering on the porch outside. A cell phone or that stubborn glint on Simone's glasses. When Oriah said, "You ready to go?" I nodded and he said, "Me too. Just need to hit the bathroom before we walk back." He excused himself, and I waited a few beats. Then, I went outside, telling myself, *This is behind you. Really, this is.* Simone sat on the porch swing, her legs crossed at the ankle, her shoes sideways on the floor. When she saw me, she said: "My feet start aching after a while."

"Makes sense." I didn't let myself think of how those bare feet led to her nakedness.

"Your hair is beautiful," she went on. "I've never been able to grow mine out that long."

I thanked her, when it would have been easy to say, *I know.*

I looked at the hunch in her shoulders. The way her eyes were thoughtful in the darkness, like maybe she was okay and maybe she wasn't. In the window behind her, a group of women threw their heads back in laughter, and I thought, You're still not satisfied are you? Nothing you've guessed about her has been right.

"I work at a salon," I said. "You get a lot of practice like that."

"Oh, right," she said, and then she gave a long, deep sigh, and I wondered if she'd been holding her breath. "I think Oriah mentioned that. Once or twice. I don't know anybody who does that sort of work. I mean, I've *been* to salons. But I never did that whole first-name basis thing. Never kept up with it. And now I feel like my hair's going to be this dry forever."

I turned away from her, avoiding her face, which only reminded me that nothing I'd done so far was enough to prove I could put everything behind me. In the house, Oriah was returning from the bathroom, scanning the crowd. Through the glass doors, his eyes found mine.

"Maybe," I said. "You could come in sometime. Let me give you a treatment."

"Really?" Her face drew into itself, and I couldn't tell what she was thinking.

Oriah was coming toward me from one side and on my other, Simone was chewing her lip, another flash of nakedness. What was she seeing as she looked at me? Calm, I hoped. A peace offering, even if only to myself.

"Make an appointment," I said, scribbling down the address right before Oriah opened the door. He saw us and cleared his throat. "Or if you're planning on walking in, it helps to get to the salon early."

I FELT KIND OF SILLY the next day and the next, as I kept waiting for her to come in. But Thanksgiving passed in a whirl of press-and-curls and flat twists, and every woman who called or entered our doors wasn't her. I thought I was making myself sick with worrying, with wondering if she remembered the address.

One December night, I rolled over in bed and felt a little tremor in my ribs and I thought, Oh she's done it now, really gotten inside you.

"What is it?" Oriah said, turning on the light. And when I told him about my stomach, he put his hands on my belly and then looked at me with a big dumb smile and asked, "Is it happening? Is she kicking?"

"The baby?" I asked—then burst into tears like I'd lost control of what went on behind my face.

"It's alright," Oriah said, pulling me against him, and I was wiping my cheeks, holding my breath, trying to get it to stop. Above me, it was like he was the brightest thing in the dark, the moonlight curving over his shoulders. But being alright wasn't the point. I'd missed recognizing it for the first time, the flutter of her kick, her announcement of her life. All because of him and Simone and the way I was still trying to be the best version of myself.

"I don't want to do this," I said, pulling back. I grabbed our sheets to steady my shaking.

"What do you mean?" His hand slackened on my waist.

"Worrying. I don't want to worry about anything anymore."

"Oh," he said. And then I saw it, how his chest started moving again, like it had breathing to make up for. "Right. Don't do that. I don't want you to worry either."

I MIGHT'VE MEANT IT. But then Simone came into the salon the Wednesday before Christmas, an hour before we opened, when I was alone. For once, I hadn't been thinking of her. I'd only been fluffing out the hair I'd twisted up and trying to remember what Nya had said about coming in late, needing to finish her holiday dishes. I supposed I could understand it. Since Tuesday had been our busiest day, this was the last bit of time she could claim for herself.

"Is now good?" Simone asked, like she hadn't already noticed the emptiness. She looked impossibly warm in her beige sweater and jeans, her hair stuffed in a bun that was unraveling.

"For that treatment? I thought you'd come in a while ago."

She didn't answer. Instead, she studied the salon walls painted their different colors, the zz plant reaching into the doorframe, my booth with its mess of flat irons and bobby pins and shears.

"I was planning to," she said. "But I had a lot going on. Almost made more sense to forget about it at this point."

She came over to my booth and started picking up my styling tools, delicately, as if they were foreign relics. I turned away from her. Breathed out. Tried to keep my hands still as I pulled a fresh apron and cape from the supply closet. I thought, I'm going to get her rinsed out, I'm going to hold her scalp in my hand and feel what my husband knew and then be done thinking about any of this. By the time I'd finished tying my apron, she was sitting in my chair, her wrists folded across her lap. "We'll start at the shampoo bowl, actually," I said. "Get you washed up."

"That's not—" Then she shook her head and pulled her shoulders back. "Alright, sure. But I'm pretty simple. You don't have to make some big production out of it."

"Simple, huh?" I shook out the cape, letting it fan into the air. "I wouldn't have thought that."

Her mouth twitched a little. Then, she strode over to the basin. Leaned back in the chair and closed her eyes. I snapped her cape, black plastic with pink trim, around her neck.

The skin at her temples pulled, and I thought, She's trying to release something too.

"Listen," she said. "I don't like when the water's too hot."

"I won't burn you. Relax, alright?"

"I am relaxed."

But I could see the ropes in her neck as I let the water wash clear through her hair. Her strands were dry, limp as they spilled through my fingers. I scratched her scalp and felt the oil there slip under my nails. She was tense, her eyes staring up at me, unblinking. But slowly she gave in, her knees bending beneath her cape.

"Oh," she said. "That's really nice, actually."

"I try," I said, "to make it feel like that. I try to be good at what I do."

She squirmed, adjusting in the chair. "Guess we all have our areas of expertise. Is anyone else coming in?"

"Not for a while. People getting ready for Christmas. You got plans?"

"No," she said, her voice tight. "No, I don't."

I kept lathering her hair, watching her look up at me. Her mole-dotted lips were slightly parted, like there was more she wanted to say. When Oriah first told me about her, he'd started with "Cherie" and then "I'm sorry" and then "I've gone my whole life without being a cliché and all of a sudden I—slept with somebody." I'd been in the middle of making breakfast. I cracked an egg, watching the yolk start out intact before erupting out of one side, spreading and spreading across the pan. "And I've already told her it's over," he said, his words running together. "And she's got her hurt, and I've got mine, but that's nothing compared to what I've done to you, and I'll do whatever you want now. Whatever you need, to make this right." I went somewhere after that. Someplace very still inside me that was gray and frayed and singed. I murmured something like, "Thank you for being honest," or I might have even said, "Well, I'm your wife and we'll get through it." Only, there was a bit of time when Oriah had his arms around me and another time when I was in the bathroom alone and my mouth was opening and closing to let something out and I thought, Once you come out of here, you'll be different.

Simone stayed quiet through her conditioning treatment, her hands stiff in her lap. I kept my own fingers moving, pumping glob after glob, working them into her hair so the salon smelled of soap and coconut. She wasn't giving me anything. Not like other clients, who'd talk of uterine fibroids or failed promotions or the route they'd walk home from here, knowing some man might kill them for being who they were. But Simone kept everything in, even as my hands worked harder, wanting to prove to myself how much I could move past this. Let this be the best you've ever done, I thought when I rinsed her and felt the new strength in her waves, moist and clumped together. Everything else is only getting in the way.

My mind kept repeating it as I got her back in my chair, as I blew out her hair, as I ran my flat iron over it until it went silky black. All the while, she watched me in the mirror, her lips chewing silent words, and I thought maybe she was finally working herself up to letting them out. She kept tracking my hands with her eyes, watching how I poured argan oil from its amber bottle and pressed it into her strands with my palms. We were alone, quiet, but everything we weren't saying sounded loud, so loud among that sunlight and glass.

"I wasn't expecting this," she said when I finished and stood behind her. Flat-iron smoke dissipated around us, and there she was in the mirror, her hair polished in neat curls. "So this was what was hiding under that mess, huh?"

I touched her shoulder, then lowered my hand again. I could do this. Be this easy, carry this too.

She laughed, nervous. Then she leaned forward to take her purse from my booth and fish for her wallet. Inside her satchel, I could see gum wrappers and balled-up pantyhose and student papers like the ones Oriah always had.

As I walked to the register to ring her up, I breathed. Thought about how I could've lost myself completely, but I hadn't. And now, I'd proved it. How *good* I was. How I never raised a fuss about anything. And this was why I had a husband and could make anyone feel good in my chair and was having a daughter who'd look at me and know that you didn't have to let things come over you. That was enough, wasn't it?

"There was something I wanted to tell you," Simone said. She was still sitting in my chair, clutching at the plastic cape. "Because at the party you seemed so happy, and I thought that wasn't right. For you, I mean. As well as me."

"I know," I said, dragging her card through the register.

But she kept talking like she hadn't heard. "Because I've done so much thinking about this. What's wrong and what's right. How awful people can really be deep down. And here you are, smiling so sweet, and I thought, Of course. Of course you're walking around here like there's nothing at all to worry about." She laughed again, this time to herself.

"Well, not anymore," I said. "I know there's nothing happening now."

In the silence, the receipt printed itself off, smudged with ink. She blinked at me from the chair. Tucked her hands under the cape and pinched it from the inside so it looked like there was a black hole sucking in the plastic. "What do you mean by that?"

"I mean Oriah told me. About you and him. Last January."

She watched me, saw me standing there looking at her. A sheen entered her eyes and then kept going. "He told you," she said, "and you invited me here."

I waited for her to understand. This is it, I thought. We're both done now.

"You invited me," she repeated. Then she twisted in the chair and looked at herself in the mirror. Reached up and patted her hair. Combed her fingers through it once, then twice. Looked down at her hands when she'd finished. They were shaking.

"Stop that," I said. "Keep your hands out of your hair."

"Don't shout at me," she said. She stood and started touching her hair again. "And don't tell me to calm down. I am calm."

I could almost see her counting to three, her eyes pinched into slits, her chest rising and falling, her hands resting on her hair. Finally, she breathed out, and her features relaxed, but only a little. I could tell she didn't want me to come any closer, not with the way her eyes opened and measured the few feet between us. Slowly, she lowered her hands. But her hair was already inflating. Ruined.

"How on earth could you do it?" she said.

"Do what?" I couldn't stop looking at how her curls weren't neat anymore.

"Just—take him back like that?" Then something shifted in her eyes. "*Oh*, he didn't tell you everything."

"He did."

"Oh, no, he didn't. He couldn't have. It was—a *long* winter. A lot of time. And even before that—with so few of us in the field, it's not like we just met. It's not like this came out of nowhere."

My thumb pressed into her credit card's edge, a sharpness that grounded me, kept me from floating too far into wherever she was leading. To the woman she'd been and what he'd seen in her and what they'd made together.

"Listen," she said, coming toward me.

"No, I don't want to hear any more."

"But you need to." She was taking her card from me, slow, her fingertips nudging my palm. "He promised me things. And then *left*. You're not understanding. He told me things I've been sick about for months."

But I couldn't hear any more. "Shut *up*," I said. Already I was yanking my hand back, peeling my apron from my body, only thing I knew she wouldn't be able to stand. "Just stop talking. Nothing you can say is going to change anything."

She saw as soon as I lifted the apron away. She looked down at my stomach, not yet as big as it would be. I watched whatever she was going to say, whatever it was that left those rings around her eyes, re-submerge. Relief, in that. I already had enough to picture her in that tent and beyond, Oriah too, all the places he'd been before he'd passed me and Nya laughing drunk outside my uncle's restaurant, "Mind if I join in on the fun you two are having?" he'd said, which might've been exciting to him then, but which probably seemed ordinary in hindsight. Only—that ordinary life was ours. We'd coaxed it out. Claimed it.

"God," she said. She took one step back. Then another. "Good luck with that."

I said nothing as I put one hand on my belly and waited for her to go. She was taking her time, lingering at my booth, her eyes not meeting mine. I stood there, imagining what else she wanted to say—*He loved me, he was going to leave you, he wanted me to go with him here and here and here, he said it was easy, being with me*—and it almost got me. Almost. But I forced myself to watch her hunched shoulders, how she was combing through her hair again. Examining her fingers.

"All that money and time for nothing," I said. "What are you even trying to do to it?"

"I don't know." She set her lips in a hard line. Then unsnapped her cape. Picked up her purse.

She was almost at the door when she added, "Actually, you know what I was thinking, when you first told me you knew?"

"It doesn't matter."

"I thought you might've tried to hurt me. Put something in my hair to make it fall out. Or burn my scalp. Or something else just as wild."

I looked at her. My own hair went cold at the roots, like pin-pricks right at the tip of me. "I wouldn't do that," I said. My heart stretched all the way up my throat.

"Maybe you wouldn't," she said, still holding the door. "Maybe." Then, with her shoulders stiff, with one hand still touching her hair, she was gone.

I watched the sun sprawl over the glass, nothing to stop it growing. It washed over the tile so I could barely even see where I was. In me, my daughter stirred and aloud I said, "Shh, s'alright." Though I wasn't sure it was. I could still feel the weight of Simone's hair in my hands. And in all that time she'd felt me too, what had she sensed there?

I DIDN'T SAY ANYTHING that night and for a long while after. A year from then, holding my daughter against me in our living room, I would tell Oriah that he'd almost killed us, that, for better or for worse, there was now a part of me that didn't trust being as patient as I'd been—that couldn't, for my own sake.

But that night I went home and watched him pore over his research, his articles. I didn't shout or soothe or ask what he hadn't told me. When I said, "I'm tired. I want to go up," he closed his book. Kissed my forehead. Went to bed with me.

We had Christmas at my uncle's, and I swallowed down goose carvings, collards that draped off the spoon, pieces of bread fluffy and high against the roof of my mouth. Oriah sat next to me, beaming, and we talked about the baby who was coming, the way our lives would change, the way it would bring us closer together, then apart again, and then, if we were lucky, closer still. "You'll do much better than your momma would have," my uncle said, and I didn't smile back.

When my mother called later that evening, she said, "When you have her, you have to bring her by. You have to bring her by for me to see."

"Of course," I said. My daughter was me and so she was my mother too. "I promise."

❋

SHE CAME EARLY THAT SPRING, pollen coating the bathroom windows again. I was showering when I felt a twinge and then a pop and then seconds later a warmer water spilling from me and onto the brown tile. I had to feel my way toward understanding what was happening. Because she'd gotten so big in me then, she blocked my view of my own feet. No way to see the water breaking.

It was Nya I called, holding the towel between my legs, Oriah away at the dig again. She pushed back her next appointment to pick me up, though by the time her red sedan sped into view, I'd already started walking up our street, was already leaning against a wooden telephone pole with my bag slung over my shoulder. My daughter was sounding her alarm now, a ringing in my body like she didn't care that first babies were supposed to come slow.

"She's not waiting," I said, hunched over as Nya scooped me against her, trying to heave me into the passenger seat. My body kept tightening and untightening, all of me sharpening to a lone searing point. "She's not listening to me."

"Come on, Momma," Nya said, her fingers shaking as she belted me in. "Breathe through it. I know you know how."

In the hospital room, I felt split in two, the mattress cool and thin under me, my daughter warm and heavy on top. Nya had gone back to the salon by then, had pressed my arm and told me to call if I needed *anything*—though I didn't have time to think about it. Doctors in blue scrubs and nurses in pink came swirling in against the room's white, probing me and rubbing my back with cold and checking to see if my baby was emerging, if I was widening enough for her. "Close call," the doctor said as he slid the needle into my spine. "She almost got ahead of you there."

I didn't call Oriah until I was under the epidural, the pain dulled and shifting beneath its chemical sheet, waiting. A nurse pressed my phone to my ear and checked my blood pressure, both of her hands firm. Above her mask, her eyes were a soft hazel.

"I'm coming," Oriah said, breathing hard into the phone. "I'm heading over right now. I'm getting into the truck and—"

"Go home first," I said. "Clean up before coming over here."

My daughter didn't wait for him, too ready, too eager. Behind the doctor's capped head, the walls went from white to purple to red as I pushed with my whole body, even with the backs of my eyes. She'll kill me, I thought. She'll really kill me if I let her.

"Keep going," the doctor said beneath me. A voice, only a voice. "You're doing fine."

"Fine?" I shouted. Louder than I had in my life. "No, I'm not fine."

And then my body clamped tighter and I rode the spiked waves of my breath and there she was. A furious spiral of dark hair, a tangle of arms and legs. She was covered in the red of me and I made a little noise and she turned her head toward the sound and shouted over it, her whole face an open mouth.

"Give her to me," I said, louder, to match her. But the nurses pushed me back. Said I'd want her clean, but I didn't, I didn't care. She was so pale beneath the red, not even sun darkened, just rolls and rolls of skin and hollering.

I would have gotten up and gotten her myself if they hadn't brought her back so quickly, wrapped in a dotted blanket, her pink nose turning from left to right, unsettled.

"I'm here," I said again, sitting up. Someone had changed me, slid a fresh pad under my hips, though the room still smelled of my deepest parts, of her. Sour and stinging like whatever was inside had been there too long.

The nurse moved toward me, cradling my baby against her chest. My daughter, feeling the nurse's breast against her cheek, turned to it.

"Hurry and pass her to me," I said, though I was so worn out that even sitting up strained my back. "She's not as delicate as all that."

I took my daughter and watched her shift toward me, scowling even as her dark eyes settled. She knew she was mine, recognized me. I pulled her to my breast and tried to get her to drink, her mouth gripping and unforgiving. She wasn't cute yet, her head pointed at the top, prodding my palm.

"Sometimes the milk needs time to come all the way in," the nurse said, reaching toward my chest. "Let me show—"

But I shook my head once, and she withdrew, annoyed, pushing her bangs off her forehead.

"It's coming," I said, too loud. I cupped my daughter's head again, feeling her matted hairs. I waited and she pulled and pulled and finally my milk came. She closed her eyes. I kept mine open, watching her. Watching myself too, waiting for the rest of me to be drawn out.

THE HAPPY LAND

HIS FATHER STILL ISN'T ANSWERING HIS PHONE.

Gideon prays for more time before the storm spirals over the Carolinas, though as he boards up the carpentry shed in his backyard, winter irks his bad knee. The sting is a promise of what's coming: heavy snow, subzero temps, a bomb cyclone. Already, the crows have fled the power lines, and over the fence, a new ink-blue tarp shields his neighbor's turnips. Gideon's spent his remaining safe hours making deliveries across suburban Charlotte, scraping together checks for his furniture business: intricate bookcases for anxious professors, dining tables for elderly women waiting for their children to fetch them. Now all that's left is putting plywood over the shed windows. If moisture slips in, it'll ruin the pieces meant to hold him over 'til spring.

Pa, in his grand woodshop a few hours west in the Smokies, could afford such a loss, his work always carrying him. After Ma's passing, the man had taken him in, ordering Grandmama to deliver him from her house to the shop up the mountain. It would become Gideon's first full memory: the armoires dark and sun drenched as syrup, the bay windows overlooking the green, layered folds of the misty Blue Ridges, the shop's rooms spread out like the chambers of an infallible heart. He was four. Suddenly, the man he'd seen on weekends stretched into a full person standing at the workbench, fashioning an end table with legs round as a greyhound's haunches.

"Hope you've had enough of your womanizing now," Grandmama said to Pa. "Lord knows, it's cost us." Then, she squeezed Gideon by the shoulders and said he was welcome at her place anytime, it was still his home.

When she'd gone, Pa said, "You just have to keep moving, boy."

Gideon stood at the window, peering over the valley of hickories and chestnut oaks. It would be an endless fall. Not at all like the hop-step down from Grandmama's back porch, where he and Ma had lived all his life, ever since she'd left Pa, eight months pregnant and hoping he'd get it together.

"Come on over here," Pa said, opening to him. "Here's how you make use of your hands."

In his backyard, now, Gideon hammers in the last nail and breaks the quiet. He pulls out his cell to try Pa again—then remembers the hammering might've attracted notice.

When he glances toward the house, the kitchen window is a shock of yellow in the gray siding, his husband encased in the light. But Darnell hasn't seen him. Instead, Darnell folds another round of dough beneath the sill, sweet potato croissants they'll bring to their friend Marie's cyclone party. Overnight, of all things, everyone taking a couch or guest room.

This is the difference between them. At the first warnings of the storm, Gideon had pictured their pair sequestered in bed, not unlike the early days of the pandemic when they'd chosen to see only each other. There'd been that slow ritual of removing their masks at their apartment thresholds, then removing their clothes deeper within. There'd been no option to be anywhere but against each other, skin to skin, nose to navel, then lower. He'd been astounded that this neighbor—remarkable smile, dimples you could set spoons in—had seen something in him like safety, had wanted more after he'd left soup cans and bottled water outside his apartment door, the coughing through the walls nonstop.

The storm could've given them that seclusion again. But for Darnell, the cyclone meant a chance for the whole gang to get together, his bakery colleagues and former roommates who'd borne witness to the parties and hookups of his twenties, friends who'd never bet on them staying together after everything reopened. "They're your friends too," Darnell had argued. "The only person who cares where you're from is you."

Which wasn't entirely true. Else Pa and Darnell would've exchanged more than a handful of conversations over the years. And there'd be no reason for him to call Pa out of earshot.

Despite the cold, Gideon lingers outside and rubs his knee, watching Darnell finish the tray of pastry dough and ease it onto the center island to rise. Then his husband leaves the view of the kitchen, heading up the stairs. And at the last minute, just as his head enters the window above the staircase, he slips. Plummets past the frame. Like a fig dropping from a tree without warning.

The space between Gideon's lungs expands. They've been meaning to fix those carpeted lumps on the stairs. So many times, they've tripped and caught themselves.

Though this time Darnell doesn't rise.

Gideon hurries across the yard, running through his stiff knee and splitting a wall of winter. Everything points toward his husband, who needs him.

"AT LEAST DO ME the favor of warming up," Darnell says when Gideon's maneuvered him to a kitchen table chair. "Instead of touching me with your outside hands."

"Just be glad you can feel them." His heart fills his ears. He'd found Darnell sideways on the wrinkled stairs, hips bent all wrong. "You weren't getting up."

"Yeah, well, if you fall and get up too quick, you give everybody permission to laugh."

"I'm not laughing."

"No, just freezing my face off. How about you get the other sheet out of the oven? They're about thirty seconds from burning."

Gideon keeps holding his husband's face, the dark skin pitted from acne scars, the brown eyes not quite meeting his. They're both in their early thirties, and a fall down the stairs shouldn't mean what it might later in life. But during his time in the Coast Guard, he'd seen civilians jabber on and on in the rescue boat, then wind up with swelling in the brain.

"Your ear's bleeding," Gideon says. Blood streams into the hair Darnell's buzzed low.

"Okay, but listen—"

"Hold still."

"Goddammit. Please back off me. For a *second*."

Gideon lowers his hands. A long moment between them: *Are you joking? Are we fighting?* They're still newlyweds, six months in. Nothing should be burning off before its time.

"I'll take care of that," Darnell says when the timer beeps. "I just wanted it to be right."

Then Darnell's moving past him. Tenderly, but moving.

Goddammit, Gideon still hears. Blasphemy.

When his husband's pulled the sheet out of the oven and padded up the stairs, Gideon busies his hands. Works around the feeling of being cored. The kitchen light flickers, and he silently adds this to the list of things he'll fix. He loads the soiled plates and mixing bowls into the dishwasher and wipes egg wash from the countertops. When he discovers flour on the beige walls, even on the framed photographs of Darnell's family—Christmas portraits of city people with designer jeans and straight teeth—he cleans those too. From upstairs, Darnell's muffled laugh reaches him. One of his friends has likely texted him something funny.

Gathering himself, Gideon studies the carpentry shed through the kitchen window, its sagging roof and peeling red paint. It isn't that he expects Darnell to pray or believe. Nor does he expect his husband to accompany him to the affirming, nondenominational church he attends on Sundays, with its rainbow banners and congregation of academics. Religion's a long road.

Certainly, he and Pa have never figured things out. It was hard to tell anymore, who was keeping whom at a certain distance. During his time in the Coast Guard, he'd visited Maywood only for holidays or the occasional weekend while on leave. But in the four years since he's gotten out, Pa has suggested they meet in towns somewhere between Maywood and Charlotte. Beers and chess pie. Easy talk of their breakfasts and drives. Eventually, he'd brought Darnell to Shelby to meet Pa, to a barbecue spot with teal booths and lacquered tabletops. Pa had wiped at the glossy surface with a napkin, occasionally answering Darnell's questions about owning a business, while Darnell talked about being the black sheep in a family of doctors, the only one opting into culinary school. Then—they talked about Ma, memories Gideon didn't even know Pa had. Like the way she always took her coffee with a dollop of vanilla ice cream. Or that she couldn't sing worth a lick but the choir let her in anyway. She just loved gospel that much. And was Darnell a Christian too?

"No," Darnell said, smiling a little. "They haven't always been friendly toward my kind."

"That's too bad." Pa's forehead wrinkled. "You've got to love all sinners, you know."

In the pause, Darnell stiffened. Then, in the tense ride back to Charlotte, he said, "I'm telling you right now I want no part of that."

To which Gideon said nothing. Pa's response would've been worse, once.

During their wedding a year later at the McGill Rose Garden, a blustery summer day that blew white petals against their wing tips, Darnell's eyes had watered, though he'd playfully announced, "Allergies," to the small crowd in the folding chairs. Darnell's friends and family filled most of the rows, though a few of Gideon's Coast Guard pals had flown in, and Pa sat solitary in the back, eyes darting toward the other guests. It had taken so much to get everyone gathered in one place, and still more to get the two of them to the altar, accounting for the fights they had about the *type* of wedding and Darnell saying, "Of course your dad wouldn't host any events in Maywood," and the different ways they were Black men and what that meant for how they showed up in the world. Still, they'd vowed to do the one thing they were good at, which was to keep respect for the places they didn't overlap, to honor them with the same reverence used for the places they did.

To swear with God's name was no honor at all.

Gideon lays the towel by the edge of the sink. Checks his phone. There's still no message from Pa.

Then he hears Darnell on the stairs, soft, as if announcing his apology in advance.

"I shouldn't have snapped at you," Darnell says, "just because you fell into your old Coastie routine. When I'm not being an asshole, I actually like that about you."

In his reflection in the window, Darnell holds a rag to the wound above his ear. Gideon studies how thin this scene looks against the gray outdoors. Though it grows denser as Darnell approaches him, lengthening by his side before becoming solid.

OF COURSE, HIS PHONE RINGS right when he and Darnell are packing up the Prius: flashlights, linens, water, canned goods, and the croissants Darnell's spent the last ten hours making. Gideon knows who's calling by the second ring. With the cold barreling over them, his numb fingers tap too slowly at the screen.

"Please," Darnell says, shoving in the last of the quilts. "Let it go to voicemail."

He can't. Perhaps he's already been a delinquent son in not making sure his old man was prepared sooner.

"Y'all, alright?" Pa asks. It is always "y'all" or "you two." Never Darnell by name. "I see I been missing your calls. Signal's patchy already."

"We were just heading out to a friend's. This get-together she's having for everybody to ride it out." Gideon keeps his gaze offshore of Darnell's face, toward their neighbors' houses, muted boxes of gray and white. The weather starkens the absence of green, how the horizon opens and opens. "You all set?"

"Work got ahead of me, but I'll make do."

"But you've got your groceries. And wrapped all your pipes." His breath fogs. The temperature has dropped that suddenly.

"I'll pick up what I can," Pa says. "I had to take care of some things. For the business. I have to say, both of us getting too old if you feel like you need to check on me."

"Pa—"

"I'm fine, I'm fine." Then Pa's voice lowers. "How'd you make out with your orders? Storm set you back?"

He can never tell if Pa means it kindly, asking about his smaller business. Or if these questions are meant to remind him that he never should've fled Maywood the fall after he graduated high school, not if he wanted to be part of the family shop, with its steady flow of customers and feature in *Southern Living*.

But there had been that boy that rainy spring, whose fingers were always wrinkled from his walks through the woods to their meeting place.

Gideon says only, "You need to start taking this seriously. They're saying the roads'll ice over. It'll be days before they can get folks out to clear them."

"I get into any trouble, and I'll head over to the church, where they've got generators. You haven't seen the new sanctuary, but you'd be impressed by it. Something to look at, with the new windows and carpeting, how they redid the ceiling. Your ma would've been beside herself, if it looked like that when we got married."

"You better make another plan. I bet lots of people will be heading to the church."

Over the line, it sounds like his father has to lug each breath through his lungs. The man's only sixty-one, though with the string of women he's kept throughout his life, he's always seemed impervious to his body's changes.

"We've both been through worse," Pa says. "Talk soon, alright?"

When his old man hangs up, Gideon stares at his phone. Slowly, he returns to the chill, to the driveway with the car's exhaust huffing over the cement. Darnell's moved to the Prius' other side, ice slivers glistening on the roof between them.

"He's gonna be fine," Darnell says.

Gideon says nothing. In his mind's eye, Pa drives down the mountain, leaving the shop and headed home, when he hits a patch of ice and skids perilously close to the guardrail. Or if he's soon to reach their old, coffee-colored house, maybe the power's already out, what little food there is in the fridge on its way to spoiling.

"Please," Darnell says. The blood above his ear has hardened to a dark bead. "Tell me you're not even considering it."

WHATEVER'S SOFTENED BETWEEN THEM bristles the whole way to Marie's, Darnell using that tone he gets when he wants not to wound, but to make it *obvious* that he's right.

"You know he's got somebody out there keeping him company," Darnell says, fiddling with the car's heat. "He's got no trouble in that department."

Gideon squeezes the wheel. Massages his knee and guides them down avenue after avenue of glowing homes, the cars and motorcycles covered or stowed away in garages, then past the breweries and restaurants with their muraled brick walls, everything duller in the gray.

"Do you even have time to make it there?" Darnell goes on. "What if this thing hits early?"

Come with me, Gideon considers saying. *Get to know him.* It isn't as if Pa doesn't give what he can, despite his coarseness. Like building that tree house their first Christmas alone together, a cedar ten-foot cube level with the roof, a strong-jawed face emerging through the sugar maples. *This ain't the home you're used to*, Pa seemed to be saying. *But I can help you love it a little.*

"I changed my mind," Darnell says when they pull up to Marie's and enter the sweep of carriage lights. Her white bungalow's wedged between two smaller homes, renovated from the ancient mill houses. "My head actually does hurt."

"Don't joke about that."

"Well . . . I'm not joking about thinking you shouldn't *go*."

Their car falls in line with the others in the drive, all at least a decade old and decorated with bumper stickers. They're out of place, next to the elegant property Marie's parents have bought her, these NoDa homes going for more than what he and Darnell can even dream of. Gideon touches his husband's hand—a test—and Darnell doesn't pull away.

"Is all this really about that friend of mine?" Darnell asks. When Gideon says nothing, he adds, "You know what I'm talking about."

"That was before us. I wouldn't disrespect you by worrying about it now."

Maybe because every moment that passes is another minute Pa's alone, his words sound truer than they ever have. Only a small part of him has sat among Darnell's friends and wondered which of them, on one drunken night in his mid-twenties, Darnell slept with. It could've been anyone, which has sometimes made his own body feel ghostly and amorphous.

"I don't know *why* you'd be worried," Darnell says. "But you could be."

"It's not that."

"I hope we could just talk about it, if it was. The first time you told me about that one boy, I mean—even I had a reaction. Like he loomed pretty large in your brain."

"I never knew that."

"It sounded awful . . . I don't know. Cinematic or something."

It feels so far away, the shelter of that tree house, the maple leaves breathing against the windows. Rain had drummed endlessly against the roof, which muffled their speaking. "Your Pa fix this up?" asked the boy he'd known then, tracing a dark smear in the corner of the tree house, where a patch of rot had formed. "Or you?"

"It's funny," Gideon tells his husband. "You being jealous of something that happened fourteen years ago."

The side of Darnell's mouth twitches. There's a faint dent in his cheek.

"Please come to the party, Gideon," Darnell murmurs.

Though when Gideon hesitates, his husband sighs and kisses him on the mouth, warm.

"If this kills you," Darnell says, before he climbs out, "I'm not calling him 'Dad'."

SKIPPING OUT ON MARIE'S was a mistake, Gideon realizes as soon as he reaches US 74, headed toward the western Carolina foothills. The pines huddle against the wind, and through the windshield, clouds spiral into themselves, as if God's drawing a deep breath and preparing to blow the whole state into the hereafter. All his time in the Coast Guard, all those civilians rescued from the watery thrash of hurricanes, and only now, on the endless road, do the hairs along his neck rise. For once, the highway is nearly empty, a handful of cars trailing its length. And whenever the Prius hits a slick patch, his share of the storm supplies rattles in the back seat. It's too dark to be just past two.

Gideon shakes his head. Concentrates on the lane lines. What would make him of more use? To have listened to his husband and spent this time with Darnell's friends, drinking spiked cocoa and binging Bravo reruns? Or to prove to his father that, yes, he has his life in Charlotte, but he's not above coming to Maywood, no hard feelings, it's simply right?

But there's something else he can admit: Sometimes, at this stage of his life, anything remotely resembling happiness is like an old dog gone to sleep inside him. Sunday mornings among the progressive congregants with their stagnant hymns. The regular jogs on the greenway, the air smoggier than Maywood's, which had felt clean enough to drink. And, of course, his carpentry business pales in comparison to Pa's.

Every now and then, that old dog in him twitches an ear and raises its head. As if looking for something more to chase after.

Gideon drives for the better part of an hour, the pines and green giants turning gray, then white, then a sort of blurry colorlessness. He can vaguely make out the exit signs for Asheville to the north, where he and Pa once delivered bookcases to an independent bookstore littered with tabbies. Flat Rock's ahead of him, where his high school went to the playhouse for a production of *A Tuna Christmas* and took turns peering down the well in the garden. And close by lies Lake Summit, which Pa had talked endlessly about: The former slaves settling nearby, calling their kingdom "The Happy Land." The log cabins they'd built. The remedies for rheumatism. The singers whose voices echoed over the hills, the mourners whose shouts did the same after their monarch's passing. The lumber and wagon businesses that would've carried them through the turn of the twentieth century, if not for the railroads. It was hard to imagine such a marvel, anyone drawing a circle of contentment that had lasted as long as it did. Now that land had become a cannabis farm.

The mountains rise into that familiar childhood sight, that feeling of being wholly and coolly surrounded, first by the emerald land, then by its blue mist. Like dwelling in a handmade bowl, the hills high and lumpen. Or a series of handmade bowls, stacked one inside the other.

Then the mountains fold before him.

A dense white curtain unfurls through the air, blocking the view of the highway and the red brake lights. Each of its parts vanishes and reappears, like a hundred small mouths whispering into the cold, making some silent wish before closing again. The curtain grows and becomes a cloud, gliding over the honking cars and moving toward him. Slowly, as if it already knows it will have the pleasure of devouring him and sees no need to rush.

His prayers have always been used on other people, a way to help when he's reached the end of what his body can do. So when he whispers, "God," he is asking for nothing.

He eases on the brakes, as if this can slow time.

The cloud embraces the car's hood, its windows. Every molecule is a press of cold.

HE IS NO STRANGER to death. Not after that phone call about Ma passing in the grocery store, succumbing to a heart attack while picking out beets for high blood pressure. Not with Grandmama going on to heaven his fifteenth year, when he'd driven to her place for their regular Thursday dinner, only to find the kitchen cold and her bedspread still high around her shoulders. Not with his decade in the Coast Guard, all those lost catamarans his command couldn't bring back, the oil spills that made turtle hatchlings look like black mushrooms quivering across the shoreline. But he's felt the certainty of his own mortality only one other time in his life.

Like this, it had come out of nowhere. A surprise made worse by the rush of his senior year. 2008, when it felt like only good things were happening to him.

Wyatt had lived on the other side of the woods with his aunt, having moved there from the Qualla Boundary and the Tsalagi relatives he rarely spoke about. Dead set on leaving North Carolina as he was, he studied everything and everybody from behind his bronze glasses, as if deciding whether they would aid or impede him. He was nineteen, always the oldest boy in their grade. Though when he stood next to his aunt, a petite woman who sometimes wore a daisy bandanna and classic rock tees and had a habit of touching his wrist, he looked at her with a patient intensity, as if waiting for her to tell him when to go.

The way Wyatt looked at people was maybe the only reason they'd started up in the first place. After a game of flag football on the church lawn that previous October, the boys gathering their abandoned sweaters from the grass, Wyatt stood beside him at the cooler. "You're wasting your time with that," Wyatt said. At first, Gideon had thought this boy with hunched shoulders and no flags in his pockets had meant the game itself. Everyone knew Wyatt would rather be reading somewhere or correcting some grown person. Then Gideon understood that Wyatt meant Charlie Morris, whose team Gideon always joined and whose blond-haired calves he allowed himself to study only in careful intervals.

The afternoon pinched around him. How small this town, and how much smaller he'd tried to make himself within it. In Wyatt's pointed gaze, he could see the whole scope of how his life would turn out. Like Mel Grayson's, the former choir director, who'd been glimpsed kissing a man at the Asheville airport, and who had afterward been the subject of Pastor's sermons about *perversions of God's roles*. Mr. Grayson's ruddy hands had grown shaky and unsteady on the organ, until they finally stopped. He never came back to church, and soon after, lost his job at the school. He'd moved to Asheville. Or maybe it was Hendersonville. A town that was not quite home, but at the edge of it. There hadn't been music for weeks.

"It's not for anybody to know," Wyatt said as the other boys entered the church ahead of them, crossing the steeple's shadow. "I just want you to understand that it's a dead-end street, fantasizing like that."

This was Wyatt, more practical than kind. Which maybe he'd learned from ignoring the way the other boys teased him about the keloid on his cheek. Or from looking after his aunt during her lupus flares. Or maybe it was that he questioned everything and therefore knew more.

"It's hard to tell if Christians are genuinely nice or if they just feel like they're supposed to be," Wyatt had said when they were walking home. They were still easing toward each other. "Simply following a rule doesn't make you good."

"You have to try, anyway. The rules are there for a reason."

"What's that Jesus line? 'If you love me, you'll do as I say'?"

"Keep my commandments," Gideon corrected, voice low.

"Sure, some of them," Wyatt said. And, unlike on other occasions, he didn't put another inch between them as they approached the main road. In the post office parking lot, a woman in a polka-dotted skirt gripped the blue side of Pa's truck and stuck her head through the window. "I mean, I think your Pa's found loopholes."

Why would this person, these particular months of his life, be so significant? It was not only the looks across the crowded sanctuary, its ceiling high and arched as a bedsheet cast into the air. Nor was it that first kiss in the tree house, when he could only remain still as Wyatt moved toward him. Nor the cool bridge of Wyatt's glasses pressed against his shoulder blades as he entered him, shuddering too soon, for once inexpert. It was learning some other way to be. *What if there is more than this?* Wyatt made him ask. *What's past these hills, past the slope of Pa's shoulders?*

"You know I called her dumb this morning?" Wyatt said as they lay side by side on the tree house floor. They could still feel the scuffs the other boys' sneakers had once made, before the gang had outgrown hideouts and put their attention on girls and recruiters. "Don't get me wrong. I shouldn't have said it."

"I'm sure you had a good reason," Gideon said, though he was half listening. They wore only their boxers, and he could barely conjure up the image of Ms. Eller at all. The damp air lulled him into sleep, as did the endless hum of the rain.

"I dunno. She's getting all fussy about her meds. She's convinced anything in a pill bottle's going to get her strung out. And she sometimes misses her old doctor."

A thought darkened in him. "What? She wants to move back to the Qualla?"

Part of Wyatt's face was hidden as he turned over on his stomach, chin tucked into his elbow creases. It was funny, given how much they'd learned of each other's bodies, what they still held back. Wyatt had never shared the reason he'd moved into his aunt's place in Maywood, just as he'd never shared the story behind the keloid on his face. *Let me be helpful to you,* Gideon thought. *Let me try.*

"I'd tell you if she wanted to move back," Wyatt said finally. "But, for now, I'm managing her alright."

The Friday before spring break, when they'd been involved for nearly three months, they'd climbed down the tree house rope ladder one by one, as had been their ritual. The clouds had retreated from the sky, so when, at the base of that sugar maple, he touched the dip in Wyatt's back—*Farewell, for now*—he mistook the pointed heat for the sunlight he hadn't felt in months.

Then he turned. Saw Pa watching from the porch. Not at the shop, for once.

That look between them. Like Pa was seeing other scenes dissipate in the mist steaming above the earth. All those shared shifts at the carpentry shop, the desks and cabinets and record stands they'd built. Sundays when they'd knelt at the altar with other believers. Those nights when, as dutiful, obedient son, he'd said nothing about the women whose laughter slipped through the den. Which maybe Pa had taken as some kind of tacit understanding of how desire worked.

Please, Gideon thought, though Pa still wasn't looking at him and Wyatt was quieter than he'd ever been. *Be better than I thought.*

"I think you ought to go see about your auntie," Pa told Wyatt.

Of course, Wyatt would argue: *My aunt's fine. And I can do what I want, you know.* But Wyatt only said, "Alright, Mr. Barnes." An obedient stranger. With one hand, he pinned his slicker's hood in place and strode into the maples. Which was the last time Gideon would see him.

"I've got somebody I have to meet," Pa said in the silence.

"Alright," Gideon said. "I can—I'll head up to the shop."

Pa shook his head, ever so slightly. "Don't worry about coming in. I'll close up myself."

Which left Gideon with hours to contemplate what his life would become. He lay on his twin bed in the silent house, studying the wooden figures on the shelf, these little men Pa had carved him every year of his life: Volunteer fireman. Lumberjack with swinging axe. Robed pastor at pulpit. Blues singer with strapped guitar. Colored Union soldier. Sorghum farmer with his bushel. So many others hidden in the second row. This year, for his eighteenth birthday, Pa would likely give him a carpenter.

Don't worry about coming in.

Gideon's throat tightened around his inhale.

The rain, picking up again, drummed against the roof. He reached into his pocket for his cell, which hadn't chimed since Wyatt left. His fingers met only emptiness.

It was after twilight by the time he found it on the tree house floorboards, his flashlight catching the glint below the windowsill. He felt his way back toward the exit, and there was Pa, some twelve feet below him, looking up into the flashlight's beam.

"You weren't in the house," Pa said, a plastic bag between his fingers. "Come on down so we can eat."

What little moon there was fell behind the violet clouds and high hills. Pa looked so small down there, with that light striking his dark, bald head. Like he was a piece of night confined to its reflection in a bucket of water. You almost believed you could face it that way.

"What'd you want to talk about?" Gideon said, still crouched and pointing the flashlight.

"Dinner, as I said."

"I mean, you didn't want me coming into the shop, you made me wait all this time, so say whatever you were going to say."

His father palmed his beard's stubby hairs, though the looseness of the gesture didn't match his eyes. "There's nothing to talk about. Nothing happened."

An old memory of Ma returned to Gideon. Her and Grandmama standing in the kitchen, mustard greens boiling on the stove. Thick-thighed women who knew themselves. "It's how he pretends," Ma said. "It's how he makes me feel like I'm crazy for knowing what I know."

"What are you saying?" Gideon asked Pa.

"Nothing." Pa glanced toward the house. "Only that maybe you ought to be mindful of how you—interact with your friends. So folks don't get the wrong idea."

"But there is no wrong idea."

"Of course there is." Pa lowered his voice. "You like your life here, don't you? How it is?"

Gideon's palms pressed into the floorboards. And when his father turned back toward the house, Gideon reached for the rope. It took his weight same as it always did, except he was faster, more insistent this time, so when the rope swung out with him, its board—rain rotted by this point in April—left the side of the tree house too. There was nothing holding him except his determination to be useful, to prove that *he* could be the one to argue things when Wyatt felt unable, though even this determination was not enough. The dark soil came rushing up to meet him, slowly and then faster, so he had time to think, Everything I've ever felt is over, isn't it? The ground slammed into him with a force identical to his own weight, which meant he was stronger than he thought. Then, an instant later, his knee landed within his leg, which meant it would never be the same. And then the flashlight, which must have rolled from the edge of the tree house, hit his skull, which meant he was looking at his father running toward him as the world blinked shut.

WHEN THE SNOW TAKES mercy on him, Gideon's heart doesn't slow. Somehow, no speeding truck or eighteen-wheeler has plowed into him in the blindness. Here is the highway, opening up, with the cars beginning to crawl. Here are the pines coated in snow. Above all this, the sky is still invisible, as if the mountains are conspiring to converge at a great height. His body takes its time unclenching. On both occasions of his life when he thought he would die, Pa has been at the root.

He drives on, hearing Darnell chide him for his foolishness. Thank God he'd kept his mouth shut and avoided inviting his husband into this winter bleaker than any from his childhood. He can't imagine Darnell in that whiteout, trapped as the wind toyed with the car.

After another hour of the Prius crawling through the snowfall, then past Waynesville and Cherokee, he reaches Maywood, his hometown even stranger to him with the flurries masking the post office, Pa's favorite diner, the dollar store, as if they all belong in some black-and-white photograph. The church at the center of town, its steeple high as a maypole around which everything spins, is the only place that glows. Shadows appear behind the arched windows, red like long wounds against the white. He can sense their presence, all his old people gathered here. People who created those gospel-laden Sundays or pressed Communion wafers into his hands or volunteered at the lock-in to keep the boys separate from the girls, which was the first time in his life that the prickly warmth inside him made itself known. He'd lain in his sleeping bag among the other boys in the chapel, listening to their gentle snores in the dark. And later, in the safety of his grandmother's kitchen, he'd asked, "Do you think most people find Charlie Morris attractive?" She'd hesitated before responding, which might've only been because she wanted to shape her biscuits precisely. "I can't speak for most people," she said. "But it's good to be attracted to somebody, whoever they are. I'm hoping you get even more than that, someday."

Out in his hometown, he wants to run into no one, stupid as he feels and not quite believing that he's safe. When he reaches a darkened intersection, the one that could take him toward the seed company that replaced the tobacco farm, he turns right, toward Pa's.

Even with the snow coating the yard, he can tell the grass has grown too long and Pa's neglected to bring in the hanging plants.

How does the place look so old, hollowed out with the absence of light, like somebody's broad chest shrinking into itself? Either Pa's holed up in there with no heat or back at the church or higher up the mountain at the shop.

Once he's inside, his father's absence meets him like a slap. It's strange, to see traces of Pa's life without the man himself: the china cabinet he carved for Ma as a wedding gift, the velvet curtains over the den windows, the wood samples arranged in a fan on the low coffee table. Sawdust powders the hardwood as Gideon pads down the hallway. Maybe the old man isn't as meticulous about cleaning as he used to be.

He reaches his childhood bedroom, then pushes open the door. His old blue-plaid comforter stretches tight as a cheek against the mattress. Those wooden men look back at him from their shelf. For the first time, he notices they share a face, the same person carved into different lives.

During the final weeks of his senior year, he'd lain in this bed, waiting for his shattered kneecap to repair itself. He had only those men to look at, those and the true crime shows he and Pa watched during quiet dinners. And in private, he and Wyatt exchanged a handful of texts:

Sry, Wyatt sent.

Its ok

You goin back to work?

idk

Then nothing for an entire lifetime of minutes, before Wyatt confessed: *Auntie & I are leaving.*

Later, Gideon would think he should've waited longer. But he immediately sent: *When?*

I mean we already did, Wyatt texted. *She needs more help.*

It felt wrong to ask what he wanted, which was *When will I see you?* They'd never named what they were. And Wyatt had not come by to see him. Which should not have stung the way it did, a needle of abandonment he'd always anticipated. Because Wyatt had his life. Had always known more. And Pa's awful silence and dismissal would only prove how limited he'd been raised to be. A Barnes boy would always be someone Wyatt had to lead.

Praying she'll be alright, Gideon sent and tried to think of something else. Wyatt sent back: *She will.* Which was the last message from him, even after Gideon sent two more over the next few weeks: *How is she?* And again: *How is she?*

When Gideon's phone buzzes, he fumbles to catch it. It's Darnell, wanting to FaceTime.

"You make it?" Darnell asks, face filling the screen. His droopy eyelids betray his drunkenness. "To your Pa?"

"It was—a decent drive. Could've been worse."

"Well, he better be grateful."

"He is." Gideon licks his mouth's dry corners. "Power's out, but we'll get a game of cards going."

"That's what these guys are doing here. They say hi, by the way."

"Hey. Everybody."

Darnell moves his phone farther from his face. It's hard to make out what's happening around him. He's sitting in front of a wavy glass sculpture that keeps flashing with distant light. Marie's has electricity, at least. "I mean," Darnell says, "you didn't even come in."

"I know."

"What's so great about that place anyway? I'm having trouble believing you went all the way out there just for him."

Gideon stretches his knee, the flare of the old injury quieting as he calms down. Through his bedroom window, he studies the thick trunk of that sugar maple, a dark strip through the veil of snow. The tree is indifferent to time, to circumstance, never mind the collapsed floorboards of the structure it holds. Even the column of space, where they never replaced the rope ladder, remains.

"You would've come back if you were me," he tells Darnell. "You would've."

"No . . . I'd only pull something like that for the right sort of person."

"How's your head?"

"I'm wondering . . . is all this saying that *I'm* not being the right person?" In the silence, he adds, "Maybe, if you can live with him, I can. Or else I'll keep pushing you to be mad at me. Or dissatisfied or restless or whatever the word. I don't know."

"Darnell—"

"Because, we're good, right? I have to ask because . . . everybody else is here."

Gideon's ear burns against the phone. How useless he is. What kind of person would leave their spouse behind, like this?

"We're good," he says. "I'll be back soon as I can, alright? At the first thaw." Then he tells Darnell to put Marie on the phone and instructs her to make Darnell drink three glasses of water before he inevitably nods off.

"Want me to text when it's done?" Marie says, her green eyes steady on his. She's piled her hair in a messy bun, which gives her face an aloof elegance. But her alto is kind.

After a beat, he nods. Out of all Darnell's friends, he likes her the most. Something about the way she runs her bakery, handling the gatherings of her customers' lives: cookies for children's birthdays, tiered cakes for weddings, lemon bars for funerals. She's learned to read people without prying.

Gideon's turning to leave when he sees through the window—Pa. Bundled in a black beanie and puffer coat, locking up some structure in the backyard. It's newly built: two front windows and a roof richly dark enough to see through the snowfall. Like a redbrick, in-law suite. Gideon hadn't seen it before. He hadn't known to look.

Slowly, managing the logs tucked under his arm, Pa heads through the woods. Soon, he's gone, a ghost fading into the white, then vanishing between the trees.

By the time Gideon reaches the backyard, the footprints are fading, too, in the falling snow. Which means there's no choice but to follow them while he can, despite his questions.

It makes no sense for the tracks to lead where they do, through the pines bending in the wind, toward the dead-end street where there's nothing but the weathered sorghum mill and Ms. Eller's old place. Confusion keeps Gideon alert, each crush of his footsteps echoing some greater hollow within him. Pa had never acknowledged the Ellers' leaving. Not even when the chair Ms. Eller had custom ordered—a mahogany rocker with a laurel wreath carved into its backing—sat in the shop for months, until some furniture collector from Missouri purchased it.

When Gideon reaches the Eller house, it's an explosion of yellow wood and bright windows, the only place in town with power, so far. Snow forms low piles on the slanted front steps, and the wind pushes the metal chimes, as if determined to remove them from their fishing lines. He supposes Pa's hunkered down with these new neighbors, circumstances being what they are.

Gideon knocks. Studies the chimes. Silver and rusting. Familiar.

Then the door opens and a man is looking at him. Average height and reedy in the middle. His sweater's baggy sleeves make his arms look like they belong on a much larger body, and the gray at his roots is faint, like age is just starting to creep up on him. Then Gideon sees the thin scar on his cheek. Not the keloid, but the marker of its absence.

"Your place lose power too?" Wyatt asks, like they've passed all other relevant questions. On his face, Gideon feels the cold like a bright sear. "I've got to be honest. I don't know how long the generator will keep at it. Wasn't expecting to get hit this hard."

"My place . . . " Gideon begins. Then doesn't know how to finish.

"You've got to hurry it up." Wyatt opens the door wider. The world stretches left: Blue Ridge watercolors, the kitchen table with a pyramid of canned goods, Ms. Eller's river-cane baskets, which she once said were passed down from her grandmother. "You're letting out my heat."

Which isn't possible because he's burning up as he enters the house, he'd take off his coat if he wouldn't feel completely naked. Somehow, here is this person he hasn't seen in half a lifetime. Saying things like *My heat.*

"I've got other supplies," Gideon says, when he can. "Back at the car."

"We've got plenty."

Pa. Ms. Eller. Whoever else has made their way here. There's a collection of men's boots by the doormat. And the closet door won't close over the coats jutting out.

Wyatt leads him around the hall corner, and there's Pa, sitting open legged on the couch before the fireplace, scowling over a game of dominoes. His coat hangs off the armrest, and only the ice glistening on its sleeves proves that everything Gideon has seen has really happened.

His father looks up at him. Opens his mouth and closes it again.

"You're here?" Pa asks, standing. Then his father's running toward him, chin ahead of his legs. When they embrace, his father's rough fingers startle his neck. It isn't that Pa's warm, just that he's warmer than outside. What's left of Gideon's breath dissolves.

Then Pa pulls back. His gaze flickers between him and Wyatt. There's so much they're not saying.

"He knocked on my door when everything went out," Pa explains.

They turn toward Wyatt, who's busied himself in the kitchen, stirring something peppery on the stove, its steam releasing. Only his back faces them, offering no explanation. Then Wyatt raises his head and their reflections in the kitchen window make eye contact.

"We should turn off some lights," Wyatt says. "Who knows if the weather will get worse."

THERE HAS TO BE a way to make this make sense. In the Ellers' den, the fire thrashes in the grate, consuming the logs his father brought over. Their trio sits on the floor, bowls of chili in their laps, the dominoes game expanded. Gideon has forgotten the rules, can't make the tiles form the sequences he wants. Though perhaps even stranger is Pa's patience. He can't remember a time Pa wouldn't hurry another player along. But tonight, Pa constantly checks his cell, relaying news of the storm when messages get through. Somebody's dog missing. The church packed with folks seeking heat. Several busted pipes across town. Gideon recognizes the names of former classmates and congregation members. Too many worlds have collided.

"But how'd you make it all the way here?" Pa asks, interrupting his own monologue.

"I drove."

"You're not going to sell me on that. You can't tell me that was a smooth ride."

Gideon says nothing. Pa and Wyatt are sitting mere feet from each other.

"I had to make sure you were alright," Gideon says carefully, and Pa goes, "Well, you know I'mma make it." A wary smile fades onto his face. New folds of skin surround his mouth.

"How are things in Charlotte?" Wyatt says, as Pa places a tile on his turn.

So Pa has told him this. They have talked that often. Though when Gideon glances at him, throat tight, Pa's frowning at his phone and muttering something about the signal.

"Charlotte's fine," Gideon says. "I've made things work."

"Good for you."

"What have you heard?"

"Everything," Wyatt says. He has a completely new face, open and assured, without that keloid. So strange, Gideon thinks, to remember the exact shape and texture of something no longer there. Wyatt adds, "Congratulations."

"You married?"

"Not yet."

"Gideon's got his own carpentry business," Pa cuts in. "And he's always taking these trips. New York. Seattle. Mexico City. He can't stay still, seems like. Though I keep telling him business would be better if he did."

These are all places he's traveled with Darnell, the last their honeymoon. "Pa doesn't visit Charlotte very often," Gideon says. "So maybe he's a little too protective of his business."

"You do what you have to."

"Fine. And I'm sure you don't have any other reason to avoid coming to Charlotte."

Pa says nothing. Then shakes his head. "It's your life. You didn't ask me to come visit you down in Galveston, so I don't see why you're so bent out of shape about Charlotte."

"You can't be serious."

"You two will figure it out," Wyatt says, studying the tiles. When he leans forward, there's a sturdiness to his shoulders, some quiet strength at his center. What has happened to this once snarky boy, who now seems distanced from what's before him? I don't need you to teach me how to be here, Gideon thinks, though it's at odds with the knot in his chest.

"Where's your aunt?" Gideon says, too loud. The flecks of gray in Wyatt's eyes are like ashes above brown ponds, a fire not quite doused. "We have to be keeping her up."

"No." Wyatt breathes in. "She passed a while back."

Gideon knows he should say, *I'm so sorry.* Or, *Was she alright at the end?* Or, *Were you?* But all he can muster is "When?" One more string binding his boyhood to him has loosened.

"'Bout four years ago now," Pa says, and Wyatt murmurs, "In her sleep. Thankfully."

Four years. Before he met Darnell, when he was still new to civilian life and living in a studio apartment within Charlotte's city limits, taking entrepreneurial night classes at the university and shelving paint cans by day. Before the old knee injury had even begun to aggravate him, reminding him that some inner scar lingered.

"She left you this house," Gideon says to Wyatt. "And you live here now."

"Well, she left the gift of the mortgage. Which I was dumb enough to accept." Wyatt matches a three to the train, shedding another tile.

"'Cause you don't want it?" Gideon asks, and Pa clears his throat and says, "Boy, it's your turn. If you're going to talk, you better do two things at once."

"A lot of reasons. It's still not easy, on a teacher's salary." The corner of Wyatt's jaw lifts. "I'd tell you about the school, but it's 'bout the same as it was when we went. Unless you want to hear about the mold. Or the fact that kids never have the chance to get bored, like we did."

"We weren't bored," Gideon says. Then understands Wyatt means smartphones.

"Well, and—" Wyatt hesitates. "When it comes to the house, Bill doesn't like it. He's traveling for work, otherwise he'd have cabin fever in this place."

Gideon doesn't ask more. Bill. A teacher's salary. A life. An entire life here in Maywood.

Without looking at his hand, he takes tiles from the boneyard. He's watching these men from his past, orange light flickering over their faces, as if the whole scene wobbles.

"So you talk often," he says. "You. Pa. Bill."

Wyatt says nothing. Pa rubs his face, and the flesh on his cheeks doesn't snap back the way it once did.

"We're neighbors," Pa says. "I don't get what you're asking."

SLEEP IS IMPOSSIBLE in this strange house, which for now holds out against the storm whirling outside. Everyone's presence reaches him through the dark: Wyatt in some bedroom down one hallway and Pa down another.

His own stiff body lies on a couch so old he could sink into it and suffocate. It is too much, this white-hot charge in him. Aside from his knee, he feels younger than thirty-two, a sudden plunge backward, like his real life in Charlotte is something foretold but not yet lived. The house holds an oaky smell, which comes to him in drifts: Wyatt's scent.

In the Coast Guard, he'd learned that the world contained pockets of surprise, never mind what you expected. A Coastie from LA, who should've had everything she wanted, was born into a Lutheran family that made her home feel detached from the rest of the city, its rainbow flags. A man from Atlanta, who had grown up with Pride parades gliding beneath his apartment window, had a mother who told him that loving both men and women reeked of hedonism. Even looking back on Maywood, Gideon could remember that two old women had once shared a home there during his childhood, both of them reading and chewing tobacco on the front porch, though when one of them passed, no one mentioned it anymore. He could remember his grandmother, her kitchen, the scent of sugared biscuits. All this, existing alongside Mel Grayson's exile. Moments when you could be welcome or not at all. Moments far fickler than any town or nation. It was nearly impossible to have everything you wanted in one place, at one time, prolonged.

On the couch, it's too easy for such thoughts to gather.

Within minutes, he's fumbled his way through the woods that blast him with damp cold, to the Prius parked at Pa's, then back again, his numb fingers looped through the insulation tape. But no matter how thick the wind or how his ears feel sucked out, he makes himself useful. He wraps the exposed pipes at the side of the house. Removes the water hose from its attachment. Checks the generator's gas. When he wipes the snow from his face and takes a few uneven steps back from the deck, the fire through the den window makes a small orange square. Like the shape of a miniature house, within the shadow of this larger one. It belongs to Wyatt, all this. It needs protecting. The storm could get worse and ruin even this bright patch.

When Gideon lets himself back inside, the house is slow to peel away the cold, and everything wrong with his knee has come back to haunt him like a lump of coal burning in the center of his leg. He ignores it. Opens all the bottom cabinets in the kitchen and hall bathroom. Turns the faucets so the water trickles. Then he shivers before the fire, blurry eyed, ice slowly retreating from the toes of his boots. If this night is choosing to work on him, let him work back.

"Were you outside?" Wyatt asks. "Just now?"

Gideon says nothing. He'd been so focused on regaining feeling in his knee and fingers that he hadn't heard Wyatt in the kitchen. When he turns, Wyatt's fiddling with the kettle on the stovetop, a shift of shadows and silver. Gideon watches him from a distance. This is a sort of intimacy they've never been allowed: Nighttime dark. Wyatt in striped pajama shorts. The left side of his hair is slightly raised, and Gideon remembers those postcoital naps in the tree house, Wyatt's cheek flattened against his wrist.

"You didn't have to do anything," Wyatt says. "Sit somewhere. Have some tea."

"I'm not big on tea."

"Me neither. But I'm not driving you to the hospital if you get frostbite."

The cabinet Wyatt opens is full of loose-leaf tins. Wyatt pushes things around, fumbling as he searches. So Bill drinks elaborate teas, owns the bass guitar in the den corner, wears approximately a size eleven in boots. Travels, apparently, but comes back.

The kettle takes forever to boil, and when it finishes, Wyatt pours two mugs. The steam is the brightest thing in the room, and when Gideon stands, not quite warm, his knee has softened to a dull ache. He grunts. Wyatt laughs softly, and it's too much, knowing for the first time all evening what Wyatt is thinking: They are both so much older than they were. At once, time has pulled them forward again.

"When did you two get on good enough terms for sleepovers?" Gideon takes the mug Wyatt offers but doesn't drink. Instead, he takes a barstool and sets the ceramic heat atop his knee.

They are doing nothing, he tells himself. They are simply talking in a kitchen.

"To be honest, I thought he'd make for the church. Though, from what I'm hearing, there are a few ladies there he wasn't too keen on spending the night with. At least not together."

In the dark, Wyatt's teeth are a curve of white. It is not, Gideon thinks, that he has never been attracted to other men since he's been with Darnell. Even in Charlotte, he's passed joggers on the greenways, some internal recognition surfacing on the men's faces, like water entering other water before smoothing out. But this is different. Some other version of himself leans forward within him.

"My life," Gideon says, deciding against using Darnell's name. "I think Pa's only visited us once. Twice if you count the wedding."

"I'm sure he has his reasons."

"'Course. He's made those plain."

"I hope you're not hating him 'cause of me."

Wyatt sips his tea across the island, the darkness sutured around him.

"Did he tell you," Wyatt goes on, "that he paid for Auntie's funeral?"

"No." But Gideon swallows. "Whatever he does with his money is his business."

"He makes furniture. How much you think he earns?"

"However much he wants." It's such a stupid conversation, given what else he hopes to know. *How does it feel, to be here? When your aunt died, did you think of her as your mother? What else have you been doing all this time?*

"You know," Wyatt says, thumb flat against his mug, "he doesn't have that shop anymore."

"He was there this morning."

"No," Wyatt says, and the old know-it-all surfaces in his posture. "Some out-of-towner owns that land now. Bought it for the view."

Snow falls against the window in a break of slowness, and a deeper understanding collects in Gideon. Pa hadn't said *the shop*, specifically. And there was that new structure in the backyard. And sawdust all in the house. And the fact that, as often as the old woodshop is on his mind, he has not been there in years.

He never got the chance to earn it back. Pa would rather it be somebody's vacation home.

"I'm trying to tell you," Wyatt says, "it was kind of him to do that for her. And I'd bet good money he wouldn't say anything about it."

"No, he wouldn't."

He's grateful for his phone buzzing on the coffee table, an excuse to put space between himself and this boy—this *man*—whom he does and does not want to touch. As promised, Marie has texted him about Darnell: *Knocked out.* But there's also a photo attached, his husband sleeping on her white couch. A dot of drool slips past one corner of his mouth, his eyelids green veined and still. He's fallen asleep in a brown scarf that makes him look like a contented animal burrowing into its nest. Gideon hunches over, his back to Wyatt.

"They're not calling it, but the storm's wearing off," Wyatt says. "We should go to bed."

Gideon turns around. Wyatt's looking out the kitchen window, toward the backyard. There is so much time Gideon holds in: Those months he waited to hear Wyatt text something, anything. Those years in the Coast Guard and his weekends grabbing dinners with men amused by how religion made him slow to sex. That moment he'd been in the cutter's common area when the news broke and the president called the decision "a thunderbolt" and some of the Coasties cried, knowing they could marry their lovers once their tours ended. So silly, to think of Wyatt, then. They'd never talked about marriage, nor would they have ever been one of those couples kissing on television outside the Supreme Court. And yet, he'd wondered what Wyatt had been thinking in that moment. He'd wondered where Wyatt was in the world.

"You got your keloid removed," Gideon says, when Wyatt heads toward the hallway. It is the only safe thing he can think of. "Never thought you cared about that."

Wyatt sets his mug on a bookshelf. It's still full, judging by the sound. "I was five when that switch caught my face," he says. "Five and careless and chasing my cousins through the woods. I guess I just didn't see why I had to have that thing forever."

Then Wyatt's gone, vanishing down the hallway and out of the firelight's reach.

And moments later, as he studies his phone on the couch, Gideon hears a second set of footsteps, shuffling down the other hall.

✳

WHEN HE WAS A BOY, he'd sometimes wake to his father watching him, ready to show him some new technique with a scroll saw or drive him into town for breakfast. Now that he's a man, he can sense Pa's attention on his face, thin and agitating as a change in the light.

"Come on," Pa says, squatting beside the couch. "It's let up enough for us to get going."

In his grogginess, Gideon shoves his feet into his boots. Follows Pa out of the fiery warmth of Wyatt's place, then out into the woods silent and laced in ice. Beneath the shelter of frozen maples, Pa marches ahead, and, inwardly, Gideon curses his own knee's stiffness. The sun forms such a bright glare against the snow that Gideon winces at the white.

As the morning wakes him, so does the understanding: They've left without so much as a goodbye to Wyatt. Or a thank-you.

"Hang on," he says to Pa. Because where the hell are they going? He can't possibly drive back to Charlotte in this. The ground's coated in snow thick as a bear's hide.

"There's no reason to talk out here," Pa says. "We get home, and you can say whatever you want. Your Ma was like that too. Picking fights at the worst times."

Gideon stops. The halt of his boots echoes through the woods. "Why're you always bringing her up?"

"You've had an attitude all night. Must be something you need to get off your chest."

"Don't you? Or are you in a hurry to get back to the shop?"

A few feet ahead, Pa turns around. His dark eyelids sag. The snow has long stopped falling, and any movement among these trees comes only from them.

"I can't talk to you about that," Pa says.

"From what I understand, talking wouldn't much help, at this point."

Pa hunches over, hands on his thighs. Though he must be fine, same as always. There's no way he has exerted himself during this short walk. And if his knees act up too, it's simply because of age.

"It's funny," Gideon says, "how you can help out Wyatt. But not me."

"You weren't here."

"I have to wonder what you tell yourself. Why you can't just be decent to everybody."

"But you weren't *here*," Pa repeats.

Everything is so still, like the whole world is a single white room. Once, he'd lived here, felt the entirety of this place. Now, even with the storm moved on, only the most brutal chill touches him.

"Are you saying this is *my* fault?" Gideon asks. How dare Pa, with his catastrophic silence that day. With how he'd made it impossible to stay.

"I'm saying, who was going to run the place? With you signing up for tours left and right, gone a whole decade."

"You didn't want me to run it. You didn't even want me to come in, that time. And every time after, even when my knee got better, you had this look on your face."

Pa squints, like the memory is thin water in the well of his brain. "I was allowed to be surprised, wasn't I? I was thinking about the business. We never got to rely on tourists and other folk, the way others did. All we had was our name, our best chances of getting somebody to buy from us. And, it came out of nowhere, how you were. Like I didn't raise you in church."

"What's church got to do with who you sleep with."

"Whatever. You're bringing up stuff from forever ago, I barely remember it."

"You do remember it. You won't even say Darnell's name."

"Horseshit. I just don't get why we have to talk about everything. I didn't understand, but I came to your wedding. I call and check on you. So why can't your private life be *private*?" Pa exhales, closing his eyes. "And the shop's gone now. How was I supposed to know you wanted it?"

Gideon stares at the endless snow around him, the thaw far off. It's drifting from him now, that imagined happiness that has been withheld all this time. His contentment in Charlotte has always felt precarious. Because the boy he'd once been never dreamed it. Not like how, during those tree house days with Wyatt, he'd always pictured being here. The furniture made of maple and pine grown not five miles away. The gospel singers who remembered Ma, when he remembered so little. The river of blood that bound you to these mountains for generations. It isn't Wyatt that he's missed. It's that Darnell and Charlotte are altogether different dreams, belonging to some person he had to grow into. No wonder that old dog in him had no choice but to lie down and wait. Or that this storm has brought out the worst in his knee. It is utterly exhausting, trying to run toward your old life and your new one.

"Whatever you say," Gideon says. He can stop himself from going, practiced as he is at chasing after Pa. But he doesn't. He heads toward Wyatt's, at least for now, until he can buy himself time to drive back to Charlotte. The Eller place is still visible through the trees, the yellow breaking up the white. There's a smear at the den window, which could be Wyatt. Or nobody.

"Wait," Pa says, catching up to him and grabbing his arm.

"Let me go."

"You have to stop. You'll ruin things, I'm telling you." Pa grips his coat sleeve, too tight. There's strength hanging around in him yet. "You can get smart with me all you want, but listen."

Gideon stares into his father's eyes, into the warning so serious and deep.

"You just can't be there," Pa says, "if the two of you are going to stand around in the dark, whispering like that. You think it won't mean much. To Darnell. But it's going to cost you. With your mother, I—" Then Pa stops.

It could make him laugh, his father's misunderstanding. Except Pa's dead serious, some prick of light in the back of his eyes, kept at bay. His father's trying to hold him here, to this place in the middle of nowhere. It's not home, or Wyatt's, or Charlotte. And yet.

This has to be enough, don't you understand? Pa's saying, pressing his thumb in deeper. *This life you've managed to have, everything you've refashioned, reclaimed.*

His father keeps his hold on him, a circle of faint heat. The man's thumb refuses to relinquish this urgency, this union, this patch of freezing earth and all that leaks outward—until it becomes impossible not to feel it.

HOW DOES YOUR
GARDEN GROW?

THAT SEED MUST'VE BEEN GROWING IN HER FOR YEARS.
Yet Claire felt it for the first time while dancing in an amber-
lit bar downtown, her ex-fiancé briefly forgotten. Her two
closest friends had dragged her out of her apartment—"Forget
him. . . . your thirties are the best decade of your life."—and
their trio got drunk on RumChatas, their bodies sour and damp
beneath the bar's exposed beams. True, she was the only Black
woman in the place. And true, Holm had broken up with her
after two years together. But the sponge of the crowd wrung
moisture into the air, and her muscles loosened as she danced,
and it wasn't possible to break if you were loose. She twisted into
the grooves of a country song. And inside her, like fruit disturbed
on the vine, something along her pelvis twisted back.

When she doubled over, Jess' sweaty palms caught her shoulders. "There you go, girlie," Jess said. "Whatever you're feeling
is fine."

Claire didn't dare look up. She didn't feel pain, exactly, but an
unsettling tightness near her groin, like a knot within her flesh.
Most likely, Jess thought she was remembering Holm. Neither of
her friends knew the whole truth about her mother, her womb,
her passing. To them, Momma had gotten sick her junior year of
high school, which was why she'd shown up to college quiet and
drawn to corners. Her friends had kindly brought her to their

homes for winter holidays, Thanksgivings with Jess' vegan pecan pie and Christmases with Allie's Ragdoll cats.

"I know we said we wouldn't call him," Jess went on, "but Allie's been on the phone with the nanny all night, so a lot of rules have already been broken."

"No phone calls," Claire said. The tightness subsided.

"Who's making calls?" Allie asked. Her burgundy oxfords returned, edging into Claire's view, among the strappy heels and leather boots. "Why's Claire down there?"

Gingerly, Claire looked up at her friends, the light stroking them from above. She could see only parts of them: Jess' tattooed eyeliner, Allie's copper hair. Yet they made a concerned wall.

"I'm fine," Claire said. And rose. "Let's not make this a big thing."

"Relax," Jess said, in that calm voice used for her yoga classes. "Breathe a minute."

"I just need water," Claire said and stepped out of reach of Allie's fingers.

In this small city in the north-Midwest, she was alternately visible and invisible, and tonight she hoped for the latter. At the bar, she sipped water—then snuck a backward glance toward the dense crowd, the white couples in plaid shirts and lace blouses swaying into one another, the grad students who lifted their drinks whenever someone passed through. Outside the long windows, the dark sky looked like the fresh water off the lake, closing around the bodies gathered. Since moving from Mississippi, she'd developed a habit of scanning rooms for other Black women, seeking that mutual live-wire awareness. Yet tonight she was grateful no one took in the fingers she placed below her navel, searching for something beneath her skin.

Should she wander back, tell her friends what she suspected? They loved her, called to check on her, canceled their classes (Jess), or hired a sitter last-minute (Allie), even when she'd said she was fine. And yet—they couldn't understand everything.

Like when she'd told them about the first time she'd met Holm. It had been a night with a darkness softer than this one, the college's halogen bulbs forming an edge of light at the campus border. The city had been getting away with a mild winter, and the sudden snowfall had taken everyone by surprise, the wait for an Uber endless. "Pool our luck?" asked a man in a navy scarf at the curb, and she'd waited to make sure he was speaking to her. She hadn't worn a coat that morning, and when he leaned closer to examine the phone she held out, it was like standing at the entrance to his cave of body heat. His pale hair collected the snow. She didn't yet know he was thirty-seven, only six years older than her and not as old as he looked.

Then the police car flashed its lights. "Alright, you two," the loudspeaker hissed. "No soliciting. Keep it moving."

In the long moment, her hair stood on end. Knee-high black leather boots, no tights beneath her dress. Which meant some people thought she must be a sex worker, next to this white man.

"This is my friend Claire," Holm said, quietly. He took off his coat and put it around her. He'd seen her name in the app's corner. "We work on campus, and we're just headed home."

When the cop car rolled along—the officer inside nodding once like he'd done them a favor—the headlights cut the night into pieces. "Shit, I'm sorry," Holm said, which he kept repeating when, shaking, she told him she was fine. He fumbled through his wallet until he found a folded piece of paper, a concert ticket. "Can I at least do something?" he asked. "You into Brahms, by any chance?"

Later, after the Uber dropped her off at her apartment building, Holm still apologizing as she climbed out, she phoned Jess and Allie. Telling them was like attempting to hand over an ancient, painfully heavy object. They gave it right back.

"Soliciting could mean a lot of things?" Jess said. And Allie: "Don't worry, he had to have meant something else. You were leaving work, for crying out loud."

In the pause, Claire said nothing. Her friends were thinking about the campus that had once been home to the three of them: naps on the quad, all-nighters in their dorm room laced with string lights. *That wouldn't have happened there*, they were silently insisting. Yet Claire shrunk. Why on earth were they trying to correct her, when they hadn't lived that moment?

"I've got to make dinner," she finally said, and got off the phone. Sometimes her friends failed her. But they were as close to family as she had, now.

At the bar, she thumbed the skin beneath her jeans' top button. The crowd parted, and there were Jess and Allie, turning their heads in her direction but not yet finding her. My mother, she thought about telling them, but they might say, *There was such a low risk. I'm sure your mother's doctors meant well.*

The seed in her pelvis pinched her again from the inside. Then released.

"FIBROIDS," HER GYNECOLOGIST SAID. It was well into September by then; she'd wasted a month trying to switch to a Black doctor. "You have quite a few, actually. Though this big girl's probably what you're feeling."

As she lay on the table, the OBGYN working the transvaginal wand between her legs, Claire felt a worm of cold in her chest. On the ultrasound monitor, globs stretched in her uterus.

"What have you been experiencing?" her gynecologist asked. She blew out one corner of her mouth and her red bangs flared.

"I—have to go in the middle of the night. Every night, basically. And I've always had heavy periods." Which she brewed raspberry leaf tea for. Though there were also the low-back twinges that had come on in her late twenties. The hardened dome of her tummy. Things she'd chalked up to her desk job or to being older. She should've known better.

"I'll send you home with a checklist. Fortunately, yours aren't the biggest I've seen. I say . . . we're looking at one the size of an apple. It's pedunculated, so say an apple on a stem. Then there's a few plums and grapes. You've got a little tree in here."

"Grapes don't grow on trees." The wand searched within her, testing her body's limits. I am all lining, she thought. And tumors. "When can I have the hysterectomy?"

"Oh we've got options before we get to that point. We could do a myomectomy, take out whatever we find. But you'd keep your uterus."

Claire watched the ceiling, how the glow around the recessed lights dilated. "That won't solve much if it's cancer."

"It's almost certainly not cancer." Her doctor smiled, and the lines on her pale face deepened, revealing all the other smiles she'd given to patients over the years. "And with a hysterectomy, if you ever wanted children—"

"That's not in the cards." Though Holm's face hadn't quite faded from her mind.

"Why don't you think about it, and I can send you home with some information?" Her doctor suddenly withdrew the wand, and Claire felt her body close around the absence. "I promise you it's not cancer. Just your regular uterine fibroids."

She sat up. Clutched the paper sheet. "Do they know," she murmured as her doctor neared the door, "why this happens?"

"You mean the cause?" Her fingers lingered on the doorknob. "Diet. Stress. Hormone levels. Maybe genetics." When Claire said nothing else, her doctor said, "It's going to be alright. We have some time."

UTERUS: ANTERIOR, SUBSEROSAL
(Size: 2.7 cm x 3.6 cm x 2.2 cm)

Maybe some meals never soften into thigh or belly meat, Claire thinks. Instead, she imagines them hardening inside a person: glasses of sweet tea with swirls of sugar, potatoes whipped with heavy cream, pie crust pressed lovingly into a scuffed pan, Auntie Glenna's macaroni casserole passed around the dinner table, burger patties popping on a neighbor's grill, slices of mud pie shared on the hood of a '94 Cadillac every Sunday afternoon. Momma leans forward and whistles through the gap in her front teeth. They'd been talking about the river before them—"Why is it so brown? . . . What makes it wind? . . . How far does it go?"—but Momma has paused. "You got a little something," she says, and Claire will miss this, the slow drag of her mother's thumb, the way it cleans her bottom lip.

AFTER HER APPOINTMENT, Claire stood in the OBGYN's teal lobby, the checkout line endless. She touched her fingers to her belly. The cold from the air-conditioning met the cold within her. How best to protect herself, to take responsibility for every inch of her body? It would take time to heal post-surgery, after the hysterectomy that seemed like her best chance. Someone would have to help her out of bed, carry her groceries up the four flights to her studio apartment. But Allie had her newborn and Jess was picking up every class she could to cover her rent.

Then there was Holm. That night of their breakup, he'd sat on her bedspread of hummingbirds, his colorless hair tied back from his face, his cheeks flushed. "You never tell me anything about what happened," he said. "Your mother *died*. When you were a child. And you have this aunt who only ever emails or sends packages. Who you never see. I—feel like I should be the person in your life who knows the whole story. I don't want to be some white guy you feel like you can't come to." And when she'd resisted, said that the past was *hers*, her mother's cancer was *hers*, he'd risen from her bed. Said he just couldn't do this anymore. He'd walked in silence to her door, that coat of his draped over his arm. Only on her apartment stairs had he turned around. "You know," he said, "I'm still here for you. In the way I can be."

But now she couldn't imagine asking for him, wanting his help with managing the pain, with guiding her out of the fog of anesthesia. She couldn't imagine his hands, those long cellist fingers that had pulled her body to attention when she'd seen him play at that concert, touching her with restraint. And he'd still want to know about the past, all the moments with her mother that shamed her.

Ahead, the line moved, the receptionist now helping a blonde woman in jeans and an argyle sweater. Claire lowered her fingers from her navel. Straightened. Maybe the surgery wouldn't be as intense as she expected, and she could manage well enough on her own. Alarms set for painkillers. Ice packs and heating pads. All her food prepared ahead of time. She might only need her landlady's son to help her up the stairs. This was life, really. How you pruned, adjusted, pinched back—all the work of taking care of yourself. No one else would.

When she reached the front of the line, the receptionist glanced at her, then back at her computer. "What's wrong? Your balance is settled."

"But I haven't paid."

Light flinched on the receptionist's purple glasses. "It was Sofia, right?"

"Claire. Coleman."

Beside the front desk, the bathroom door squeaked open and a woman stepped out. Immediate: the eye contact. The woman was shrouded in a green pullover, hood over her ponytail. She was two inches taller. They were both Black women. They looked nothing alike.

"I'm so sorry," the receptionist said. She looked Claire in the face, then Sofia. "It's just been a crazy day, and I wasn't paying attention."

"S'alright." Claire handed over her card for the co-pay. At the sound of Sofia's short laugh, her shoulders tensed.

They wound up in the elevator together, watching each other without looking. In a different time in her life—Mississippi summer, Momma and Auntie Glenna sharing sandwiches along the brown tendril of the Pearl River—it would never have felt like an *event* to pass another Black woman on the street. Yet, in this steel box, the stitches in the air tightened. They had only seconds.

"It's funny," Sofia said, toying with her hoodie's ties. "You take the whole morning off, drive all the way here, and they can't get it right." Her voice was deeper than Claire had imagined: no drawl, but textured, like a soft carpet rolled out.

"Where you from?"

"Alabama. Well—the Gulf. You?"

"Jackson. I could tell you didn't sound like Mississippi."

"Well," Sofia joked. "She sorta got the region right."

The elevator nudged the bottom floor. When the doors parted, the glass hallway let in a breath of autumn, the hickory and elm leaves easing toward their fiery shades. Sofia shouldered her tote, and Claire saw that she, too, wasn't wearing a wedding ring.

"So, twin of mine," Sofia said shyly. "You hungry? Or you have somewhere to be?"

SOFIA CHOSE A THAI RESTAURANT downtown, a box of dark hardwood and red tablecloths and lace flowers bursting into white stars. On the east side, thankfully, Claire thought. At least when she texted Allie and Jess an apology for missing their monthly Thursday lunch—*Sorry, something came up last minute*—she wouldn't be caught in a half lie. How could she explain this to them? It was just that most of the Black women she talked to existed on Reddit or other online forums, far from her life.

"You into spice?" Sofia asked, peeling off her hoodie. "They don't tone it down here."

Claire nodded and twirled her straw, the condensed milk fogging her tea. "Been a while, though. My ex always wanted to split every dish, but he'd have maybe two minutes before his forehead started sweating."

"I can give him credit for trying. Unless you're gonna tell me he doesn't deserve it?"

"No, he does." She sipped. Wondered if Sofia would care that Holm was white—though maybe it didn't matter since he was no longer hers.

"Okay . . . " Sofia's face dimpled a little as she smiled. "Maybe we'll get to that."

Claire looked at the menu, its print running together. The week before, she'd seen Holm lugging his cello across the west parking lot. She'd stood under the administration building's stone arches, gripping her office keys, watching their differences thin out like the near-gray strands of his hair: their ages, his friends' obsession with travel and fine dining, his large Danish family over in Chicago, his relentless desire to be relied upon. All of that vanished in the wake of the love that split her in a bright bolt. That love should've made a noise, a crack. He should've looked up and found her at once.

"Wow, Claire," Sofia said, her menu long set down. "He did a number on you, huh?"

But Sofia didn't push. The waiter, a teenager in black slacks and green high-tops, approached the table and took their orders of panang curry and pad kee mao.

Maybe, Claire thought as Sofia ordered in an assured alto, it was too easy to believe that a friendship could come from any Black woman who invited her out to lunch, a friendship where there'd be less to explain. Carefully, she folded her hope into a manageable size. They could turn out to have so little in common. They could disagree on politics, have different family lives, possess vastly different ideas about music and movies. She couldn't just assume she would be understood. Neither race nor shared blood had kept Auntie Glenna close.

Yet she could sense Sofia wanting something, too, the woman leaning forward as soon as the waiter removed their menus.

Sofia talked through the twenty minutes it took the food to arrive. She'd been born and raised in Mobile, daughter of a veterinarian (mother) and history teacher (father). But she'd been living *here* for just over a year, since starting her PhD in ecology, which sucked more than she thought it would, plus the fact that none of her peers got why she didn't want to join them for morning swims—it'd take forever to detangle her hair, no thank you. Really, when she wanted water, she wanted home. Her walks over the wetlands at dusk, the Mardi Gras celebrations, the crab boils at her brother's.

"I'm guessing you don't miss home?" Sofia paused, her noodles languid over her chopsticks.

"Parts." They *were* different, she and Sofia. Neither Momma nor Auntie Glenna had been to college. "I guess Ma was pretty determined about me leaving."

"What? She was from someplace else?"

"No. Jackson born and raised." Claire hesitated, but Sofia was still listening. "Buried."

"I'm sorry, I kinda got that sense. You don't have to talk about it, if you don't want."

Outside the table's window, a steel crane rose into the sky, preparing to deliver pipes to a construction site. Claire swallowed. Yet—there was a relief in the way Sofia had respected her privacy.

"She was just always tired," Claire murmured. "And she had this crazy heavy period. Once, she put my hand on her belly, and you could feel this hard thing in her stomach."

"Uh-uh. Hang on." Sofia leaned back. "You are not saying your momma died of fibroids."

"No." Claire drank her tea, and the cold froze her throat. "They misdiagnosed."

"Oh, thank God. I mean, not *thank God*. But I just can't hear about anybody dying from that right now." Sofia rested both palms on her stomach, which sloped out a little.

The restaurant closed around them.

It felt like someone had cupped them between two palms, so everything they weren't saying hummed, shared a warmth. She had only wanted similarity, a moment of respite in this town that could be hard, sometimes. And now Sofia was mirroring her.

"Two grapefruits," Sofia said into the silence. "Though I don't know why they have to call everything a fruit."

"I've got an apple," Claire said quietly. "A few plums and grapes. Maybe more."

There was a new openness to Sofia's face, like a bellflower revealing its nectar.

These weren't the stories you wanted to trade, not the connection you wanted to another person. And yet.

She'd already let them scrape her out twice, Sofia confessed, and now they wanted to remove her whole uterus. But she wanted *babies*. And even if there wasn't yet a man in the picture, she had to look out for her future self. There had to be something. Some natural remedy or diet that could shrink these doggone things.

At this, Claire decided.

"I'm having a hysterectomy," she said. "Until they take them out, they can't completely tell what's going on." Her fingers twinged with the longing to reach across the table, to take Sofia's wrist and say she'd talked about babies with Holm too. But she refrained; maybe that would be too much.

"I'm just saying," Sofia went on, "these doctors don't know everything."

"No, they don't."

"Even you and that tea. All that sugar, the little suckers feed on that stuff."

"Sure. I've heard that."

"Oh, come on. I don't sound that woo-woo, do I?"

The afternoon was going so well. Maybe she could try. "Ma and I used to live with my aunt, this big healer. All these herbs and jars in her house. This garden big enough to get lost in. So I guess that's one thing I miss. Big yards."

Sofia sat perfectly still. "Only your aunt?"

"Hmmm?"

"Only your aunt was the healer? I mean, not *you?*"

A shadow grew against the table. Their waiter, bringing the bill. Sofia didn't even glance down. Her lips were half-parted, more words waiting at the edge of them.

"No," Claire said. "My aunt always said you either had the gift or you didn't."

Slowly, Sofia broke eye contact. Then scanned the check. Before Claire could stop her, Sofia pulled out her credit card and closed it within the holder.

"You'll have to tell me about her," Sofia said. "Next time."

UTERUS: POSTERIOR, INTRAMURAL
(Size: 2.4 cm x 6.7 cm x 4.3 cm)

Auntie Glenna's garden grows larger than the house it sits behind. Rooms of azalea and sweet shrub, halls of twisted beautyberry. From its bounty and from Auntie Glenna's travels, the women in her family make walnut oil to cure athlete's foot, fig juice to heal ringworm, clove oil to soothe gums red and swollen as parachutes above loose teeth. If a friend or neighbor wants to pay in conversation, they let them. Otherwise, they sell their remedies for ten to twenty-five dollars a vial in their nursery in downtown Canton, among their other plants and perennials. But this morning, Claire has woken to find her mother and aunt home in the greenhouse, rolling burlap sacks on the healing table.

"I don't see why she can't go to Canton High like everybody else," Auntie Glenna is saying, wiping her hands on her black jeans. "And I sure as hell don't see why you've got to bend over backward to send her across town."

In response, Momma's voice is as soft as her hands on the leaves: "Isn't that what you're supposed to do for your child?"

Auntie Glenna brushes a gnat from her freckled skin. Her hand leaves behind a smear of green. "Since you're over there eavesdropping," she says, "tell my sister you don't want to go to private school, not if it means she'll be up all night cleaning floors."

Is her response the first real decision of her life? Or did the trouble begin even earlier, the first time she agreed to help Auntie Glenna dry herbs or the first time Momma quizzed her about the difference between a remedy and a poison?

Right now, she is thirteen. She always chooses her mother's side.

"You're thinking private school?" she asks.

And Momma winks, her brown eye brighter than her green one.

THE THING ABOUT ROUTINE: You could rely on it. Like a steady river, it could carve deep grooves into the bed of your life, allowing trouble to pass on through.

Claire had long mastered her late-fall rituals. Her quarterly trim and silk press. The annual camping trip with Jess and Allie. Her seasonal tonic, composed of ginger root, horseradish, and homemade apple cider vinegar, meant to ward off campus colds.

She needed such control. On the phone, when her doctor had resisted her request for a hysterectomy, she'd said, "I'm not asking. I have family history." Her doctor presented more evidence against it, said she'd seen her chart, but leiomyosarcoma wasn't genetic, and the way her fibroids looked on the ultrasound, there was no vascular indication—"I've already decided," Claire had repeated, and her doctor relented. The surgery was scheduled for January, the first week of the new year. Until then, she would rely on her routines. She would take care of herself, as she always had.

In mid-October, she received the expected email from Auntie Glenna. Her heart swelled:

Hope you're keeping well. I'm making it. Got my hands full with the new nursery hire. She'd rather be doing anything else but working. I got back from the Carolinas (the bay trees aren't what they used to be) and she's in the shop tapping away at her phone. You would think nobody's been in for months.

All this made me think about you, those kids you're helping. Am I the problem? I just need somebody to run the place right.

Expect a little something in the mail from me.

Love,

Auntie

Claire mulled over her reply for a week, wondering if she should write the sentences that so often stirred in her: *I did the best I could for Momma. I would've done things differently, if I'd have just known.* But it wasn't as if her aunt had ever said, *I know you tried, child that you were.*

The last time she'd seen Auntie Glenna had been years ago at the Jackson airport. August. Her seventeen-year-old self pulling her two college suitcases out of the trunk and Auntie Glenna helping. The sun hovering in the distance, both of them sweat smeared. "You'd better go on in," Auntie Glenna had said and hugged her so quickly that it was a brief meeting of moisture. "Before you're soaked." Claire had nearly said more: that she was always waiting for her mother to tell her what to do next, that it was *wrong* that her mother wasn't alive to see her off. But Auntie Glenna had already pulled back—and at the same time, they exhaled. The sound of relief. After the months of her mother's slow passing, each of them just brought up so much for the other. "Alright then," Claire had said, reaching for her suitcases as the planes roared overhead. "I'll let you know when I land."

Now they sent these emails only a handful of times per year, the rope of their familial bond reeled out. In her response, Claire wrote that she hoped Auntie Glenna had enjoyed her trip, that the weather was fickle in the Midwest too, that she should be nicer to the new employee. *With my students* . . . Claire typed, and shared stories about the undergraduates who came into the Diversity & Inclusion office burdened, wondering where all the people of color were, if it was a mistake to leave home for an island of white people who often said the wrong thing. Then she thanked Auntie Glenna for the Dr. Bird cake that had arrived. "Why do they call it that?" Momma had asked every year, then plucked off her candles and ate. This year, she would've been fifty-six. Which, in her own quiet way, Auntie Glenna was acknowledging.

Claire sent the email. It felt like tossing a coin into a fountain: habit, rather than belief.

As the weeks crept along, Claire felt change arrive in cool drifts, passing through the carefully wrapped cloth of her life. Allie's child turned one, which meant a birthday party where all of them took turns helping the infant remove glittery wrapping paper. Jess kept going on and on about a Christmas meditation retreat in Mexico, apologizing for how she'd miss their usual get-together this year.

Claire only nodded. Holm was gone, which meant no talk of visiting his family for the holidays.

But there was Sofia, this new, chronically online person. The details of Sofia's life trickled into Claire's timeline, tiny shoots pushing their way through tender soil:

Sofia in the field with fellow grad students, her bare feet on a deck railing as the others dragged nets through dark waters.

Sofia making notes beside a plate of weed brownies in a cherrywood library.

Sofia and some handsome dreadlocked man taking a selfie at a local movie theater. Then taking another in what looked like Sofia's apartment, given the casement windows behind the ochre couch, the man's gaze failing to find the camera in time.

When Claire sent Sofia an article about pleasurable sex post-hysterectomy, Sofia immediately messaged back: *Did you know there are whole forums about shrinking fibroids with green tea extract?*

Sure, Claire responded. How to be kind, to this person you wanted to know? *But how many times has it worked?*

Sofia didn't reply. A few hours later, she changed the banner on her profile to a *Vogue* photograph of Rihanna, radiant in a red-lace bodysuit and sprouting a baby bump.

When Auntie Glenna's cake arrived, Sofia came over to the apartment to share. The last time somebody was in here . . . Claire thought, then couldn't figure out the math. Because of the baby, Allie always asked if the three of them could meet at hers.

Claire arranged the slices onto two petal-pink plates, watching Sofia take a slow turn through her apartment. What did Sofia think of her, now that they'd had several online interactions, a few more hangs in coffee shops, walks down the narrow sidewalks of Sofia's neighborhood, the honey locusts now bare, their leaves coating the ground in bright yellow? This newfound friend stood with her hips to one side, arms crossed as she studied the coral walls, the cream carpet, the study abroad photographs with Jess and Allie in Argentina, the Beyoncé vinyl stacked by the record player. "Am I crazy for still hoping she'll win album of the year?" Sofia asked, turning over the black cover.

Over cake, they talked about the man Sofia was seeing, who apparently was also from Mississippi, a graduate from Alcorn State with a degree in biology. But the jury was out on whether she could be serious about him, Sofia said. She'd asked if father-hood was on his radar and he'd balked—but who had time to beat around the bush?

"Which part of Mississippi were you from again?" Sofia asked. She'd finished her slice of cake and nudged the cinnamon crumbs from her plate. "Sometimes people say Jackson when they're really from someplace else."

"Canton." Claire flaked off the glazed crust, and the spiced pineapple smell wafted between them, until Sofia asked for more.

You would like her, Claire thought, and hoped her mother would hear it, wherever she was in the afterlife.

She brought slices to Allie and Jess during their next lunch, delayed because the baby had given Allie a cold and Jess had picked up extra classes to pay for the meditation retreat. (The irony, Jess muttered, of quitting her teaching job to be healthier, then working herself to death to relax in Playa del Carmen.) Under a black umbrella, they ate linguini with mushroom sauce, the weather clinging to the last of its warmth.

"You know, you don't have to keep your little secret," Jess said, and flicked the bow on her blue bandanna. "We're not dumb."

Claire kept her face even. "What secret?"

"Come on." Allie's mouth crinkled. "We wanted you two to work things out."

Her friends, so attuned to her, to changes she didn't even know registered. They waited for her response, all those years in their faces.

"It's not Holm," Claire said. "There's—a friend I'm getting to know. Her name's Sofia." Maybe she would introduce them all. Soon.

Some shared light flickered in Allie's and Jess' eyes.

"Ignore us," Allie said. "It was just a stupid thought."

UTERUS: ANTERIOR, INTRAMURAL
(Size: 5.4 cm x 5.1 cm x 3.6 cm)

Momma makes herself integral, a practice that began with the pink bind of pregnancy and now refuses to unwind across time. Every morning, she drives Claire down the I-55 corridor toward Madison and Ridgeland, to the white-columned private school. In the afternoons, Momma works at the shop, and in the evenings, fries catfish or chicken for dinner while Auntie Glenna finishes the last of the healings. A small corner of Claire's mind is reserved for tracking her mother's whereabouts, which is how she can feel Momma lingering in the doorway, watching as she reads AP textbooks until she's blind, her old friends, her old life falling away. This sort of studying, her mother has told her, will open up the world, if only she can play the right games. So she ignores the strain in her eyeballs, the ache in her jaw, which she will do for years. "You don't think they're smarter than you, do you?" Momma asks, resting a hand on the doorframe. She hasn't yet headed back to the school for her nightly janitorial shift. "Do they know anything they haven't read about? Do they even care about really learning it?" Those hands, tapping out their impatience. They are forever red and chapped, yet Momma still paints her fingernails lavender. Somehow, despite the fact that her mother barely has time to eat a complete meal, her torso curves out. When Claire says nothing, Momma says, "You can survive this for three more years." Which Claire silently recites as she sits in classrooms where her teachers pass over her and her peers plan parties in their Madison manors. Claire grips the desk her mother cleaned the night before, its polished surface a raft without which she'd drift downriver.

THEN—DECEMBER ARRIVED. AND Sofia was suddenly gone. All their lunches and online interactions vanishing like the last of the leaves.

It hasn't been so long, Claire told herself as she left for work each morning, entering the campus gates, the chill. Two days since she'd texted Sofia about the hysterectomy: *U scheduled yours?* Then three. Then four. Then more silence after a follow-up: *U doing okay? U get my text?* Usually, Sofia was always on her phone, always quick to respond, even when they were disagreeing. Now, her online posts had ceased. In response, Claire's own timeline slowed.

You really do have only yourself, Claire thought. Then buried herself in work.

In the free yoga class Jess gave her one Thursday, ninety minutes in a steamy room where she kept picturing her to-do list, she felt that inner knot as she bent and twisted, her body warning her not to move the wrong way. "You alright?" Jess whispered behind her as the regular yogis took headstands. Her friend's fingers adjusted her hips, coming dangerously close to her fruit tree. "All good," Claire said, though Jess lingered before moving on to the next person.

She was not quite ignoring her body, Claire told herself in moments she felt the apple shudder within her. She was merely waiting out the days where she passed undergrads juling nervously on the quad during finals, the meetings where her colleagues worried about cuts to their programs. All of which she would tend to. Just after she could tend to herself.

At the end of one workday, the heaviness in her lower abdomen increased, like a stone sinking deeper into mud. She walked to the pharmacy on the campus outskirts, the serviceberry trees now skeletal, every human padded in a wool coat. When she checked her phone, Sofia still hadn't replied.

But what was she hoping for? Maybe they were not really friends. A quiet fear had grown in her each day without a response.

She walked down the pharmacy's egg-white aisles, searching for pain relievers, something instant that she wouldn't have to brew. For the upcoming hysterectomy, she'd still planned only for her solitary recovery, though it frightened her that there would be days in the hospital, then weeks in her apartment when she couldn't lift anything, perhaps not even herself off the toilet. Maybe part of her had been harboring some fantasy that, if Sofia decided to get the surgery too, they could take turns helping each other, understanding what it meant to go through this. But maybe even that was too intimate, too soon.

She toyed with the box of Aleve and calculated how much was left in her account. With her salary significantly lost to student loans, it was already an effort to cough up the five grand for the procedure.

But you had to adjust. She decided on generic pills and lifted them from the shelf. Then—felt a warm pressure on her face.

There, on the other side of the row, was Holm. Pale hair pulled into a ponytail, a sheen in his blue eyes that could've come from the overhead lights or from within. In this moment, he looked younger, face soft and unlined because no smile shifted his skin. Then he did smile, a little.

"You alright?" His gaze lingered on the painkillers, then her.

"Surviving." It could've been true. Anything could be true, if he kept talking. She'd missed his voice these three months. "Your elbow again?"

He lifted a plastic box that contained a mesh brace. "Among other things."

Silence pooled between them, and they stood unmoving in its center. It has been so hard, she thought, and saw it in him too.

Then he murmured her name.

WHEN THEY WERE IN her apartment, she knew he wouldn't stay. Each glide of his body into hers and out again was practice for a much longer leaving. She knew it, just as she knew he wouldn't have approached her if he'd been seeing someone else, that he wouldn't have suggested her smaller apartment if he wanted more than this one night. Still, she surrendered, feeling his index finger hook around the back of her knee and open her body to him. She ignored the tree quivering inside her. So much of what she held threatened to drop.

But when they'd finished, he did not get up. He lay beside her, hidden within her dotted sheets. She'd loved his quiet, how it contained some deeper knowledge, a way of paying attention.

Once, he'd massaged her lower back when he saw her bending stiffly over groceries, and another time, he'd bought her an art book of iris varieties because she'd lingered before it in a bookstore. She'd always thought he'd liked their shared quiet too.

"I kept thinking," he said. With the sun abandoning the windows, the blond hairs on his chest looked like they were dwindling. "That maybe you didn't have room to talk about your family because I was always so caught up in mine. All those stupid holidays. And that time I dragged you to Copenhagen. And we were always at my place."

"I loved your place." She'd loved Copenhagen, too, those few weeks they'd spent eating cardamom buns in outdoor cafés, taking the immaculate trains through the bisected loop of the city, biking along the water with his cousins, whose last names matched his first, his mother having given him her maiden name.

"Those were just examples," Holm said. "I'm saying, maybe I shouldn't have said you were isolating me. It's allowed to be your business, not wanting to say more about your aunt or your mother or anyone else."

The pillow cradled her neck as she leaned back. She'd tried to keep her life so small. She'd never wanted it to grow beyond her capacity to tend it herself.

"I . . . like your life, honestly," Holm was saying. Her hair softened under his fingers. "And I like me *in* your life. If you do too."

UTERUS: FUNDAL, INTRAMURAL
(Size: 6.2 cm x 7.1 cm x 4.7 cm)

Bone weary as Momma is, Claire asks for more as a sixteenth birthday gift. It's seventy dollars for a relaxer at the neighborhood salon, and this will make her less of an anomaly at the private school, where the popular

Black girls have oil-slick hair and avoid her, wanting no association with somebody who'd worn a gris-gris bag her first day. They should be her people. They should see her, in those hallways, and offer what sanctuary they can.

"A relaxer?" Momma says from the couch. "Does anyone know what they put in that stuff?" But Claire argues that she got straight A's last semester, that she deserves this, that Auntie Glenna is traveling again, taking long camping trips in wetland forests to gather elusive herbs, and isn't here to protest. This is how she and Momma talk now, presenting a tally of things each of them has done for the other. This time, Momma, whose wrinkled eyes are half-closed, doesn't ask more questions to make her reconsider.

In the salon chair, Claire tips back and feels the beautician's hands parting her hair in neat sections, then the medical tingle of the relaxer, then the fire that makes her scalp feel like scorched earth. Still, she does not whimper. She has asked for this, she will be less alone. And Momma's in the shop corner, napping with her face against the glass. Already, spring has sapped what's left of her energy.

Claire knows she is beautiful when her hair is a flat sheet against her face. Who cares if Momma says nothing as she hands the beautician a hundred-dollar bill? Everyone in the salon is getting the same style, and already she is growing used to the sharp, hydroxide smell that hovers in a cloud around her face. She will think nothing of it again until she is twenty-six, when she reads an article in ESSENCE magazine linking hair relaxers to uterine troubles.

But the relaxer won't be the worst part of this day. It will be her and Momma walking across the glittering parking lot, Momma ahead of her and moving with a strange sort of determination. The wooden heels of Momma's clogs collect dark-red splotches. And when Claire's gaze trails higher, the sight pierces her.

A thick fluid streams from her mother's full thighs. In the sunlight, it looks like water before it looks like blood.

THE MORNING AFTER THEIR REUNION, she woke to Holm in her kitchen. She lay still on the bed, watching him fuss with her coffee maker, not nearly as svelte and modern as his. Here he was, popped back into her life, bringing everything, including his easy annoyance. And Jess and Allie had predicted it.

"Why are you laughing?" he said, and when she shook her head, he asked, "Is it some Beyoncé thing?"

Her laughter dissipated as the hours passed, as he lingered in her apartment and streamed a recent Oscar winner on her laptop. Ordinarily, his cinephile nature would've made him insist they use the larger TV and ornate speaker system back at his place, yet she could sense him not wanting to leave her bed, too much time lost.

I'm having surgery, she considered saying. And yet—in the snap of a single evening—she'd grown unsure. They'd always assumed their relationship would end in children, so perhaps he would try to talk her out of a hysterectomy. A frightening thought, given the part of her that now wanted other things. With him.

My mother, she began inwardly, and against her back, he shifted, his arm around her waist. The laptop screen displayed a family in identical shades of blue setting up a picnic in a cherry orchard.

She was barely watching. If they try the myomectomy and they're wrong, she thought, and he murmured, "Tell me, what's been going on with you?"

So he wasn't watching the movie either. She thought of telling him about Sofia instead, about her hope that they were still friends, in a way that went beyond merely being useful to each other.

Claire shook her head. Said only, "Nothing. I missed you like you wouldn't believe."

A few days later, they walked to Allie's townhome for dinner, her friends brimming in the brick doorway. "You better not lose your mind again," Jess said and swatted Holm's shoulder when he flushed. Allie, who'd been about to join in, went, "Hold on," and whipped into the house, where her husband shouted for help with the baby.

As everyone sat around the dinner table—Jess refilling the rosé and Allie nuzzling the baby's downy ring of hair and Allie's husband bringing out the lasagna and Holm making faces to the baby's gummy delight—Claire laced her fingers in her lap. Why did her body have to trouble her now, in this season of her life, filled with potential?

Everyone helped themselves to seconds, except Jess, who quietly announced that she'd made vegan cheesecake, if anyone was interested. Claire said sure and Jess smiled at her, grateful, and said, "I worked on it a long time."

Claire's phone rang as she was helping to clean, carrying saucers across the den to the corridor kitchen, the sink full of loopy baby plastics. Sofia's name flashed on the screen. So here she was, reaching out after all. And through a phone call, no less.

"Don't be mad," Sofia said.

Claire glanced over her shoulder, as if Sofia were somehow close by and could see her face lighting up. On the other side of the pass-through and across the den, the baby was crawling toward Holm, flat hands on the carpet, bum swiveling. Everyone watched her like they'd never seen anyone move. "Why would I be mad?" Claire said.

"Your auntie's shop is Coleman Herbs and Remedies, isn't it?"

Claire's pulse stilled in her neck. After three weeks of Sofia not responding to her texts, she'd wondered if Sofia had simply changed her mind about wanting to know her. Or if the fibroids had degenerated and one of Sofia's grad school friends had rushed her to the ER. But this.

"Why are you asking if you already know?" she said.

"I just had to try. I searched your last name. And Canton. I know you think surgery is the only option, but there's—"

"You do need surgery." She moved deeper into the kitchen, toward its corner. "We do."

"I spoke to your aunt. She's saying she can help. But you didn't ask her."

Claire braced herself against the counter, knees slack. She was seeing the family shop, the red shelves and gray-green walls. The violation of Sofia reaching out to that space. Now Auntie Glenna's freckled face appeared before her in Allie's cabinet glass.

"She told me," Sofia said, voice low. "About your mom. But that was different."

"I have to go. I can't deal with this right now."

"She says she'll help me, if you'll come too. I can ask her . . . if she'd do it just for me. But she said both of us."

In the distance, her friends cooed to the crawling child: *Over here, over here.* Inside Claire, some long buried place emerged from its sinkhole, and she swallowed it back down. Auntie Glenna had said nothing to her, not even over email. She could scarcely remember the last time she'd heard her aunt's voice. Aloud she said, "She doesn't want to talk to me."

"She does."

Claire hesitated. It was too much, Sofia calling. Saying things that overwhelmed.

"Do it for me?" Sofia's voice grew higher. "I'd pay for everything. I'd—feel so grateful. I wouldn't be asking if it wasn't important."

Claire said nothing. All this time with Sofia. All the small ways they'd confided in each other. Only now could she hear the underside of Sofia's questions: "Only your aunt was the healer? . . . Which part of Mississippi were you from again?" She'd been used. Or—maybe Sofia was relying on her, as the only person who could help.

From far away, Holm called, "Claire? Where'd you go? Jess wants to take a picture."

"Please?" Sofia whispered. "I know you think it's crazy, but it's my body. No one knows what's better for it than me."

✳

UTERUS: SUBSEROSAL, PEDUNCULATED
(Size: 8.2 cm x 9.3 cm x 6.7 cm)

They have been in the emergency room too long. Around them, patients cough into their shirt collars or hold crying children or stare, dazed, at the receptionist's desk. Claire's helped Momma clean up in the bathroom and brought her coffee, and now Momma's perked up a bit, interrogating the woman next to her about her sudoku strategies. After Claire's paced for twenty minutes, Momma says, "You want them to get you a room too?" But Claire, who only has her permit, drove them here, drilled through with the awareness that everything depended on her. Even though Momma's herself again, it's hard to relinquish the role of adult.

"Ninety-nine percent chance they're uterine fibroids," the doctor says when, three hours later, they finally have a room and the ultrasound results. He's black haired and hazel eyed, taking in Momma's belly at a glance. "They're pretty common in your community."

"My community?" Momma asks, and Claire's ears prick. She has learned to hear beneath words.

"Yes. African American." The doctor presses on Momma's belly gently, then firmer. "The bleeding's contained?"

"I've got a napkin on."

"Let's do iron pills. And I'll give you something to stop that bleeding altogether." The doctor sighs and removes his hands. "Listen, we can do an MRI, but I don't know your insurance situation, and nine times out of ten, these tumors are benign. Only you can decide what you want to do. Usually, it's surgery or live with them."

Claire watches this man, who glances through the door's window. "How much is the MRI?" she asks. If she had known this was coming. If she just hadn't begged for a relaxer, for what connections it might offer.

The doctor says, "That's between you and your insurance."

"Here we go," Momma says and leans back into her pillow. "Calling those grifters again."

Claire watches this moment, as she will continue to watch it for years. She has been raised by two women who have bent an impossible world toward them. She knows that black cohosh tea can soothe cramps (but can be harmful in high doses) and that primrose oil can ease heavy bleeding. She has been raised to be studious, to use her textbooks when her teachers' lectures confuse her, and to trust her instincts on exams. How can she not offer what relief she can, when Momma has looked after everything for so long? She can do this, brew the elixirs that help the body heal itself, that keep tumors from getting out of control. At least until they reach the summer, when school's closed and Auntie Glenna is back to help Momma decide what she wants.

"Let's get you home," Claire tells her mother, whom she convinced to come here in the first place.

WHEN SHE STEPPED THROUGH the airport doors, Mississippi flung its damp warmth around her. She'd forgotten this, the mild December nights of her childhood, the erasure of dusk at the horizon. Throughout the plane ride, she'd shivered beside Sofia, silently rehearsing what to say to her aunt and to this person who'd convinced her to come back. But now that she'd arrived, the words vanished.

"So this is you," Sofia said. She pulled her new braids off her face.

Around Claire, sixteen years slowly dissolved. People in jeans and T-shirts passed her and Sofia on the sidewalk, gliding along with their luggage. A father nudged a child toward a waiting vehicle, his speech slow and rhythmic. This, she remembered, was what it was like to stand in a flow of other Black folk. There was recognition beyond skin. You could see somebody in the particular loop of a businesswoman's silk scarf or a man leaning against a street sign, waiting for his lover. "It's time to get something to *eat*," said a rail-thin woman in purple who stood next to her and Sofia. So what if they were strangers, her lined eyebrows said. Point was, they'd all journeyed to get here.

As the Uber carried her and Sofia onto the interstate, Claire imagined she was being unborn, moving backward through time—or perhaps being reborn, entering a city adjacent to the Jackson she remembered. Before leaving Holm's apartment, she'd told him, "I'm going to Mississippi for a few days, to help a friend with some health troubles." He'd hesitated, wondering if he should come with her, so she said, "I'll tell you more when I get back." For once, he refrained from protesting. Instead, he made her promise to call, to tell him what she wanted. But what could she say about these thick oaks and dogwoods lining the freeway, the orange haze of downtown in the distance? How low these buildings looked compared to other capital cities, their glow like a series of tea lights. Occasionally, when some story made national news, she'd pore over articles about the old pipes and boil-water notices, the climbing homicide rates. But the Uber driver rode with the windows down, the air seeping into the Honda and moving around her face familiar. Her hair rose into it.

Their Airbnb sat tucked off State St. in the Fondren District, and approaching it felt like entering a different world entirely. "Hurting land," her mother had once called the area, since it had housed the insane asylum and the patients whose grave markers the earth had swallowed. Even during her childhood, Claire remembered Fondren as a collection of vacant buildings. But now there were restaurants with bright neon signs and long farmhouse tables. Tourists crowding the wide sidewalks. Rainbowed canvases in art galleries and vintage clothes in the windows.

"You alright?" Sofia asked, pausing her conversation with the Uber driver, who'd been chatting about meeting his friends when he got off work. Claire said nothing. She'd come all the way here for a person who checked on her only as an afterthought.

They pulled onto a side street, their driver guiding them around a pothole. The rental property peered back at them, a dove-gray cottage sheltered by dormant crape myrtles.

"Don't worry, I got you," their driver said, carrying their luggage to the front steps. Despite all his talk of meeting his friends, he suddenly didn't mind that he had somewhere to be. As he smiled and set their bags in the entryway, his white teeth were like a wedge of bright fruit in his mouth. "Y'all be safe, alright?" he said. And left them.

"What a sweetie," Sofia said, closing the door, though Claire was looking at their digs. Some other family had made room for them, the décor too personal. That herringbone couch was something else. So were the framed pictures of poodles.

"I think the food in here is theirs," Sofia said as she stooped into the fridge light. "Though I'm so hungry I'd pay them for leftovers."

They walked twenty minutes to a restaurant off Duling, Sofia oddly silent now that she was on the verge of getting what she wanted. There was no wait for the oyster bar they'd chosen, its seashell and colored-glass fragments pressed into the walls and picking up their shadows. Even this place had been changed, Claire realized, studying the grid of windows, the long narrow hall through the restaurant's side doors. It looked like an old elementary school.

"This might be dangerous to ask," Sofia said when their oysters were delivered, glistening in their shells. "But we cool, after I dragged you back here?"

A little space opened in her chest. So Sofia knew what she'd done, cared about the impact. "You can't bet on this healing, Sofia," Claire said.

"Why not? Your aunt was telling me a good deal of it is intention."

"The only intention you should have is doing everything you can. So it doesn't matter if somebody else makes a mistake."

"I hope you get that I'm trying to do that. And it's not cancer. I couldn't have the biopsy, but my doctor's pretty sure."

Biopsy. Something in Claire reeled backward. Her doctor hadn't mentioned that option. Even when she'd pushed for the hysterectomy, her doctor hadn't said a biopsy was something they could do.

"How you feeling about seeing your auntie?" Sofia asked, taking another oyster.

It took Claire a long while to return. Biopsy. "I don't know."

Sofia tipped back her oyster and returned the empty shell to its bed of ice. "I don't understand you two. If somebody was my family and we'd been through something together, you couldn't separate me from them."

"Maybe. It's easy to think that."

But Auntie Glenna had returned from traveling, her suitcase bulging. She took one look at Momma and said, "How long she been like this? Can't you tell what you're giving her ain't working?"

"She wanted to get mom to this doctor she knew," Claire went on, lowering her voice. "Though it had spread by then."

She and Sofia were the only ones in the restaurant, the waitstaff engaged in their own conversations beside the bar. Still, it was hard to look Sofia in the face. *Cancer or no, I would be there for your surgery*, she wanted to say. *I would be there so you could have something that works.* Because how many elixirs had she made her mother that spring? How many times had she drawn Epsom salt baths or massaged cypress oil onto her mother's hard belly or made beet juice to cleanse her blood, which flowed and flowed. Nothing shrank, which maybe was the cancer and maybe was not. "We should call Auntie," she'd said, though Momma kept saying not now, wait, let the school year end, let things settle down. Momma hadn't listened. Like Sofia wouldn't listen now, on this eve of her attempted healing. How on earth did people stand baring themselves to other people? You always met the wall of how they saw the world.

"I don't want you to be disappointed," Claire said finally. When she looked down at the platter of oysters, she had no memory of eating, though a film that could've been salt coated her mouth. "I just want everything to work out for you."

"It has to."

"I know."

Silently, they drank water. Then, Claire said, "The weeks you didn't respond, I figured you were sorting something out. But I didn't think it was this."

Sofia said nothing for a while. Then pressed two fingers to her belly. Almost the way she'd done before—but higher this time, above the navel. "You remember that guy I was telling you about? Well . . . *surprise*."

Claire couldn't see anything. Then she understood. Sofia was touching something small and loved and still growing.

"I'm six weeks along," Sofia murmured. "Apparently."

"You're going to be alright," Claire said, which was the only thing she could give. There could be no surgery now.

"You too," Sofia said. Then smiled. "You and that white dude on your timeline."

Claire reached for her glass. Her small grin rose, despite herself.

"Mmhmm," Sofia said. "Queen of secrets."

THE LAST FIBROID, TOO SMALL TO PICTURE.
She has spent so much time trying to
understand how bodies decide their
growths, their patterns. But there
are rules that will forever elude her:

Like why fungus finds her aunt's rose blooms late that summer. Or why neither the earth nor the doctors can save the most important person in the world. Or why her mother, between stretches of sleep, will wake and ask her endless questions, the person she was still wrapped in the person who is ending.

"But why would I be born your sister?" Momma asks with slitted eyes as Auntie Glenna rubs aloe into her hands, no longer chapped, but peeling. Claire stands in the doorway. Her mother is an infant swaddled in white sheets. She does not even fill the square of light coming through the window.

"And why are you looking like that?" Momma says, finding her in the doorway. "And what are you bringing me now? And why can't you just leave me alone?"

THE NEXT MORNING, the Uber deposited them at the house in Canton. Same clay brick. Same garden growing thick and dense behind its frame, like hair teased from the back of a scalp. Tree roots pushed through the sidewalk, and the sun sliced onto the crooked porch. It hurt less than she thought it would, looking at it. This place had long dwelled in her.

"That your aunt?" Sofia asked, voice low.

Claire let herself see the figure on the porch. That high yellow skin and that stern nose. The litter of freckles and the brown hair finally lightened to white. Auntie Glenna had already found her, facing in her direction. For an entire year after Momma's passing, they'd communicated mostly in half phrases: *Yes. No. I can't. Dinner's on the stove.* It was so hard to take care of somebody else, outside of the obvious ways. Especially when you'd so keenly felt your limitations.

A lagoon of skin contracted at Auntie Glenna's collarbone. Then she raised one hand and pointed, the same gesture she'd once used for customers: *Around back.* If the years since they'd last seen each other were collapsing, they fell on her aunt's hunched shoulders.

The garden plants touched her and Sofia as they passed through, stroking their wrists and upper arms. Their pair pushed through the green, its force above the stone path.

"Keep coming around," Auntie Glenna said from a distance. "You remember where it is."

Which she did.

"I can't," Sofia said behind her. She bent beneath the low branches, and there were the soft mounds of her breasts, the larger mound of her belly. "I can't even see."

"It's here," Claire said, and pushed the final branch out of the way. The greenhouse shone in the winter light. And beneath it— Auntie Glenna, holding the door open. Saying, "Hurry along."

When she and Sofia lay side by side on the healing table, Claire felt the pressure in her abdomen rise, her tree tipping up. Once, when she'd been an infant, new and mewling, her mother had lain her here for naps, the table endlessly wide. Though she was so much bigger now. Sofia breathed heavily. This table could scarcely hold them both.

"Relax," Claire said, and cupped Sofia's hand. Sofia's fingers gripped back.

Auntie Glenna's face eased overhead, the deepened lines around her eyes echoing the furrows between her brows. There was so much that face held in: the long nights that year, the valerian root that did nothing to help them sleep, their first Christmas apart, Claire at Jess' tinseled home and Auntie Glenna on extended travels along the Florida coast, all the separate holidays thereafter.

Oh, Auntie's face said now. *You're so different.*

Except she wasn't. It was familiar, the glass ceiling caked with dry leaves. So was Auntie Glenna murmuring her starting prayers. This was how things got done.

Her apple tree grew heavy, resisting. Sofia tightened her grip.

There would only be a short while of this. Twenty minutes, if what she remembered of healing was the same. She would stay in this spot, alongside Sofia. This was what they demanded of each other: the showing up, the bearing witness, the honoring of the need for belief.

"Beloveds," Auntie Glenna said, "you have to let go now."

When her aunt pressed her stomach, Claire felt the tree stir in her, the apple bobbing to the surface of her skin. Not pain, but the edge of it. She braced herself, gripping the table, her neck sinking into the basin between her shoulders. Beside her, Sofia made a sound stranded between a moan and a gasp.

Claire closed her eyes against her aunt's hand. Then—when she opened them, her aunt watched her, separate from the healing. Such a long journey in that look, some truth held back.

This was the whole point, Claire understood. She'd been summoned here to be touched like this, because her aunt wanted to reach her in the only way she could. Auntie Glenna could make a wayward husband come back, could make fertile the soil of a woman's belly, had once taught a reluctant tooth to grow in a toddler's mouth. Yet she was saying she could not fix this and understood why Claire could not either, back then. Nor could she speak about any of it.

But imagine being here, a voice in Claire said. Back in Mississippi. Back home. Imagine having collected so many other hands in your absence—Jess and Allie and Holm and Sofia—and lying on this healing table with the memory of them. Imagine the accumulation of such flawed care, how you'd keep trying to receive it. And still, that didn't mean you couldn't tell people to do better.

"You feel this?" Auntie Glenna said, voice wet.

What she felt was a folding beneath her navel. Later, she would think it was her tree bowing in knowledge of all that would come: She would fly home and tell Holm about her mother, so it would no longer divide them. Jess would return from Mexico with food poisoning, and Claire would pick up her antibiotics and sit with her while she cried about the classes she was missing, when she so needed the pay. Allie would confess that she didn't know herself anymore, that parenthood had pitched her into a life she didn't recognize, and could they please go somewhere, the three of them, so she could remember?

In January, Claire would demand the biopsy, her OBGYN insisting she take painkillers for the cramping, the suction. "I thought so," her doctor said when the results came back negative. The phone made her voice strangely small. "I just didn't want to try anything invasive, before. And if you'd been right . . . if it was cancer—. Well, I didn't want to make things worse."

By July, Sofia would give birth to a wisp of a boy, a determined little thing who'd grown around the crags of her body. "At least your aunt gave me this," she'd say while Claire stood beside her in the neonatal unit. "At least she did what she could."

And all these people in Claire's life would be there when she had the myomectomy during summer break. She was shocked by how light she felt weeks after, her belly emptied. Her doctor would text her to check in. Holm would help her into bed and rub the gas from her shoulders and whisper about them finding a place together. Jess would bring fruit and fresh-baked salmon. Allie would curl beside her on the couch and say, "Please tell us everything from now on," and Claire would hesitate before saying, "Please make it easy to."

One morning, Claire would wake to Auntie Glenna in her apartment kitchen, making peppermint tea for the discomfort. "Don't argue," Auntie Glenna would say. "You know mine's better than yours." And Claire would think of her mother, who'd been better than them both.

Between her aunt's hand and the healing table, that tree in Claire's body shifted, as if to tell her what it could.

Or else that feeling was simply another part of her body, shriveling in this moment, in the face of this small healing being offered. She did not want to remove herself from it. If she could grow even a seed of belief, she did not want to be removed.

TILL IT AND KEEP IT

IN THE BEGINNING, THERE WAS HER SISTER'S BREATHING. Which meant neither of them had died.

It was faint, a slip of sound in the truck's stillness. But it reached into the front seats and nudged Brie awake. She lay over the console, an ache in her ribs, sweat on her eyelids. Against her wrist, morning light fell in a thin orange beam. So she could see colors again, which meant the illness was fading. She'd been smart to pull off the road—sometimes, rest was all you needed.

"Harper," she said, "wake up. We're still a long ways out."

Her sister's breathing quieted. Brie felt behind her, arms weak, neck too stiff to turn. If she could just touch Harper, surely she'd wake too?

This was hardly the worst they'd been through—unlucky as they were, born into prolonged summers and floods rushing deep into the coast and dwindling federal relief. There was the land they'd worked in Low America for years, the trees more branch than fruit. The miles of brown fields after they'd fled Randall's farm and the masses of white tents clustered outside silver cities and along freeway exits. On more than one occasion, thin-hipped walking men waved down their truck as it sped past, but who knew if such men carried viruses or meant them harm: any kindness had to be carefully doled out. After the sisters had flashed their vaccine cards and passed the health inspection at the Arkansas line, they'd stood in a shallow creek while Brie shaved Harper's deep-honey curls. The green city lights wavering in the distance made Harper's hair shudder on the water's surface. "I don't care what it looks like," Harper had said, gripping Brie's elbow. "Just so I don't feel his hands in it."

"I got you," Brie murmured, tying a wrap, red as a caul, over her handiwork. "It'll look good." She finished right before the outage drowned them in darkness.

In the truck, Brie finally twisted to glimpse Harper behind her. The wrap fell over her sister's cheek, flattened against the back seat. Who knew anymore, how a virus would go. Some filled your lungs with fluid and made your muscles go liquid for weeks; others made your skin ache even in moonlight. This one had made Harper break out in hives once they were well into Tennessee, then start asking why the sun looked as brown as the trees. As she drove, Brie said, "Just hang on. We'll stop soon," and passed her sister a canister of tea leaves to chew. But whatever was ailing Harper hit Brie too. As the hot pressure spread through her skull, she eased off the road, into woods blurry as gray flames. She cussed. Then prayed: *Lord, cover us.* It was different from her usual prayer: *Lord, let us get the chance to taste something green.*

Brie repeated her sister's name. They hadn't survived so much for her to lose Harper now.

Then she saw the orange and green shapes outside the window. The orange globes, dimpled and striped pink. The green, a sharp tip. It took her a minute to recognize them, long as it had been since she'd seen such fruit.

"Harper," she said. "There's peaches out there."

As if he'd heard, a man appeared at the window, the peaches vanishing behind his brown face. He opened the door, cool air rushing in. Then he lifted her against him, and her whole body split with pain. Her neck couldn't hold her head, which tipped over his arm. "God almighty," he said. "There's two of you."

She sank her teeth into his shoulder. Held tight until she felt his skin break.

He cussed. She felt him grip her thighs, trying not to drop her. Then his grip was gone, and so was everything else.

SHE WOKE IN a wooden shed that smelled of grass and sweat. In the bed beside her, Harper slept curled against the rose-patterned sheets, her fingernails dull in the moonlight falling through the window. When Brie woke again, it was to the sound of splashing: the man stood at the sink, scrubbing her patchwork jeans with a bar of soap. She yelped, fearing her own nakedness before him. Then he was moving toward her—or toward Harper—the lone light bulb swinging above his low curls. She aimed her fists at his forehead, striking once before he caught her wrists. His hands were cool and damp, and this brought her back to her senses. Someone had dressed her in a thin blouse.

"Nothing's going to happen to you," he said, though he didn't let go. His shirt had slipped in the tussle, exposing a white patch covering his shoulder. "Go on back to sleep, and I'll get Lauren in here soon as I can." But Brie didn't sleep, not for a while. She studied the scythes and rakes hanging on the door he'd closed behind him. Beside her, Harper's fingers twitched once.

She woke the third time to a white woman bent over her, kneading her calves. The woman had a gray braid that swept Brie's thighs, her knuckles bony and blue veined as mountain ridges. When Brie moved, the woman adjusted the bandanna over her nose and mouth, then turned to two steaming mugs sitting on a crate. She offered one to Brie and moved to the bed's edge, far from where Harper slept with half-parted lips.

When Brie sniffed the rim, the woman said, "It's just tea. And it hasn't killed you yet."

After the woman introduced herself as Lauren, Brie asked, "You live here?"

She shook her head. "Got my own to take care of."

Her own, Brie thought. It could mean a sibling, a spouse. So many ways to have a family. She took a careful sip, the brew bitter and piping hot.

"Mind if I work on your friend while you drink?" Lauren asked.

Brie let Lauren massage Harper's thighs, thin above the sheets. "Who lives here, then?"

"You took a bite out of his shoulder. May want to apologize for that. He took a lot of risk, letting you stay here. And quarantining you." Lauren's hands pushed and pushed against Harper, stuffing life back in. "Seems like whatever you had makes a real mess of your nerves. But I figure you're out of the woods now."

Brie lowered her mug to her stomach. "My sister—" She breathed deep and touched Harper's shoulder. "Will she be alright?"

Lauren's eyes flickered. Of course she'd doubt they were siblings, comparing Harper's yellow skin to Brie's mahogany. Lauren was older than their mother had been, old enough to remember a time before most people were brown, either by sun or by blood. "She's—making it," Lauren said, and lifted Harper's arm toward the ceiling, working her thumbs into flesh that went pink under the pressure. "Between the two of you, you got the stronger genes."

Brie felt for Harper's free hand. When they'd been girls in East Texas, Brie had gone under the floodwaters, dry leaves plugging her nose. Harper had yanked her into the boat by the wrist, the skiff swirling in the chaos: "You're not allowed to die, you hear me?" Water streamed down her sister's face. Then she rowed the two of them to something like safety, to drier ground some twenty miles from the government complex where their mother had died with her lover.

"Don't worry," Lauren said—and when she patted Brie's arm her hand was hot with her exertions—"You're both safe here."

THE WHOLE PLACE was a dream of green. The farmhouse with its clean panels and long windows, the surrounding shrubs like woolly-haired children. That evening, she took dinner on the porch steps, a plate of venison and beans on her knees. In another time, she'd have avoided the meat—who knew what it carried?— or eaten slowly to disguise her hunger, but there was already so much her mind couldn't swallow. The trees bending in the breeze, threatening to drop their fruit. The soil dark and loamy enough to hold a footprint. Even the men on the far edges of the porch relaxed as they ate. They sat with their backs to her, dirt settled on their shoulders. Had she not known she and Harper were somewhere in Tennessee—and had it not been for the cloud of heat—she would've thought they'd made it to Maine. Which meant Harper had been wrong when she said Low America was finished, that—if the cities would not let you in—you had to get north to have a home that would flourish and last.

Behind her, someone said, "You looked better passed out."

When she turned, the man with the patch on his shoulder was toweling off his face. "Calmer, at least," he added. He must've come from around back, too close to the shed where Harper slept. It was thirty seconds away. Twenty, if she didn't let her full belly slow her down. She kept her hand on her fork. Said, "Only a crazy person would say somebody looks better passed out."

"Bad joke. Didn't mean anything by it."

He flopped the towel over the railing, then leaned on it with one elbow. The men behind him murmured greetings, gratitude for the meal. Had this happened on any other farm she'd worked? The owner feeding them? The men called him Colton.

"Where you two headed?" he said, when his attention returned to her.

Brie, chewing, kept her eyes on her plate.

"Fine," he said. "It's none of my business."

She looked over his shoulder. Up the dirt road, a few mares grazed, their tails flicking in the air. Their black coats were so shiny it made her eyes prickle. "How'd you come by this farm?" she asked.

"My parents, who got it from theirs. Prices weren't so high, once."

And it had survived all the storms. "But how do you manage to keep affording it?"

"We treat the soil right. Grow no more than we can handle and shield during freezes. Take help, if the right sort of people come along." He glanced at the men behind them, still intent on their plates. "Not saying we don't get trouble like everyone else. Or god-awful weather. But we get by."

He moved closer, and his shadow touched the knee of her jeans. She tightened her grip on her fork. "I won't hurt you," he said, brows relaxing. "I just want to sit. Right there, next to you."

She didn't protest. He smelled the kind of clean that meant a bath every day or every other. *Waste of water*, Harper would've said, but Brie let herself enjoy it for a few breaths. The money some people had.

"You know," he said, "my shoulder's kept me out of the picking three days."

She ate a sliver of deer so fast her fork barely met her tongue.

He sighed. "Listen, we won't get anywhere like this. Your truck's still on the edge of the farm, 'bout a mile off. Maybe you've got ten miles of fuel in there. Been forever since I've seen anything not electric."

"Didn't really have a choice."

"Not judging you. I know a guy with a fuel reserve. In town. I can get some for you."

Around her, these trees, bursting with life. A man could be tolerated, if he had all this. "We'll work for it," she said. "I'm guessing those peaches'll rot if you leave 'em too long."

His whole body became an apology, head dipping down, smile hanging off his face. The spots on his forehead put him anywhere between twenty-five and thirty-five, given how Momma once said people aged faster than they used to, the sun being what it was. "I wasn't asking for anything. The guys'll haul a few gallons over tomorrow, so you don't have to worry yourself. You and your friend—"

"My sister. I'm telling you, I'll work. Least 'til she's awake."

Her eyelids lowered. Imagine. Time spent on this place as rich as something out of Momma's old photographs, the previous century, with its regular crops, its more manageable seasons. Just wait until Harper saw it. Maybe Maine could wait a little while.

When she looked back at him, the dark color in his eyes gave way, like the earth easing beneath her boot.

ON THE FIRST DAY of work, she waited in the orchard, calves quivering. She'd arrived earlier than anyone, before the sun would drain her further, and she thumbed the bark of a tree as she tried to contain herself. Then she gave up and grabbed a low-hanging peach. It burst in her mouth, its juice stinging her tongue. When she turned, Colton was a few feet away, studying the trail on her chin. She wiped it, clutching the rest of the fruit. Then he approached with a small jug and rinsed off the peach's remains until her hands were soaked. "You've gotta clean 'em," he said. He grabbed a peach from a branch near her cheek. Rinsed that one off too. Bit in.

The second day had all the hard work of the first. It was May, and the laborers had long developed their routines, leaving behind families in camps to pile into electric sedans or ride three to a horse or bike the full five miles to Colton's farm. All eleven of them went right to work, reaching into the trees. Because her legs were still weak, Brie stood below Colton and made a tent out of a blanket, catching the peaches he tossed down and carefully lowering them into crates to avoid bruising. His wound bled through its dressing and onto his shirt.

On the third day, they traded places. He had to steady her on the ladder, his thumb pushing into the back of her knee, his flesh a damp circle beneath her stiff shorts. Imagine being hungry for touch, of all things. "You know," he said, "for a while, there was only my family to help out with all this. Either we killed ourselves or a lot went wasted."

He was waiting, she knew, for her to ask more. But she wouldn't. When she was fifteen and Harper twelve, their mother had begun whatever-you-wanted-to-call-it with the new water monitor. Sex. Convenience. Love. William had appeared out back of the government complex, where Momma pinned a sheet to the community clothesline and Brie and Harper played cards on the Astroturf. He knelt beside the filtration unit and installed new canisters, all the while looking back at them. Above her playing cards, Harper rolled her eyes, though she went still when he said to Momma, "Decades ago, I had my own house around here. Though I have to say, you look better than my memories of that place." "That might not be saying much," Momma said, though the lines in her face went softer than they'd been in years. Nights later, from the bedroom allotted for the teens, Brie and Harper heard Momma and William laughing in the den, louder than the other adults. Beneath the door, candlelight flickered. "Didn't they assign him his own unit?" Brie whispered, and Harper answered, "Who cares. Momma promised we'd head out before the next hurricane anyway."

Against Brie's knee, Colton's thumb sweated. Or she did. In the distance, she saw Lauren heading toward the shed, preparing to tend to her sister.

"I can manage," Brie said, and he let her go.

On the fourth day, Lauren returned to cook for the workers. Three miniature chickens and corn hash stewing over a fire, which stretched toward the sunset like it was kin. Brie had learned by then that the men never stayed late, wanting to get home to their families before full dark. By the time the sky turned pink, they'd stacked their empty plates in neat piles, and the ones who had to walk plunged their faces into the water buckets so they'd be cool for the journey back. She watched from the front porch until Lauren's laugh floated through the house's open window. Brie turned. Lauren stood with a man in the kitchen, his mouth mashed against her neck. So her family was her husband. His hair grew in black patches, and his red-spotted hands pulled her against him. No wedding band, but then again, it was smarter not to. In the complex, everyone crammed together on their assigned floors, anything valuable could become someone else's. Once, when the mess hall had run out of proteins, she and Harper had slipped a silver necklace out of a newcomer's backpack. Easy to bribe a café worker with something so flashy. "We might have the chance to pay her back for it," Harper had said as they picked at their hard-boiled eggs, icy from the back of the fridge. Though of course the newcomer had been gone days later, already checked out of the complex and on her way elsewhere.

"What you thinking 'bout?" Colton said, sitting beside her. She shook her head, and he said, "Hey, now. Your sister'll be fine." Her heart pounding, she let him maneuver her into the tender pad of his shoulder. His breath caught. Could've been pain. Or the closeness.

The fifth day, she saw the damage she'd done. She'd knocked at his front door, waiting for the usual breakfast of eggs and toast, and he'd come out with his shirt half-askew, his wound exposed. Bridges of skin stretched from one raw side to the other. "Come in?" he said. "Cool off?"

Four chairs at the kitchen table, only one pulled out. A pair of leather boots, about his size, by the door. It was already marvelous, that landline plugged into the wall, a sign of what else he could buy. Probably he had a cell phone stashed away somewhere, one of the nice, expensive ones from a company that could afford to keep its data centers cool.

But God, this air-conditioning rushing over her. So long since she'd been in a real house, not a shed or barn attic or truck.

She allowed herself to sit in one of the chairs, slow. If she leaned against its pillow, would she smear it with grease? No matter how many times she scrubbed herself, dipping her sponge into the bucket of soapy water outside the shed, she was dipping into her own filth. He placed the eggs before her and took his cup of coffee near the stove. She asked, "You live here alone?"

"If I answer that, you'll answer one for me?" When she nodded, he said, "Yeah, alone."

She let her fork break the yolk of her egg. Finally, he said, "Where'd you and your sister come from? And where you headed?"

Two questions, but she let him get away with it. "Left Texas after Hurricane Bev. Spent a few years working farms in Mississippi. Earning what we can 'til we get to Maine."

"What's in Maine, aside from crazy winters?"

Permanence, she thought. Water. Greenery. She said, "Well, what's here?"

He twisted toward the window, and something in her knew his body often reclined against the sink this way, waiting, his gaze on the road. After a beat, he said, "What's not?"

On the sixth day, when she returned to the shed, her body reeked of peaches. There it was: Harper turning on the mattress at the scent. All the fear that had clutched Brie's heart uncoiled.

"You?" Harper murmured. "You were gone?"

Brie rushed toward her sister. With her cleanest fingers, she pulled back the sheets, then retreated.

Harper's chest rose and fell. "Why are you way over there?"

"I don't want to get anything on you."

"Like . . . I care about that."

"I'm filthy. You just can't see."

Harper squinted at her. Then said, "I can see it" and closed her eyes.

By the time Harper fell asleep again, everything was bright, everything a peach, even the sun, half-crushed against the horizon. Brie closed the shed door behind her and walked toward the house, limbs alight. The men were gone when she mounted the stairs. There was only Colton, sitting on the railing, reading a big leather Bible. "Thought you were in for the night," he said.

"Harper's awake. And I want to hug her but—" She looked down at her hands, then the rest of her body.

"Oh," he said, lowering his Bible. "I see."

The bathroom was far nicer than the ones in the complexes, the tile mint instead of cinder, the shower so hot it burned off her dry parts, flakes of skin and dirt disappearing down the drain. She could feel the soap foaming on her scalp, lifting the crusted sweat so her hair fluffed. She showered for as long as she could stand it, half wondering if he would come upstairs to remind her about the water regulations. But he didn't.

On the doorknob, he'd left a black dress with four pockets and a bra a size too big, like hands hovering over her breasts. Left over from some cousin or sister or somebody else? A wife? A woman who had things. Brie clothed herself, then sat at the top of the stairs and tucked her chin on her knees until the sun went down. In its fading light, she could see the hairs curling on her arms. When Colton appeared beneath her, at the stairs' foot, she sat up to regard him. They remained there, considering each other in the gathering darkness.

"I have to go up now," he said. "To bed."

She said, "Show me."

When they lay beside each other on his mattress, not yet naked, he touched his shoulder's ruined skin and said, "I'll have this scar for the rest of my life."

"Guess it'll match the others." So hard to be sure of him or of this long-suppressed heat inside her. But there was no denying this mattress. It was even softer than his chest.

"You mean this?" he asked. "This one's from where a dog nipped me. And I've got this one near my ear from when I was out on a delivery. This desperate kid with a knife." As he spoke, she pressed her ear to his heart, letting only half his words enter her. She shouldn't have mentioned the scars; she didn't need to know about them.

"Can I?" he asked, his fingers tilting her chin toward him.

They kissed and she thought, This, too, is rest. Soon, he removed her dress so she was naked and clean against his own clean body, and she remembered how she'd purposefully forgotten this: to have somebody other than Harper.

On the morning of the seventh day, she returned to the shed and found Harper standing beside the bed, both her arms outstretched, like two wings, for balance. Brie wiped the grime from her sister's forehead.

She thought: Well, I guess we have to go now.

She said: "Harps, I tried. But we're low on fuel, and we can't leave 'til we can pay for it."

TO BE SAFE and headed nowhere, for once. The illness left Harper's skin stiff with sweat, and Brie helped her bathe with the bucket outside the shed. With a towel, she made a fuzzy curtain, shielding her sister from the house and its fields.

"Shit, shit, shit," Harper said, laughing, her blonde eyelashes damp, "promise when we get to Maine we'll make sure our farm's got warm water. No more freezing like this."

"You want to shower in the house?"

Harper shook her head. Cleaned herself furiously, cold water flying off her hands and slapping Brie's feet. Harper's body was all bones and caverns. Like some long, slender rodent lost to time, the hairs on her legs like quills. "I must look god-awful," Harper said.

"You should've seen yourself before."

"At least you look good." Harper exhaled, scanning the rows of peach trees. It was Sunday, no picking, and maybe this would make it easier for Harper to appreciate the beauty.

"You see the colors?" Brie asked. "How bright the peaches are?"

"Sure." Harper shrugged. "I see them."

They ate Lauren's chilled sunflower soup, which did nothing to stop them from sweating. Then they walked, Harper's body sharp as it leaned against her. Brie talked about Colton and the harvest schedule, keeping her voice neutral. Almost two weeks they'd been here, and maybe two more would get them what they needed. It was about a quarter mile to the dirt path that ran right up to the house, then another quarter mile on the other side. Once they'd finished, Harper was panting.

"God, I'm sorry," Harper said. "I wasted so much of our time."

"You didn't." Brie wiped her forehead, felt a drumbeat of shame. Being here was the best time she'd had in a while—and what did that say about her? "If the High checkpoints are as strict as they say, you wouldn't have passed, sick like that."

"Still, if he'd hand over the fuel, we could be on our way. But somebody's always bargaining."

Brie pressed her lips together. Colton was coming out of the house. He paused on the porch and pulled at his collar, the heat getting to him all at once.

"That him?" Harper asked.

"Yeah." She squeezed her sister's shoulder. "You know I bit him? At the truck, I thought he was coming after you, so I took a chunk out of his shoulder."

"Look at you," Harper said. Then she shook her head and laughed until it sounded like crying, so loud you could believe it—and not the wind—stirred the trees. She quieted only when Colton approached.

"Glad you're feeling better," he said to Harper. His hand hung in the open air between them. "We both worried about you."

"Well, you wouldn't know, but I always make it."

"I believe it. House is ready, whenever you are. I've got extra rooms."

Yes, Brie's body said, but Harper went, "We're fine in the shed," and tugged her away.

They had the whole afternoon before them, all the laborers having remained home with their families in the camps. Possibly, the bright emptiness was even better than being permitted into the cities, because inside Dallas or Little Rock or Nashville, you would have reliable water systems and sturdier infrastructure and your own space, though it would not be this much. Brie and Harper lay on a blanket in the orchard and let the peach trees shelter them from the heat. Colton hung around, standing over the blanket so they were in his shadow. He was trying to win Harper over with talk of how his family had been Tennessee natives for centuries—slaves, then sharecroppers, then farmers, then Low America nationalists and, blessed, for now, from disaster, though when Harper kept complaining about the gnats, he quieted. "And your family?" he asked. Neither Brie nor Harper answered. He picked at his shirt, mumbled something about dinner, and retreated into the house.

"What makes him think we want to know about his life?" Harper asked. "His family didn't have the sense to move north, and he doesn't either, apparently."

"I don't know. This farm's not nothing."

"It's peaches, Brie. And who knows if they'll even grow next year."

"Not just peaches. Sweet potatoes on the other side. Okra. Tomatoes. Not to mention the chickens and everything Lauren's got at her place."

"He still eats chicken? Gross."

Brie folded her hands across her stomach, which rose fuller than it had in years. She couldn't admit that she'd eaten chicken alongside him. Pork, too, with everyone else, and no one had gotten sick, the way Harper had always warned. But Harper had always known how to survive: Leave the complex. Take the electric trains. Get work on farms when they could. Save and work and save and learn until they could get to Maine and buy land at least worth the impossible price, until they could choose a life that gave them a chance. Even the uncertainty of High America had to be better than here, which was always hot and had the tornadoes and floods and mosquitoes and viruses to prove it.

"Place is nice, I'll give you that," Harper said, grabbing her hand. "But even Randall's was nice, at first."

❃

THE NEXT MORNING, when it was time to resume picking, Harper refused to join the others. "Tell Mr. Man I'll be with Lauren in the kitchen today," she said as she shrugged on her denim overalls, newly washed. The color in her face was returning, though she'd eaten around the pork on her breakfast plate.

Brie didn't tell Colton. Instead, they spent the day at opposite ends of a row of peach trees, keeping all the men between them. Was he being sensitive to what she needed, letting her wear out her fingers like everyone else? Only days before, when they'd lain together, he'd mumbled into her ear, "I think I might love you." Which felt absurd, unless he meant he could see his way to something like love. With her. Even her own body opened to pleasure around him, some ancient room inside her unlocked. Though— it was also like they fit only because he was a man and she was a woman and they were in this beautiful place.

Her sister would say, *One room ain't a whole house.* Or something like that. Once, at seventeen, a boy from the complex had been assigned to plant onions beside Brie in the communal garden. He wasn't special, aside from the fact that he hadn't been sick in the past year and didn't let his temper get the better of him in the heat. It was one shiny coin of a moment: rocking with him in that storage facility. When she told Harper, her sister paused sewing the arm back onto a jacket. "You know what they used to do centuries ago, when they wanted to keep slaves on plantations?" Harper said. "They let them get married. Or let them call it that anyway." Her sister had never taken to William, whom the other women couldn't lure from Momma's bed for long.

Brie descended the ladder before her allotted tree, then wiped her brow with the back of her hand. The day was ending, and when she turned, Harper stood in the house's doorway, that wrap on her hair, her body a red-tipped match at the edge of the fields.

Come dinner, they ate with Lauren in the kitchen, the men outside. Lauren and Harper had made soybean casserole with pepper and dehydrated herbs, which they laid out on the table. *Don't you miss this, Harps?* Brie thought. It had been forever since they'd eaten someplace that didn't require sitting cross-legged in a dry field or in a truck's cramped cabin. But Harper only nibbled, leaning toward Lauren, which was always how Harper got with women.

"Your place must have a lot too," Harper said. "You don't come here every day."

"I wouldn't say a lot." Lauren smoothed the cap of her hair to where it tightened into a braid. "It's only the two of us."

"At least you don't have kids." When Lauren laughed, Harper blinked. "What? There were so doggone many in the complex."

"It's nothing," Lauren said, and her newly soft voice made Brie press her foot over Harper's; you could never tell what people had lost. "You'd manage, if you had them."

"Maybe we want more than managing." Harper freed her foot and cleaned her plate. Brie wondered if there was more casserole. It'd be careless to ask for meat in front of Harper.

"How long you two planning on sticking around?" Lauren said as she skinned a peach.

"Just 'til we earn fuel," Harper said. "Get our truck going."

"Who's got fuel?"

"Colton knows somebody," Brie said. "We're working off the cost to him."

The peach skin Lauren pulled away wrinkled like her mouth. "He's honest. He'll make good on whatever he told you." She said nothing else for a while, and Brie felt caught in the net of her stare. "But in the meantime, I'd appreciate help with the canning. We'll wrap up harvest soon, and whatever doesn't get sold in town will need preserving. Think you'd be interested?"

"We could be," Brie said. Harper studied an ant wandering over her plate.

That night, as they faced each other on the shed mattress, Brie said, "There's a lot we can learn in a place like this, if we both work."

Harper curled her fist under her cheek. "We been working and learning for years. At some point, you just have to go."

Brie rolled onto her back and stared at the ceiling. There had been cobwebs in the rafters that morning, and now they were gone.

"I don't think peaches grow in Maine," Harper said, her voice softer. "But maybe apples? Potatoes? Would that make you happier, staying through the canning?"

BRIE DID NOT RETURN to Colton's room that night, but she thought about it during that third week, as she and Harper joined the others in the peach orchard. It felt wrong to think about his shower, his plush bed. Anybody else would be making sure their sister didn't tip over during the harvesting, given how Harper yanked the fruit hard enough to snap branches.

Colton didn't approach her in the fields until Thursday afternoon, the sun overhead a white, unflinching eye, the others taking lunch and Harper gone to use one of the outhouses. His knuckles brushed the loops of her jeans. "You've done enough now," he said. "I'll get the fuel tomorrow."

"Still too much to do. Like the canning. And probably more."

His shadow nodded on the tree in front of her. "You know you're welcome to anything in the house. Whatever you want. Whenever."

That night, as Harper slept, Brie went to him. She showered and slipped into a strawberry-print dress he'd left for her, though she ignored the bra. From Colton's bed, she imagined the woman it once belonged to moving down this hallway, her feet gentling against the floorboards. Brie sat on the bed and looked out at the pristine dinner plate of the moon. When Colton crawled in beside her, she chose to stop thinking about anybody else.

After, she asked him to show her around, and he obliged. A series of rooms: an office with piles of papers, a bedroom with a blue gingham comforter and sewing machine on a round table, one entirely empty room that he closed the door on, quick. The hallway had a long table covered in a yellow runner and glass figurines of animals she couldn't identify, ghostly in their long-necked translucence. A photograph of a grinning, gray-haired couple stared back at her, their arms extending from the frame as they angled the camera toward them. In the background, a city of canals.

"My parents," he said.

"You must be ancient."

"I wouldn't say that. A lot of people wouldn't."

She lifted a teacup, its trim curving silver in the moonlight. In the complex, what little she and Harper owned had been lost. They'd waded knee-deep through the partially drained flood-waters, where everything shelved had been coaxed out: the R&B records their mother inherited from her parents, Brie's baby shoes curling with pink ribbons, the framed photograph of their family eating quesadillas at the canteen on Harper's twelfth birthday. All of it ruined.

"Yours," Colton said, and closed her fingers around the tea-cup. "If you want." She nodded. In the distance, she heard a horse's wet neigh. "Will you tell me how old you two are?"

"I'm twenty-four." She wouldn't tell him Harper's age. *No part of me is any of his business,* Harper would say.

"That's about what I thought," he said. "Though I wish I hadn't needed to spend so much time guessing."

She didn't ask about his age. Nor about the woman who had lived here before.

"I'm thirty," Colton murmured, releasing her fingers. "I need you to know I'm not so much older."

THEY'D BEEN THERE SIX WEEKS when the picking ended. By mid-July, the summer fleshed out and the laborers had fleshed out too, growing partners and children who appeared on the horizon for the final, celebratory dinner. Lauren and Harper had spent hours on the knotted rolls of bread and creamed potatoes and the pig, slaughtered and then garnished with peaches, though this last task had made Harper vomit on the back steps. A mess of a gathering, at first. The cast-iron pots and pans jumbled on the table. People knocking against one another as they filled their plates. The children working their way from lap to lap, only to scramble back toward their parents. These families, vibrant under the string of golden lights buzzing on and on.

They'd figured something out, something different from the thrown-together families of the complexes, where everyone belonged to everyone, no room for it to be any other way. But here a laborer with hair only a shade redder than his face had two wives, their trio occupying one corner of the long wooden table. A pair of men in identical plaid shirts, who arrived and left together daily, lay on a blanket, the taller man's arms around the shorter one. And then there were the endless man-to-woman couples, chasing their children down the dirt road, dust coating their hair.

On the porch, Brie watched as Harper's wry half smile settled into wary amusement. Even in Brie's earliest memories of her sister, Harper was this watchful. Eleven years old and studying their mother parting the pale heart shells of the crabs that washed up after Hurricane Sharunda, her callused hands exposing their tender pink flesh.

"Makes me think about William," Harper said. "That night he taught us how to do that dance from the cities." They'd never known why Momma attached herself to him. He couldn't find a crab on a doorstep. He took most of the money for who-knew-what and ate more than his share of their rations. Maybe he was simply a source of warmth that first winter. And he did dance.

Brie remembered: the four of them in the common area, her own voice providing the bass of the old music, Harper's soprano carrying the melody, their mother and William harmonizing as they rolled their feet against the floors and wound their arms in the air. But she couldn't speak about it, not with how much she was already holding inside. One of the laborer's wives, a sun-kissed woman with brown curls plastered to her face, began singing, "My old man sleeps with one hand on his gun, the other 'round my heart."

A surprise, when Harper started singing too, her voice unfurling like a cool mist. The woman smiled at them, and Brie thought for sure Harper would stop, but no, Harper rose, swaying, her wrists plumper, her fingers pulling the air's invisible strings.

The woman moved her hips, raised her fingers too. But Harper closed her eyes, her lashes a veil to another world inside her: their old bedroom, shared with the other teens, the sketches of the solar-assisted cities copied from the common room television, the packed classroom where they wrote out their plans for something better. Brie closed her eyes too, let the spin of lights fill the darkness. Maybe Maine will be like this, she thought, when we get there.

By the time Brie opened her eyes, the woman had abandoned her interest in Harper, settling against a man in a wooden chair, his grin lost in the tangle of his beard. Across the yard, in a huddle of other men, Colton's eyes met hers, as if Harper's dance, the arc of her arms, plucked a taut string between them. He mouthed something: *Stay*, maybe. Or, *Wait*.

Her sister was turning, dragging one boot in a circle through the dirt. She stopped. "Just dance with me," she said. "For Momma?"

WHEN THEY WERE BACK in the shed, they splashed water on their faces. Harper unwound her head wrap, and Brie fought the urge to even out her sister's hair, which stood up in spikes and looked so much worse than it had that night at the river. Harper picked at the flyaways as she studied the teacup resting on the windowsill. "That's pretty," she said, and Brie splashed the water harder.

"Something's on your mind," Harper said when she was combing out Brie's tight kinks.

"You seemed happy tonight."

"Guess I was."

"You ever think about staying here? Even beyond the canning?"

The comb met a knot. Harper pulled hard, then gentler. "Hey," Harper said, and the brightness in her voice wasn't what it should've been. "Don't ask me that again, alright?"

Brie dug her nails into the mattress. Stupid, to forget the point of all this. In the silence, the laborers called out last goodbyes.

"You remember that little garden snake we found in the complex that time?" Harper asked. "I would've fed it forever, if Momma hadn't made William kill it."

"She was afraid. Can't really blame her for that."

"That's what I'm saying," Harper said. "You were scared too, at first. But you got over it."

She supposed so. Harper's fingers were in her hair, tentative, searching.

A few nights later, when Colton pressed his own fingers to her scalp, she shrugged off his touch. She'd snuck out and lost herself under him, but now his sheets felt thin, her shoulders cold. He rolled toward the other side of the bed.

"I wasn't telling you to go away," she said.

"Truth be told, I've got no idea what you want, half the time."

She sat up. Slid both legs over the bed and toed the tops of her boots.

"See?" he said. "There you go."

When she turned, his face was more crushed than she was expecting, his wrinkles drawn out. "I'm trying," she said, and he set his chin on her shoulder and said, "At least tell me what happened to you two. The whole story."

She made herself inhale. What rushed into her body felt like a flood itself: William saying, "There's no better place to be," even when they were the last ones in the complex, the common area empty after the calls to evacuate. They had a shaky peace those first hours, playing cards on the concrete floor until the power went out, then quietly wondering where everyone else had hunkered down, until the wind outside grew louder than their voices and Harper shouldered her emergency pack and said, "I told you," and climbed the stairs to the adult quarters on the second landing, then the teens' on the third. "Get some rest," William said, as they each took a bunk, the slate walls around them shuddering and Momma, beside him, pulling the blankets overhead. Hours later, sleepless, Brie twisted on the mattress and her arm draped over its edge and met warm water, already rising toward her shoulder. Her scream was silent inside her, and she would've sat inside that silent scream forever if Harper hadn't pulled her away, leading everyone through the hollering wind and the waist-high water up the next flight of stairs to the storerooms with cans scattered over the floor, then up the escape ladder to the roof, where the emergency boats were chained. "You can't release it 'til after you're in it," Harper shouted to William and Momma through the fury of rain, but either William didn't hear or he'd grown desperate because the second boat was loose and slowly sliding away from him and Momma, then blown out of reach and over the edge, the way their bodies would've blown over if they weren't on all fours. Where, Brie whispered, had her attention been at the moment of William and Momma's vanishing? The water rose too high too fast, already dragging her from Harper, then sealing her beneath. And out of that black water and screeching wind, Harper reappeared, grabbing her wrist and hoisting her into the safety of the boat, which rocked against its chains, then shot away the instant Harper unclipped them, away from the patch of roof where Momma and William had once been. That roof soon vanished entirely, just like the other roofs across the development, the lightning flashing against the black water hell-bent on clearing the earth.

It did not make her feel better to tell Colton. Nor did it make her feel good to explain what came after: The government acknowledging that, despite the flooding it would cause to adjacent regions, they'd had no choice but to release the water from the reservoir, which could not keep up with the rainfall. The promise she and Harper made never to depend on anyone but each other, to get all the way north before settling down. Still, she talked. Of the farmwork that bent her back like a blighted tree, the money dwindling from the cost of food and water. Of the viruses that didn't kill them but took them out of commission for weeks. Of how Mr. Randall's farm hadn't been so bad, until Brie saw him pull Harper against him in the cornfields, one large, pale-knuckled hand gripping the hair long and wilting as wheat. They disappeared into the stalks. Brie raced to his truck, which was parked outside the barn, and after gunning the engine, raced toward the figures in the field, honking the horn until Mr. Randall leapt up, his glasses lost in the dirt. "Enough," she'd yelled while Harper climbed in, covering her face in the swirling dust. In the rearview mirror, Brie could see him shouting after them as he ran, obscured by the dust until he was out of sight. Brie's hands shook as she drove, swerving out of the fields and onto the road. "I was supposed to kill him," Harper said, and it was the first time Brie had ever heard her sister sound unsure. "I told myself I would, the next person. You grow up, you get older, and you think—" Brie clutched Harper's hand, and the two of them drove, drove, drove into distant states, none as far as they wanted to be.

Brie stopped. How long had Colton been holding her arm?

"Let me come with you," he said. "Make sure you get to Maine alright."

"Why would you leave all this?"

He pulled her against him and squeezed. She closed her eyes. God, to love her sister yet want this comfort. When she looked out the window, she saw that the land was still green, even after its trees had been picked clean.

THE NEXT MORNING, Brie couldn't look her sister in the face, as if, in telling their story, she'd removed all their clothing. She stood with Harper on the porch, her mind aware of Colton watching them as he fixed breakfast in the kitchen. She'd let Harper borrow her teacup, but it was hard not to read into her sister scowling at the gray haze over the farm and its promise of rain. It came as they sipped their tea. So did the woman on horseback.

She was a white blouse and straw hat in the distance, a ghost floating on the horse. Brie, alert, noticed Harper stiffen. The woman was too tall and dark to be Lauren, and anyway, she did not wave. Instead, she reached the front of the house, slid off the horse, and hauled a drenched canvas bag over the dip in the animal's back, before it shook rainwater from its mane and trotted off to a soggy patch of grass. Only then did the woman's gaze flicker over them—then return once more. She opened her mouth, slow, a tiny hole appearing at the very center of the world. Finally, she called, "Col," and the intimacy of the sound made something in Brie tip over completely.

From inside came Colton's approach: a collection of footsteps, the fumble of the doorknob. Brie breathed in deep; Harper's brows furrowed over the teacup.

When the door opened, he said, "Alice," his hands flexing beside his thighs. The woman stood on her toes and kissed him quick on the mouth, and Colton went still.

Brie thought: I let you all the way in.

"This," he began, not looking at her. "This is my . . ."

But Brie knew. She stepped away from him, deeper into the porch's shadows. The woman tipped back her hat and studied— what? Her outfit? That strawberry print dress, the fruit dark with rainwater.

"Looks good on you," the wife said.

BRIE THOUGHT: How did I ignore it? In the kitchen, Alice took off her hat and laid it on the table. Shook out the short, fuzzy dreads that jutted over her ears. Kicked off her boots and left them in the middle of the floor. She went through the cabinets and pulled out bread and a jar of peaches Lauren had canned only the day before. As she ate with her fingers, she said, "These are better than I'd have expected."

Colton couldn't decide whom to angle his body toward. The four of them sat at the kitchen table, a kettle of tea at its center. Because Brie couldn't look at him—everything, after all this time, belonged to this other person—she turned toward Harper, who, for once, was relaxed, even inside and even without Lauren. Harper rested one wrist on the table, the other against her face. Brie's mug burned her fingers.

"You tired out your horse," Harper observed.

"Had to, with every camp leader flagging me down for water packs."

"Where were you?" Colton said. He still hadn't touched his mug.

"Outside Etowah," Alice said. Then, more quietly: "Then outside Valdosta. Gaffney, then Hillsborough. 'Bout a four-month loop."

"More like two years," Colton murmured. And Brie felt his words hum in her ears. He meant them for her.

"I meant this leg. I was checking on some farmers we knew." She pushed one of her dreads out of her face. "Before that, I . . . spent some time in Nashville."

"You survived their so-called 'quarantine'?" Harper asked. Her lips failed to hide her smirk. "How'd you get them to let you in?"

"They're trying to grow peaches inside their nursery." Alice smiled a little, a warmth rising through the wrinkles in her face. "And a few other things I could help them out with."

"You didn't leave here 'cause you wanted to help out somebody else," Colton said.

"No. I suppose I didn't." Alice pursed her lips. "Don't worry, I just need a place. At least for a little while."

Colton pushed away from the table, and the tea shook in their mugs. He'd almost made it to the stairs when he paused and said, "What do you mean by 'farmers we knew'?"

Alice folded her hands. "Know. The Rogers stuck around. And the Tanners."

"Jesus." He pulled hard at his chin. Then his eyes said to Brie, *Come?* And he went upstairs.

Brie didn't move. Alice sat back in her chair and licked her perfect yellow teeth. "How long you two planning on staying?" she said.

"At this rate," Harper said, and leaned in, "who knows?"

HOW LONG WOULD she have to stand it? She sat, listening to Alice talk about how much rain there had been near Bristol, how much harder it was to find a hotel with reliable power. Harper goaded Alice on: How far north have you traveled? How strict were the state checkpoints in High America? Why would you ever leave a city, given its resources and healthy populations? "Even those won't last forever," Alice said, and inside, Brie felt some seedling wilt within her.

When Alice had finally gone upstairs, Harper following and asking more questions, Brie rose, her ankles loose. She thought of how much she'd told him, this man she'd known only seven weeks, and this was what he'd held back? She was almost outside when Colton grabbed her arm. "Please," he said, his hand a band of heat. "I never even thought I'd see her again."

She yanked her arm away and stomped down the porch steps. In seconds, she was soaked.

"How was I supposed to know?" he shouted.

Later, the shed where she lay beside Harper was boxed with the scent of rain.

"She's lovely," Harper said. She sat on the mattress and picked at the hairs on her legs. "No idea why she's with him. If they are together."

Brie grabbed the sheets beneath them. "It's been a long time since I met somebody who talked that much."

"Is that all you have to say?"

Brie turned so her hair, dense from humidity, covered half her face.

"Wow," Harper said. "I don't think you've ever tried to hide anything from me."

THE RAIN DIDN'T STOP for five days, a sheet of water walling them in. The phone rang, and when she answered, Brie could hardly make out Lauren's voice: "Will come when—. Rain too—."

"Wait 'til the connection's better," Harper said, and padded barefoot into the living room.

Since Alice had arrived, Harper had stopped asking about the fuel. When Colton appeared in a room to find Brie, he'd speak her name. If he caught her alone, he asked questions: Will you just talk to me? Don't you know that she's not even sleeping in my room?

In the meantime, Brie scalded, sliced, and jarred the peaches, using instructions pieced together from Lauren's calls. At some point, she let Colton stand beside her. He stirred the syrup, then poured the finished mixture into sterilized jars. There was the prolonged quiet, the few charged inches between them. Don't, Brie thought. Don't you dare. She was wearing her old jeans and the plaid shirt she'd worn upon arriving. Only once had she been alone with Alice. The two of them were making breakfast together, and Alice touched her back and said, "Oh, honey, he's just a man," and flipped a pancake.

Harper always curled up with Alice on the couch, propping herself on one elbow. Or else she sat across from Alice on the ledge of the living room window, swinging her legs side to side.

What happened, Brie thought as she looked at her sister, to our own talking? Then again, people needed . . . some shining link to other people. Or at least they told themselves this.

Halfway through a Tuesday that turned the fields to lakes, the crops covered, Alice nodded at Harper's head wrap and said, "You must get hot under that."

"Not the hottest I've been." But Harper untied the wrap, and that awful hair emerged.

Alice tugged at her own locs. "I'm thinking of cutting mine that short. Practical."

"Yours isn't so bad. Not so long you'll waste water getting it clean."

To Brie, Alice said, "How do you keep yours from tangling?" and Harper answered: "Me."

It was the kind of comment that used to make one of them touch the other in affection.

AT THE END of the rain, the sky ashen, Alice and Harper made their way into the flooded fields, heading toward the empty peach groves. Brie watched from the kitchen window, how Harper kept covering her patchy scalp with her arms. Alice caught Harper's elbows and brought them down, until the tufts of hair were exposed. Which was maybe alright. Maybe Alice could make Harper understand how easy it was to long for certain things. Even if it made you foolish.

She felt Colton behind her, a coolness that pricked her neck.

"Did I say it?" he asked. "That I was sorry?"

Brie watched Alice and Harper pause near the trees. Fireflies circled their shoulders in a queasy green. She and Harper would have to go soon. Nothing here belonged to them.

Colton breathed above her hair, the strands rushing from his mouth. "Alice is just one of those people," he said. "You know what I mean? They never have enough, and so they go and you let them. That's not my fault. This whole time, I've never lied to you."

Standing here with him. In this house. All the water out there. For so many nights, before they came to this place, she'd shivered under such weather, and for a time, the truck cabin felt like enough—was dry at least. If she and Harper had left for Maine already, they'd have been caught in this torrent, the cabin smaller than ever.

Her body surprised her, turning toward him: *Touch me now,* it said. *While there's time.*

BECAUSE SHE AND HARPER had gone so long without speaking honestly, Brie did not immediately worry about Harper's absence a few days later, when the fields had dried. She woke in the shed with room to spread out, Harper's side of the mattress empty. When Brie did not hear the splash of the water bucket outside, she assumed Harper had already started the day's work.

She began her own tasks, packing the jars and listening as Colton talked to men who'd come in from town, black-suited government suppliers who wanted to know about getting some chard. True, Harper's head was absent from the orchard, but Alice was gone too, and there was Colton to think about, how they'd lain together three times since that evening the rain stopped.

Harper's absence alarmed her at lunchtime. Even the cool pleasure of the kitchen couldn't dispel the strangeness of the empty chairs.

"She'll be back," Colton said when he saw her face. "Alice probably took her on a walk."

They both heard it from the house: the low growl of a truck with too many miles on it.

Brie went out to the porch. Their truck, that old blue beast, plowed down the dirt drive, growing louder as it approached, as if eager to move on. She felt Colton behind her and spun around. His eyes were already widening to hold hers.

The driver's door shot open and Harper hopped down, legs steady. In the passenger seat, Alice made a visor of her hands.

"We got the fuel," Harper said. She walked up to Brie, her gaze so intent it was like their foreheads were touching. "Alice traded the horse in town. And got enough to get us a long way."

"To Maine?" Brie asked.

"Or close." Harper looked over Brie's shoulder, past the house. She licked her mouth's dry corners. "We can head on now. Don't even think I have much to pack."

Harper walked toward the shed; Brie did not realize she'd followed until they were inside. "I think," Harper said, sweeping her backpack over her shoulder, "we can at least make it near Richmond today."

Brie looked around the shed. So many things were hers now: the dresses, the extra underwear, the teacup. Slowly, she filled her backpack until it no longer drooped. Her wooden comb rested by the sink, and when she didn't move to collect it, Harper dropped it inside her backpack for her.

When Brie got to the truck, she expected Alice to climb down from the passenger seat. But Alice didn't. She leaned over a map on the dashboard, whispering to herself.

Brie hesitated. Tried to understand what it meant for the three of them to be going. Maybe Alice knew the checkpoints or had ways of getting into places. Or maybe Harper simply pulled people along. In Brie's hesitation, her backpack dangling from her fingers, Colton lifted her from behind. He crushed her upward into him, so her feet left the ground. Like he was trying to say goodbye. Or to lift her into the truck himself.

She said, "Hang on."

Harper tossed her own backpack inside. Extended a hand for Brie's.

"I can't," Brie said, and clutched her sister's hand, "go yet."

Harper gestured with her fingers, impatient. Alice looked up from her map, eyes fluttering. "Brie," Harper said. It was not a question.

Colton lowered her to the ground, one inch at a time. Her toes pressed into the soil. "Later," Brie said, and stepped back until her head met Colton's neck. "I'll meet you later."

Harper's face flushed. She opened her mouth, closed it again. "What about one more night?" she said finally. "And we leave in the morning?"

"We can come back for her," Alice said. "Some other time."

"Come back and get me?" Brie asked. "I'll be ready, by then."

Harper didn't answer. And that look on Alice's face: the boredom everywhere but the tight mouth. Brie rummaged through her backpack and pulled out the old tea canister, the teacup sharply silver in the sunlight. "Take these. In case you get sick again."

Colton walked up to Alice, who shook his hand, then bent to whisper into his ear. After a moment, he said, "Yeah, you too."

Alice said something like, *Don't I always.* Or maybe it was, *It's a long way.* Brie couldn't tell. Harper pulled her into an embrace. "I'm not watching this happen again," she whispered. "Don't be fucking stupid."

"I'm not," she said. "No hurricanes here, right? And maybe— you'll find a good phone. In the meantime." She kissed Harper's shoulder so hard it hurt her teeth. Then she pulled away. She pressed her backpack to her chest, over the warmth Harper left.

She stared down until Harper's boots vanished and the truck door slammed and rattled. When Brie turned to face Colton, she saw his relief.

Though she might as well have looked behind her. When Harper and Alice drove off, the truck was louder than anything.

INSIDE THE HOUSE, Brie was alone with him. She wobbled as she walked into the kitchen and set her backpack on an empty chair. I live here, she thought, looking at the white cabinets.

Colton put his hands on her arms. Then let them fall. "Your sister," he said.

"She was—" She sat down in one of the empty chairs. It was like the backs of her knees had been scooped out. "We found her. At the complex. This group brought in from another part of Texas, this town that had run out of water. Momma and I, we'd gone to pass out food and Harper had nobody. Was just sitting in a tire with her knees up. And so we kind of made her ours. But she was never—" Her fist loosened. She couldn't even believe the sentence enough to finish it. Harper had refused food for days, snarling at the adults, throwing dirt at the children. But not at her. She'd approached Harper with an onion. Polished it on her shirt and took a bite before offering it. Harper had watched her. Then held out her fingers.

"Oh," Colton said, his shoulders relaxing. "So you're not really sisters then."

When he saw her face, he stepped back. "Don't look at me like that," he said. "We can't start like this, with you looking at me like that."

FOR THE LONG MONTHS AFTER, when the phone rings and she hears the inhale on the other end, she waits for the caller to speak. "I'll swing by?" Lauren will say. Or one of the laborers will go, "Y'all need somebody?" She tells them to come on. Surely, if someone can call, Harper can too, whether she got ahold of a phone in some city or reached a Maine cell tower not destroyed by a storm.

For now, Brie thinks, there's the work of living for the life she has. Going into the fields, sometimes with Colton and sometimes without him, all the crops to rip up or plant anew.

Evenings with Lauren and her husband across the kitchen table, bellies delightfully warm from roast or nauseated from the latest vaccine, the power flickering around them. Nights when Colton thumbs her navel and talks about the land surviving, bountiful forever. She wonders about children. She has never had to have her own answer, about whether or not to have them.

In other moments, her mind reaches elsewhere. She'll twist from the kitchen sink and study the shed, always wanting its door to open, for Harper to step out. *What if it were the very beginning of the world?* she imagines Harper saying. *You'd choose me then?* Easier to think of that than the days after Harper's leaving. She'd gone walking, and something crunched in the dirt beneath her boot. She'd stooped. Found a piece of the teacup, a jagged slice of white and silver, her gift hurled against the trunk of a peach tree.

Maybe Harper would ask nothing, would return with no warning at all. The truck kicking up dirt. Harper leaping down, her hair grown back and landing around her shoulders. She'd holler across the green space. Come rushing toward her so fast the wind would meet her before they collided.

It's hard not to come up with such stories. The waiting, long as it is. It's long enough to remember how eternal a love she had once. How difficult a time it'll have finding a way back.

CREDITS

I AM NOT A SCHOLAR, but I have relied on the work of academics, journalists, and historians in crafting this collection. I'm deeply indebted to Nikole Hannah-Jones' *The 1619 Project* and Imani Perry's *South to America*, which inspired me to be unflinching in incorporating historical and contemporary realities into the lives of my characters. Their work gave me permission to be bold, to not look away. All mistakes are my own.

"WHEN WE GO, WE GO DOWNSTREAM"
Thank you, Lee May, for answering my questions about Hill Country ecology. I loved learning about the differences between prairies, savannas, and grasslands and how the Hill Country's ecosystem has changed over time. This story might be a work of fiction, but I wanted to be as precise as I could be.

Barr, Alwyn. "Sabine Pass, Battle of." *Handbook of Texas Online*, Texas State Historical Association, 1952. Updated September 14, 2021. https://www.tshaonline.org/handbook/entries/sabine-pass-battle-of.

Brown, John. *Slave Life in Georgia: A Narrative of the Life, Sufferings, and Escape of John Brown, a Fugitive Slave, Now in England*, edited by L. A. Chamerovzow. London, 1855. https://archive.org/details/06374405.4802.emory.edu.

Burnett, John. "A Chapter in U.S. History Often Ignored: The Flight of Runaway Slaves to Mexico." NPR: *All Things Considered*, February 28, 2021. https://www.npr.org/2021/02/28/971325620/a-chapter-in-u-s-history-often-ignored-the-flight-of-runaway-slaves-to-mexico.

Charpentier, Marisa. "One of Austin's First Black Communities Has Largely Been Erased. This Building Tells Its Tale." KUT NEWS, February 25, 2022. https://www.kut.org/austin/2022-02-25/one-of-austins-first-black-communities-has-largely-been-erased-this-building-tells-its-tale.

Drewery, Laine, director. *Underground Railroad: The William Still Story*. PBS, aired February 5, 2012.

Duncan, Madeline. "The History of Wheatville: The Black Community That Originally Settled in West Campus Area." *The Daily Texan*, October 2, 2023. https://thedailytexan.com/2023/10/03/the-history-of-wheatville-the -black-community-that-originally-settled-in-west-campus-area/.

Gordon-Reed, Annette. *On Juneteenth*. Liveright, 2021.

Goudeau, Jessica. *We Were Illegal: Uncovering a Texas Family's Mythmaking and Immigration*. Viking, 2024.

Hill, Sharon. "The Empty Stairs: The Lost History of East Austin." In *Intersections: New Perspectives on Texas Public History*, edited by Bonnie Tipton Wilson. Texas State University-San Marcos, 2012.

Levitz, Dena. "Park View: It's Not Petworth." *UrbanTurf*, August 3, 2012. https://dc.urbanturf.com/articles/blog/park_view_its_not_petworth/5851.

Mateum, Stephanie. "The Ghost Lights of Marfa." In *Cowboys, Cops, Killers, and Ghosts: Legends and Lore in Texas*, edited by Kenneth L. Untiedt. University of North Texas Press, 2013.

Parry, Tyler. "The Role of Water in African American History." *Black Perspectives*, African American Intellectual History Society, May 4, 2018. https://www .aaihs.org/the-role-of-water-in-african-american-history/.

Penningroth, Dylan C. *Before the Movement: The Hidden History of Black Civil Rights*. Liveright, 2023.

Pohl, Eric W. *Texas Hill Country: A Scenic Journey*. Schiffer, 2017.

Teston, Jacy, and Mason Meek. "Yellow Fever in Galveston, Texas." East Texas History. Accessed September 3, 2024. https://easttexashistory.org /items/show/251.

White, Clarence Cameron. "Don't You Let Nobody Turn You Around." In *Forty Negro Spirituals*, Theodore Presser Co, 1927, via the Bluegrass Messengers website. http://bluegrassmessengers.com/aint-gonna-let-nobody-turn-me -round--white-1927.aspx.

"COTTONMOUTHS"

Thank you, Thomas Lockyear II and Elaina Gyure, for answering my questions about Collier County history. You were invaluable in helping me put the finishing touches on this story.

"The Ancestors." Seminole Tribe of Florida. Accessed November 7, 2024. https://www.semtribe.com/history/the-seminole-ancestors.

"Big Cypress: Deep Lake." National Park Service: U.S. Department of the Interior. Updated May 1, 2020. https://www.nps.gov/bicy/learn /historyculture/deep-lake.htm.

Butler, Deanna. "History of Tamiami Trail." Florida Seminole Tourism, April 1, 2022. https://floridaseminoletourism.com/history-of-tamiami-trail/.

Casey, Constance. "The Smartest Snakes: The Strange Myths and Even Stranger Reality of Cottonmouths." *Slate*, September 8, 2014. https://slate .com/technology/2014/09/cottonmouth-natural-history-myths-research -feeding-and-mating-habits-of-of-water-moccasins.html.

Gyure, Elaina. "Collier County's Golden Age of Railroad." YouTube, uploaded by Naples Parks & Rec, April 5, 2022. https://www.youtube.com/watch?v=eBY-6Gm7w8s.

"Historical Events in Collier County." Collier County Centennial. Accessed October 25, 2024. https://www.colliercounty100.com/history/.

Lockyear II, Thomas. "Celebrating the Black History of Everglades City," presentation given June 15, 2023. Museum of the Everglades, Everglades City, Florida.

Manley, Don. "Black History of Everglades City." *Coastal Breeze News*, June 29, 2023. https://www.coastalbreezenews.com/news/community/collier_county_s_centennial_celebration/black-history-of-everglades-city/article_49d9815e-1629-11ee-9d48-d77220bc2f9f.html#anchor_item_2.

"ALL SKIN IS CLOTHING"

Leonhardt, David. "Middle-Class Black Families, in Low-Income Neighborhoods." *New York Times*, June 24, 2015. https://www.nytimes.com/2015/06/25/upshot/middle-class-black-families-in-low-income-neighborhoods.html.

The folktale that Brayden's mother references is modified from a folktale titled "Out of Her Skin." Though I've made changes to the tale, I'm grateful to the following sources for documenting oral traditions and for guiding me through stories of boo hags and other Sea Island myths:

Murray, Chalmers S. "Macie and the Boo Hag." In *The Annotated African American Folktales*, edited by Henry Louis Gates Jr. and Maria Tatar, Liveright, 2018.

Parsons, Elsie Clews, and Maria Middleton. "Out of Her Skin." In *The Annotated African American Folktales*, edited by Henry Louis Gates Jr. and Maria Tatar, Liveright, 2018.

"SURFACING"

My deepest thanks to Emory Rooks, Henry "Chip" Wilson, Sheree Atkinson, and Maurice Wilson at the St. Simons African American Heritage Coalition. Your knowledge of history and the changing St. Simons area were invaluable for sharpening this story, and I appreciate you answering every question. All respect to and gratitude for those who have been on St. Simons for generations.

On page 83, Olivia uses two Gullah Geechee terms. Because the language is primarily oral, the terms have a variety of spellings (ex. "comeya" or "cumya" and "beenya" or "binya"). I've used "come-here" and "been-here" to emphasize meaning, as well as Grace's experience as an adopted daughter.

The clock-themed dance that Grace's troupe performs is a reference to *EN*. Choreographed by Jessica Lang. Composed by Jakub Ciupinski. Performed by the Alvin Ailey American Dance Theater. Zellerbach Hall, Berkeley, California. April 12, 2018.

Kai, Corinne. "Vaginismus Can Cause (and Be Caused By) Emotional Trauma, But Healing Is Possible." *Allure*, January 28, 2019. https://www .allure.com/story/vaginismus-mental-health-causes-painful-sex.

Maltz, Wendy. *The Sexual Healing Journey*. 3rd ed. William Morrow, 2012.

Roberts, Amy Lotson, and Patrick J. Holladay. *Gullah Geechee Heritage in the Golden Isles*. History Press, 2019.

"MORNING BY MORNING"

I wrote this story in a fit of inspiration after listening to Solange's 2019 album, *When I Get Home*. The transition between two tracks—"We Deal with the Freak'n (intermission)" and "Jerrod"—forced me to think about God one moment, then sex and desire the next. I wondered: *If God has made your incredible body, then what does it mean to share that body with someone else, especially given religious norms? How do different types of love intersect with one another?* I'm deeply grateful for Solange's careful curation and for the sheer power of her art, which turned me inward.

The story borrows its title from the hymn "Great Is Thy Faithfulness," specifically from the line "Morning by morning new mercies I see." Chisholm, Thomas O., and William M. Runyan. "Great Is Thy Faithfulness." Hope Publishing Co, 1923. https://www.hopepublishing.com/W3208_GREAT_IS _THY_FAITHFULNESS/.

Fick, Emma. *Snippets of New Orleans*. University of Louisiana Press, 2017.

"From the Graphics Archive: Mapping Katrina and Its Aftermath." *New York Times*, August 25, 2015. https://www.nytimes.com/interactive/2015/08/25 /us/mapping-katrina-and-aftermath.html.

Oberman, Mira. "Remembering New Orleans Chaos, 10 Years after Katrina." Agence France-Presse, August 27, 2015. https://correspondent.afp.com /remembering-new-orleans-chaos-10-years-after-katrina.

Staten, Annie, and Susan Roach. "'Take Me to the Water': African American River Baptism." Folklife in Louisiana: Louisiana's Living Traditions, 1996. Accessed October 25, 2024. https://www.louisianafolklife.org/LT /Articles_Essays/creole_art_river_baptism.html.

"GATHER HERE AGAIN"

Fessenden, Maris. "The Ku Klux Klan Didn't Always Wear Hoods." *Smithsonian Magazine*, January 13, 2016. https://www.smithsonianmag .com/smart-news/ku-klux-klan-didnt-always-wear-hoods-180957773/.

Katz, Andrew. "Unrest in Virginia: Clashes Over a Show of White Nationalism in Charlottesville Turn Deadly." *Time*, August 2017. https:// time.com/charlottesville-white-nationalist-rally-clashes/.

McWhiney, H. Grady, and Francis B. Simkins. "The Ghostly Legend of the Ku-Klux Klan." *Negro History Bulletin* 14, no. 5 (1951): 109–12.

O'Hare, Erin, and Evan Mitchell. "In Less Than a Decade, More Than 100 Black Residents Moved Out of Starr Hill." Charlottesville Tomorrow, October 4, 2022. https://www.cvilletomorrow.org/in-less-than-a-decade -more-than-100-black-residents-moved-out-of-starr-hill/.

Sainato, Michael. "100-Year Anniversary of the Hanging of Leo Frank." *Observer*, August 17, 2015. https://observer.com/2015/08/100-year-anniversary-of-the-hanging-of-leo-frank/.

Young, Patrick. "Were the Ku Klux Ghosts of Confederate Soldiers? Mississippi 1868." The Reconstruction Era, November 20, 2019. https://thereconstructionera.com/were-the-ku-klux-ghosts-of-confederate-soldiers-mississippi-1868/.

"IN THE SWIRL"

"Birmingham Officials Announce Plan to Close City Parks Rather Than Permit Racial Integration." Equal Justice Initiative: A History of Racial Injustice, On This Day—October 24, 1961. Accessed November 7, 2024. https://calendar.eji.org/racial-injustice/oct/24.

Hackman, Rose. "Swimming While Black: The Legacy of Segregated Public Pools Lives On." *Guardian*, August 4, 2015. https://www.theguardian.com/world/2015/aug/04/black-children-swimming-drownings-segregation.

Hansen, Jeff. "Birmingham Changes as Blacks Move to the Suburbs." *Birmingham News*, March 27, 2011. https://www.al.com/spotnews/2011/03/birmingham_changes_as_blacks_m.html.

The movie referenced in this story is based on the 2012 film *Savages*, directed by William Oliver Stone, distributed by Universal Pictures, and featuring Blake Lively, Aaron Johnson, Taylor Kitsch, and Salma Hayek.

Wiltse, Jeff. "Segregation & Swimming Timeline in the United States." POOL: *A Social History of Segregation*, exhibited at Portland Center Stage at the Armory, Portland, Oregon. https://www.pcs.org/features/segregation-swimming-timeline-in-the-united-states.

"NATURALE"

Agha, Andrew, and Nicole M. Isenbarger. "Recently Discovered Marked Colonoware from Dean Hall Plantation, Berkeley County, South Carolina." *Historical Archaeology* 45, no. 2 (2011): 184–87.

Cooper, Leslie. "Colonoware Jar with Pedestal Base, Curriboo Plantation, South Carolina." Digital Archaeological Archive of Comparative Slavery, Thomas Jefferson Foundation. Accessed October 27, 2024. https://www.daacs.org/galleries/colonoware/.

Finkel, Jori. "The Enslaved Artist Whose Pottery Was an Act of Resistance." *New York Times*, June 18, 2021. https://www.nytimes.com/2021/06/17/arts/design/-enslaved-potter-david-drake-museum.html.

Hauser, Christine. "Florida Woman Whose 'Stand Your Ground' Defense Was Rejected Is Released." *New York Times*, February 7, 2017. https://www.nytimes.com/2017/02/07/us/marissa-alexander-released-stand-your-ground.html.

Hedgpeth, Dana. "This Tribe Helped the Pilgrims Survive for Their First Thanksgiving. They Still Regret It 400 Years Later." *Washington Post*, November 4, 2021. https://www.washingtonpost.com/history/2021/11/04/thanksgiving-anniversary-wampanoag-indians-pilgrims/.

The book Cherie is reading is Toni Morrison's *Beloved*, first published by Alfred A. Knopf in 1987. Morrison, Toni. *Beloved*. Alfred A. Knopf, Everyman's Library Edition, 2006.

Ranky Tanky. "Ranky Tanky." *Birthright: A Black Roots Music Compendium*. Craft Recordings. Released February 17, 2023.

"THE HAPPY LAND"

The Bible verse Gideon and Wyatt refer to is from John 14:15, which, in the New International Version, reads, "If you love me, keep my commands," spoken in Jesus' words.

Brashear, Ivy. "Keep Your 'Elegy': The Appalachia I Know Is Very Much Alive." In *Appalachian Reckoning*, edited by Anthony Harkins and Meredith McCarroll. West Virginia University Press, 2019.

Catte, Elizabeth. *What You Are Getting Wrong About Appalachia*. Belt Publishing, 2018.

Dulken, Danielle. "A Black Kingdom in Postbellum Appalachia." *Scalawag*, September 9, 2019. https://scalawagmagazine.org/2019/09/black-appalachia-kingdom/.

Duncan, Barbara R., ed. *Living Stories of the Cherokee*. University of North Carolina Press, 1998.

Elliston, Jon. "The Happy Land: Former Slaves Forged a Communal Kingdom in Henderson County." *WNC Magazine*, Winter 2021. https://wncmagazine.com/feature/happy_land.

Gilly, Steve, host. *The Kingdom of the Happy Land*, video podcast. *Stories of Appalachia*, YouTube, February 16, 2024. https://www.youtube.com/watch?v=QhAi_8iLVkM.

hooks, bell. *Salvation: Black People and Love*. HarperCollins, First Perennial Edition, 2001.

Izard, Missy Craver. "Kingdom of the Happy Land." Flat Rock Together, *Good News* (blog), February 6, 2021. https://www.flatrocktogether.com/good-news/kingdom-of-the-happy-land.

McCarroll, Meredith. "On and On: Appalachian Accent and Academic Power." In *Appalachian Reckoning*, edited by Anthony Harkins and Meredith McCarroll. West Virginia University Press, 2019.

Obama, Barack. "Remarks by the President on the Supreme Court Decision on Marriage Equality." Obama White House Archives, The White House: Office of the Press Secretary, June 26, 2015. https://obamawhitehouse.archives.gov/the-press-office/2015/06/26/remarks-president-supreme-court-decision-marriage-equality.

Pruitt, Lisa R. "What *Hillbilly Elegy* Reveals about Race in Twenty-First Century America." In *Appalachian Reckoning*, edited by Anthony Harkins and Meredith McCarroll. West Virginia University Press, 2019.

Turner, William H. "Black Hillbillies Have No Time for Elegies." In *Appalachian Reckoning*, edited by Anthony Harkins and Meredith McCarroll. West Virginia University Press, 2019.

Wilkinson, Crystal. *Praisesong for the Kitchen Ghosts: Stories and Recipes from Five Generations of Black Country Cooks.* Clarkson Potter, 2024.

Zimmerman, Martin, Jacob Horr, and UNC Charlotte Urban Institute. "NoDa Perceived: Past, Present and Future of a Mill Village." UNC Charlotte Urban Institute, October 28, 2020. https://ui.charlotte.edu/story/noda-perceived-past-present-and-future-mill-village/.

"HOW DOES YOUR GARDEN GROW?"

Claire and her mother have a difficult time accessing the medical care they deserve and long for, but I am so grateful to have amazing healthcare providers. Thank you, Dr. Jennifer Rumpf, for answering my many questions about uterine fibroids and leiomyosarcoma—and for your impeccable care.

"About Fondren." Find It in Fondren. Accessed October 27, 2024. http://finditinfondren.com/local-links/about-find-it-in-fondren/.

Chedekel, Lisa. "Black Women with Fibroids Face Elevated Risk of Endometrial Cancer." *The Brink*, March 24, 2016. https://www.bu.edu/articles/2016/black-women-endometrial-cancer/.

Eltoukhi, Heba M., Monica N. Modi, Meredith Weston, Alicia Y. Armstrong, and Elizabeth A. Stewart. "The Health Disparities of Uterine Fibroids for African American Women: A Public Health Issue." *American Journal of Obstetrics and Gynecology* 210, no. 3 (2014): 194–99. Accessed November 7, 2024. https://www.ncbi.nlm.nih.gov/pmc/articles/PMC3874080/.

Gaspard, Whitney. "Can Hair Relaxers Cause Uterine Fibroids?" ESSENCE, October 28, 2020. https://www.essence.com/news/hair-beat-can-hair-relaxers-cause-uterine-fibroids/.

Holohan, Meghan. "Mom, 42, Had Heavy Periods for Years. Doctors Dismissed Her. It Was a Rare Uterine Cancer." *Today*, March 14, 2023. https://www.today.com/health/womens-health/mom-42-details-symptoms-rare-uterine-cancer-doctors-dismissed-years-rcna74731.

Kail, Tony. *Stories of Rootworkers & Hoodoo in the Mid-South.* Arcadia, 2019.

Lee, Michelle Elizabeth. *Working the Roots: Over 400 Years of Traditional African-American Healing.* Wadastick, 2014.

Leibovitz, Annie, photographer. "Oh, Baby! Rihanna's Plus One." *Vogue*, April 12, 2022. https://www.vogue.com/article/rihanna-cover-may-2022.

Nanna, Paul Joseph. "Herbal Treatment of Uterine Fibroids—Part 4." *Guardian*, September 6, 2018. https://guardian.ng/features/herbal-treatment-of-uterine-fibroids-part-4/.

Pelonara, Daniela. "Cypress Essential Oil Profile." *Native Essentials* (blog), July 7, 2017. https://www.nativessentials.com/blogs/clean-beauty-notes/cypress-essential-oil?srsltid=AfmBOop6lUUFHoohnXyinglkX6UyaFiI sqdIngGsaOokBnK2hpJa9RAl.

Walker, Adria R. "Beauty Influencer Jessica Pettway Died of Cervical Cancer Following Misdiagnosis." *Guardian*, March 21, 2024. https://amp.the guardian.com/us-news/2024/mar/21/jessica-pettway-death-cervical-cancer.

"Welcome to the Asylum Hill Project." Asylum Hill Project. Accessed November 7, 2024. https://asylumhillproject.org/.

Wirth, Sara Rush. "Inside Saltine." *Restaurant Business*, October 14, 2014. https://www.restaurantbusinessonline.com/inside-saltine.

Wolfe, Anna. "Development Catches Fondren Residents Off Guard." *Jackson Free Press*, February 11, 2015. https://m.jacksonfreepress.com/news/2015/feb/11/development-catches-fondren-residents-guard/.

Villarosa, Linda. "A Relaxer Reckoning." *New York Times*, June 13, 2024. https://www.nytimes.com/2024/06/13/briefing/hair-relaxers-health-risks.html.

"TILL IT AND KEEP IT"

This story owes its structure to the Bible, specifically the Modern English Version (MEV), which contains the following language for Genesis 2:15: "The Lord God took the man and put him in the garden of Eden to till it and to keep it."

Despite the imagined viruses and geographical limitations within this story, it bears some resemblance to our contemporary world's disasters, including Hurricane Harvey and our most frightening COVID-19 years. I'm grateful to the following journalists for their coverage of the storms, as well as for their coverage of the quarantine restrictions in the administrative region of Hong Kong, which I've exaggerated for the southern American cities in this story.

Fernelius, Katie Jane. "After Two Climate-Decimated Harvests, Southern Peach Farmers Wonder How to Regroup." *Guardian*, August 29, 2023. https://www.theguardian.com/environment/2023/aug/29/peach-harvest-southern-united-states-farming.

Gura, David, and John Ruwitch. "He Loved Hong Kong. Its COVID Crackdown Made Him Leave without Even Saying Goodbye." NPR, February 20, 2022. https://www.npr.org/2022/02/20/1081557870/hong-kong-expat-exodus-covid-restrictions.

Hoskins, Peter. "Hong Kong Covid: The Cathay Pilots Stuck in 'Perpetual Quarantine.'" BBC, December 6, 2021. https://www.bbc.com/news/business-59370672.

Klein, Ezra, host. Ghodsee, Kristen, guest. "What Communes and Other Radical Experiments in Living Together Reveal." *The Ezra Klein Show*, *New York Times*, June 9, 2023. https://www.nytimes.com/2023/06/09/opinion/ezra-klein-kristen-ghodsee.html.

Springer, Kate. "Hong Kong's 'Zero Covid' Strategy Frustrates Travel-Starved Residents." CNN Travel, August 10, 2021. https://www.cnn.com/travel/article/hong-kong-travel-restrictions-cmd/index.html.

Texas Monthly Staff. "Voices from the Storm." *Texas Monthly*, September 2017. https://www.texasmonthly.com/interactive/voices-from-the-storm/?_ga=2.112665217.480637240.1704989781-1051370202.1703006682.

Texas Monthly Staff. "Voices from the Storm, a Year Later." *Texas Monthly*, September 2018. https://www.texasmonthly.com/news-politics/harvey-survivors-one-year-later/.

ACKNOWLEDGMENTS

LIKE ANY LIVING THING, a book makes demands. For over ten years, I tried to give this collection everything it asked of me, and many people made that work possible. What's more, they gave me everything I asked of them, in turn.

During my undergraduate days, when I was questioning what it meant to *know* something, my professors taught me research, caution, and craft. Thank you, Elizabeth Tallent, Dana Johnson, and Susan Segal for teaching me the foundations of fiction writing. Thank you, Michelle Gordon, Shana Redmond, and Francille Wilson. You showed me how to read, taught me how to think, and pushed my writing to be more complex. I'm forever grateful for every conversation, lecture, and office hours discussion. You made me want to take my time and do the best work I possibly could.

Thank you to the following workshops, fellowships, and awards for their instructional and financial support: the Tin House Summer Workshop, the Community of Writers, the Sewanee Writers' Conference, the Skidmore Summer Writers Institute, the Martha Heasley Cox Center for Steinbeck Studies, the 2021 committee for the Keene Prize for Literature, and the Steinbeck Writers' Retreat in Sag Harbor. When I didn't know how to be an artist—I'm still learning!—you gave me the space and time to figure it out.

Many of these stories contain difficult subject matter, and my community has been integral to my mental and physical well-being. Thank you, Melissa, Julie, Rollie, and Seth, for the therapy that made it possible to write; literature is healing, but so is the work you do. Thank you, Madeline, for hearing out every anxiety and believing in my work when I questioned it. Thank you, Ashley, for all of your encouragement and help with my website. Thank you, Bri, for every phone call and inspiring card that taught me to keep going. I love y'all so much.

Thank you, Sundai and Josh, for your friendship and for giving many of these stories your careful reads. Publishing is always hard, but you showed me what more I could do, and therefore made me more comfortable with letting my work out into the world.

Without the tireless work of many magazine editors, these stories would be in far worse shape. Thank you, Karen Friedman and Patrick Ryan (*One Story*), Paul Reyes (*Virginia Quarterly Review*), Carolyn Kuebler (*New England Review*), Sacha Idell (*The Southern Review*), Michael Koch (EPOCH), and Adam Ross and Eric Smith (*The Sewanee Review*). I thank every editor and staff member who helped these stories become the best versions of themselves.

Thank you to Valerie Borchardt, the best agent in the world, for believing in my fiction and guiding me through every stage of the publishing process. I'm over the moon that I have a home at the Georges Borchardt Agency.

Thank you to Elizabeth DeMeo at Tin House Books for finding these stories and for, a second time, finding the best stories within them. Years ago, after understanding what it meant to publish a book, I developed a strong fear of not being edited, of putting into print less-than-ideal versions of my work. Thank you for being a person I could trust with these stories, for your exacting eye and incredible care. I couldn't have asked for a better editor.

Thank you, Meg Storey, Lisa Dusenbery, Jacqui Reiko Teruya, Becky Kraemer, Nanci McCloskey, Masie Cochran, Isabel Lemus Kristensen, Beth Steidle, Justine Payton, Alyssa Ogi, and the rest of the Tin House team for all of your incredible work. You turned my Microsoft Word drafts into a beautiful book—and caught errors I never would've seen on my own. I'm so happy that I got to publish with you.

Thank you, Uzo Njoku, for your stunning artwork, for your patterns and portraits that are rich with their own stories. Your painting gave me a cover greater than what I could've imagined.

For so long, my dream was to attend the Michener Center for Writers in Austin, Texas, and the reality surpassed my fantasies. Thank you to every Michener and New Writers Project fellow I shared a class with and who taught me to be a better writer. Thank you, Holly, Blake Lee, and Billy, for making it possible for me and the rest of the fellows to focus on writing. Thank you, Rickey, Stephanie, Brynne, Megan, and Reena for the gifts of your own work and for your invaluable friendships. I'm deeply grateful for every comment and suggestion that made me revisit these stories and make them better. Thank you to the professors whose teachings and guidance changed my life. Maya, Deb, Elizabeth, Amy, and Bret, all I wanted was to learn, which means that I got everything that I wanted for three whole years. I'm still trying to use every grain of wisdom you imparted and wrote by example.

My dearest Scriptrices, thank you for reading nearly every piece within this collection, for our conversations that could've continued deep into the night. Ana, Becca, Caroline, and Neval, you inspire me so much, teach me attention to detail, and make me laugh when this writing life gets hard. I can't wait for our next workshop.

Thank you to my Wilson family, for years of support and for welcoming me as your daughter. Thank you for instilling in your son a love of reading; now I get the privilege of picking his brain and reading with him too.

Thank you, Victoria, for teaching me to be confident and demonstrating what it means to love yourself. Thank you to my grandmothers, for all you survived with joy and resilience, for letting me read on your kitchen floors. Because of you, I wanted this work to be right.

Thank you to my parents; those childhood road trips formed the foundation of this collection, and you showed me so many parts of the world through Big Bertha, your own stories, and your life experiences. Thank you, Dad, for every trip to Waldenbooks, Borders, and Barnes & Noble, for teaching me to put God first and live with the biggest heart. Thank you, Mom, for what you said when I was in the first grade and you saw me stapling pages together. You said: "Maybe you'll be an author someday."

Hannah, you are my best friend, my best reader, the person who taught me that there's more than one way that souls can be linked in this world. I remember our first summer writing in Saratoga Springs, and since then, you have become an inseparable part of my life. This work bears your fingerprint. Yet beyond our pages, our friendship will stretch to the grave.

And thank you, Jonathan, my husband, my home. We built our love from scratch, and every day it gets bigger. You heard every fear, talked me through every story, moved halfway across the country, and helped us make temporary sanctuaries whenever my writing took us to yet another town. Sometimes, people think they see traces of you in my characters, but truth is, you are far too marvelous to capture in words; every day I remind myself that you are real. Our life together is greater than any romance that fiction could make exquisite.

MATT VALENTINE

CARRIE R. MOORE's fiction has appeared in *One Story, New England Review, The Sewanee Review, Virginia Quarterly Review*, and other publications. A recipient of the Keene Prize and the inaugural writer-in-residence at the Steinbeck Writers' Retreat, she earned her MFA at the Michener Center for Writers. Born in Georgia, she currently resides in Texas with her husband.